"Sukey Hughes's young Dutch lacemaker, Saskia, takes us on an enticing, moving, frightening journey to her new life in South Africa in the 1740s. Looking for a new experience, she accepts a post as a childminder-cum-servant of a wealthy winemaking family, but then . . . well, read the book! Saskia's interactions with people of diverse ethnicities, social standings, and backgrounds make for a thrilling ride through life.

On each page I find myself marveling at the beautifully crafted writing. I was particularly taken by the author's imaginative similes and metaphors. She's obviously done her research too, as attested by the convincing detail and imagery. If you've never visited eighteenth-century South Africa, this book will make you think that you have."

—Dr. David Barnes-Hughes, University of London.

"I was totally absorbed and amazed by the details and passion of the time, place, and characters. The skillful writing put me in a time and place I had no way of knowing without Sukey Hughes's artful crafting. This is a powerful novel of important historical and universal themes. I am grateful that I had the experience of reading this novel, not an easy read, but a deepening understanding of the necessity of following one's destiny."

—Dorothy Jardin, creative writing teacher, poet, author.

"I read historical fiction to learn something of a particular time and place without having to do the slogging research myself. How much more luxurious to learn through a novel, with perhaps a bit of romance, what life might have been like on a wine plantation in South Africa in the mid-eighteenth century. Sukey Hughes has done this for us beautifully with her new book, Diary of a Lacemaker. Not only is it a delicious read, but it is also a stirring glimpse into the quasi-caste system of the time. In some ways the story works as a kind of 'Upstairs/Downstairs' tale. The slaves and servants, and their owners/employers live entangled lives.

Our heroine, Saskia, arrives with the mistress of the plantation and her children from Amsterdam, as no better than an indentured servant. When the mistress finds out that she is a lacemaker, and therefore a money maker, she is further enmeshed in the Big House. She befriends the slaves and the other servants. A nanny, she is able to move between the two worlds but belongs to neither. As an outsider, she is able to see most clearly the social, political, and emotional inequities of her surroundings. Much the way Anne Perry does for the Victorian era, Hughes takes us behind the facade of the times to the lives of the people who are suffering while others posture. Her research was phenomenal. I felt enmeshed in the color, flavor, noise, smells, and language of the different settings of the book. And as for that love story, you will have to read Diary of a Lacemaker for yourself."

—Ariadne Weaver, PhD in Cultural History, University of Chicago.

“Diary of a Lacemaker by Sukey Hughes is a deeply emotional novel that delivers Saskia Klaassens and the readers onto the shores of Dutch-ruled South Africa in 1749. She has known only a hard life in Holland and what unfolds here, with great grace and beauty, is a girl becoming a woman, learning life in a beautiful and dangerous land of owners and slaves, and keeping the secret at the center of her heart. She is a lacemaker—for the love of it, for the magic in her hands, guarding this from people who would use it for their own gain. Saskia moves into your heart in the first paragraph and lives there still when the book ends.”

—Gerald DiPego, screenwriter.

“Sukey Hughes takes us on a trip in which life for all members of society is inescapable—except for the heroine who, despite incredible danger, follows her heart—despite the price. You don’t want to miss this eloquent, elegant adventure into the past—and you won’t forget it or the elegant and opulent word painting of the author who spares herself nothing so that we can BE THERE!”

—Zoe Keithley, novelist.

DIARY OF A *Lacemaker*

AIA PUBLISHING

SUKEY HUGHES

Diary of a Lacemaker
Sukey Hughes

Published by AIA Publishing, Australia
ABN: 32736122056
http://www.aiapublishing.com

All characters in this publication are fictitious and any resemblance to real persons, living or dead, is purely coincidental.

ISBN: 978-1-922329-23-3
Cover design by Rose Newland

For

Michael Ondaatje

A Note to the Reader

Please note that some words and terms that are today considered offensive are included in this book because they were commonly used at the time in which the story is set. Their use is necessary to paint an authentic picture of the racist thinking of the times.

Chapter 1

There is in God, some say, a deep but dazzling darkness.
—Henry Vaughn

April 1749 (Autumn)
Windroos

Mama once told me that an invisible silk thread connects us to those we are fated to meet. We were sitting at our snow-white pin-studded pillows, talking about how she and Papa met. We were working the lace together, and I was quite young, but I never forgot what she said. It is Fate that chooses when and where and how the meetings will occur. The thread of destiny may stretch or tangle or tighten, she said, but it never breaks, for it is our souls' will. Now I know she was right.

Soon after her death I had one powerful yearning: to get as far from home as possible. Now, as our ship dropped anchor in Table Bay, I had done just that. I'd sailed from a civilized land, a land I could no longer bear, to the end of a far continent. Sailed to another earth.

I stood on deck, heart ablaze, gazing out at rugged cliffs and white beaches ribboning a deep azure sea. What beauty spread out before me! A strong sun, nearly blinding us, glanced off the white-limed homes of Cape Town. Fierce sun, bitter wind. Imposing mountains flanked the town like a fortress. Boats circled the ships in the bay, and thick-armed, dusky-skinned men, stripped to the waist, their torsos gleaming with sweat, unloaded cargo. They shouted to one another in a strange kind of Dutch that rose and fell in staccato rhythms. No longer were we in the Netherlands! With Cape Town sparkling before us and our journey ended, a wild soup of hope, doubt, joy, anxiety, excitement all tumbled about inside me.

Months ago in Delft, Mistress de Witt had interviewed me for the position of nursemaid to her children Pier and Catryn. I spoke with care that day, safekeeping the truth about why I wanted to leave home. Whatever I said must have pleased her, for she sat back in her chair and leveled her china-blue eyes on me. "Miss Klaassens, are you ready for an adventure?"

I'd blinked. "What do you mean, *mevrouw*?"

"I mean journeying with us to a wondrous land. You, me, the children. A great travel adventure, Miss Klaassens, a glorious and mighty adventure. We will sail to Africa, to the Cape."

My heart soared. At that time I would have punted down the canals to Rotterdam in a boat of river rats to get away from Papa's new family. Raggedy clouds of fear pushed forward with images of twisted jungle, man-eating natives, ferocious beasts. But we Dutch would have conquered those. *Af-ri-ca*. I savored the feel of it on my tongue, let it melt there like a sweet.

Now I looked around. Sure the Mistress was below deck, I ripped off my cap. Wind tore at my hair and whipped it across my neck. Despite her friendliness in earlier months, I now hardly existed for her. Not much had gone well on this voyage.

There'd been challenges, like how to entertain my bored charges, and how to please a difficult mistress. But in nearly five months at sea, we'd also battled storms, sickness, filth, and bad food. A birth gone wrong. That boy who fell overboard, and only the mother rushing to save him.

I had survived, yes, and learned a few things. I'd learned to be silent and meld into my chair at the Captain's table while the Mistress held court, learned to fetch sherry for her every afternoon at four bells, and learned to pretend her fickle moods were normal. I learned when to challenge and when to hold back. I could suggest a plainer dress for her for dinner, one with less lace. I might suggest she back me in admonishing Catryn for stealing jam. But what I could never do was challenge how she pampered Pier, no matter how outrageous his antics. And yet I was responsible for him.

Only my dreams sustained me. At long last, I felt sure that this Cape of Good Hope was the place my life would turn bright. I would make good here. As soon as I was settled in my own room, I would pull out the bobbins and thread and once more make lace.

Lace. What purity it has! Back home I would hold it to the glass, letting the summer town below fall into wintry softness. The dirty canal and beggars who hobbled by on crutches became frozen in white. That is how I made my world beautiful, by viewing it through a gentle haze of lace. Then the world became whole again, tied together in harmony by orderly threads of white.

"Stop kicking your boots on the side of the ship, Pier! She will remember you. You don't have to leave your toe marks too."

What a handful the boy has been. How many times on the trip out had the Mistress caned my knuckles, not his, for some mischief he'd gotten into? I prayed that being with his father again would steady his wildness and temper his tantrums. But whenever I reached out to him and mentioned that reunion, Pier turned a sour back.

His little sister padded to my side and held my hand. "Katje," I called her. "Kitten." At nine, Catryn was wide-eyed, with corn-colored frizzle that streamed down her shoulders. What a dear nature she had, though she could also be stubborn. Like me, I suppose. We had our tugs-of-war over bedtime, but I drew the line when she insisted we nurse the flying fish that had crashed on deck. Anxiety made her pull at the hairs of her eyebrows. I tried to comfort her during our months at sea, but it was no use. Now her eyebrows were almost bald.

The *Windroos* eased a path into Table Bay, and crew and passengers hooted, whistled, and threw their caps into the air. We had joined other Dutch ships, British and German too, lying anchored in the harbor. High flags and colorful pennants snapped in the rough breeze, awaiting the signal to enter. I looked up. Angry clouds swept across the skies like goaded sheep.

The Mistress gripped the balustrades a few yards away. To protect her skin from the sun, she wore a linen face mask, sunbonnet, and long gloves. How strange, for I worshipped the sun. She stared at the city, and I could almost hear her brain click away, assessing, judging. And this the woman who said Africa would be an adventure. I herded the children over to her, to shiver together in the chill morning air.

On the wharf, rows of armed guard of the VOC, the governing body at this outpost, lined the curve of waterfront. Alert guns pointed up at the blue sky. On deck, an officer made the rounds. Be patient, he told us. We'd have to remain on board one more day.

A cannon signal roared from shore and rocked the bay. We jerked back. A ship's call to enter. With sullen ease, a tired-looking *sloep* glided close and dropped anchor. The echo of cannon died down. But for the *lap-lapping* of water against the ships, all was eerily still.

Then, in a flurry of movement, the sloop's crew scuttled below deck. That was when we heard them, the moans that crawled out of the hold.

"What kind of *schoener* is that, Mother?" Pier was tall for his twelve years, and from the way he clipped words, you would have thought him head of the family. But he held himself awkwardly, crushed in at the chest, a boy still terribly unsure of himself. At nineteen I was nursemaid to children old enough to be my siblings.

"That?" Above, gannets screeched and wheeled on gusts of wind. My mistress scanned the ship up and down. "That, my dear, is a Slaver."

I grasped the ends of my shawl and knotted them tightly across my heart. We stood and stared, slouching away from the slave ship, clutching the railing's brass hitches.

A sudden commotion of noise, blustery movement. The wind rose and hit us with ungodly stenches: disease, human waste. Out of the bowels of the ship the sailors hauled them—men and women, native, Black, with matted hair, emaciated, naked, tethered to one another by ankles. Some were scarred and crusted with blood. A sailor broke open the chains as others lowered the slaves one by one into the longboats.

I'd seen a few Black people back home, servants to the wealthy—boys dressed in little corduroy suits smartly holding trays of drink, and Black women who nursed babes. But I'd never seen a slave. My ears grew alert. The cries seemed to dissolve the very air.

A Black man lurched free of his captor's grasp and dashed for the side of the ship. Sailors cried out, several sprinted after him, but the slave leapt over the railing and crashed into the water below. Three crew, hands fumbling, scrambled to gather up a huge net. They waited, poised at the balustrades across from us. In the water, a vortex swirled. The echo of cannon died down. The moment the Black man crested the surface and gasped for air, the sailors leaned back, aimed carefully, and heaved their net. It splayed wide, with giant grace, fins of a ray, plunging down over the water and snaring him.

We stood there, dumb. Everything moved at leaden pace. Catryn whimpered and hit me with her fist. I grabbed hold of the hot wet hand, as much to comfort myself as her.

Pier laughed. "They caught the dirty heathen!"

Sailors bolted into action, cinching the cords swiftly, flinging an end over a boom. The rusty winch cranked and complained as they hauled the Black man out of the bay. Water streamed from the bundle. He grappled on the cords and thrashed about, trying to clamber up the net, but it was useless—he was a pendulum spinning helplessly in the fierce wind, swinging precariously over the water. The sailors jerked him higher and higher, until his head hit the mast. Below, sailors jeered in triumph. For a moment I lost my sense of balance—it was I swinging from that boom.

Catryn squinted up at the Mistress. "Is that a human being, Mother?"

Mistress de Witt settled a hand on her daughter's neck. A kind of darkness shuttered her eyes. "That's a poor African, my dear. They work the grapes in your father's fields and help us run the estate. We give them everything they need and try to make good Christians of them. They cannot do without us. Yes, I suppose they are a kind of human."

I turned and stared straight at my Mistress. "A *kind* of human?" She answered with a glare that could have bent an iron stake. I looked down.

Catryn's brow wrinkled. "If we're helping him, why was he running away?"

The Mistress turned her back to the slave ship. "Go to your cabin, dears, and be sure your things are packed. We disembark early tomorrow."

I knew I should have gone with them, if only to avoid what I knew was coming, but I could not take my eyes from the Black man. He bobbed back and forth in his net, a possum in a deathtrap. Something wrenched in the pit of my stomach. Hadn't this land belonged to these natives not so long ago?

The Mistress watched too. Then her satin skirt whipped against my wool one. I felt something powerful and cold well up in her. "How dare you, Saskia Klaassens! We are at the Cape now." Blades of her *chinees* fan flew past my face and pointed to the guards across the bay. "Has the sight of those soldiers eluded you? They are here to enforce the law of the land. And the law here is slavery. Never again question me like that, young lady, nor speak one word against what is. You are not irreplaceable."

I stepped back and took a deep breath, heat rising from the base of my skull. So—we were in that other world again. On the voyage out, I had almost forgotten something I should never forget: the world does not care what lies in the heart of a servant girl. We must never challenge those above us. And almost everyone was above us. In fact, we must never challenge authority at all—certainly not White authority over people of color.

I shivered. A coldness had entered me, and was swirling about inside like a blast of autumn wind, chilling full these bones.

Chapter 2

April 1749 (Autumn)
Windroos/Cape Town

The sea, the sea. Sometimes it rose like tides in my blood. We Dutch are a water people, our fates ever wedded to the sea. With our dams holding back the press of ocean, water has been our benefactor—and greatest source of fear.

As our ship sat anchored in Table Bay, I watched the ocean, smooth, lustrous, and as gray-green as water in a pewter bowl. Yesterday a group of enormous fish, the leviathans called whales, loomed close as if to greet us. How thrilling to see several breach the crest of water, then dive back under, their great tails slapping ocean spray upon us. Pier howled with delight, but he was nervous too—here were the monsters he had long feared, yet longed to see. One was so close we beheld its ancient and unfathomable eye. It stared at us, expressionless, as if made of glass.

We hoisted our colors and several shots bellowed out from the fortifications, acknowledging us, and the *Windroos* answered. At last, this was the day we would disembark, assuming we could pass the health inspections.

Midshipman Soolmans came to our side and leaned his lanky frame against the railing. He was several years my senior, with a gentlemanly manner and kind eyes set deep in his skull. His presence always put me at ease. "You know, children, we have survived one of the world's wildest oceans."

Catryn pointed at the horizon. "That mountain's on fire!" Majestic Table Rock loomed up from the hem of town, smoke-thick clouds scudding across its back.

"Nay," he laughed, "Sometimes the clouds will cling to the ridge like that. Like a white tablecloth, they say." The Cape had provisioned ships with food and water for the last hundred years, he told us. And farther south, winds of two great oceans met and fought it out at the most southern tip of Africa.

Pier gave a haughty jerk of his chin. "I already know that."

"Pier!" I said. "Be respectful." I put a hand to his shoulder, but he shrugged it off.

As the *Windroos* pulled closer to the jetty, a strange excitement shot through me. Here, under a thickened sun, the air seemed to fairly bristle.

The night before, late, I had come up on deck. Only a few crew were about, on watch. I gazed up into the night, and the Southern Cross, trying to stare through the stars to the other side of the sky. Was Mama, lost these ten years to me—was she out there? The islands of stars glittered like rivers, pinpricks glowing through a paper lace pattern. A map of constellations, stars tied together as if with cosmic threads. As to my own life, well, that seemed to have no design at all. I pulled my cape more tightly around me and listened to the water lap against the bow.

If God had a plan for me, I prayed it included lace. I'd kept my skills secret from the Mistress, for I'd been warned of girls becoming lacemaking slaves to greedy employers, and I loved the craft too much to fall into that trap. Lace! Long before

I worked it with the lay Sisters, it was my obsession. One of my first memories was of Great-Grandmother's bed jacket in cream-colored silk, yellowed and crisp with age, but lace still supple and soft. Fountains of ivory as delicate as snowflakes. When Mama was out, I used to lift it from her trunk, grasp it by the hem, and whirl around her bedroom until it billowed out, cloud-like, riffling the air like the wings of a moth. Then I would jump upon the bed and let it fall from above until it blanketed my face.

Dutch law forbade servants to wear silk and jewelry, or too much lace. Would this also be true at the Cape?

Someone was watching. I wheeled around to see the Midshipman, arms crossed, leaning against a mast. A lantern high in the rigging lit his smile. He had been my one true friend on the voyage out.

"Apologies, Miss Klaassens. I interrupted your reveries."

"How long have you been standing there, Mr. Soolmans?"

"Not long," he said, though I sensed otherwise. He stepped close. "I was just noticing how like a child you look. Staring up at the night like that with such innocence."

"*Ja*, such innocence."

He was quiet for a minute. "I don't know what that scoundrel did to you, but it's over now."

Blood rushed to my face. I turned and stared into the blackness of water. He means well, I thought. The image returned in one disturbing flutter: that early morning in one of the ship's storage closets, when this very officer heard my cries and pulled that sailor from me—Claus, a young man I'd once also considered a friend.

"And I'll always be indebted to you, sir."

He bowed slightly. "That kind of thing is more common than shipping companies like to admit. Try to put it all behind you."

Behind me? An assault that shamed me deeply. That morning, as they took him below to a cell, he'd cursed me. Cornelia, a British girl, was leaving an officer's cabin adjusting the laces of her bodice. She threw him a rude gesture. "Don't ye mind his bluster none, lassie. They always do that when they feels guilty. Always blame the woman, they do." I decided that if I could ever get Cornelia alone, I'd gather my courage and tell her what happened. Ask her if I were still a virgin.

Now Mr. Soolmans moved closer. "As you will travel inland and my work keeps me in town until we sail on to Java, it's likely we'll never see one another again. Will you permit me a little counsel?" His eyes grew soft. Even though his breath smelled faintly of ale, I trusted him. "Women are rare at the Cape, Miss Klaassens, especially unmarried ones. I've watched you these many months. Oh, I know, you can use your tongue on that young lad Pier. But I've also seen your gentle nature. The Cape can be a rough place, and men will pursue you." He paused, looking out over the water a moment. "Prey upon you, most probably. Please take care."

I glanced at him under lantern light, then laughed uncomfortably. "Gentle nature, Mr. Soolmans? A bitter nature more likely. Bitterness under a calm facade."

"I can hardly believe that."

Oh, how little he knew me. We stood side by side in silence, staring out over the night ocean, eyes on the cliffs illuminated by the moon.

~

The Compagnie physician was an abrupt, officious man with a crooked wig. His sailors separated out the sick and hauled them into longboats to be whisked away to the town hospital. I thanked the Lord that the family and I, from better food, were healthy. Others less fortunate suffered the loosened teeth and open wounds of scurvy.

Still, we had to submit to rude examinations. We women flushed when they probed mouths and poked about under clothes for vermin and disease. Only Cornelia tittered and laughed with each feel, teasing the doctor mercilessly. "Consider yerself fortunate, sir. Normally ye would be paying me for this privilege." The Mistress pulled back in indignation. I muffled a giggle.

Later in the day, when the children were taking their naps in our cabin, I lay in my hammock bunk content to listen to the gentle rattle of their snores. Did they dream of Africa? Lately, sailor stories of marauding beasts and captives boiling in cannibal pots gave them nightmares. I'd told them I was absolutely sure the East India Compagnie and church *predikants* had a strong grip on things—all the time wondering how well they really held back the wild tides. How many miles I'd traveled! Not just in ocean expanse, but in ways of the world.

In the morning, as crewmen brought up the last of our trunks, I supervised their placement around me. One eye watched that nothing was pilfered, the other on the children playing tag in the tangle of sails. The Mistress excused herself. "A little courage," she muttered, clambering below. I sighed, knowing her courage took a liquid shape.

I was looking out over Table Bay, watching for returning longboats to carry us ashore, when my friend Carra slid to my side. She was a small, modest girl with fine green eyes, an open face, and clothes too large for her. Her fingers shook. Soon she would join her Cape Town burgher, an older man she had never met, to whom she was betrothed. An orphan with no money, family, nor prospects, Carra had agreed to an arranged marriage. He'd paid for her passage from the Netherlands and would be at the quay to greet her. But now things were complicated. On the journey out, she and the ship's Purser, Mr. Jan Graaf, had fallen quite in love. Now she stood silent, her face as pale as the white Cape cliffs.

"What will you do, Carra? Do you intend to honor your contract?" Her Purser, who stood with the other officers, paced nervously. "Bugger the old burgher!" I cried. "You two should elope. Hide below, Carra! You two can sail on to China!"

She winced. Her tortured eyes scanned the wharf. Little sobs rattled her chest like winds.

"Oh, Carra, I'm sorry. What you do is not my affair. God be with you."

Suddenly she turned and scuttled down the companionway. Her Purser flew after her. Then before I could tell them how much I hoped to see them again in this life, before I could say farewell to the ship that for months had been our home, we were hustled into longboats and churning toward land, about to touch sea-crazed feet to ground for the first time in months. On African soil.

Chapter 3

April 1749 (Autumn)
Cape Town

"There's Father!" Pier shouted.

A man in a corduroy suit and wide palmiet hat strode down the quay, two slim hounds at his heels, with a small, barefoot Black boy carrying an impossibly tall sunshade. Commanding the boy to wait, he swept a path through the crowd, wielding a walking stick. He looked distinguished and trustworthy, like one of the fine gentlemen who used to commission art through my father. At least, that was my first impression.

The Master, perhaps in his forties, a satiric twist to his mouth, smiled and opened his arms. Catryn ran into them. "Sweetheart. What a fine lass you've become. How old are you now? Seven. Or is it eight?"

She pouted. "I'm nine and a half."

"Nine, and plump as a porpoise. Your mother indulging you with sweets, no doubt. What happened to your eyebrows?" He spun around. "You've grown tall, Pier!" I frowned when he tousled his hair, locks I had so carefully combed. Pier wasn't a little boy any more. "Stand up straight, lad. We'll make a gentleman out of you yet. Once we've cleaned the green from your gills. Ha!"

The children flushed and squirmed. My poor fishes.

The Mistress smelled sweetly of musk and jasmine oil she'd been saving. When she lifted her sunmask, the Master grazed lips across her cheek. "How are you, Annetje? And the journey? Not too hard on your nerves?" She flashed him a tight smile. He barely looked her in the eye, this wife he had not seen in a year.

He took her hand tenderly, a hint of apology in his eyes, saying he had a few small gifts waiting for her at Rustigvallei. The Mistress flicked her lashes at him. Was she flirting? She introduced me. As he looked me up and down, I dared study his eyes: proud brows over gray steel walls. I lowered my lids and curtsied. "Pleasure," he murmured, touching his straw hat briefly with his stick, then turned quite away. I felt like a bruised melon in a fruit stall.

The Mistress must have known this meeting would be strained—she'd downed the last of her sherry just before we disembarked. Still, what an elegant figure she cut! Slender and handsome, all the while as cool and untouchable as her thin porcelain teacups. Before the voyage out, her skin had been as white as sugar-iced cakes. Despite her precautions, it now was freckled and tawny.

The Master forged a path through the crowded docks, the Black boy shielding the Mistress from an intense sun with his parasol. I took up the rear. At every step the earth seemed to betray us, moving beneath our feet like the sea.

I spotted Carra on the wharf. A portly man in a wig was bowing to her, taking her hand. My heart sank. So she was going to be with her burgher after all. Well, perhaps he was a good man. Perhaps he would even make her happy. I looked again. At least she'd have security.

The Mistress took precarious steps, dodging puddles, tottering, perhaps from the liquor as from the unmoving land. In high-heeled shoes she hadn't worn in months. She steadied herself with the help of an ebony walking stick, refusing the Master's arm.

Some rough men who worked the docks sidled up behind me. So close! How tall and beefy these African Dutch were! Trying to block recent memories, I determined not to get rattled. Where was a sharp-tipped parasol? Hadn't Papa warned me? "A serving girl is fair game for any manner of scoundrels, Saskia. If anything happens to you, do you think for a minute the courts will be on the side of a maidservant?" He'd never wanted me to go into service in the first place, and certainly not in Africa.

How fierce the wind blew! When it flirted with my petticoats, I gripped my bonnet, walking closer to my protectors.

At our carriage, I glanced up at the driver. Thick arms. And was that nose of his mashed? "To the Castle, Jaco," the Master barked, tapping his stick above the window. He slipped off his hunting gloves. "Have you children been good?"

Catryn said *she* had, but Pier set fire to a closet of sails. He glared at his sister, then shifted nervous eyes to his father.

"What's this, Pier?" The Master sat erect. "Is this true, Annetje? Well, where was Nanny?" I looked down and flushed. The Mistress had given my hands the caning, not Pier's. After that I had to watch the boy as a dikesman watches a dam for leaks.

"You're supposed to behave like a young gentleman, not some thug." The Master slammed his fist against the carriage door. "You have the family name to uphold. Mark my words, Pier de Witt, you will be punished!" Pier's eyes darted furtively out the window. When his knee began twitching, I felt alarm. Clearly this master suffered no fools.

"You should have seen the tarboy swinging from a net on the Slaver, Father," Pier said. But the parent he had traveled halfway around the world to be with only stared at him.

We were to spend the night with a friend of the de Witts, giving the Dutch East India Compagnie time to handle our papers. Meanwhile we would turn sightseers while our men stocked up on supplies.

Our carriage approached a massive circular building with gray stone walls, and solid bastions that shot out like cogs on a wheel. "This is the Castle," the Master announced. "It's also our prison." We stared at this ugly fortification boasting armed soldiers out front, and for a moment I feared he was dropping Pier and me off for lockup.

The Castle, we learned, housed the High Governor as well as soldiers, batteries of cannon guarding the harbor, and criminals. Master de Witt told the Mistress that the High Governor and his wife were throwing a party for her here tomorrow. Her face lit up. "Everyone of importance at the Cape wants to meet you." She glowed. But when he muttered that he couldn't stay for most of it, as he had to get on the road selling his wines, she looked away coldly. I felt for her. Just when she needed him most.

We alighted, and walked on crushed seashells along the Castle moat. The Mistress and Catryn strolled down a path to inspect the roses, while the Master, Pier and I peered through an iron grill. I started, for right before us loomed a high platform with crossbeam—the gallows. And beyond, a great horizontal wheel, the breaking wheel, used to tear apart limbs. Pier pumped his father for details. He wanted to know all about these implements of torture.

As we walked toward the gates, a foul odor permeated the air and strange statues came into view. But no. Pier and I froze. Impaled on stakes, encrusted with blood and flies were two heads, one African, one European, flesh peeling and rotting in the sun. Viscous, lifeless eyes stared inward. I inched backward, the ground falling out from under me, my last meal cresting my throat. I ran as fast as I could to the carriage, sinking into a corner, shivering. Why in God's name had the Master brought us here?

Pier clambered in looking nauseous. The Master stood outside, smirking like an eel, sucking on his meerschaum pipe. "Town fathers here mean business. They tolerate no rogues. I can tell you many a story about slaves and murderers tortured in those prison cells." He looked toward me intently. "Why, a dairymaid was burned here just three weeks ago for threatening her mistress with an ax. She'd gone quite mad. A sobering thought indeed, is it not, Miss Klaassens?"

I gritted my teeth. Who did he think I was—a common criminal? What kind of country was this, anyway? And what manner of man my master? A dread entered me then, a dread that often was to sneak up on me in this new land, like some ghost frightening me from sleep.

On the road again, I peered out the window. What a marvelous patchwork of people walked the streets! Natives of every continent, the Master said, many conversing in tongues I'd never heard. The burgher families dressed years behind in fashion, while dusky natives paraded by like luscious fruits in green silks and lemon-colored cottons, blue cocked hats with grand feathers, or mountainous headwraps. How I wished I were able to sketch them! The children pointed and tittered.

"Mind your manners!" the Mistress snapped. I nearly laughed myself.

And again, powerful odors! This town fairly cooked in them—smells of decaying fish, a beached whale, the scat of penguins. The 'Cape Doctor,' the Master told us, was a powerful wind that blew odors out to sea, while heady fragrances like *koffie* and spices vied to scent the air. The East India Compagnie stored vast quantities of spices from the Orient awaiting ships bound for Europe. Once settled, I would make little packets of cinnamon and clove, and place them among my clothing. For if I could no longer smell of French lavender, at least I would smell sweet with the East.

Master de Witt told us about such intriguing places as the Compagnie Gardens, the Malay Quarters of the Bo-Kaap, and the Slave Market. He talked of that barren Isle of Robben we passed offshore, where prisoners, exiles, and lepers go, never to return unless they can swim faster than the sharks.

"Mama!" Catryn thrust a finger out the window at a barefoot Black man. He wore ragged breeches and a strange conical straw hat that peaked on top. My mouth fell open to see a chain cinched around his neck; a White man pulled him like a cur. Memories of the Black man swinging from the spar pressed in on me.

Slavery was not illegal in the Netherlands, but I never heard of any slaves there. My parents used to debate slavery heatedly, Mama saying it was the height of colonial arrogance. Papa agreed, but argued it essential to the economy of our empire. And besides, we Calvinists doubted natives even had souls. "Miserable creatures, baked black with the sun, no more than animals," they had said. And everyone knew animals didn't have souls.

The *predikant* at our Reformed Church in Delft had spoken frequently about our divine necessity as the elect of God to save heathens from sin by showing them the good Christian way. I had looked around the congregation. How many churchgoers here were really that good? When I tried to discuss such things with the lay Sisters as we made lace, they snapped at me: "Never

ever question the Church!"

In the carriage that afternoon, I decided I would get to know some slaves and decide for myself if they had souls.

The Master pointed to some small, wiry San Bushmen, their skin like wrinkled leather and with skinny eyes, wearing only skins. "The most primitive people on earth," he insisted. "Those ostrich egg shells are probably full of beer." Ha! As if half the men back home weren't sotted with beer most of the time. As for their cousins, the Khoi-khoi, or Hottentots, the Master called them thievish, idle, dirty beasts who rarely came to town for fear of being accused of crimes and forced into labor. Many had been wiped out by the pox in 1713. "Local *kaffirs* are useless as slaves. They refuse to work no matter how much they're punished."

How clever of them.

"What's a *kaffir*, Father?"

"A *kaffir*, son, is a heathen Black infidel who does not believe in God. They're hardly more than animals. God has placed them in our hands, to do what we can with them."

I averted my gaze, holding my tongue.

"Will they eat us?" Catryn asked.

Pier swatted her arm. "Oh, shut up. They might give you a disease, though." His father's eyes flashed at him, then relaxed, as if agreeing. "Mother," Pier said, "when can we have our sugar cakes?"

The Master leaned in. "Then there's that other kind of *caffer*. Slave convicts who strong-arm for the city magistrates. Stay clear of *them*."

Suddenly, approaching an intersection, we heard a chorus of young voices. I stuck my face out the window. Native children, girls, dressed in spice sacks, stood against a wall and filled the air with song. A couple of them looked very light in color. The Master signaled the carriage to stop. We sat and listened.

What harmonies! Except for their sad faces, I thought heaven had dropped angels down upon us. When the singing ended, one child approached with a tin cup. Her brow was smooth and high, and her small eyes bright and brimming with, yes, intelligence. As I reached for my purse, the Master looked at them with little darts. He rapped, and the carriage lurched forward. I looked back at the choir of children, and a great sadness shrouded me. Couldn't we have given them at least a few coins?

The Master had other thoughts. "Miss Klaassens, as simple a maid as you are, here you will be considered superior to the noblest person of color on all the African continent, solely on the merit of your pale skin."

I scowled. What merit was there merely in being born White? I gazed out the window, remembering a line I once copied from a book by a certain Mary Astell: "If all Men are born free, how is it that all Women are born slaves?"

I, a contracted servant girl, ever under the control of some man or other, was but one step removed from the slaves who walked by this very carriage.

Chapter 4

April 1749 (Autumn)
Cape Town

It was early when I snuck outside to catch the first light of morning as it glanced off the mountains. We'd spent the night at the house of a friend of the Master's, Dr. Buehl, a German physician. Palm trees swayed softly around his large home, which was high in the foothills. It gave a grand view of town and harbor, or what I could see of it, for a veil of fog hovered over tile and thatched-roof homes and pressed onto the cobbled streets of Cape Town. Large birds screeched strangely from the sycamores, making me start—a sound like metal grinding metal. On what manner of planet had we landed?

Last night at dinner, when he wasn't looking, I scrutinized the doctor. Tall, middle-aged, portly. His right foot was swollen and bandaged, and he walked bolstered by an olive wood stick. "Gout," the Mistress had muttered to me under her breath. "A glutton, I'd say."

I blinked as she downed her third glass of sherry.

Dr. Buehl boasted wide, grizzled hair, a wrinkled coat, drooping stockings, and shoe buckles long overdue for a polishing.

Throughout the meal, he joked and teased, often beaming at the children and me, mumbling apologies for food spilled into the crumpled fits of his cravat. After dinner he rummaged through a large waistcoat pocket, a hole burned through it, doubtless from tucking a lit pipe there, and pulled out pieces of marzipan for us. His face reminded me of those old woodcut prints of a full moon that smiled down benignly from the sky. I loved the man.

I went inside to rouse the children. They shivered and fretted at the cold. Though April, it was autumn here, a world moving fast toward winter. Once we crossed the equator, all seasons became opposite, so we were cheated of spring. Now the tulips would be opening back home. How I missed them!

Master de Witt announced he would not accompany us into Cape Town today, and that after his required hour at the High Governor's party this afternoon, he would begin his trip north to negotiate the sale of Rustigvallei wines. The Mistress fastened him with a look of betrayal, but I was relieved, for that meant Dr. Buehl would be our guide and protector.

An hour after breakfast the children and I were in the carriage, suited up and ready for our trip into town, waiting for the Mistress. Dr. Buehl was waiting too, sunning himself on the front *stoep*. The better part of an hour passed. I jumped in and out of the carriage, fretting. She used to treat us with more respect. On the journey out, I had become her confidante, privy to family secrets, such as their rebuff from Delft society. Business contracts her husband never won, parties to which they were never invited. When I looked questioning, she only muttered it had something to do with Master de Witt's forebears. Did they carry some shame? Was that why we'd sailed far away to Africa? As their servant, was I now shamed too?

The Master had left the Dutch Provinces for the Cape months before I was employed, to prepare matters at the estate.

He'd taken along several servants, including the Housekeeper, who was also the Governess—Mistress Cingria. Cingria. Such a foreign name.

In the carriage the children kicked the bottoms of their seats and breathed onto the windows, running fingers through the moisture. I led them in a game of Cat's Cradle, and we passed the time picking webs of yarn from each other's fingers. How it made my hands itch to work the bobbins again! To see the beautiful tracery of threads emerge like magic on the pillow. "This is so like lacemaking," I murmured.

Catryn looked up, excited. "Do you know how to make lace, Miss Saskia?"

I fell silent. "Let's get out and let the sun warm us."

Pier swaggered to the top of the ridge. By now the fog had lifted, and the town sparkled from housetop to beach. A puppy bounded across the drive in front of us, chasing some noisy guinea hens. We giggled when the hens suddenly turned and chased the frightened puppy back to the house.

Oh, where was the Mistress? The children were about to hurtle the carriage down the hill in mutiny. I walked inside to her room. She was sitting at a dressing table, still in her bed gown, while a slave dressed her hair. I stared. "We've been waiting in the carriage, Mistress."

"I'm coming, I'm coming. Just go downstairs. Wait, Saskia. Pull out my green satin gown and lay it on the bed, would you? Two lace petticoats. And hoops. And the green mules."

For the most part, she'd been a gracious employer, but there were times onboard I wanted to push her into the sea. When I'd bring afternoon tea to her cabin, she'd complain it wasn't hot enough. Or, as I stood in the wind above deck, she would point to a tendril of hair that had blown from my cap. We were on a merchant ship on the high seas, for goodness' sake, not sitting in her parlor in Delft. I thought of the guinea hens chasing the little dog. *Pick pick pick, peck peck peck.*

Many an afternoon, when I'd take the children above for fresh air, she'd retire to her cabin and sip liqueur in her chemise, *en déshabillé*, until she fell asleep. Sometimes I had to dress her and take her arm, she was falling about so, just to climb the short steps to the Captain's dining room. I don't remember her drinking like that in Delft. She had refined sensibilities, I decided. Ship life was too much for her.

But she'd been generous too. She'd given me a couple of her old linsey frocks. Sure, she'd stripped them of lace and braid, but that was only fair, for I was a servant and not allowed such excesses. Once on the journey out, unable to stand ship food one more minute, she took over the galley and cooked *pannenkoek* for all the officers, improvising from the pantry. She laughed and jested the whole time. The children and I knew, for we were her assistants. Everyone truly enjoyed her then.

At last she entered the carriage with the doctor. He settled deep into the leather seat and stretched out his gouty foot next to Pier, who cringed and turned away. And so we set out for Cape Town.

I watched Catryn press her face to the glass as we rumbled through town. Persimmon-colored leaves blanketed the streets. Great oaks, sycamores, and trees unknown to me lined the walkways in front of tidy homes. The inhabitants seemed larger and rougher than they had yesterday. Perhaps Mr. Soolmans was right to warn me. Did separation from one's mother country give license to become shaggier at the edges?

How excited I'd been to board ship bound for this far Dutch outpost! I'd said my goodbyes in Delft, feeling like some heroine traveling to a far land where my destiny awaited. In truth, the moment we pulled from Amsterdam harbor, my eyes grew moist.

I watched the redbrick skyline of the city, the church spires, and wide-winged storks disappear from sight. Family, friends, the Calvinist Sisters who taught me to make lace, every person and thing that defined me rushed further and further away. I loved my country, but I couldn't stay. After Mama's death, Papa remarried. And when they had a babe I felt evicted from their little family.

Now I saw Dutch gabled buildings, limed brilliant white from crushed seashells. Streets cobbled with—stones! We have so few in the Netherlands. Bricks we make, but there are few large stones. Some of the red-tiled roofs were weighted down with them, and I could see why, for the wind was growing fierce. Suddenly rocks and roof tiles soared through the air, crashing down around us. Jaco steered the carriage under cover of eaves until the wind died down, much to our relief.

After fruit and rusks at a *koffiehuis*, we visited the Compagnie Gardens. What an exuberance of beauty and bounty! Not only flowers, but apple and pear, almond, orange, quince, and lime trees—every kind of fruit imaginable. We strolled down palm-studded paths bordered with flamboyant, spiky plants, succulents, but also orchids. All planted and tended by slaves. The Cape had nearly lost it all two years back, when a plague of locusts attacked city and countryside, eating every leaf in sight. But most came back.

What truly amazed us, though, was a menagerie of animals from the African veldt. We were thrilled to stand so close to giraffe, great apes, ostriches, snakes, and the African tyger they called leopard, all caged behind bars, of course. A magnificent lion roared so powerfully that the children, Mistress, and I fell back, clutching one another in fright, which made the doctor roar too, with laughter. I shuddered. Would we chance upon such beasts in the bush?

The Mistress wanted to find her favorite white *chinees* tea, so the doctor instructed Jaco to drive us to the Bo-Kaap, a part of town where free people of color lived. Jaco parked the carriage at the crest of a hill, and we sat waiting while the doctor headed for the Asian stalls.

How colorful the market below us looked! I asked if the children and I could run down just for a look, but all the Mistress allowed us was to stand beside the carriage and hold hands while Jaco left to fetch grapes and cheese.

Then a most peculiar thing happened. We could see it all from the hill. A man the color of dried figs was trudging up, balancing a wide basket of apples on his head. At the same time we could see another man, also colored, climbing the other side pushing a cart piled so high with rags it was a wonder he could see where he was going. Well, he couldn't, for at the crest his cart crashed right into the appleman. Blue and white rags, trousers, and skirts winged through the air like birds, then fell, littering the street. Blood-colored apples rolled everywhere. The men screamed at one another, voices louder and louder as they cursed and swore at feverish pitch. When they threw up their fists, my heart began racing. A fight! Catryn grabbed the hem of my jacket. I held her close.

"Jaco, Jaco, where are you?" The Mistress, frantic, peered up and down the street. "Children, Saskia, get into the carriage." But we weren't about to move.

By now a crowd had gathered. They shouted and goaded the men on, flush with battle fever. That's when I spotted her, an older colored woman walking with a Black man. She was lame or something, but made her way quickly enough toward the two men. She grabbed the upraised fist of the ragman and clasped it to her mouth, kissing it. I couldn't believe my eyes. She let go, then grasped the other man's fist and kissed it, too.

Everything stopped. Murmurs rippled through the crowd. Both men pulled back their fisticuffs. The young Black man, who must have been a slave, took off his hat and leaned down, filling it with shiny apples, and dropped them into the man's basket. The ragman hesitated, then scrambled after apples too, and the appleman rushed to gather up ragcloth, folding striped shirts and flowered petticoats neatly onto the cart. Bystanders also bent to help, until each man had his load back in place. I turned to where the Mistress sat. She was leaning out the carriage window, fascinated.

I looked again. The moment he picked up his last apple, the slaveman glanced toward us. He was but fifteen yards away, and for a brief moment I thought our eyes met. He bowed crisply, spun on his heels, grabbed the older woman by the waist, and lifted her over a curb where they disappeared into the crowds.

Chapter 5

April 1749 (Autumn)
African Interior

Our carriage stumbled over cobbled ruts. How sad to leave Cape Town! A fierce sun peeked in and out of the clouds, and I gazed back at this city wedged between mountain and sea. We were heading for Rustigvallei, the wine estate, our new home, hours inland. The Master had arranged for us to meet up with our traveling party at Cape Town's outskirts. Two ox-drawn wagons loaded with provisions greeted us. His slaves rode in donkey carts or walked alongside, prodding the animals on with switches of hippopotamus hide they called *sjamboks*.

The slaves seemed to wear a mantle of invisibility and did not look us in the eye. But one old man returned my smile. The others called him Oom Samuel, "Uncle." A small, wiry man whose teeth reminded me of the stained ivories of a spinet my aunt kept in her attic.

Our entourage traveled beyond the wild meadows that drifted up the foothills of Table Mountain. Our carriage groaned down dusty roads, and the land opened out into wide plains and grassy hills. Oh, this was a country of summers! For us

Hollanders, for whom water is an ever-present currency, the air felt parched. Yet my heart filled with joy at patches of green that burst with life, and the red of Cape lilies.

"Those flowers are like a woman just entering middle age," the doctor said, almost to himself, as he parted the carriage curtain. "Fading but still in bloom." He smiled at his witticism, then looked with alarm at the Mistress's frown. "Begging your pardon, Mistress. I was not referring to you. My dear lady, you are young, a rare orchid among weeds." I suppressed a grin. When he shifted the conversation to the party they had both attended at the High Governor's yesterday, she beamed, for the Cape's elite had gathered in her honor.

The road threaded a path behind Table Mountain, through sand dunes, then marshland. Dry dirt spit into dust clouds or turned to stoney mud. We gaped in wonder at wild antelope and striped horses called zebra dotting the distant valleys. We passed forests of fir, majestic, towering trees. I heard a screech, and looked to see hawks circling. All the while my eye locked fleeting frames of countryside into lace designs: a meandering road became a chevron, a spread of leaves a fan. At times like these, when my hands were helpless, the lacemaker in me grabbed the rhythm of things, weaving nature into motifs of my imagination.

At a great river, we alighted to cross a stone bridge. The men fought to push the carriage and wagons over rutted cobbles. Jaco the driver wore his three-cornered hat at a jaunty tilt, and when the Mistress gave him a disapproving look, he straightened it. I smiled when, out of her sight, he tilted it back again. I took the children by the hand and stepped down to riverbank, mesmerized by a bevy of blue water lilies, and we splashed water on our faces. Water, clear water! Water safe to drink. What a wonder! On the road again, more mountains sprang up on the horizon. Would we have to cross them?

The journey from Cape Town to Rustigvallei would take four hours. We were well into it when Jaco stopped the carriage on a high ridge. We looked down into green valleys of fields, rows of grapevines burning with red leaves. Here and there a farmhouse punctuated the countryside. Catryn turned and asked the doctor about her new Governess. I searched his face. I too wanted to know about the woman under whom I would be working.

"You mean Mistress Cingria? She's the Housekeeper too, you know. That woman is one holy terror," he cried. "They say she turns into a panther at night and prowls the house looking for sweet morsels of children to eat!" His hands flew up and he scratched the air with claws. "Aaaaaarrrrggh!" Catryn stared in horror, then burst out laughing. I waited for the doctor's qualifying statement, but it never came. Nor did the Mistress admonish him. What manner of woman was this Mistress Cingria?

We spotted a Hottentot *kraal*—a great thorny fence with circular mud huts, and goats, oxen, and natives moving about. How different this was from home! The sun burned hotter as we progressed until the sky cleared and cupped itself over the landscape like a vast blue bowl. Jaco jerked the carriage to a halt and cocked his rifle. We jumped forward in our seats as several shots rang out, shots that bounced across the hills. A slave loosed the hounds and they took off, padding back with a brace of plovers in their teeth. "Well done, lad," the doctor said.

Our party plodded on. Jaco had put us at ease earlier promising that dangerous beasts mostly stayed clear of such well-used roads. So I was a bit nervous when he called out from his high seat. "Shall we take our guests along the trail up the *kloof* then, Dr. Buehl, sir?"

The carriage veered to the right, and we teetered up a steep slope, entering a cleft between two great hills. Dr. Buehl bent forward, his eyes dancing. "Sorry to go a little out of our way, Mistress, but I wanted to show you the *real* Africa."

At a clearing along a high cliff, our party alighted. I inhaled sharply. A rush of vertigo ripped through me. Never before had I stood at the edge of an abyss. Far below, at the bottom of the craggy slope, wild animals sauntered across the savanna toward a distant lake, shimmering like ghosts in the dusty heat.

"Rheebok," Dr. Buehl said, pointing to a herd of elegant antelope. He swept his arm along the horizon. "There, over by the thicket, wildebeest. And can you make out the buffalo? Magnificent horns!" We stared and stared. "Those fat animals in the water are hippopotamus. Dangerous beasts when stirred. At sunset the giant elephants will come by the hundreds. Some day, Lord willing, you will get to see them."

Only in nature does such wildness happen, I thought—such force of life!

"I'm going to ride out with Father and shoot them all," Pier announced.

The doctor's eyes rested on him. I held my tongue. A cousin of mine back home once bragged he'd shot all the crows and squirrels he could in the woods that week. "Well done, Henkie," I'd said. "And every one of them killed, I'm sure, in self-defense."

Suddenly a thousand flamingo, wading in the water on stilt legs, broke into flight, splintering the stillness like a barrage of coral arrows. We gaped in wonder. Even Pier was absorbed to the bone. Below us, the beasts trod the parched veldt, every footfall, it seemed, reverberating across the savanna like pulsing blood. If I put my ear to the earth, surely I would hear the beat of their hearts.

That moment on a high ridge was when it lay claim to me.

Africa! It had entered me now. Driven itself into my marrow.

A band of natives strode across the plains, Black silhouettes on the horizon. They moved as gracefully as tall grasses. Heat flickered their forms like flames in the wind.

"Hottentots," the doctor said. "When you Hollanders first encountered them, their language sounded like the stuttering *click click* of 'hoet-en-toet.' So that's what you called them."

The Mistress's hands shook. She stepped back. Yes. We Dutch thought we could tame anything. Now standing at Africa's interior, I knew how deep the roots of wildness cut.

Driving back to the road, one thing became terribly clear. From here on I would be forced to live wide-awake. For this land was infused with a spirit too large for me to hold.

~

After several hours' journey, tossed about so that our bottoms tingled and our teeth rattled, we entered rolling green hills. The children moaned of being tired and hungry. I was too.

"Perfect timing, children," Dr. Buehl said. "I've arranged with a house*vrouw* just down the pike to prepare us a light lunch."

A slaveman opened the gate. A thick-waisted woman in a plain dress and white cap stood cross-armed at the door of her cottage, her Dutch face earth dry, guarded. Our "light lunch" consisted of fish soup, pigeon, stewed turnips and cabbage, rice, dumplings, beer and a large milktart, all spread on a table beneath her one tree. A slavewoman with a strange iron contraption over head and mouth offered us soup. I tried not to stare. She was quiet, but I could smell the resentment.

"What's that thing on her head?" Pier demanded.

"That's not our business, Pier." The Mistress settled into a high-backed chair the doctor had brought from the house.

The *vrouw* looked him straight in the face. "To teach her not to talk back."

I stared from house*vrouw* to slavewoman. What monstrous punishment was this?

"A mouth trap," Pier punned to his sister, and they giggled. I glared at them in warning, but then the *vrouw* laughed too. Somehow I got through the meal, but food seemed to stick to my throat. That slavewoman had more grit than I had.

Back on the road, I glanced out at brilliant hills of farms and vineyards, and the chain of ragged mountains beyond. Formidable mountains. The Mistress slumped in her seat, napping. A fanciful thought took hold: what if I had married the wealthy boy Papa had chosen for me? Like her, I might already be a mother, mistress of a fine home, and comporting myself grandly. But fine clothing and a grand home meant nothing to me.

Pier sprang forward in his seat and pointed a finger down the road. "Look!" Atop a two-foot anthill a few yards beyond squatted a great old ape. It bared its dagger-like teeth and shrieked. Catryn screamed, and the Mistress wakened with a start, recoiled, then fanned herself with her bonnet. We sighed with relief as the monkey crashed off into the underbrush.

Dr. Buehl laughed. "That, my dears, was a *bobbejaan*—a baboon. Do you know what the Hottentots say? That baboons can speak, but they don't let the White man know for fear he'll put them to work."

Catryn and I laughed and laughed. Until we saw the Mistress scowling at us. "Really, Miss Klaassens," she snapped. "If you can't act with more decorum, perhaps we should put you on the next boat back to Amsterdam."

I clenched my fingers and buried them in my skirts. How

she had changed toward me!

"Madame," the doctor said, bowing slightly, "please forgive me. It was a joke, but I'm afraid in poor taste." The Mistress gave him a minimal nod, then stared out the window. As we traveled on, she pressed him with questions about her frail health, her nerves. He listened attentively, promising to visit whenever he could and bring medications. A grateful smile lit her face.

"Ladies and gentlemen," the doctor suddenly announced, "I give you Rustigvallei. Here is your 'Peaceful Valley.' "

At last!

Sitting in the lap of towering mountains, it emerged like a dream: a great gleaming white Dutch manor house. My breath caught in my throat. Acre upon acre of grapevines radiated over fields and hills in even rows, stalks bent with the weight of purple-black grapes. A long stand of oaks bordered the estate, while to the east a forest of conifers ran up the mountain.

We rode through an elaborate portal crowned with a sculpted cornice and up a magnificent drive with arching trees. As our carriage neared the house, my heart thumped. So this was where I was to live and work. I thought I would faint from the beauty.

Chapter 6

April 1749 (Autumn)
Rustigvallei

The manor house loomed before us, grand, handsome, whitewashed, with the clean lines of our finest farmhouses. Ornately stuccoed gables presided over its front, and the sweeping roof was tightly thatched. And two stories.

The door opened and men and women, colored and European, poured outside to greet us. Colored maids in shabby dresses dipped into curtsies, murmuring greetings in a striking singsong. Catryn grabbed onto my skirt. "There, there, Katje," I reassured her, though I too was astonished to walk within touching distance of so much dark skin. But, as they say, the natives were friendly.

"Welcome to Rustigvallei, *mevrouw*. I'm Johanna." A Dutch maid with sunbaked cheeks smiled and curtsied to the Mistress. "I been asked to show ye round."

Where was Mistress Cingria? I thought the Housekeeper would be the first to greet us.

Johanna was about my age, with bushy eyebrows and untidy dark hair that kept spilling from her cap. Not a beauty, somewhat broad in the beam really, but alert. She gave me a cool eye.

Inside, the ceilings were high, the floors wood, the gallery elegant and spare, stretching out into one very long room. Like many country manors, other rooms stemmed from its sides in an "H" pattern. It was grand and Dutch, with hints of the Orient, such as the *japanees* porcelainware, and Javanese louvered doors that folded against the wall.

The Mistress glided through the rooms, an imperious arch to her neck. She paused before a massive chest with fine brass hardware. "Furniture mostly made by our Malay slaves, of African woods," Johanna said with pride. Then she dug a toe into the carpet. "Real Persian. And on the floor!" The Mistress gave her a sideways look. Poor girl. She probably thought good carpets were only for tables.

Johanna showed the Mistress her bedroom at the front of the house, indicating this was her realm, a place to sleep, write letters, and receive female guests.

"Are you saying I'm to live in this one small room?" the Mistress demurred. As if she'd just been escorted to her cell at London Tower. Johanna curtsied, fidgeting.

I loved seeing so many fine paintings on the walls, much like the ones Papa used to broker in his art business. But these looked like copies, though good ones. Down the gallery through the back door loomed an immense yard, with outbuildings and grapevines that seemed to go on forever.

Suddenly it hit me what a daunting enterprise this was! Surely, I told myself, once I understood my duties, I'd feel more comfortable. I was proud to be Assistant Nursemaid—not as high in rank as Housekeeper or Nursemaid, but certainly above most servants. Like this girl Johanna.

The Mistress, exhausted, made for her bedroom.

Johanna beckoned us. "Come along, children." But they

lingered in the entryway, marveling at a rack of flintlock pistols and rifles that hung above the family Bible. "Don't even *think* of touching those!" I barked.

The kitchen was a large room with stone-flagged floor, two great tables, and walk-in hearth. Water in a kettle suspended from the chimney crane simmered over crackling logs. Scores of kettles and ladles, copper pots, brass pans, skimmers, silver mugs and trays flashed over wall and hearth. Several hutches boasted massive amounts of pewter, porcelain, stoneware, and that precious commodity, glass. Every piece was a work of art.

"You're to help with tonight's dinner," Johanna said. I began to protest. "Mistress Cingria's orders."

I frowned. Where was that panther of a woman, anyway? When Catryn and Pier burst into the kitchen, Johanna herded us up a narrowly twisting staircase. At the landing, Johanna nodded to a room to the right. "For dry storage. And a few extra coffins, just in case."

Catryn's mouth fell open. She shot me a look of exaggerated alarm. Pier leaned into Johanna's face. "Are you telling us our rooms lie next to coffins?"

Johanna paused, a smile curling her lips. "Well, they don't have no bodies in em! Yust sacks of grain. Keep it from the mice. We'll move em outta there, dearie, if it gives ye the creeps. Come on, children, I'll show ye where you're to sleep."

Two slavemen lumbered up the stairs behind us, straining under the weight of trunks. Johanna and the children entered the room on the left, but I continued down the hall, looking for mine. Above, lashed-together bamboo and wood beams supported exposed thatch—a sudden fragrance of cut grass. An eerie mood enveloped me. Just as I reached for the door latch, Johanna yelled out, "No!" I jerked back, but not before I heard the latch click to a lock from inside. "That's Mistress Cingria's room," she whispered.

The *kinder*room, where the children would study and play, was wide but shallow, with bedrooms on opposite sides. Walls shone with the blue of robin's eggs, and sun poured through low gabled windows. The room boasted—oh, luxury of luxuries—a fireplace. How the children and I would enjoy spending time here! Catryn dragged me to the window and pressed her forehead against the panes.

Below us, extending for miles, loomed the magnificent yard with tall, wide-armed oaks and gnarly camphors, outbuildings, and beyond, mountains and fields. I even spotted a river with a mill. Pier gave a cursory look, then fished through his trunk to find the toy forbidden to him for months. He grabbed his *kris*, cackled like any good pirate, and slashed at the air.

"Put that away, Pier!" What kind of parents made presents of real daggers to their children? The Javanese weapon had a sharp, wavy blade, making it all the more terrifying. Unpacking, Catryn lifted her French dolls from our trunk when a round woman padded through the door. Her face was gentle, remote. Catryn stumbled back. I rubbed her cheek.

"This is Black Lucy, children," Johanna said. But the slavewoman had remarkably light skin. "She'll be a kind of auntie to ye, your *aya*, caring for you when Mistress Cingria or Miss Saskia cannot."

"I don't need anyone to take care of me," Pier growled.

"Hush, Pier," I said. "You're still a babe in many ways."

Johanna regarded him for a long moment, like someone assessing a gift they're not sure they want. "Help the children unpack, will ye, Lucy?" She tapped me on the arm. "I'll show ye where you're to sleep." What? Wouldn't I be sleeping by the children?

I told Catryn that Lucy would be kind. "You are becoming

a young woman now. How would a grown up girl act?" A ploy, yes, but it often worked.

I followed Johanna through the kitchen and down the yard, entering a small cottage. "Here be where us domestics sleep, the White ones, that is." A tiny sitting area and the smallest of stone hearths. "That's Cook's room. This be mine and Anna's." Her voice trailed off adding, "And now yours too."

My heart fell. The room smelled damp. Sagging curtains enshrined two sagging beds. One homely chair. Cracked chamber pots and foot warmers stuck out from under the beds. Certainly better than our cramped cabin onboard, but a far cry from the clean, light-filled room I'd had in Delft. Heat crawled up my neck. The Mistress had promised me a room of my own.

A young woman our age slipped through the doorway. "Anna, meet your new roommate, Saskia."

Anna. A thin, gaunt-faced Dutch girl with a mouth full of donkey teeth. Her chin bent upward toward a long thin nose, as if they were trying to meet. She frowned. The girls drew straws as to whose bed I would share—it was Johanna's. I unpacked a few essentials, then lay down. It was as if I'd swallowed a stone and it had somehow slumped into my heart.

The girls sat and gawked at me. "Did ye know," Johanna said, "that Anna here tried walking down the stairs backward when she first come to the manor? Close yer mouth, Anna, you look like the village idiot." Anna's pale lashes looked down. "It's true, ain't it, girl? You slipped and dropped a tray of porcelain cups. Yust about broke your foot too, ye did." Johanna cocked her head toward the girl. "She were used to coming down ladders, backward, where she live before, being the farm girl she is." Johanna chuckled.

Poor Anna. Green as the tender grass. Wasn't Johanna being a little mean, though? Later I would see them together in the sitting room, Johanna helping Anna with a pile of mending she was behind on.

A slavewoman called at the door—I was needed in the kitchen.

The aroma of herb-infused stew and freshly baked bread filled my nostrils and beckoned my stomach. Two light-colored slavewomen stood at the table, one mincing onions as tears coursed her cheeks. A large, top-heavy Dutch woman with pale, pink-rimmed eyes tossed a hefty knife onto the table, pointing to a huge bowl of turnips. "Chop."

I stared at her. "Who, me?"

"Yes, you. Don't get uppity. Mistress Cingria's orders." She shuffled across the floor like a crab.

"Saskia Klaassens, if you please. Assistant Nursemaid." I picked up a turnip and sliced in heavy blows, vexed to be doing kitchen work.

"Well, Saskia Klaassens Assistant Nursemaid, I'm in charge of this here kitchen. So chop." We chopped and stewed for an hour until, suddenly, a bell rang outside, so loudly I lurched forward, nearly shaving off part of a finger. "Yust the slave bell, dearie. Calling workers from the fields."

When dinner was ready, I padded after Cook and her slavegirls, all of us bearing pots of stew or bowls of seasoned vegetables. Down the yard, not far from an outbuilding, sat two great long tables. White, Black, and caramel-colored people were settling onto the benches under great oaks. Behind the tables loomed auburn fields, and a burning sun began its descent behind the mountains.

A slaveman lit rush torches mounted on stakes around the tables, and some yards away, another cranked a spit skewered with wild antelope. I was ravenous!

"Attention, you rogues and scruffies," Cook bellowed. "This

here be Saskia, a new maid shipped in from the homeland. Miss Saskia to most of ye, if you please." Many nodded a wan greeting, so I curtsied. Everyone laughed, including Cook, her great breasts shaking. "You don't have ta curtsy none to this lot, girl. This be family."

I sat next to Johanna, trying not to blush. The fall evening was crisp, and I wished for my shawl. Just before the sun sank behind the mountains, it grew huge and fiery, throwing long rays of orange-lavender across our motley party. White skin turned peach, colored skin bronze. I was suddenly tired from our travel, and my throat was dry. I gulped at my wine.

So many new faces. Johanna tried to teach me their names. There was the Malay Anthonij, the short, stocky Foreman; and the tall, lanky White Overseer, Mr. Pesser. Colored Manassa with a blind eye, and burly Black Sladie. The Malays, Luther and Josiah. The slaves smiled gently, averting their gaze but for one, a pretty slavegirl, Jezza, who loped down the yard with a purposeful swagger. Her delicate features and lichen-colored eyes made me think the blood of several races streamed through her. "Calls themselves *bastars*," Johanna later told me. "Come in every shade of *koffie* and cream, don't they?" Jezza glared at me, slammed a pot of hot greens and turnips on the table before me, then turned abruptly, sniffing the air. *Choose your battles*, Mama had counseled. Well, tonight it wouldn't be Jezza.

Johanna talked on about slaves coming from Batavia, Ceylon, Bengal, Macao, and the Celebes, all called Malays. Darker natives hailed from Angola, Cape Verde, and other parts of Africa or Madagascar. Most of them spoke a funny *taal*, Dutch with native words thrown in. Johanna said most houseslaves were light-colored, and ate and dressed better than the field slaves. "Then there are us White indentured servants. Slaves as good as."

She turned to her friend. "Hey, Anna, remember when you thought if you touched a Black man, their color would rub off on yer fingers?" Johanna howled with laughter. Most workers smiled, though not Anna. Frankly, I might have once thought that too.

"Where is Mistress Cingria?"

"Out stealing horses." I looked at Johanna askance. Her grin was gleeful. "Got ya! She doesn't eat with us. Maybe dining with the family tonight. Or hidin in her room." Before I could ask why, Cook called Johanna. She jumped up and ran into the kitchen.

Next to me sat Sara of Mosambiek, a gentle girl. Her Dutch was limited. And my Mosambiekian did not exist. But I managed to understand that she'd only recently arrived. By torchlight, her slender fingers made shadows that danced on the wall—grasses in the wind. Above us, the first stars of evening glittered in the sky, while a great yellow moon rose from behind the mountains.

Oom Samuel sat apart, slumped in the depths of an old chair, chewing on a battered pipe. His face was like a worn leather satchel. He wore clothes more patches than original cloth and stroked a mangy cat. When he nodded to me, I smiled and nodded back. Then I was squatting at his side.

"Hello, Oom Samuel." He sat up in his rickety chair, giving me a toothless grin. His eyes wore a quiet I had not seen earlier. "All of this is so new to me—Africa, I mean. Where are you from, Uncle? Do you have family here?"

"I be from here, my daughter. And these people," he nodded around, "they be family." His faded eyes turned to me, mischievous. "Why is you ask it, Miss Saskia? You wantin to my family be? Wantin to court this old old man, isn't it?"

I threw back my head and laughed, and he giggled. I liked him, and the funny way he spoke. Yet his eyes bore a sadness. As if bones had been broken around the heart they were meant to protect. For a while it was lovely just to sit with him, listening to others chatter.

A young European approached. High eyebrows arched over narrow eyes, billowing hair stuck up in front, like a startled cockatoo. It was the Master's valet, Egbert. He gave an extraordinary bow, then proceeded to educate me on the finer points of winemaking. It was as if I'd pulled some switch and set noisy gears into motion. But I didn't want the lyceum lecture. When he pulled his chair closer and said he'd take me under his wing, I chirped my apologies and flew off.

I headed back to the table. Despite teasing Anna, Johanna seemed a genuine lass, down-to-earth. I liked Anna too, though she had a silly way of looking away and giggling any time a man spoke to her. Even Jaco's "Pass the turnips."

"Found out somethin today." Anna beamed. "Seems that a fine lady in Cape Town, she so wealthy she drunk hot cocoa two, three times a day, even durin her confinement. When her time come, she give birth to a babe the color of chocolate."

We were speechless. Titters, then laughing so hard that tears rolled down our cheeks. Anna looked flustered. "Oh, Anna," I said, "you really had us going for a minute, pretending you didn't know better." I decided to take her aside later and explain the facts of life. And chocolate.

Just as dinner broke up, as people started drifting off into the evening, I saw a candle put to flame in the upstairs room beyond Catryn's. The silhouette of a woman appeared at the low window. She must have picked up a shawl and thrown it over her shoulders. I shivered, thinking of a giant raven flapping black wings. That had to be her.

In the kitchen, just as I started to go upstairs to the children, Cook told me to clean the dishes. Indignation welled up inside.

That wasn't one of my duties! I stayed, though, and scrubbed sand on the pots so hard, I thought the brass would come off. At last, washing done, I headed for the steps, but Cook took me by the arm and told me to fetch two watermelons from the garden. Blimey!

"I'd really best check on the children, Cook."

"That's all taken care of." She handed me a tin lantern and pointed toward the garden. What were my duties around here, anyway? And who gave the orders?

I stumbled around in the dark, tripping over broken brick, until at last I found the arched gate. I was standing amid the prickly vines, reaching down, touching a slick green melon when I heard a sound. I spun around, holding up the light. There, a few feet away, was a slavechild, perhaps seven years, in cutoff breeches and an ill-fitting woman's bodice. He jumped up and stared at me, large eyes burning in his skull.

"Hey!" I shouted. "Caught ya!" He dropped a fist of red melon, thrust hands to his hips and fixed me with a look both scared and defiant. Pink juice trickled down his chin. "Are you stealing from your master? Wait!" I yelled as he tore away into the night. "I won't tell."

It was late by the time I checked on Pier and Catryn. They were already in their beds, dozing soundly, with Black Lucy asleep on the *kinder*room floor. In the hall a light leaked from under Mistress Cingria's door.

At the cottage, Anna and Johanna were stripped to their chemises. Anna's hair fell like stalks of wheat, but Johanna's stood out from her head in a horizontal frenzy.

I hesitated. I hadn't undressed before anyone since I was small. I unlaced my jacket, then slowly let fall my petticoats. As I stood awkwardly, about to unlace my stays, the two girls stared at me. Brazenly.

"It's not fair," Johanna complained. "How did ye get such a womanly figure?" She settled into the chair, looking me up and down while Anna picked little somethings out of her hair. Lice!

"My mother poured me into an hourglass every night before I went to bed." They barked with laughter.

Johanna patted hands over her bulging midriff. "My mother and sisters had to beat me into my whalebones. Always afraid the laces were gonna burst. Seems like every few months I had to sew in more fabric."

"Never woulda had to if ye kept away from all those tarts!" Anna grinned. "Cherry tarts, *melk* tarts, apple—"

"Oh, shush," Johanna snapped. "I'd rather be soft and fleshy than a flimsy bag a bones like you. Hey, Saskia, let's see yer bosom."

"Yeah," flat-chested Anna cried, jumping off her bed in anticipation. "Bo-som. Bo-som," they chanted to my horror, and rushed up as if to strip open my stays. "Bo-som, bo-som."

"Stop it!" I shouted, throwing my arms across my chest.

"Shut up in there, you lot," Cook yelled from the next room. "It's late!"

We looked at each other and giggled. Suddenly I felt mischievous. "All right, then." With a boldness that surprised me, I grabbed the necklines and pulled them down, exposing my bosom for two seconds—then covered myself up. How glad I was to have them laughing.

As we plunked down on our beds, Anna and Johanna asked in lowered voices about my family. When I told them about the sickness that took my grandfather and mother, they nodded solemnly, saying they too had lost family to disease.

"My father remarried soon after Mama's death. *Very* soon. My stepmother . . . well . . . she made my life difficult." They waited for more, but I could only look down.

Johanna spoke of her father's death, how the family and farm fell into dire poverty. Anna said enough for me to suspect she'd been severely bullied. A heavy silence enveloped us.

At last I pulled out the locket with Mama's portrait. Johanna stroked the sterling frame, then fixed me with a skeptical gaze. "Saskia, how is it you come to be a Nursemaid?" Was she sensing the chasm between their upbringing and mine?

I paused. Do I tell them the whole story? Would these be the sisters I'd never had? I lay back into the pillows. "One day last June, riots tore through our town. I decided that was my chance."

I'll never forget that day. Militia on horseback thundered down brick lanes, shooting at anyone thought to be looting the homes of tax officials, who were all corrupt. I grabbed the bags I'd packed weeks before, hoping for such a break, and, nearly killing myself, climbed from my second story window onto a shed below. As I ran along the canals, strange things bobbed by in the waters: account books, torn-up coats and gowns, even a harpsichord and a waterlogged wig. A glass eye glittered eerily in the setting sun, its blue iris winking at me. I dashed across town, the summer air snowing with feathers of coverlets thrown from upper-story windows. At one point, in a brilliant cloud of color, an aviary of blue and red parrots flew free into the skies.

"I dodged bullets and drunks and ran across town to the Charity House. For years I'd dreamed of joining the good Sisters there. I used to help them, you see." The girls stared at me, wide-eyed. I didn't tell them how the lay Sisters and I used to make lace together, nor the part about teaching lacemaking to orphans and fallen women. "But they wouldn't let me join their order. They said I was too willful." My eyes became moist. "Instead they called for Papa to fetch me. I hated having to go back. But then the Sisters found me employment with the Mistress. She asked me to come to Africa with them. Had to work hard to persuade Papa to let me go. But here I am."

Johanna and Anna exchanged glances, then Johanna eyed me narrowly. "That's quite a story," she ventured. "You sure it be true?"

"Cross my heart and hope to die, stick a needle—"

"Stop, we believe you. That rhyme makes my hair stand on end."

Once in bed, sharp pieces of straw poked me from the mattress. The two of them warmed themselves in Anna's bed, whispering about men, especially some slaveman. I liked these girls, but more than ever I determined to have my own room. How else would I be able to make lace again?

I tossed and turned. Thoughts rubbed against my mind and images of everything fierce in this new land hit me like buckshot: the native dangling from the mast, the heads impaled on stakes, the slave pulled about like a dog, the chorus of children, the woman in the headtrap. How fierce the Cape was! The distance between here and home gaped like the yaws of hell, and I'd burned all the bridges leading back. What would be demanded of me? Should I have come at all?

I lay awake for some time, fighting to calm these fears while the girls chattered on. "For heaven's sake, you two, let's get some sleep," I finally snapped.

Johanna moved into my bed, her body offering warmth, and soon she was lost in snores. Then, when my brain had exhausted every disturbing memory, sleep pulled me down and down, under its soft veil, deep into the shadowlands.

Chapter 7

April 1749 (Autumn)

The blare of the slave horn, then clang of a piercing bell outside stirred me out of deep slumber. Someone jerked at my shoulder.

"Wake up, Saskia. Won't *do* being late your first day."

I slumped out of bed, bare feet jolting on icy floors. And so began my first day at the wine estate. I splashed cold water from the basin on my face, dressed quickly, then ran across the yard to the kitchen. Somewhere in the trees above, a Cape pigeon cooed its throaty song. I drew deep breaths—this was my life now, for better or worse. I silently prayed I'd be ready.

Savory smells of fried sausage and apple porridge wafted through the kitchen, but Cook informed me that before I could have any, I had to report to the Housekeeper, who would apprise me of my duties. Mistress Cingria was the one to whom all domestic staff, servant and slave alike, had to answer.

Johanna took me aside. "Don't cross that one, dearie. She not be made of flesh and blood. Spanish steel more like. She's the one rules this household, after the Master that is, and she don't put up with nothin from no one." I was thinking I needed to set this woman straight about my duties, but now . . .

Mistress Cingria sat rigidly at a desk in her tiny office next to the rear foyer, a dark-haired, dark-eyed woman, about the Mistress's age. So this was Dr. Buehl's panther. She was handsome, I suppose, in a severe sort of way. Her nostrils flared and eyes sloped upward—a hint of the Levant? I curtsied.

She peered up with chilling confidence. "Miss Klaassens, is it? Wait."

I'd heard she'd been widowed recently. No widow's weeds now. In fact, the way she dressed looked too stylish for a servant. Brown silk gown with white collar and lace, a simple pin, and lace edging her cap and sleeves. Back home, lace was forbidden to servants. My eyes honed in, trying to guess which weave of lace, until she caught me staring.

"Young lady, your first duty of the day is to start the fire in the *kinder*room—on very cold days only, mind you. All winter, slavemen go out daily scrounging for deadwood, so don't waste it! Then you are to scrub the floor and windows thoroughly before the children rise. After you help Catryn dress, bring their breakfast on a tray to the *kinder*room. Cook will instruct you on what they eat. And, for God's sake, scrub your hands first."

As she spoke, she ran a long, fine finger down a list. A set of large keys hung from a chatelaine at her waist, and when she fondled them, they jangled. That's when I saw a strange physical aberration: the stub of a barely formed sixth finger, poking out of her right hand. Good Lord, just like King Henry's mistress, Anne Boleyn. The hairs on my arms shot up. Was this woman a witch?

"After the children's breakfast, take the tray downstairs and Manassa will go up to care for them. After that you may take your breakfast—ten minutes and ten minutes only. Manassa is the tall slavewoman in the yellow turban, the one with the blind eye. Black Lucy may look after them when the Mistress doesn't need her."

She rattled on and on, enumerating all my duties in a clipped voice: clean the *kinder*room, change the linens, help Cook in the kitchen. And on occasion lead Pier and Catryn in their lessons. Long before the litany had ended, an internal bell was ringing, and the top of my scalp burned.

"Begging your pardon, *mevrouw*," I said in a voice rising with emotion. "There must be some mistake. I contracted to be Assistant Nursemaid with a few light duties. Not a housemaid who occasionally attends the children."

She glared at me with an expression so cold it could have cracked ice. "You're underage, Miss Klaassens. You cannot make contracts." I watched in horror as a satisfied expression crossed her face.

"But it was my father—"

"Forget about contracts! These are the Master's instructions. It seems to me you were brought here at great expense to this family, and unless you intend to pay them back now for your passage from Amsterdam, I think you'd best keep your mouth shut and just do the work." In a precise and final gesture, she smoothed back her dark hair. "Your pay will be the same." And she waved me out of her office.

My face felt hot. So that was their game—they offer an attractive position, and when you arrive, treat you however they want. Back in the *kinder*room I lit a fire and scrubbed the stinkwood floors with a vengeance those planks had never known. Knuckles white, fury streaming from every pore of my body. How could they cheat me so?

I breathed deeply as I went about picking up toys and laying out the children's clothes. By the time I wakened the children and got them ready, my anger was cooling. I fetched them a tray of porridge, fruit, and cheese in pewter bowls. They ate upstairs at the low table in the *kinder*room while I gazed out the window, ravenous. I should have stolen a bite of their food on the stairwell. How unfair! For now I could only do as I was told. Sun pierced through tall windows and flooded the blue walls with light. At least this was a pleasant room, with a grand view of rougey mountains.

By the time I got downstairs for breakfast, the hearth was blazing and the kitchen flooded with warmth. The sausage was gone. Cook handed me a bowl of porridge spiced with nutmeg. Most everyone had already eaten.

Jezza stood at the hutch, arranging food and flowers on a silver tray. Her pale frock was patched and ragged at the hem, but laced tightly enough to show off her tiny waist. A purple headwrap, knotted at the neck, covered her hair. She fussed over the dishes, shuffling them unnecessarily. "When do Titus come back?"

Oom Samuel was scrubbing the breakfast dishes with sand. "Any time from now, child."

"Uncle, that's slave talk," Johanna complained. "Don't tell us nothin."

I rinsed my hands under the waterbarrel spigot, then stepped to the hearth and plucked a dried peach—a string of them hung there shriveling. Ah—sweet and chewy! "Just who is this Titus anyway?"

Jezza turned to me and glared. "Can't spend all day gossipin. Gotta git this to the Mistress." She thrust out her chin, spun on naked heels, and strutted off with the tray.

"We don't talk that much about him, do we?" Johanna asked. "He's Stable Master here, ye know. We're all quite fond of him."

Cook stood before a crockery bowl, so corseted and top-heavy she made me think of an immense popover. "Say," she said to me, "you been the one stealing all me peaches?"

"No, ma'm, this is my first."

She looked at me long. "Titus *is* a fine lad. A slaveman as Black as you are White. In charge of all the horses. He's smart, mind you. Has some learnin too. Some missionary taught him things, reading and writing, accounts. Mark my words, he'll be Master de Witt's clerk one day. He's to get his freedom afore long. He works hard, takes care of a lotta things round here."

"Where is he?"

"Out stealing horses." Johanna swung the hearth crane toward her, dipped her ladle into the great iron pot, and slopped porridge into a bowl. I jerked around to see her grinning again. "He's upcountry hirin hands, carpentry types, that's where." She slathered butter onto bread and stuck it into her porridge. "Master needs a lot of wine barrels made. Been gone over two weeks now."

A lone slave trusted to be gone for weeks?

"*Ja*, and all these maids, they do missin him. Cause he a big handsome buck, and they all wants a roll in the hay wit him, isn't it?"

"Go on, you old fool," Johanna protested, pummeling Samuel with her fists while he chuckled. "What do you take us for?"

"Johanna, sweetie," Cook said, "you'd follow a meerkat down a hole if it smiled at you."

"Oh, thanks," Johanna snapped. I grinned.

Later, Johanna and I were stripping linens from the Mistress's bed. I ran admiring fingers through the fine lace curtaining the canopy. I'd wanted to touch this silky gauze from the moment I'd set eyes on it.

"Why so glum, dearie?" She glanced around to be sure we were alone. "Has the Spanish Terror gotten to you?"

I told her how I'd signed on to be Assistant Nursemaid,

not this. I scowled. "Now I'm just another rotten little skivvy." I punched a pillow into its case. "Oh, Johanna, I mean no offense . . ."

She looked me full in the face. "None taken. Not the first time I heard that happening. Not hardly fair, is it? But they gots the power—can do anything they damn wants." She stomped over to an immense teak chest and started tearing out clean linen. "Nothin to do but make the best of it."

I flung a pillow onto the bed, saying nothing. If Papa knew, he'd raise holy Cain. But I wasn't going to tell him. He had warned me about the pitfalls of going into service. For a minute, we worked in silence.

"Is what Samuel said true then? Are you and Anna sweet on that slaveman?"

She slipped a pillow into its case. "I don't know. Maybe we're all a little soft in the head when it come to Titus. But he don't feel nothin special for me, so's just as well. Anyway, White maids shouldn't even think of bein with a slave. But *you'll* fall for him, once you meet him."

"I will not."

"What kinda man ye lookin for, Saskia? If ye're looking at all."

I tossed dirty sheets into the wide wicker basket and paused, staring far out the window toward the canopy of oaks. "Oh, I'd like to meet someone special, like Papa. Smart and honest and gallant and fun. Someone people look up to. He'd have to treat me as well as Papa treated Mama, that's for sure. I won't know him until I meet him. But a good man."

"A good man? Is that what ye wants? Not me, dearie. The good ones, they're boring. I suppose it's all right to have em respect ye and all." She sighed, pitching a clean sheet across the mattress so crisply it snapped at the air. "I want the man who'll make my skin tremble when he touches me, ye know?" She lowered her voice to a whisper. "Those good ones don't even touch you. Ye may be waitin for just the right man, Saski, but I'm waitin for just the *wrong* one."

We giggled, grabbing opposite handles of the linen basket, and stumbled down the gallery and out the kitchen door toward the laundry. At the paddock, the Master was taking leave of a gentleman just mounting a sleek horse. He looked like a younger version of the Master, but with a broader brow and more open face. Fine-looking. When he glanced our way, Johanna and I, still holding the basket, dipped into curtsies. Was it my imagination, or did his eyes linger on mine for just a moment? Mr. Soolmans had told me European girls were prized at the Cape. The young man grinned, kicked his mount, and trotted around the house toward the road.

"Master's nephew, Adriaan," Johanna whispered in my ear. "Speak of the devil." Her eyes pierced mine with meaning. "We yust spoke of him, girl. And don't he yust appear. Spooky."

Then she dropped her side of the basket and ran around the corner of the house, padding after him. Foolish maid! By now he'd have cantered out of sight, far down the road to Cape Town.

Johanna! Don't you know better than to act so desperate? I thought of a dog chasing carriages. In the faint chance it ever caught one, would it then know what to do with it?

Chapter 8

April 1749 (Autumn)

Not yet dawn, but I was quite awake. I rose and dressed, shivering, careful not to wake the girls. After so many months at sea, I could at last wander on and on, across open fields. Why not explore the estate?

I stood outside in the bracing air, watching glimmers of morning push back the night. There was that lovely rush that comes knowing one is the first to see the new day. Sunlight began penetrating leaves. They flickered in translucent greens. How wondrous lace would be if it too could grab hold of sunlight, changing pattern with the rustle of a breath. I felt at the cusp of a new, fuller life, my *own* life now, not an extension of someone else's, with all their calculations for me. I vowed to work hard and excel, that my employers would not regret bringing me all the way to Africa.

Now farm animals were braying, lowing, snorting. Then a cry like a stricken babe. I listened, then stepped toward it. The *kraal* fence, a marvel of gnarly roots and thorn branches, penned in the goats. Then I saw it. In a far corner a young goat had caught its hoof in the fence and hung there precariously. I found the gate and rushed in.

Cutting through the smelly herd I unloosed its leg from the tangle of thorns, the animal bleating piteously, and placed it down. Then, out of nowhere, *bam!* Square in the buttocks. I shrieked. A bearded old black billy goat with large horns and bulging eyes menaced me again, tearing up the ground with its hooves, then charged. *Bam!* Again! I dashed for the exit. Suddenly I was surrounded by men I'd never seen before.

One grabbed me by the arm and half jerked, half lifted me through the gate, then slammed it shut. The old goat charged, ramming the fence. The men burst out laughing. I steadied myself. My rescuer was a short, dark Malay with powerful arms and a kindly face. Slavemen were not supposed to touch you, but thank God he had. I looked at the European laborers. Why hadn't one of *them* lifted me to safety?

"Here, let me dust you off," one said, winking a sly eye at the others while he jostled his hands over my hips and breasts.

I jumped away. "Get off! Don't touch me!"

The men leaned against the fence and laughed. Very funny! My Malay rescuer offered me his neckcloth for the blood on my arm just as the Foreman arrived. They followed him out the arches.

I stumbled back to the cottage. Damn! One of only two chemises I owned, torn and stained. So much for my little foray into the new world. Johanna was in our room, lacing up her bodice. "What the blazes happened to you?"

"Blasted goats! Blasted laborers!" The girls chuckled hearing of my encounter with the billy.

"We'll help you change," Johanna said as I rummaged for my other chemise. She plunged my bloodstained clothing into a basin of water. The girls had just left when I heard a scream from outside. Johanna was pacing up and down the yard, hands flying about. "Saskia!" she shouted. "Did you leave the goat pen open?"

O Lordy! Outside, mobs of goats were wandering about the yard, my billy too, tearing up grass and thrashing at bushes. Several had pushed their way into the cutting garden, eating masses of flowers.

I looked at Johanna in horror. "I'm sure that slave closed the gate. I'm *sure* he did."

"What? You didn't latch it?" She picked up a prodding stick and smashed it to the ground. "Saskia, you are the most ignorant maid I've ever known! Blast it, girl, what were you thinking? Now help me get these beasts back into the *kraal*."

A tall Black slaveman, Isaiah, joined us in herding the goats back into the pen. Johanna shook her head. "Can't leave you city girls alone for ten minutes with my livestock, can I? Try, will ye, not to bring the estate to ruin afore dinner."

I flushed to the roots of my hair. Would Johanna tell everyone what I'd done? I scanned the disaster: great holes eaten through neatly pruned bushes—*imported* bushes, Johanna informed me—and in the garden, carrots pulled out, jeranums laying in red tatters. Isaiah grimaced. Lordy! And this my first week.

~

The morning passed, but Mistress Cingria never called me into her office. I watched her, though, huffing and puffing the length of the backyard, muttering expletives under her breath. Later she told Johanna to show me around the estate. I suppose she thought that if I knew the ropes, I wouldn't get into so much trouble.

At afternoon break I met Johanna in the back foyer. "Touch nothing!" she said as we peeked into the Master's bedroom at the rear of the house. I knew his study was up front, across from the Mistress's room. Johanna fished in a bowl in the foyer, stealing a fistful of dates, then grabbed more and pushed them into my hand. Was accepting stolen goods also thievery? I slipped them into my apron pocket, to enjoy later.

"Most of the slaves sleep in the Slave Quarters, but in winter Cook and her girls put mats by the kitchen hearth. And ye know where Mistress Cingria sleep upstairs." I quickened to the name, still expecting the axe to fall any moment.

Outside again, the yard thrummed and buzzed with industry. So Dutch! The sawing of barrel staves, the cranking of water being hauled from wells, the squawking of geese, the ringing of iron in the smithy, the snapping of linens as Black laundresses hung them on the line. The Master, Johanna said, often lectured on estate efficiency.

" 'Rustigvallei is like a well-oiled instrument,' " she quoted in a low voice, her jaw almost to her chest, " 'and if one gear misses its timing, the whole mechanism breaks down.' " We giggled. "I think he wants this farm to be as efficient as any back home, Saski, but I don't think Africa be ready for it."

"Not if it gets as hot as they say."

"Right, dearie, right." She clapped me on the shoulder.

Johanna was kinder now. Perhaps we were becoming friends. A down-to-earth girl, quick and savvy. More importantly, she had heart. Two years ago she'd arrived as a housemaid, but when the Foreman discovered she was from a farm in Friesland, he put her to work milking the cows and goats, tending poultry, and working with the slave Isaiah tending asses and pigs. She helped in the house too, but early in the morning her work was with the beasts.

"I don't mind it, lass. I'd rather be with animals than people any day. Beasts don't boss you around, or talk mean to ye. As for the cleanin and ironin, well, no thanks."

"Just don't come to bed with any more lice and fleas, I beg you."

"But we *like* to pick em outta each other's hair. That's our social life, dearie." I laughed, then stared soberly into her face, afraid it was only too true.

Johanna told me that Rustigvallei was built in 1710 by French Huguenots escaping persecution, and at two hundred acres of land and fifty slaves, it wasn't the largest Cape estate, but neither was it the smallest. The harvest had taken place just before I landed, she said, with almost fifty extra workers hired for the picking, making an army of almost a hundred in the orchards and fields.

"The grapes are in now, 'cepting for the port grapes that stay longer on the vine. Oh, dearie, what a grand festival you missed! Lotta them White indentured workers are unattached, ye know. We had a high old time. Never mind, you'll get your kicks in next year."

Standing on a graveled drive, about to enter a long building spanning the southern breadth of the yard, I glanced through one of the two great arches and drank in the blazing purple and red-leafed vineyards beyond. And orchards, with oranges, mulberries, lemons, quince, apricot, peach, almonds, olives and—oh, yes, figs. "Ye could never starve here," Johanna said. "What a blessing."

"The stables over there are Titus's domain." She nodded toward the carriagehouse, then took me through the winery buildings. On the porch, slaves sat before great baskets, tearing purple-black grapes from their stems, while others sorted them with wooden rakes. Juice spattered their clothing, as if they bled from the inside out. We walked past an enormous wood press from India, then marched down to the cellar with its hundreds of barrels of wine waiting for their time. A sour smell assaulted my nose. At the end of the room, two slaveboys hovered above great vats on precarious ladders, stirring something with enormous wooden paddles, while others fed fires below.

"Fermentin the grapes," Johanna called back over her shoulder. "No way ye want to fall into that stew of juice, or ye can kiss this here world goodbye." There were great copper cones, convoluting tubes, and other strange devices. I sensed there was something quite artful and mysterious to this whole winemaking business. I stumbled, woozy from the fumes. "Yust the alcohol ethers," Johanna said.

She pointed a thumb above us. "Wine laboratory up there. We won't bother the Wine Master." Just then a young man ran down the steps, and Johanna introduced me. But I already knew Jaco. "Once was a boxer in Rotterdam," she said, grabbing him suddenly by the biceps. He pulled away, embarrassed. "He gots a wife who's a domestic on a neighboring estate, don't ye, dearie? So don't go settin your sights on him, Saskia. He's already hitched."

I smiled. I wasn't intending to set my sights on this kind, mashed-nose hulk.

"Hey, Johanna," he said, poking her ribs with a finger, "I heard ye left something open this morning. And some loose beasties chewed up half the garden, not to mention the Master's favorite ornamentals. Guess you're in one heap a trouble!"

Johanna poked him back. "Even goats need a little freedom, dearie. Best time they ever had."

I stared at Johanna. She was smiling, but scratched her thumb nervously against her finger. So that was it. She had taken the blame! An act too generous. But if the de Witts came to know the truth, would they dismiss me? Where could I possibly go?

Johanna led me past the pond where waterfowl floated contentedly. "Ducks eat the snails," she said. "Then we eat the ducks." I glanced at them, but hardly heard her. What should I say to her?

At the Chandlery and Soap Kitchen, female slaves smiled and nodded but kept stirring large pots of plant and animal tallow, adding wood ash. I asked Johanna when I could take a bath. Probably not soon, she said. The de Witts felt that too much personal cleanliness in servants was not healthy. "But slaves get a few candle and soap scraps. Better not be caught stealin nothing more, right girls, or Anthonij will come after ye with his *sjambok*." One slavewomen swatted a hovering fly. The others gave wan smiles and shifted uneasily on their feet.

We passed the cooperage where men sawed and planed wooden slats for wine barrels. Beyond this was the Slave Kitchen, which cooked for the field slaves as well as the manor. At an outdoor oven, an iron box encased in wattle and daub, a slavewoman baked bread. What aroma! Bending over the coals, she turned to regard us. One of her eyelids was sewn shut. Manassa smiled shyly, then turned the eye away.

A hefty Black woman, older, trudged out of the kitchen bearing a pan of batter. "A *melktert*, Sladie?" Johanna clapped her hands. "Oh, goody."

"Sladie is Titus's aunt," Johanna whispered as we left. "She's also a woman of the herbs. Keeps a garden in the Quarters where she grows healin plants and such. Gathers stuff from the forest too, like sap for turpentine. Dr. Buehl buys from her. If you get a bite from a black adder, or even a stomachache, it's Sladie ye go to."

Black adder? You mean there were poisonous snakes here too?

Under the eaves of the Slave Kitchen hung ropes of drying antelope—*biltong*—and corn, and below that a wooden mortar for grinding *mielies*. Up the yard, a variety of black and white spotted pigs special to the Cape wallowed in pens of muck. I moved to get upwind, but Johanna talked to them with affection, reaching into her apron pocket to feed them dried apples.

After an hour of touring, I could see that Rustigvallei was more than the cultivation of grapes and making wine—it was a living, thriving community. How wealthy this family must be! While they paid us meager wages, or, to the slaves, nothing. Did the family only care about themselves? Resentment started to cast its black shadows . . . But Johanna was right. I needed to make the best of things, not start feeling bitter.

When we wandered onto some slavechildren, I brightened. They were scouring the ground under the oaks, trailing dusty sacks behind them. "Findin acorns to feed the pigs," Johanna explained.

Oh, there was the child from the watermelon patch! "What's your name, little one?" He rose and stared at me, swaying back and forth, tapping his arms.

"Hey, Digger. That's Black Lucy's child."

Digger turned away. When I reached into my pocket and offered him dates, he paused, looking at them with cautious eyes, then snatched them up as swiftly as a chameleon's tongue. When the other children threw me burning looks, I distributed the last of them. It was worth it to see pleasure glowing from their eyes.

"Nice of you, lass," Johanna said. "They don't get many treats."

In the center of the yard, bees and flies swarmed over leftover crusts of meat on the spit. Johanna told me the Master believed in feeding his staff well, sometimes the slaves too, not because he was kind, but because he got better work out of them. "Every two weeks or so, like last night, he give us an ox or goat or antelope to roast. Also on sacred days."

"If they're going to roast goat, let me know. I've already got a nice old billy picked out." Johanna threw back her head and laughed. My eyes caught a slavegirl walking into the house. "I've been meaning to ask you, Johanna. That slavegirl, Jezza—is that short for Jezebel?"

"She say it's from Jessamine, the flower. Don't suit her like Jezebel, though, do it? Jessamine's no name for a slave anyways. Cook named her Jezza."

We walked through two gardens toward a sad compound fenced high with thorny branches. Beyond loomed the forest of pine and fir. The compound's only entry seemed to be through the wide door of a long building facing us. Johanna called out, then knocked. No answer. She lifted the latch.

"This is one of two Overseer buildings," she whispered. "They takes turns playing guard. Nasty fellows. Have to be, job like that."

Was this what I thought it was?

Directly opposite, another wide door opened onto a little village of huts and two long buildings. We tiptoed through cool darkness into blinding sunshine.

A grouping of wattle-and-daub huts, their thatch falling in and outer walls crumbling. Hempen sacks covered the windows, and tree stumps were chairs. Two thin trees for shade. Disheveled chickens wandered in and out of doorways. My heart fell into my stomach. More poverty and squalor than an Amsterdam ghetto. "Slave Quarters?" I asked.

"We shouldn't go in. But no one's here now. Mistress Cingria *did* say to show ye the estate. Well, this be part of the estate. Let's do it." We stuck tentative heads through the door of a long stone structure. It smelled of moldering fruit and dank clothing. Rough beds strung with leather thongs, piled with musty rags for blankets, or the occasional moth-eaten hide. On a table sat sticky, gravy-coated plates. Under it, decaying quinces moldered away next to broken pot handles. Rat leavings. How brutish!

Our Calvinist Church proclaims that those who have are the ones who deserve to have. The wealthy are the chosen of God, and as for the rest. . . Well, they are just the rest. We stood there, clasping our arms, growing quite still as a gloom descended over us.

"Come," Johanna said. "I want to show ye something."

At the other end of the courtyard, past dried stalks of corn, stood a small hut with a smoke-stained chimney. "Titus?" Johanna called out, then poked her head through the door. "Knew he weren't here. Just checking."

The hut smelled sweet from cords of tobacco and dried fruit hanging from bamboo beams. A simple bed with a thin mattress, rough wool and antelope blankets, neatly made. Small stone fireplace and a high window. Table and chair. Instead of sacking on the window, there was a frame of waxed muslin, and shutters. It was clean and tidy.

Johanna turned to me. "More exalted quarters, wouldn't ye say? Poor, but don't seem it."

An African drum decorated with a strip of leopardskin dominated a corner. I was surprised to see a creased etching of a horse, quite beautiful, pinned to the wall. Hide shoes like I saw the Khoi-khoi wear rested neatly next to a wooden box that jutted out from under the bed.

"I thought slaves weren't supposed to own things."

"The Master, he don't care, long as they don't overdo it. This ain't much, really."

Johanna trooped over the threshold and, to my astonishment, went immediately to the box. It made scraping sounds across the floor. "Can't resist." I uttered little protests, but she had already thrown back the lid. Inside lay a brown journal with bent corners, a quill, inkwell, and stub of candle. A tattered blue book on Dutch grammar and a black Bible.

"So he's a Christian."

"He's a slave," Johanna admonished. "Can't be a *real* Christian."

I leaned over Johanna's shoulder as she flipped through the journal, stopping on a page of carefully penned alphabets. The *s*'s and *f*s were particularly graceful. "Is this slave literate?"

"Not just literate, dearie, he's—what's that word—liter*ary*. Ain't common for a slave, ye know. In fact, ain't usually allowed."

Just who *was* this man?

Johanna rifled through the box, stopping on what looked like a poem written in a neat, masculine hand. She whispered the first words slowly. "*It's written in our bodies . . .*" I wanted to hear more, but we were invading this man's most intimate world. Footsteps echoed across the courtyard. Hastily we placed everything back into the box, shoved it under the bed, and scrambled outside.

Someone moved out from the shadows. Johanna and I breathed with relief to see it was only an old slavewoman. She looked beaten down, in the way trampling beats down grapes, robbing it of vital juice. I stared into her eyes, and froze: I was sure I'd seen those eyes before. Had I dreamed them? They looked vacant, as if hollowed out by some blade of fear. As she passed, she murmured, "Hello, Mama. Hello, Mama," in respect. I started, for one of her arms was shriveled and misshapen, like the broken wing of a bird.

"That's Hannah," Johanna whispered when we'd walked past. "Works in the fields, so you won't see much of her. Got that arm mangled in a wine press when she were a kid. Then some men took advantage of her. The other slaves let her be. She's had one hard life, she has. Maybe a little off in the head."

A cold wave shuddered up my back, along with some vague, troubling premonition that Fate had something to play out for me and this woman Hannah.

~

Just before dinner I found Johanna propped up in bed, her arms crossed. "Thank you for not telling on me, Johanna," I said at last. "I owe you."

"Yes, dearie, I think you does. I thought it best ye not start work here in a heap a trouble. But mind ye, I won't take the blame a second time."

When Johanna did not appear at dinner, I questioned Anna. Johanna had been denied food all day for allowing the goats to run wild. The color drained from my face. We stuffed biscuits and cheese into our pockets and brought them to Johanna. Then I fished through my trunk and presented her with one of my best handkerchiefs, fine white linen that I'd edged with silk lace. "Never in my life owned a handkerchief this fine," she said quietly, and reached for the handkerchief with fingers that shook. That's when I saw her red and swollen knuckles. A caning! When I turned to leave, she was dabbing her wet cheeks. Something in my brain clicked into clarity.

Though it was late, I marched to the main house, knocked on Mistress Cingria's office door, and confessed to her it was I and only I who had left the farm gate open this morning.

Chapter 9

April 1749 (Autumn)

Dearest Cousin Gertruyd,

I just received your letter dated four months ago, and was so happy to receive it. My second letter at the Cape, the first being from Papa. Did you get mine? I described our long journey out and all the dreadful things that happened. It's only in you, dear Cousin, that I can truly confide. Please, tell no one, no one!

I'm doing well enough in this beautiful new land, after a clumsy start, and word going around is that my employers appreciate me, for the most part. But there's so much to learn. Rustigvallei still seems vast, but I'm getting to know it. It's like a self-sufficient village, really. They work me hard, but I'm used to that. As are you, farm girl. I've had a few frustrations concerning my position here. I'll just say I don't know how much I can trust my employers.

But Gertruyd, this land would amaze you! I've already described some of the fantastic beasts, but lately I've learned about the wild dog called hyena. Some say it can change its gender. Regardless, they are loathsome creatures, and sometimes make mournful howls at night, disturbing our sleep, as do the spotted tygers. The children get scared half to death. The lions have mostly fled this area, for they won't live close to men. But let me tell you of an encounter I had the other day with my own wild beast.

All the farms here have orchards, yet we staff don't always get much of the harvest. Wild fruit trees, however, abound throughout the countryside. My friends here told me about an apple orchard in a high valley south of the estate. So one free afternoon, I set out to find it, as it's autumn here, and trees are red with apples ripe for plucking. I carried a shoulder pannier with baskets on each side, thinking how lovely it would be to bring back sweet fruit for my friends, for this week our master sold the last of our apples. No one would go with me, so I took off by myself, deciding the yoke of my pannier was enough weapon against any ferocious animal. After a half hour's walk I found the wild copse, and thrilled at all the fragrant apples filling the trees, blanketing the ground in red.

I was humming happily, Gertruyd, and filling my baskets when I heard the most horrible snorts from the bush. In a flurry of dust, a huge African boar exploded from the long grass and tore down upon me, snarling and gnashing its giant teeth.

I jumped like a monkey into the low branch of an apple tree, the beast so close I could feel its hot breath on my feet. It grabbed my petticoat with its sharp incisors and tugged with such force it nearly pulled me out of the tree. This warthog, as they call it, had enormous tusks that grew from beneath its snout like a bony mustache. So dangerous if they gore you, Gertruyd. And long, dry, thin stuff you could barely call fur, and a tail that shot straight up like a flagpole. And it smelled foul.

I rocked about precariously on a low branch, finally managing to wrench my petticoat from its teeth. Quickly I scrambled onto higher branches, and prayed to God the beast couldn't climb. It snarled and stomped about the trunk in fits of temper, like a deranged dog. I suppose it thought itself owner of the orchard, and I a criminal interloper.

It would not leave, Cousin. I really began to wonder if this was the end of me, if I would ever make it out alive. I thought of all the people I love back home, especially you and Papa, and regretted the many times I acted selfishly, or in anger. Surely God was punishing me by never letting me live to see you again.

After a time, I just got angry. I shouted and cursed,

yes I did, and plucked apples and threw them with all my might at the beast. Occasionally my missiles hit their mark, but that only made the beast more ill-tempered. Does this remind you of anyone?

Gertruyd, that warthog held me prisoner for hours, determined not to let me escape. I ate apple after apple to relieve my hunger, and the hog did too, crawling oddly along the ground, front knees bent, gobbling up the fruit.

I was worrying how I could possibly spend the night in a tree without falling out when there was a rustling sound from the bushes. Someone called my name. A savior! It was Egbert, the Master's valet. When I hadn't returned, Cook told him to check the wild orchard. I was never in my life so happy to see someone—and this a young man I detest! I shouted a warning just before the warthog charged. Egbert shot at the hog, for which I was almost sorry, but after only one report from his pistol it took off in a whirlwind of dust and disappeared into the thicket.

When we got back to Rustigvallei, the Housekeeper was quite upset with me, but Egbert confirmed my story about the beast that held me hostage. I wasn't punished. Apparently the boarish owner of the wild orchard is well known at the manor, but no one had bothered to tell me. Now I can't stand the taste of apples. Every time I see one I nearly retch. I only thank the good Lord it wasn't a panther, which would have hunted me to the treetop, and you would no longer have a cousin to write this letter you hold in your hands.

As for Egbert, he has been insufferable. He follows me everywhere. When he finds anyone who will listen, he puffs up like a peacock displaying its plumage and tells how he rescued me from certain death. All his talk of his heroics has nearly taken the good out of it. Though he expected what he calls his "due"—and I assume he means no more than a kiss, disgusting enough with this fellow—you can be sure my gratitude was limited to a handshake and hearty words of thanks.

I hope this finds you and your family well and in good health. Give my regards to everyone.

Affectionately,
Your loving and still living cousin, Saskia

Chapter 10

April 1749 (Autumn)

Alone in our room, I took out my portfolio of pages. "I journal to come to terms with my soul," Midshipman Soolmans had told me. "When you become both priest and confessor, life becomes clear." I dipped my quill into ink.

My first two weeks at Rustigvallei have seemed like two months. I labor sunup to way past sundown, but it's not the hard work I mind. What bridles is being more Housemaid than Nursemaid. I like being with the children, and I'm hoping to guide their young minds aright.

On sunny days, and there are many here, I sometimes get to take the children for walks. We like to wander out as far as we dare, chasing one another on the hills, playing shuttlecock, or shooting clay marbles. Pier brings along paper boats he has made, and we sail them on the river, or play hoops or kolf, letting loose before going home to "the house of many rules." The children seem happiest then, Pier less scornful. Sometimes he even shows some kindness, letting us ride his pony while he leads. Once he even made a necklace of wildflowers and placed it around my neck. I should be with them often, for that is what was promised me—and promised them. Regardless, my days are cheerful enough, and at the end I stumble into bed, sometimes nodding off even before I've removed my last petticoat.

But in moments of quiet, a secret heart reaches out in longing for something to soothe this restlessness. I suppose it is love. Love like Papa and Mama had. Like Carra and her Purser had onboard ship. Maybe I long for that love, and at the same time, fear getting it.

Someone was coming. I threw powder over the ink and slammed the journal shut. By the time Anna walked through the door, I'd stashed it away. Close! Oh, how I needed my own room.

In my own room I could journal in private. And secretly make lace. How I longed for it! At odd moments throughout the day, like sitting at meals, my hands wandered under the table, tracing the movement of bobbins they dared not hold.

One evening after dinner I came back to the cottage only to discover Johanna pawing through my trunk. "What are you doing?" I shouted hotly. "Those are *my* things!" She pulled herself up, looking both guilty and indignant. "Sorry, Saskia, but I can't find my sewing scissors. I thought you might have a pair."

I fished through my folded clothes, presenting her my childhood shears. "Don't you ever again go through my things, Johanna!" Another narrow escape. Surely she'd have questioned me if she'd found the lace pillow at the trunk's floor.

Later, in the kitchen, unable to stand it one more minute, I snatched the tray of sherry from Black Lucy's hands, astonishing the poor woman, and whisked it off to the Mistress's room myself, where I boldly reminded her she had promised me a room. "I have nothing to do with the running of the manor," she said peevishly. "Ask the Housekeeper." As if she couldn't even speak her name. But I didn't want to ask Mistress Cingria. I wouldn't give that woman yet another chance to quash me.

Finally, on Saturday night, after prayer hour and supper, I served the Master his nightly beaker of beer. Before retrieving the tray, I thrust my fear into my pocket, knocked, and entered his study. He sat lounging by the fire, reading. I picked up the tray, put it down again, and stood facing him.

"Well, what is it, girl?" He hit his pipe into a dish, loosening old tobacco.

I curtsied. *Don't lose nerve, Saskia.* "Begging your pardon, *mynheer*, but I wish to ask something of you." Fingers fidgeted with the corner of my apron.

His eyes grew small. He squinted up from his spectacles. "Well?"

"Sir, it's about having my own bedroom. The Mistress promised it to me in Delft. I wouldn't have come out here without it being agreed upon, sir."

"Why bother me with such matters?" He pulled out his pocketwatch and glanced at it, as if saying he had no time for this. "Ask your Mistress."

"I did, sir, and she told me to ask you." I averted my eyes. If he saw into them, he might see I fibbed. Just a little fib.

When I looked up, his eyes were blazing. *Hold your own,* I commanded myself. "Mistress gave me her word, sir. She promised." That was true.

I thought his eyes would bore a hole through my forehead. Should I mention my contract had been broken as well? He sat in silence, then jumped up, startling me, and marched to the fire. "Why do I have to deal with servant problems!"

I took a deep breath. "Because you, *mynheer*, are the head of the estate, the person wisest and most capable of handling problems the women cannot." He turned and shot me a wry look. But the flattery seemed to appease him.

Tap into their interests, Papa had said. I stepped to a table where bronze microscopes and instruments glinted in the candlelight. "Pardon me, *mynheer*. What is this?" I pointed to a cushioned box with a shiny brass disk. It was palm-sized, magnificently crafted. Dials within dials, intricate hooks, grids, and strange symbols. I'd often admired it while dusting.

"That's an astrolabe from Arabie. Fifteenth century. Measures the distance between sun, stars and planets. Islamites used them to tell time, so they knew when to pray. Do such gadgets interest you?"

"Oh yes, sir. They very much interest me."

He opened the leaded window and pointed the astrolabe up at the night sky. "Come here." For the next few minutes the Master became teacher showing this curious child an elaborate toy—how to direct the pointer at the brightest star of the Southern Cross, then calculate the distance to the closest planet. The night air blasting through the window chilled me, but I followed as best I could his talk of tympans, azimuths, degrees of arc. He looked at me intently. "You didn't really understand that, did you?"

"Of course I did. Well no, sir. Not really."

"Never mind. So you want your own room, do you?" Blue

smoke from his pipe floated past, its fragrance permeating the room. It was the same brandy-soaked tobacco Papa smoked. For a moment I softened, letting the sweet smell fill me. "You're bright enough, Miss Klaassens. You have good manners, are modest in demeanor, all pleasing qualities. I've been told that you work hard and the children like you."

Really? Pier liked me?

He strutted to his desk. Then, abruptly, "In a godforsaken land such as this, Miss Klaassens, it's important we rear children according to the Lord's dictates of hard work, loyalty, piety, and decorum. There are too many vainglorious people at the Cape for my liking. Free Black women parading up and down the streets of Cape Town in hoop skirts and parasols. Servants too, in silk, jewelry, lace. An absolute abomination!"

I stood there, stunned, for did not Mistress Cingria wear those things? What did all this have to do with getting my own room?

"Especially lace. I cannot abide it! The devil's thread, that's what it is!" My eyes fluttered, and I looked down. Best never let him find out I make the stuff!

"Your mistress rebukes me for not wearing lace. Says that even the Grand Executioner in France wears lace to the scaffold. That's France for you. But I'm a Deacon of the Church." He had been staring out the open window. Now he walked over and shut it quietly, as if suddenly aware of his rant.

"So my wife promised you a room of your own, did she? Well, there aren't any."

My heart plummeted, and a slow heat began crawling up my neck. So much courage mustered for nothing.

He studied his pipe, then looked in the direction of the kitchen. "Except for that drafty little space near the children's rooms. Perhaps it *would* be useful to have you closer to them at night. Then they won't have to bother the Housekeeper with every little nightmare. Just an attic, but Abraham and Josiah could help you fix it up."

Elation flooded my body. "Oh, thank you, Master de Witt." I grabbed the sides of my skirt and gave my deepest curtsey.

"It's right over the kitchen, you know. You'll be cozy enough in winter, but it's beastly hot in summer. I think bats and mice have the run of it. You might not find it suitable."

Oh yes I will.

Later that day Johanna led me a few steps up from the upstairs landing. Yes, it was a ruin of a place. Warm indeed, but it had two windows. I'd be comfortable for now. The ceiling slanted so on one side that I could not stand, and it was littered with junk, but it was my own. I'd make it work.

Johanna and I pried open the windows. "Ach! Forgot them coffins. The men will take em out."

Giggling and screaming, we chased bats out the windows with brooms. As for the mice, I would invite up Oom Samuel's cat. From the south window I had a magnificent view of the mountains, vineyards, orchards, and countryside. From the eastern one, the Slave Quarters, and the forest and hills beyond. I took a pail and water and scrubbed the wood floor until it shone.

Cook suggested we look over some furniture left by previous French owners, stored over the gallery. There was a bed with a horsehair mattress and chipped headboard, stuffed chair, an armoire with a long looking glass inside, a table and chair, and a moth-eaten Persian carpet. The Mistress came up and scanned the items—too rococo, outdated, or damaged for the family, and I was welcome to them. To their delight, we even found pieces for Johanna and Anna.

The next day Josiah and Abraham helped me place the furniture. I smiled at Josiah, my billy goat rescuer. He had a flat nose, dark, exotic eyes. He'd once carved wood in Java. Now he assisted the carpenter, especially loving to make furniture. He ran his nut-colored fingers over the carving on the headboard, as if to memorize its curves. Abraham was a simple African who worked in the smithy. Wide-shouldered and tall, he cried out whenever he knocked his head on the low thatch. The men emptied the coffins of grain, and I decided to keep them. Stacked, they'd be grand window seats.

In a trunk I found long panels of blue *chinees* silk with frayed embroidery. The men mounted it on a wall for me, hiding a crack. Then I asked them to make a canopy for my bed with drapings of linsey-woolsey, to hold in warmth and keep out any insects falling from the thatch. There were shutters but no curtains, for Calvinists believe curtains might be hiding something. Once I take out my lace bobbins, I *will* be hiding something.

From Mistress Cingria I obtained bed linens, an oil lamp, a candleholder, and other essentials. On the wall I pinned a Rembrandt etching Papa had given me, *The Flute Player*. I stared at it for a few minutes, choking up, remembering how we would play recorders together for Mama. Mindful of beauty, I arranged my few personal belongings, making this room mine—a nest in which to dream, to write—and later to make lace. When my friends saw it, tendrils of envy crept into their faces, so I reminded them I had the onerous job of having to tend to the children any time of day or night.

A week later, the Mistress mounted the narrow steps. "What have you put together here, Saskia, a room in a *bordeel*?" I gave a wan smile. I thought my lodgings magnificent. Bedraggled maybe, but magnificent. Finally she laughed and shook her head. At least she let me keep it.

Late at night, I brought out my lace pillow. With the glee of a criminal, I set up my pattern and pins, then wrapped the flax thread around the bobbins. Such devilish satisfaction knowing I hid a secret. Later I would hide my lacemaking things in a coffin.

Once I found some glass globes, I'd make a set of flashes that would reflect extra light onto the lacemaking. Tonight I would make do with the light of two candles. It had rained all afternoon. Perfect! Cool and damp keep the lace supple. Tomorrow I'd prepare a foot warmer with hot coals. Now, fingers fluttering, I paused and breathed deeply, ready to make my first lace at the *Kaap de Goede Hoop*.

I call this "lace writing," for the threads seem to weave themselves back and forth, crossing and twisting across the pillow like words on paper. Arcane words in a secret alphabet. A personal language whose meaning I know but cannot explain. Here my mind ceases its talk. Here there lies peace.

I roll the bobbins over palms, stopping to set the pins, and lines of thread plait themselves into stitches. I put my love into the working and the lace blooms forth like flowers, out of nowhere. The bobbins *click click* in my fingers. Two bobbins cross over the right one, another between two on the left, back and forth, until a lustrous web emerges across the pillow. This is the time I feel clear and serene and most deeply myself, for I've entered another world. Under the gentle clatter of bobbins, another way of being pushes forth, and I arrive before knowing I've departed.

Without questions being put, answers come. Without articulating what is in my heart, my heart speaks. Without this, without feeling the music that is my own sound well up and take me over, how will I know who I am?

Chapter 11

The spider taketh hold with her hands, and is in kings' palaces.
—Proverbs 30:28

April 1749 (Autumn)

I was sitting at my lace pillow at the end of the day, feeling serenely cozy, a cup of hot *rooibos* tea at my fingertips, a foot warmer of hot coals at my petticoats, when suddenly she was at my door. God help me! Of course she could come, it was the rule that my employers could come to my room anytime—but they never did. There I was, fingers flying, wrapping the little nooses of linen, so lost in work I hadn't heard the door open.

I had been thinking how this was the last of the thread Mama had bequeathed to me. When I was little, she'd hold me in her lap and sing as she worked the lace, gently rapping my knuckles if I grabbed the bobbins. Then, a swish of silk snapped me back to the present. And there she was. "Mistress!" I jumped up, planted myself in front of the lace.

"I thought I would come see what you get up to late at

night," she mused, surveying the room with sea blue eyes. "My, there's a lot of light in here. How did you get—what are you hiding there, Saskia?" She pushed me aside. Stared down at hundreds of hours of lace splayed like a web across the pillow. My heart beat furiously in my chest. Blast it!

"Dear girl," she said, "I didn't know you made lace. Why didn't you tell us? This is exquisite!" Then her eyebrows arched. She stepped forward and drummed polished fingernails over the glass globes. "You stole these from the winery, didn't you?"

The day before, I'd persuaded Jaco to 'borrow' them from the cellar for me, to make flashes, or lamps. I told him they were for reading. He'd hesitated. Then, with his roguish smirk, "I guess a little larceny now and then is good for the heart." I'd filled the globes with water, corked and sealed them with beeswax, then inverted them onto candleholders at my table. The candles before them reflected water-light onto my work. Glass is horribly expensive here. I suppose I could have made lace by candlelight, but . . . how I'd coveted those globes!

The Mistress leaned over the cushion and traced the pattern with her finger. "Peacocks! Arabesques!" Then her eye caught something else. "Did you make this too?"

My favorite red jacket hung on a wall hook, and draped over it a sheer linen *fichu* edged in filigree lace. I'd made the piece months ago in the Netherlands, but never dared wear it. She flung the scarf over her shoulders, and, picking up my handmirror, turned, preening. I had to admit, it did look extremely fine lying across her aristocratic shoulders.

"A maid in my employ with such a talent! You won't mind if I take this to show Master de Witt, will you?"

I bloody well *did* mind.

"No, no, please take it, *mevrouw*." My voice was cracking. *Say farewell to that scarf, Saskia. The only place you'll see it again will be against her skin.*

"You know, my dear," she said, flirting with the mirror, "we could make good use of a lacemaker."

"Oh, no, Mistress de Witt," I said quickly. "I make ever so many mistakes unless a teacher is standing over me, directing my every move." A lie, but I was paddling for my life here. I couldn't let her force me to make lace for her.

"Don't play games with me, Saskia. You don't have a teacher here tonight. *You* know what you're doing." Her mouth hardened. "Next time you need glass globes, ask." And she sailed down the steps, my scarf floating about her neck.

That night sleep wouldn't come. I opened the shutters and sat on my seat of coffins. Moonlight spilled into the room, illuminating the lace spread over its pillow like a taught, spidery web. Would I have to make lace all the time now, for my employers' profit? How could the Mistress, who never performed any needlework at all, understand the demands?

First there was designing the paper pattern, pricking out every point, then pinning it all onto a pillow. Winding threads around dozens, even hundreds of bobbins. Then the long labor of crossing and twisting, staying alert and heedful of every pattern change. For fine work, you might complete a square inch in a week's night of labor—if there are no mistakes to undo and rework, nor piles of bobbins to untangle, which so often there are. Lace edging is one thing. Making a set of ruffles or a bed curtain is something else—months and months, a year, more, of devoted work. Nuns make lace, for they have all the time in the world.

And take into account the aching fingers and burning wrists. The neck stiff for days. Often, for the lace's sake, working in near darkness with strained eyes. Some lacemakers go blind from the close work. If I became the de Witts' lace slave, I'd come to hate lacemaking. But that was how my hands expressed themselves, how they found beauty.

Some, like the Master, say lace promotes excess, for lace is expensive. But a white cloud framing the breast and face is refinement itself. A cascade of lace softens and beautifies. It lifts clothing above the common. Lace edging soft white pillows and sheets, lace veiling one's privacy in curtains of a bed—delicacy of living at its best. The Mistress understands this. Yes, we could all exist without this whim of airy stuff, this froth of gauze caressing the skin. But how much more elegant, more beautiful, more magnificent life is with lace!

To have no skills at all is better than having one for which people can exploit you. On the ship sailing to this new land I should have thrown my bobbins into the sea.

My head fell back against the window, and that was when I saw it: a great silken web stretching across thatch and beam. A shimmer of silver in the tangle of moonlight. A furry spider hopped about, as if to some rhythm only she could hear. She was a lacemaker too, weaving webs in darkest silence. I watched as she drew silk from out of her belly, out of a secret self, spooling it across the thatch. Servant or slave to none, free to ply her art or not.

I wouldn't touch her masterpiece, even if it gave birth to a hundred spider babes. Not if the web stretched there for years clogged with dust and broken wings. For she and I were sisters in the craft.

~

After breakfast, the Master called me to his study.

I was greeted with a blazing fireplace throwing light on his Cabinet of Wonders, with its sun-bleached whale teeth and mammoth bones. There was the table of microscopes and armillary spheres, shelves of folios and black-letter quartos, all entries into mysterious worlds. Much as I admired these trappings, I sensed what was coming. Right now his office felt like a court of law, and I had to defend myself.

Master de Witt sat at his desk, lighting his bulbous pipe, the Mistress standing behind him, all smiles. My beautiful *fichu* covered her shoulders like fresh snow. One hand, heavy with diamonds, rested on the scarf, the other on her husband's shoulder, as if holding fast two important possessions. I felt confused, even fearful at this sudden solidarity between them.

I curtsied. Master de Witt rose and paced the room, the hem of his scholar's robe rustling about his ankles. *Chinees* silk, it looked.

"Miss Klaassens, as you know, I'm not a great fan of wearing lace." Confidence and authority settled about his eyes. As ever, he did not speak so much as lecture. He strutted about the room sipping on his pipe, and when he settled on the edge of his desk, the robe slid across his ankles like water. "I abhor excess. All that flaunting one's wealth—the devil's fripperies."

He paused. I cast my eyes down so they wouldn't seem wide with amazement. What about he and his wife? "Still, nearly everyone of consequence wears it, even I, when forced to." He glanced back at the Mistress. "But there's nothing wrong with lacemaking." What? Didn't he feel that vine of hypocrisy wrapping around his heart?

"My girl, you apparently have a special talent, but you say it needs improving. Cook has told us of a woman in Cape Town, mulatto, but reputed to be a fine lace teacher. We will pay for your lessons. You can go on your days off, after every eighth day of work. In exchange for this kindness on our part," he said, punctuating his words with little blue balls of smoke, "all the lace you make in your lessons and during your free hours will belong to us. What do you say to this generous offer, girl, eh?"

Outrageous!

"What about my salary, *mynheer*? And my workload?"

"The same, of course."

I looked from husband to wife, my cheeks burning. They looked quite pleased with themselves. So they would make me their lace slave after all. I would be working every minute of my waking day, for the same low wages, and making good money for them with my lace. I was under contract; I couldn't just sail back to the Netherlands, even if I had the money. I stalled for time while I thought.

"How am I to get to town, *mynheer*?"

"We'll see that you get to Cape Town. The men go frequently on errands."

Tension rose in my chest, but something willful too. Papa always said, if you don't like the terms people offer, then *houd vol.* If I didn't take a position now, my life would be a misery. I curled my toes into my clogs, roots of strength burrowing into the earth.

"With all due respect, sir, madame, I don't know how I can accommodate you. If I ride to and from Cape Town on my days off," I reasoned, "and work from dawn to eight every workday, when will I have time and energy to make lace? Lacemaking is brutal work, hard on the eyes and hands. I could go blind. My fingers will fall off. You ask too much."

There. I had said it. They stared at me, then at each other.

"Fingers fall off?" the Master barked. "Go blind?" He leapt up, thrusting his pipe in my face. "Stupid, insolent girl! You'll do exactly as you're told!"

"Philippe," the Mistress implored.

"Wait outside!"

Beyond closed doors, I heard their muffled voices bat words about. Oh, they were angry. What a fool I was! Maybe standing your ground worked for men, but . . . for young maids? They'd sack me for sure. But didn't I have something they wanted?

Minutes passed like hours. Finally the Master opened the great doors and motioned me in. I braced for the worst.

"We have come to a decision. After your early morning tasks with the children and other duties—tasks we will decide upon—we will allow you to spend the late morning hours at your bobbins." My shoulders relaxed. At least I wasn't going to be fired. "You may work at the window in the back foyer, which has plenty of light. You will be released from duties hard on your hands. Any free time during work hours, you will be expected to make lace for us as well."

From behind his chair, the Mistress nodded. "Yes, Saskia, beautiful lace that we can keep as heirlooms, or give as gifts to special friends."

Translation: *We will sell it and take a handsome profit.*

"Titus knows Widow Huyskens well. He can arrange for lessons. Remember, any lace you make there also belongs to us. Well? Is this not a generous offer?"

I paused. So I wouldn't have to make lace *all* the time. I'd be free from most housework. And I would be going into Cape Town. But how unfair that they would get beautiful lace made on my piddling salary. Yet I suppose that's the fate of most lacemakers.

I cast my eyes down and curtsied. "Begging your pardon, *mynheer, mevrouw,* but I really should have extra pay if you use my lace skills."

"What impertinence!" he shouted. "We just paid for your passage out. I would say you owe *us*."

I blanched, and thought quickly. It would kill me to be in

their debt. With their plan, my skills were bound to improve, and I could make more money later, when I left this employment. "There's also the cost of extra bobbins, thread, and pins." He waved his hand impatiently. "I'll need paper patterns from Europe. And the back foyer can only be used for the largest weaves. Perhaps I can find a cool, damp room under the house, or work in my room. Not too near the kitchen—the cooking could discolor the lace and the heat dry—"

"*You* choose the place, then," he interrupted, waving his hand in annoyance. "Charge what materials you need to my accounts in town. The Mistress will tell you what to make. Don't bother me with details!" And dismissed me.

All day my head buzzed, wondering what my life would soon look like. Not exactly a promotion, but at least it would release me from menial work. And I was still employed.

~

That night, as I put my hands to bobbins and thread, I mused. What would happen if the de Witts gifted my lace to certain high officials? What if the High Governor of the Cape himself pronounced my lace so exquisite, so magnificent, that he'd honor me with a special prize? In time, like our famous portwine, my lace would find its way to Europe and capture the hearts of the nobility, who would sing praises to its singular beauty. Staggering fortune and acclaim were mine! Why, the sun would weep with envy at my brilliance!

Ja. As if in the real world that ever happens. What lacemaker has *ever* known fame or fortune? My dreams burst like a sheep's bladder overloaded with wine. It was more like me to die penniless and obscure with nothing but arthritic fingers and rheumy eyes for my efforts. And so my dreams and fears balanced accounts.

Then anxiety seized me. What was really in store for me?

I breathed deep, emptied my mind, studied the work before me. *Guide my fingers, Lord, that they create beauty for love's sake.*

I wrapped the bobbins with my best white silk, all the while studying the paper pattern until it entered me. Cross the first bobbins, weave, secure the pins and cap them. Making stitches stilled my mind. I rolled the bobbins easily over my palms, crossing and twisting pairs, weaving to the rhythm of an inner song, forgetting all that might upset me. One stitch here, another there, one pin to anchor the lace while pulling out another, as if tying my life together. Oh, the magic of numbers! Order emerging out of chaos. Lacemaking placed my fears in the hands of something greater, released my tight grip on this little life. And I was safe again.

I worked for hours into the quieting night.

Chapter 12

I am Black, but comely, O ye daughters of Jerusalem,
as the tents of Kedar, as the curtains of Solomon.
Look not upon me because I am black,
because the sun hath looked upon me;
my mother's children were angry with me;
they made me the keeper of the vineyards;
but mine own vineyard have I not kept.
—The Song of Songs

May 1749 (Winter)

I was standing in the kitchen early that morning, pouring myself a mug of milk, reflecting on my first weeks at Rustigvallei when I heard a *click click* of metal. The top half of the door to the yard squeaked open slightly and a hairy arm pushed its way in. I stared, frozen. Fingers with curved nails scrabbled around the jamb, groping further inside. Suddenly they tore a string of dried peaches from its hook.

I raced to the door and flung the top all the way open. "Drop those peaches, you—!"

All at once I was nose to wet nose with a smelly creature. Its small, glistening eyes burned like glass buttons under a brow of fur. It bared incisors and snarled. My mind swirled in confusion. This was no human. It had to be one of the Master's new greyhounds perched on its hind legs.

Just then Cook shuffled in from the hall. "What's going on?"

The animal dropped on all fours and bounded away, the string of desiccated peaches bouncing in its mouth. I grabbed a poker from the hearth and dashed outside. "Stop, you thief!"

Cook stuck her head out the door. We watched the animal lope down the yard in the direction of the forest. Cook leaned against the doorjamb, breathing hard, her hand on her heart.

"That has to be the strangest dog I've ever seen," I said, reaching down to pick up two peaches. The Master's hounds started barking in their kennels.

"Dog?" Cook exclaimed. "Dog? Damned if that don't be nothin less than a baboon monkey, me girl, a *bobbejaan*."

"Baboon?" I stood up, dumbfounded, then ran down the yard as far as the garden. Only distant bushes still trembled where the monkey had bounded through. On the *stoep*, I collapsed next to Cook, sweating, my mind a muddle.

"Biggest I ever seen. What cheek, stealin me peaches like that! Vicious they are too. Coulda taken your face off with one swipe of its paw, dearie." The corners of a smile crept into Cook's face. "Dog, my arse." She started laughing, then laughing louder, and soon I was laughing too, laughing at my stupidity, laughing in relief that I'd escaped a close encounter with a dangerous beast.

Throughout the morning, as I went about my duties, servants and laborers in the yard all seemed to turn to each other and snicker behind their hands. Were they laughing at *me*? Later, in the foyer, Egbert jumped in front of me, crouched down and scratched his sides like an ape, shouting "Woof! Woof!" then convulsing in laughter. I turned and ran upstairs for refuge, but when I entered the *kinder*room, even the children were guffawing. "All right, you two, what's so funny?"

"You are," Pier jeered. "Thought a monkey was a dog! You're the monkey." Even my dear Catryn let out a good belly laugh.

"Watch your tongue, Pier! If you don't show more respect, I'll give your ears a good *klop*!"

I took a deep breath and walked out. All right, I'm new to Africa—have pity! That Cook! I guess she loved having a good story by the tail, and now she was telling it to everyone she met. Just when I'd begun to gain a little respect here for my hard work, just when I thought I was comporting myself with confidence and grace.

Pier was right. I was the monkey.

~

In the afternoon, the children's lunch tray hot in my hands, I saw him—the slave the girls had been talking about. He was leaning against the door to the pantry, tall and proud, his face in profile. Sun poured through the window behind him, obscuring his features. Little shafts of light caught on the round of his hair like a sun in partial eclipse. I stared, blinded.

Cook was pulling jars of crockery from a wooden crate and handing them to him, who ordered them high on the pantry shelf. As he moved, I thought of a lion, like the great caged one we'd seen in the menagerie—powerful, still, with something raw that slept just below the skin. He was young, and so Black the hollows of his face dropped into blue shadow. He moved with precision, light glancing off muscles in his forearms. I suppressed something instinctive, something responding to him bodily.

He caught my stare, stepped back from the blinding light and fastened his gaze on me. Eyes dark and warm as hot *koffie*. "Ah, do this be the new maid from the Netherlands, then?" His voice was burnished, velvety. When he flashed a white smile and tugged at the corners of his neckerchief, anything left of my composure leaked away. "Welcome, my sister. I hope that all go well for you here." He bowed.

Sister indeed! Still, his words seemed kindly meant.

"Saskia, this here be Titus." Cook, preoccupied inspecting jars, did not look up.

I nodded gravely, lowered my eyes, and curtsied. He gazed at me with a puzzled expression, then grinned. Oh, why was I curtsying to a slave? Again! What a fool he must think me. I plunked my tray onto the table. The porcelain cups rattled in their saucers. It was *his* fault. Over my shoulder I saw him smile, his gaze following me. How bold!

"Be you needing my help later, Mistress Cook, in taking from this place these crocks? I think this shelf be too high for you to reach it well."

"*Ja*, Titus. I'll let ye know when I'm ready."

I studied him from the corner of my eye. He was handsome, as the girls had said, his nose sharp and well formed. When he smiled, his face was gentle and steady, but then there was that puzzling intensity. Was this the face of a poet? What did poets look like? He passed me, making for the back door, then spun on his heels and stepped close, a mischievous smile playing over thick lips.

"I think I hear about you. You be the maid who face down the vicious baboon."

Not him too! Cook chuckled. My eyes fluttered and I turned away, folding and refolding a napkin. He's a slave! How dare he? "I know how to handle wild beasts, thank you. I've been around men all my life, haven't I?"

A big grin spread across his lips while a quiet laugh hummed in his throat. He looked at me again, as if for the first time. He smelled of darkness, of something thrilling. I grabbed the tray and scuttled off.

~

For the rest of the day, despite myself, I kept thinking of Titus. In truth, I could not *not* think of him. Images of him lingered in my mind. As I filled the bedroom chests with linen, I thought of his large, clean movements. As I arranged Catryn's dolls in the *kinder*room, I remembered his fingers—fine fingers with pink nails and a pale underbloom. Fingers that could form a perfect letter *s* in a notebook, and pen lines of poetry. Could a slaveman be that clever? How could he fluster me so?

I listened as the slavewomen chattered in the garden, thinking how different his Dutch was from theirs. His curiously stilted, as if learned from old books. His speech had a peculiar lilt, making me think of greenly growing things. And then there was that brashness, unbecoming in a slave. Strangest of all, he seemed familiar, as if I'd met him before. Of course that could not be.

I volunteered to pull the clean clothes from the line, normally slave work, but I wanted some fresh air. I navigated the stone path between lines of laundry, basket at my hip. A movement in the distance caught my eye: Titus was riding a horse, bareback, into the vineyards. That very moment I heard a booming sound, like rolling thunder. I scanned the sky—bright sun, no clouds. I heard it again, more subtle this time, then started. That thunder came from within. A strange rumbling was gathering force in my brain like a storm warning, an excitement, a portent. I snatched up the dry sheets.

~

It's embarrassing to confess, but in the afternoon I had a scuffle with Pier. The children and I were in the *kinder*room cutting out paper costumes to sew and paint for a play the children had written—a war drama, the only kind Pier liked. He picked up his *kris*, shouted "Charge!" and flung out an arm, ripping his costume. I swallowed my annoyance and sewed it back together again.

Then Catryn revolted—the play had to be a romance. Pier shouted what a stupid idea *that* was, and began slicing the air about her head with his *kris*. I jumped up and twisted the sword from his hand. That's when he jammed an elbow into my stomach and kicked my shins. "You must have suckled on wolves, Pier de Witt!" I yelled, grabbed his wrists, and jerked them behind his back. He shrieked and shrieked.

Of course the Mistress heard, and burst into the room. "Miss Klaassens, just what do you think you're doing?" I released the boy, who ran into his mother's arms. "What's wrong with you?"

"He swung his sword at my face," Catryn sobbed.

My face burned. "He punched me. Kicked me."

I reached out a tender hand, but Catryn flew to her mother, who cradled both. "Then you did something to deserve it."

Pier stared up at me, smirking. Triumphant. Oh, he would lord it over me now! How could I manage a child if he would not obey me? I'm sure my behavior, not Pier's, would soon reach the ears of the Master.

~

Later, as I helped prepare the noon meal, Titus's face appeared in the window. He smiled—white teeth, a flash of sun. For a second I was reminded of that Renaissance painting, a young Italian leaning against the sill, chatting up a maid.

"How do the day be treating you beauties? Mistress Cook, Manassa. What fine cannibal stew be you stirring in that pot?" They giggled. He didn't even glance at me.

"Gonna stew up some tender young Black man, you're not careful." Cook laughed.

For the rest of the day I went about my duties while the children played in the shade of the oaks. In the evening I trudged up to my attic, exhausted and depressed. So hot! The sun in its lowering arc had baked its way through my windows, and along with the cooking downstairs, my room was an oven.

What was this? A long yellow sash hung next to my bed attached to a couple of pulleys along the wall. And above, a waxed muslin banner suspended from the ceiling.

I tugged gingerly, felt some resistance, tugged again. There was a rasping sound, and the fan *swish-swish*ed overhead. A cooling breeze blew over me. I tugged again, letting the air caress. Whoever did this, God bless them! I scrambled downstairs. Johanna was in the kitchen, sipping cider.

"Johanna, there's a fan in my room!"

She smiled mischievously. "It were Titus. He knows how hot the attic get, and suggested it to Cook. She told him to go ahead and try his hand at it. Titus. He's a genius with mechanical things. Ain't you the lucky one!"

No man but my father had ever gone out of his way for me like this. Titus, whom I had thought so haughty. Tomorrow I would seek him out and thank him.

In the deep of night I awoke from the cold, remembering the opened windows. I wrapped myself in a quilt and sat gazing out on the inky darkness. A cloud of stars drifted down the black of sky—nomads of the night. Orion, my old friend, and the Southern Cross. All the white, bright, glittering stars crowded the vaults of heaven.

A noise below. Two men carrying lanterns tiptoed across the yard toward the Slave Quarters. I fell back into the shadows. Minutes passed. They emerged with a slaveboy. Was that Digger, my watermelon thief? My fig boy? Muffled cries as one man clamped his hand over the child's mouth. Should I call for help? When he raised his lantern, a profile I knew stood out in silhouette—the Master! The kidnapper slunk down the yard with the boy while the Master crept back to the house. What in blazes was happening?

I sat in silence for a long time, but nothing more stirred. Had the Master sold a slavechild in secret, not telling the mother?

A withering feeling churned my stomach.

~

The next morning when I entered the kitchen, Manassa and Oom Samuel sat huddled at the table chopping apples, unusually quiet. Cook was at her hearth, throwing apples into *pannenkoek* batter.

"Is little Digger still around?" I asked. Manassa nodded. I breathed with relief. "And the other slaveboys?"

"*Ja*."

After tending to the children and their breakfast, I came down for mine. I pushed at the fish. Cook had left the *galjoen*'s head attached, and a glazed eye stared up at me.

Afterward, I took the basin of dishwater outside to pour under the trees. At the ox kraal, the slavechildren were combing the ground for cowpies. Digger was not among them. "Hey,

Eli," I called. "I'll give you a penny if you help with lunch today."

He said nothing. His shoulders were tight. He moved leadenly, as if in pain.

"What's wrong? Let me see that face." A wound puffed up his left eye, reddish blue.

"Did you get into a fight?" He turned back to his work.

In the kitchen, I asked Manassa what had happened to her child. She rose from the table. "I's got work to do," she murmured, heading for the hall.

"Me too." Samuel cleared his throat. "Got no time for gossip gossip, isn't it? No, suh." And he stumbled out into the yard like a man thick with sleep.

And then it dawned on me. "Cook, does this have something to do with men in the yard last night?"

She whirled around, waving a copper spoon at me. "Never you mind! It's none of our business!"

~

Later that afternoon, as the children and I returned from a walk, I caught sight of Titus at the irrigation wheel. He lay prone on the grass, oily rag around a coach wrench, yanking a greasy gear. We walked up to him. He gave us a brief glance.

"Titus, I want to thank you from the bottom of my heart for the fan. What a wonderful surprise! How ingenious you are!" He did not speak or look up. His thick-padded fingers flicked grit from the wheel's rim. "Titus. I'm trying to thank you."

He rolled to his knees, rising slowly, wadding the cloth in a fist. He was taller than I remembered, imposing. Still, he did not look me in the eye, but out across the fields. "Pleasure, Miss Saskia. I hope this fan, that it work well for you." Not even a smile.

"Oh, yes, it works beautifully, and when I pull the sash—"

Titus jerked around and glowered down at Pier. "And how do you be today, Master Pier?" His face was brooding. "Is your father taking good care of you? Keeping you from the harm?"

Pier scowled. Titus swung on his heels and marched away.

How dare he speak to the little master like that? What a strange man! What on earth was going on?

Chapter 13

MAY 1749 (WINTER)

"I feel like a rat caught in a trap," Johanna sighed when I entered the kitchen.

"That's how I felt all those many months onboard ship." I shivered before the hearth, flicking water from my cape. How I had taken for granted the fine autumn weather.

It had rained and rained for over two weeks. June already, but at this end of the earth, that meant the depths of winter. Every day, in a crash of thunder, the sky cracked open and unburdened itself upon us.

I had just run out to the garden to pull up some leeks for Cook when I looked up and saw the Master standing at an upstairs window. He was looking out over his vines, and I could imagine him grinding his teeth, afraid the soil would wash out from under the plantings. The kitchen workers were just as upset, for they had to run through puddles to fetch water from the well. The laundresses fretted for they had no sunshine to dry their wash, which hung damp now on indoor lines. And I was cross, for the mud-soaked veldt and pelting rain meant I couldn't go for the walk I'd promised the children. The cold rains were affecting all of us—as if we'd been caught in an enormous linen press that squeezed us into ill-temper.

I stoked the fire in the *kinder*room, then stood at the window watching the rain pound the mountains and mist that rose from the warm earth. I gave the room a thorough cleaning, scrubbing the yellowwood floors to a gleaming shine. My hands were raw from the harsh, soapy water. Should I really be doing this work? Shouldn't I be protecting them for lacemaking? Mistress Cingria either didn't know or didn't care.

As the morning drew on, I watched the children at play. Catryn was the easy child, laughing often, sometimes in a high-pitched giggle. Still such innocence! Sometimes she would put affectionate arms around my shoulders as I sat at the low table. But whenever her brother threw a tantrum or played fiercely, which was often, she would get upset. Perhaps her heart was too kind, for she cried at any small injury to any creature. The other day a couple of Cape pigeons landed on the open windowsill. When Pier grabbed one and twisted its little neck, she screamed and cried so hard, I had to carry her to bed and rock her back to calmness. What a scolding I gave Pier! He'd wanted to roast it on a spit. Instead, we buried the bird in a plot of earth next to the roses. I made Pier dig the soil himself.

Pier was playing with his lead soldiers and Catryn and I cutting paper into lacy designs when Mistress Cingria suddenly shadowed the door. She would be busy today, so could I lead the children in their geography lesson? At last!

I brought out books and attacked the lesson with relish, pinning a large map of the world to the wall. Mistress Cingria had instructed me to teach the children the names of all the sub-Saharan nations. Did I know them myself? Soon the children were banging their feet against the chairs, sneaking peeks at the rain beating against the glass. Then, with a sudden sweep of his arm, Pier sent his geography book flying across the room.

"Pick that up, Pier! Books are expensive! You know, if this is the way you children are going to act, I might as well be in my room reading, or making lace."

"Well, go do it then," Pier snapped. Catryn covered her face with her hands, muffling laughter.

"Don't be insolent, Pier de Witt!" In my own childhood, I'd fought for every morsel of learning I could get. People thought education wasted on girls. But I too would have been bored with this lesson. Then I remembered something. "Keep studying those maps, children. I'll be right back."

I returned bearing a large portfolio. Page after page of painted etchings fell open, revealing headhunters from Borneo, turbaned maharajas from India, *chinees* farmers with wide reed hats and bamboo yokes. I quickly flipped past pictures of people in scant clothing, stopping on a page where Zulu hunters lunged their spears into the gaping mouth of a lion. Catryn and Pier pushed against each other to get a look.

"Children, I'm going to tell you a story about some people like these." I paced the room, trying to remember the African tale that Oom Samuel had told me. "Once upon a time there was a native boy who took care of his father's cattle."

I recounted the tale of Jambo, who released a lion from a trap after the lion solemnly promised to do him no harm. But the moment it was freed, the lion licked its lips. "That's when Jambo knew the lion was thinking what a delicious meal he would make. He took a few steps back. 'You took an oath not to harm me!' The lion replied that after struggling in the trap so long, he was hungry. The promise didn't matter."

Catryn started shivering. "He didn't eat Jambo, did he, Miss Saskia? He promised."

I paced the room. "Well, wily Jackal happened along and

cleverly tricked the lion into stepping back into the trap. And so Jackal saved Jambo's life." Catryn laughed. Even Pier grinned. "So you see, children, never break promises you make to anyone."

For a minute the children were silent. I could almost hear their little brains grinding away. The rain stopped and a warm sun crept out from under the clouds. Pier rose and gazed out the window. "You don't keep *your* promises, Miss Klaassens."

"What?"

He spun on his heels to face me. "You promised me things would be better once we got to Africa. You promised me everything would be fine with Father!"

I turned away, wishing myself gone. "I'm sorry, Pier. I really thought things *would* be better. I shouldn't have promised what I can't control."

The rattling of keys. Mistress Cingria stood at the door. "I want Pier to write an essay for his father." She pulled out paper, ink, and quill. Her movements were sharp, officious. "Three pages on what you've learned today about countries." Her eyes fell upon the portfolio. "What's this?" She flipped through pages, pausing at an etching of a Javanese woman with naked breasts. Her cheeks flushed. "Miss Klaassens, did you take this portfolio from the Master's library without his permission? And show this to the children?"

"Well, not *that* picture . . ."

She snapped the portfolio shut. "Shame on you! How dare you do such a thing?"

"We really like the book, Mistress Cingria." Catryn pulled at her eyebrows.

The Housekeeper shoved the volume into my hands. I was to take it to the Master and apologize. Then go clean the floor of the Slave Kitchen until it sparkled. And if Pier's essay did not satisfy the Master, I would be punished further.

"Clean the floor of the Slave Kitchen?" I echoed in disbelief.

"This minute! After you return the portfolio. Now get out!"

I grabbed Catryn by the hand and stormed down the steps. There was something seriously wrong with that woman.

The Master was in his study. I curtsied and scraped. How angry he was! But Catryn ran up and rested a hand on her father's neck, telling him what a grand book it was, and how happy she'd been to hear the story about Jambo and the lion, and how important it was for people to keep their promises. He drew her to his side and buried a kiss in her cheek. It must be true then: even the hardest of men can melt in the company of those they love.

I suited up: white apron, white cloths, and even white gloves, looking for all the world like the living dead. Cook was aghast at my mission while Manassa volunteered to help. The slavewomen stepped aside in wonder as we entered their kitchen. I was so furious that I scoured that peach pit floor on hands and knees like a demon. And thanked Manassa for helping me.

"Ain't no work for no lacemaker, that for sure," she frowned.

Later, Mistress Cingria inspected the floor, but said nothing. For the rest of the day I fumed.

At tea in the *kinder*room, I asked Pier if the Master had liked his essay. He threw me a nasty look. "Couldn't find one good thing in it, that's how he liked it. Said I couldn't write worth a damn, that I was shiftless and lazy, and he was ashamed to have me as a son. It's your fault. What a useless geography lesson! You're just a useless whore." And he kicked me under the table.

I jumped up. "Pier de Witt! You're a spoiled, ungovernable child, and not too old for a good lashing."

"Just try it then." My mouth went dry as a stick. "You're no better than Father!" I grabbed him by the ear, but Catryn cried out, so I let him go.

The Mistress would take his side anyway. She allowed him to disrespect anyone without fear of punishment. In Delft he had gotten into all kinds of trouble, once pushing his little sister into the canal, for which I was caned. Servants there told me he was wild and rebellious because the Master was overbearing. And after the Master sailed ahead to Africa, no one punished him at all.

I'd witnessed the Master at work. "Stop slouching, Pier," he'd shout. "Stand up like a man, not some cowering hyena!" He believed in the going theory that criticism without praise would make his son strong. Between the Master and Mistress, no wonder he was a mess.

Mistress Cingria sent me to my room without dinner. There would be no breakfast tomorrow either. I sat on the corner of my bed, her words burning my ears. The last time I felt this crazy was when Grandfather was alive.

I pulled out my journal pages—perhaps if I wrote down my early memories, I'd loosen some tangled threads.

Most of my early memories are happy ones—at least in the years Mama was alive. I was not yet so angry.

I put down my quill, surprised. When did anger enter me, then?

I used to be as carefree as any child. I led my friends in games through the brick alleyways, flew kites in the park, and skated on frozen canals in winter. Mama taught me to sew and read and write a little, and to make lace. On evenings when he was in town, Papa and I played the recorder after prayers. That and evening walks along the canals were our special time. My family thought learning would make me vain and impertinent, and perhaps they were right. But I was keen for it. It was my aunt, cousin Gertruyd's mother, who taught me to read beyond my years and to pen a fine hand. She also taught me to play some viola, and what I lacked in skill I more than made up for in ardor. Of this further education my parents never knew.

When I turned nine, my easy child-world came to a halt. Papa was frequently away from home on business. Grandfather ruled the house, and could not stand the noise of children. There was but one of me. Just how much noise could there have been?

"I am a scholar!" he would thunder. "Can't I have peace in which to read and study in my own house?" He yelled often and ever quoted scripture, frightening me with warnings of damnation. Always, I felt on guard, afraid to make a mistake. I grew quiet and sullen. If I squirmed in my chair, Grandfather scolded. If I raised my voice or laughed loudly, he came down hard. His canings blistered my hands so that I could not play my recorder, nor make lace for days.

Mama was not always well—something about the dampness and her lungs. She took to her bed often. I turned sullen and would not speak for days, but no one seemed to notice. I felt bottled up and waxed over, like a jar of preserves.

When Grandfather wasn't around, Mama would take me in her arms. "Hush, hush," she would whisper. One night when I was particularly distressed she walked me to the window and, lifting me onto the table, pointed up at the night stars. "These are your guardians," she said. "See how they smile down on you? Think of them and you will never feel alone."

I put down my pen and breathed deeply. A painful journey indeed, going back in time. Could I recall the real truth of things? The Sisters of Charity had taught me that to be honest, one must be vigilant. And memory resists vigilance. I picked up the pen.

When I turned eleven, Grandfather told Bertje to lace me tightly into a long dress with stays, to develop the posture of a lady. It had a deep bodice that jabbed my thighs and a starched white collar that scratched my neck. And very old-fashioned.

"Now don't you get them clothes dirty, missy," Bertje would instruct, "cause that's extra work for me, and we both gets into trouble." Bertje was tall and strong. I liked the smell of cinnamon and clove on her hands after baking. But when I tried to talk, she told me not to bother her.

Soon I was of an age to help. There was always cleaning. Bertje fitted me with a servant's smock and put me to work, even washing floors. At least then

I was allowed to loosen my stays. As long as I can remember, my head has rung with the sound of water hitting tile, known the smell of lye soap and feel of reddened hands.

I preferred sewing, making music, and especially making lace, pleasures allowed me once my work was complete. Even when tired, I got in a little lacemaking, but I wasn't so serious about it then. Grandfather said there was time enough for the gentler arts when I was older and grooming myself for a husband.

When I turned twelve, everything changed. A great sickness ran wild through the country, frightening everyone. It was the pox. Everyone barred their doors, but people succumbed. Then it gripped Mama and Grandfather. We fetched Papa, and he stayed home more, but always pacing, attending to them as I did, and sleeping little. I cleaned with more fervor than ever. But my spirit was squeezing smaller and smaller each day, until it felt no larger than a nut compressed in its shell.

Then Grandfather died. One afternoon I snuck into the room where he was laid out and pulled back the sheet, starting at this thing called death. The pox-scarred face looked like Grandfather's, the body too, but he was not in it. Just a statue of clay.

For weeks Mama lay in bed, feverish, breathless. I prayed for her constantly. Disease wove its threads *around her like a demon spider. Pustules grew and burst on her skin. She grew pale and weak as she fell toward death.*

I moved about the house ever so quietly, afraid that if I made too much noise, Mama's breath would stop. And then it did. Papa said it was neither our will nor hers, but God's. All the same, just as I came into my first month's blood, just when I needed Mama most, she took the outstretched hand of Death and was gone. That's when fear became a squatter in my heart. Fear that burrows there still.

I could write no more. The memories were brittle, and I about to break.

I lit a candle and set up my lace pillow. As I fell into the rhythm of wrapping thread around bobbins, my thoughts began to soften. I entered the cycle of bobbins crisscrossing palms—two between two, *click*, around and back again. *Click click.*

Mama used to say we can change painful thoughts by replacing them with grateful ones. As I worked the threads, I pulled in everything glad that had happened since coming to this new land. In these few months, there'd been many happy moments. Like when the de Witts praised me for my work with the children, or for my lace. There had been days when fine gentlemen looked at me with admiration. And times when I'd had all the staff laughing.

I thought of early mornings when I'd open the shutters and look out on a sea of mist sweeping the countryside, or watch leafless vines march like soldiers up the blue mountains. Late afternoons striding alone through the fields, tall grass tickling the skin beneath my skirt, catching sight of a family of springbok. Times like these, I'd be awash with a sense of beauty, and I floated in a sea of gratitude that the world is as it is, and me right there, that moment, a part of it. I remembered this, and felt now as I felt then—whole again.

Chapter 14

May 1749 (Winter)

"You all right, Miss Saskia?" Samuel chuckled. "You so quiet quiet being. Thought you musta fall off the back at the last pothole."

I sat braced on a cracked leather seat in the bed of the fourteen-ox wagon, self-conscious and chilled to the bone, while Samuel rode up front with Titus. The sun was just rising, casting lavender mist over the hills. The men were making their regular run to Cape Town, and instructed to deliver me to my lace lesson. What could this mulatto possibly teach me? No matter. I would enjoy spending more hours at my bobbins. And get to see more of Cape Town. So far I'd avoided becoming a lace slave to my employers. Or had I?

We rumbled down the dirt road with its deep ruts, wheels and oxen kicking up pebbles. I blinked away the dust, shook it from the folds of my blue woolen shawl. The twenty-mile drive would take four hours at best, perhaps longer. I was told the springs on this wagon cushioned somewhat better than the carriage that brought us here. Still, I prayed that my teeth and bones would survive the rattling.

Frankly I was nervous about sharing a wagon with Titus. He had a brooding, bristling energy, and I think I feared him, but I was curious about him too. Thank goodness he sat up front, focused on driving the team. With Oom Samuel it was different, easy. For miles we rattled along, the two Black men up front talking, me in the back, clutching my walnuts and my lace kit. Until Samuel's question.

"Still here, Uncle," I called out.

"Not like Miss Jezza riding wit us, isn't it, Titus? That gal she talk and squawk like the ostrich in heat! One bag a flirtatious chatter, isn't it? 'How you like my new hat, Titus?' 'When you play drums to me again, Titus dear?' " he mocked in falsetto. "Can't wait to lose her at the market yust to get some peace. Or maybe you like attentions dat girl, son. Mighty pretty she be, isn't it?"

What a long speech from this old man! Titus was smiling grimly, like someone teased fairly but too much. Everyone knew Jezza was besotted with the fellow—in Cook's crude expression, she had an "itch in her linen" for him. In the kitchen, the slavegirl hinted they were sweethearts.

I sank into a pleasurable dreaminess, looking out over the land, trees leafless and hunched like specters, grapevines brittle and brown. Every now and then, particularly approaching a pass we could not see beyond, Titus would crack his incredibly long bamboo whip. The leather thongs split the air like a rifle shot, echoing through the hills, warning approaching wagons of our presence.

Although it made me freckly, I pulled back my straw bonnet and let the sun burn my skin. Brown faces were for farmers, I've always been warned, but to me it looked healthier than the ashen, powdered look of fashionable women. Ah! That's something I'll never be . . . Lying back, I studied the white clouds as they swarmed above, lost in them, mapping out their lacy threads into patterns.

After what seemed hours, on the promontory of a high hill, Titus pulled the wagon over. Without a word we alighted, unpacked our blankets and lunch baskets, and set up a picnic under the shade of a wild fig. We sat in silence, eating fruit, bread, and dried hake. Eagles soared and glided above on invisible currents, while down the valley earth-colored elephants lumbered over the mudflats. There is nothing on earth as grand as animals in the wild, especially these ancient beasts.

Samuel pointed to a mountain slope across the valley. I caught my breath—an old male lion and his mate sat sunning themselves sleepily on an outcropping of rock, as haughty and indifferent to us as if they owned these slopes, which I suppose they did. My body gave a little shiver. I feared them, yet thrilled to see them.

"The lions, they once come to the edge of Rustigvallei," Titus said. "But no more. Leopards—that be another matter."

Titus's dark profile stood out against the glazed blue sky. How like a lion he looked himself—and just as proud. We ate in silence. Much later, back on the road, just as I was lost in the movement of firs blowing about in the winds, Titus spoke. His voice was burnished, taunting.

"So, Miss Saskia, do this be the way we go along always?"

I sat up. "What do you mean?"

"Is it always to be like this? Samuel and me up front like groom and footman while you ride behind, the grand duchess."

Samuel sucked in his breath, and I released my grip on the wagon. "Well you're a bold one! I'm just going to pretend you never said that."

He cracked his long whip smartly but needlessly. "Miss Saskia, do not take the offense. It is the conversation with you

I want. Perhaps you do not be in the habit of conversing with slaves."

Was he baiting me? "I'm new here. I don't have any habits." Awkward silence. "If you want to talk to me, Titus, why can't you just say so?"

"But I did say so! *Ach*, women! No winning with them. What do you think, my uncle?" Samuel chuckled and shook his head. "I do be sorry, my sister," Titus said. "I was just having with you the fun. Let me try again." He cleared his throat loudly. "Miss Saskia, would you do these poor men the honor of the sitting up close for the purpose of the pleasant conversation?"

He turned his face, smiling. Sincerely. When I moved to get up, he reined in the oxen. I crept forward, lowered myself onto a sack of grain behind them. "This better be worth it," I muttered in a voice any martyr would have admired.

"*Ach*. So I have to prove myself now, do I?" When he flashed me a good-natured smile, I grinned and looked the other way.

We climbed above the veldt, red and gray shale jutting up onto the road. Midway up a high pass, we heard the immense crackle of a whip splitting the air. Titus answered with the crack of his, then maneuvered the lumbering oxen to the side of the road to make way. The top of a covered wagon came into view, then two drivers, rough-looking men in laboring clothes and wide, flat-brimmed hats. *Voortrekkers!*

As they passed, we stared at one another. Their faces were creased with ruts, parched as earth-red as the rocks, eyes baked from the sun. Muskets, rifles, powder horns, cast iron cookpots, leather buckets, and tools banged against the sides of the wagon, along with leopard pelts, crocodile skins, and the skulls of wild beasts. A cross between roaming natives and proud Dutch settler. When they grunted and nodded in greeting, we called out, "*Goedemorgen*."

"You do not see the many trekkers much now," Titus murmured. "Since they stop the land grants and explorations inland. Hard men. They carry the religion hard too."

I looked back over my shoulder. A small brown hand parted a slit in the wagon's canvas and two young Bushwomen peeked out—wives or mistresses, I presumed. The wagon disappeared into a wall of dust. I'd heard of these frontiersmen. They'd spurned the Compagnie and all its laws and regulations, thumbed their noses at Dutch society, and set out for the interior, mostly desert or mountains, to scratch a living from the earth.

"Please tell me about this lace teacher, Widow Huyskens, Titus. You know her, don't you?"

"The remarkable woman. The free mulatto, aging now. Dutch, African, and Malay. Poor as the mouse in the chapel. Did you know she walks with the crutch?"

A handicapped widow, and of mixed blood. I flashed on all the disadvantaged women I'd known, mostly rough and brutish. Bitter women, some crazed. They filled the Spinhaus shelter in Delft where the Sisters and I had often carried food, clothing, and prayer to them. Sometimes we'd be able to teach them enough needlework so they'd earn a few guilders. We'd pray they wouldn't sneak out and spend it on drink, but they often did. I wondered, was the widow like these? Couldn't be —she made lace!

I was beginning to warm to Titus. He spoke well and with heart. When he gave his whip a sudden crack, it sailed ever so lightly across the yokes of the oxen, barely grazing the hairs on their shoulders. I held my breath as I glimpsed his strong hands and the muscles of his forearms. Never before had the sight of a man's body moved me.

We were an hour back on the road, when out of nowhere a boy stumbled in front of us. Dressed in the rags of a field slave, he was dark-complexioned like an East Indian, his blue-black hair askew. He spun back and forth before us like a thread from its bobbin. Did the gourd he brandish contain wine? Stolen from his master?

Titus reined in the team and called out. I grew nervous. The boy staggered across the lane toward us and—I couldn't believe this—pulled himself out of his breeches and pissed on our front wheel. Titus questioned him in Dutch, then English. Hearing Portuguese, the boy's face brightened, and he keeled over, sprawling onto the road in front of us. Titus jumped from the wagon, rifled through his pockets and opened the slave's shirt. Was he robbing him? Titus heaved the boy onto the wagon boards, barely an arm's reach from me.

"Titus!" I shouted, almost jumping onto the backs of the oxen.

"We be taking this one to the home of the owner," Titus announced, whipping the oxen hard. And then, almost under his breath, "If we can find that place."

My gut wrenched. We were playing with fire picking up this slave. "You don't even know where he lives."

"It must be the Brill estate. It be the closest."

"Titus, get him out of here!" And finally, in my most commanding voice, "You're only a slave, Titus. You have to do what I say. Now get him out of this wagon!" But he did not. He drove on, steering the team down a side lane lined with poplars. I folded my arms over my chest.

"Miss Saskia, the life of this boy be in our hands."

We drove past vineyards until we glimpsed a great manor house. Suddenly I felt a tug on my skirt. I screamed. Samuel and I restrained the boy under grain sacks. I was sweating marbles, scared of the boy but more terrified we'd be caught with an escaped slave. Just when Titus and Samuel jumped out, a troupe of gray baboons boldly plunked themselves down on the dusty road next to us.

"Hey! You're not going to leave me alone with him? Baboons too! Samuel! Titus!"

"You be all right," Titus called back. "If any give you the trouble, yust hit them with the shovel over the head." And they raced across the fields.

"Whatever happened to chivalry?" I shouted after them.

The shovel was half buried under the boy. Gently I pried it loose, heaving it skyward, weapon readied. The baboons fled. I watched the slaveboy closely. He didn't stir, though strange guttural noises were coming from his throat. He was snoring! Too insensible to even notice me. Soon Titus and Samuel returned with Blacks and Malays who gathered up the boy and scurried off with him through the grapevines. On the road once more, Titus said that clearly he was a slave. He'd been looking for a tag or papers when he found the mark branded on his chest. He was from Ceylon.

"If they find him missing, drunk, and far from home, the situation for him, it be bad. Very bad."

I shuddered, glad we'd saved that boy from punishment, though I would have left him reeling in the dust. I turned around angrily. "Damn it, Titus! We could have been stopped and accused of trying to help a slave escape. You put us in such danger!"

"He be the slave, and so he be my brother. I take the chance."

Of all of us, Titus had the most to lose. He would have lost the freedom soon due him, and worse. Yet he'd put that slave's welfare before his own. But before ours too. Such a man I have to watch.

Chapter 15

There was an old woman lived under the hill
And if she's not gone she lives there still.
—Traditional Song

June 1749 (Winter)

"We must walk across the city." Titus and Samuel were outspanning the oxen in the field bordering Cape Town. His Black fingers pulled the harnesses loose with assurance. "Do you have the basket of yours?"

"*Ja*, Titus. Of course."

I grabbed my lace basket from the back of the wagon and scurried after him. I was nervous, and breathless too, as I was late. We trotted in the direction of the Malay Quarter, Titus and Samuel stepping a few paces behind me. That is the rule, it seems, when White women walk with slaves. Samuel scrambled off toward the wharf to pick up mail and supplies.

Bo-Kaap homes, painted in brilliant hues of rose, melon, parrot green, and lavender, straddled the southeastern hills, commanding magnificent views of Table Mountain and Sugar Loaf. Streets vibrated with the noise and activity of an Amsterdam ghetto, teeming with the same odor of poverty and neglect. We sprinted over ditches of fetid water that cut through stone streets. Shops and people looked patched together, barely one step up from slavery.

Black and cinnamon-colored people ambled about in exotic costumes—Malays, Indians, and other freepeople of color made their homes in this district called the Bo-Kaap. Titus told me on the trip in that many were *hindoo* or *islamite*, their religions not sanctioned by our Governors—in fact, barely tolerated. The Compagnie allowed them no temples. I know nothing of these peoples. Do they believe in God?

But what color! Cries of barter in foreign tongues invaded the market air. Syrupy smells of cracked-open fruits and exposed sacks of clove and *kumin* pulled at our noses. We stumbled to avoid stepping on blankets crowded with green porcelain. "As jade green as the China Sea," Titus remarked, and I turned to look at him, wondering how he would know. Stalls were piled high with crushed silks and printed cottons. We hurried past lengths of gaily embroidered ribbon, wedges of coconut candy, slivers of dried antelope—all tempting, all easily had for a coin. I was enthralled.

Titus directed me through narrow alleyways where pungent aromas of *kerrie* poured from kitchen windows. "Widow Huyskens's mother," he explained, "had the mixed blood—Javanese, Dutch, and African. She was mistress to the Dutch merchant captain who sailed the route of Cape-Asia." After his wife's death, the captain brought his mistress and their children from East Africa to live with him in Cape Town. A bit awkward, I mused—but probably less so in this land where people seemed to invent their own codes of living.

"Effie was not born with the lameness," Titus continued. "She be very beautiful when young, though crippled. No matter, she marry the fine Hollander and perfect her Dutch." The widow's husband, he said, had been highly esteemed in the Bo-Kaap, a mediator between the coloreds and the government. After he died, Effie Huyskens had only a cottage and small stipend, so she made lace and gave lessons to make ends meet.

We made our way up and down hilly streets, my wood shoes clattering over cobbles. "Mistress de Witt told me some people won't buy lace made by a mulatto."

Titus stopped. "If that be true, then they are the stupid people. Effie Huyskens give many years to teach and encourage the young in this place. Now everyone, they call her 'Auntie.' My parents knew her. I love her just like my own *aja*."

I walked on, feeling bad. There must be more to this woman than I'd first thought.

We climbed a steep hill, and Titus halted before a small stuccoed cottage on Longmarket Street, its walls a chalky blue with orange-yellow shutters. A lovely vine of leaves was painted around the threshold. A small woman with lively eyes opened the door—carved out of polished fruitwood, she seemed. Her smile lit up like a child holding a *chinees* sparkler.

"Come in, dear children." Leaning on crutches, she wrapped gentle hands around mine. "Saskia—what a lovely name. Call me Aunt Effie, or just Effie."

Titus apologized for our tardiness. "Not to worry," she said. As the two spoke, I noted that her Dutch was better than Titus's, but with the same lilting rhythms. Like other old lacemakers, she stooped at the shoulders from years of bending over her lace pillow—and also, I guessed, over her wooden supports.

She offered us rusks and *rooibos* tea infused with flowers. I was glad Titus was staying awhile. They settled into speaking of old times, so I took a turn around the room. It was humbly furnished. Students' practice pillows sat piled in a corner with their crude, newly formed lace. I liked the funny yellow of the walls—it made me feel I was floating around inside a daffodil. I listened to snatches of the conversation: Titus had been born at the Cape, though his parents and aunt Sladie had been captured as slaves from some country on the Indian Ocean called Mosambiek.

A large niche in the wall drew me. It was crowded with flowers, a small etching of the Virgin, and a tile with some strange oriental script. A piece of copal burned in a dish, sending out fragrant smoke. And—idols! I traced a finger along a statue with many dancing arms, wondering what they were all for. And an elephant head on a man's body! Our church in Delft had been spare, lofty, empty of icons. Papa often said our Dutch churches were stark vessels for the Void. Yes, and void of mystery too, I thought. What dark mysteries did these heathen idols hold? If the de Witts heard about them, would they let me return?

All too soon Titus rose and asked if he might come for me in four hours. *Four hours!* In a strange house in Cape Town with a pagan I'd just met? I flashed him a distressed look.

Widow Effie Huyskens and I settled into armchairs and sat for a moment, regarding one another. She said she'd learned lacemaking from a French Huguenot. I nodded, for I knew of their skills and long persecution in France.

Could I see some lace she'd made? She slid a piece of brown fabric onto her lap. Against her white apron, the dark pattern of the lace stood out starkly. I knelt close to examine its wispy threads, which were the color of wet earth. It had an angular, block-like style, very unusual, with beasts and natives roaming a palm-studded landscape. Large birds filled the trees and ascended toward a sun. And all edged in a bold geometric pattern. Goodness, so primitive! Did daemon spirits inhabit this work? It was so wildly different from anything I'd ever seen. I sank back on my haunches, speechless.

"Did you bring any of your own lace to show me, my dear?"

I pulled three silk pieces wrapped in tissue from my basket and laid them out over black cloth. I was proud of their fine weaves and graceful designs.

Effie ran a finger along the panel of cupids and studied them for some time. "My word, child, well done. Very well done indeed."

I bit my lip to squash pride. "Do you make traditional lace too, Widow Huyskens?"

"Call me Effie, or Aunt Effie. And yes, I do." She rummaged through a drawer at her side, showing me several pieces in white silk thread. Exquisite!

"Widow Huyskens—Aunt Effie—you humble me. I'd love to see you work those African motifs."

I fetched her lace pillow, and watched her study the pattern for some time before picking up the bobbins. With assured fingers, she crossed the brown thread around itself, swiftly looping, turning, and twisting. Her hands hypnotized me—the bobbing of two small birds. A bold web plied across the pillow. Gone, then all at once, her fingers stopped—she was back.

"Are you ready to weave your first Cape lace, Saskia?" The widow brought out tissue patterns from her collection. I searched among them, choosing a European design, though curious about the African ones. As I sat at the table, tracing one of her designs onto thinnest *japan* paper with a pen, she asked me about Dutch lacemaking.

In Belgium and the Netherlands, I explained, orphan children as young as five wove lace. I told her how the children were thrown together in dank cellars and forced to sit at their lacemaking pillows for up to twelve hours a day. How they sang songs to pass the time and to keep the rhythm of the bobbins. I told Effie about the middlemen who bought from the lacemakers, then turned around and sold their lace to wealthy buyers. These middlemen were often mayors—and they were the ones who made all the money. The lacemakers, for all their skill and efforts, received a pittance.

Effie looked up, brow wrinkled. "I suppose the middlemen supply them at least with thread and pins?"

"Nay! Have to pay for those themselves. Hard for them even to come up with pin money. And never allowed to wear any lace at all."

Effie shook her head. "Poor darlings. Like that fairy tale. Locked in a room and forced to turn straw into gold." I laughed.

Now my eyes again fell on the strange idols in their niche. "Effie, do you pray to that elephant on your alter?" I was hoping to God she wasn't a heathen pagan. Whatever that was.

"No, child." She laughed. "I don't worship them. In some religions, those figures are messengers to the divine. Though I do like the idea that animals might mediate between heaven and earth."

Something in me relaxed. Soon I was telling Effie about my childhood in Delft and my father, who spent a lot of time traveling as an art broker. How the business went downhill as the economy got worse, art being considered a luxury—although Papa insisted people needed art for their souls. I told her about Mama's death, and that it was difficult later, under Stepmother's rule. Effie listened kindly.

After some time I rose from the table, stretching. And saw something that startled me—her skirt had fallen back, exposing an empty place where her right leg should have been. My heart dropped into my stomach. I sneaked a sideways look. Yes—Effie was missing a leg! A wave of compassion fluttered through me. Back at the table I made hasty pricks on the pattern, but my hands trembled. Titus had not said she'd lost an entire leg! I decided I would absolutely, positively not look again at that hollow in her skirt.

After an hour or so at our work, Effie rose. I stretched my legs, then self-consciously pulled them back under my skirt. I was thinking too much about legs, about gimpiness. "Effie, where did you get the colored thread you use in your lace?"

"It's from agaves grown right here at the Cape, my dear. I spin it myself, then dye it brown with walnut hulls."

"How wonderful. And the tough gimp?" I blushed a beetroot red. Oh, no! Would she think I was referring to her being a cripple—or know I meant the lace term?

"I use a thick linen imported from Friesia. And yes, I probably am a tough old gimp."

I put down my pricker and covered my face with my hands. I wanted to crawl under the table and die. Effie started laughing. I looked at her, then started laughing too, that wild laughter that only comes with embarrassment.

"Help me with the tea, Saskia. Then I'll tell you my story."

In the kitchen I was still laughing. Then we settled into our chairs again, cups in hands. "When I was in my early twenties, Saskia, I was pretty full of myself."

One night her uncle was driving them home from a wedding in the Bo-Kaap. "He'd had lots to drink at the reception. I think he was in love with the bride, or something, and decided to drink all the wine in Cape Town." He drove the horses so hard that a wheel broke off. The wagon collapsed, and they flew out onto the road. An oncoming carriage had no time to stop—it ran over Effie's leg. She was bedridden for months. The break healed, but not the wound. Infection spread and they had to amputate.

"High up, very high up." Effie put a hand on her skirt, folding it over a bone just below her hip. "Sometimes I feel it, as if the leg were still there—alive and complaining." She laughed, reaching for her tea.

I breathed in deeply. "Oh, Effie. How horrible!"

"I felt so too. Then I began to appreciate my unique situation." I gave her a blank look. She sat calmly, then picked up her lace pillow. "Now let's get back to the lace."

Instead I got up and looked for ways I could help. I fetched water from the outdoor furrows and washed our dishes, then scrubbed all the dirty pots in the basin for good measure. There was a knock on the door. A Malay woman, all but her face draped in fabric, placed potted orchids into my hands. Effie looked pleased when I brought them into the sitting room. Only then did I pick up my paper pattern again.

"Hold it to the window, would you, dear?" Against the glass, light poured through hundreds of pinpricks that shone like constellations. I brought the pattern for her to inspect. "Good work."

I'd only known this woman a few hours, yet how quickly I'd come to trust her. I began pouring out my heart. I told her some about the ship coming out, how many lives we'd lost to scurvy. Told her about the young Jewish boy who fell overboard—he and his mother had been on their way to Java to start a new life. How she'd screamed, trying to unlash the lifeboats, but the crew held her back. At sea, very few were worth the dangers of attempting rescue.

We were quiet for a minute. "There's this slavegirl, Jezza, at the estate. We were alone in the kitchen last week when she began telling me very personal things about my friend. Like how Johanna got pregnant, and had a slavewoman take care of the problem, if you know what I mean. Suddenly I was agreeing with Jezza and judging Johanna. Then felt awful."

Outside, wind whistled through the alleys. I ran pins through a lump of beeswax, but in my agitation I'd pricked too many holes in the paper. Effie leaned over, smoothing down errant holes with the back of her fingernail. "So you took part in a conversation you say you hated."

I sighed, shifting in my chair. Be honest about your motives, Mama always said. I rarely did, but here, with Effie, it felt safe. "I guess I was just trying to make friends with Jezza. We haven't really liked each other much."

"Do you think real kinship can ever come from bonding with someone against another?"

I paused, then looked down in shame. "I guess I wasn't being loyal to Johanna."

I must have looked pretty miserable, because Effie reached over and patted me on the wrist. "Be gentle with yourself, child. This is how we learn."

I rose, walked to the window, and pulled back aching shoulders. Outside, a wretched-looking slaveman struggled up the hill with a cartload of dead rock rabbits. "Effie, I feel like telling everyone what a troublemaker Jezza is."

"Leave it alone, Saskia. She's a slave; treat her gently. Her life has been unspeakable. People in pain can't help sometimes hurting others, especially those they envy."

I'd never thought that Jezza might envy me. "But life has dealt *you* hard blows, Effie. I doubt you go around hurting people."

"I'm not perfect, Saskia. Just old. Had time to work a few things out."

"Jezza is so confident, so sure of herself. It throws me." A clock on the shelf struck three—Titus would be here soon. I covered my lacework with a cloth and started packing my basket.

"I trust joy in a person any time over confidence," Effie almost whispered. I looked at my teacher, ashamed of my pettiness.

When I asked, Effie pulled a ruffle of her African lace from a box. It too had a primitive motif, but woven with more finesse. I stared at bold elephants, clouds, mountains, and wide canopies of trees, all woven in strange proportions. A shiver rushed down my arm. All of a sudden her designs made sense. Her lace wasn't merely simple. It was vigorous. Honest. The animals seemed to be marching right out of the cloth.

"This is how I think of Africa," she said. "A little rough, perhaps. But we Africans are a rough people, don't you think?"

"Not rough." I struggled for the words. "Alive." Then, standing in the front room of her home, excitement rushed like fire up my spine. I'd love to make lace like this!

"Aunt Effie, your lace . . . *sings*." She laughed. "Why can't I come up with something original? I always weave the same old sentimental deer and cupids."

"Be patient, my dear. One day you'll create something new, but you must let more of life happen to you. It's like sap coursing through a tree, making leaf then bud then flower. Just keep your heart and eyes alert to what is around you."

When Titus arrived, he was surprised to see me with my arm around Effie, her fingers clasping mine. I smiled up at him. "Titus, I think I've found a long lost aunt."

~

We rode home in the late afternoon, I up front with Titus. Samuel lounged in the comfort of sacks of rice they'd bought at market.

"Titus, I love that woman. As easy to be with as an old pair of gloves—or book of confidences." But then I had to ask him. "Her leg was amputated so far up!"

"So she told you of that thing, did she?" He looked straight ahead, shifted the reins. "I think she not mind if I tell you. She suffers much, you know, after the leg it is taken. The pain. But also the young men, they come no more to court. Many friends do not come. One day she decide, 'This be too much.' She goes to the roughest part of town, a tavern by the wharf. Sits down. Orders many gins. Never drank before, mind. The more she drinks, the more the bitterness, it bubble up. She picks the fight with the biggest, meanest White man there. Tells him he be weak, has no manhood. She does it on purpose. For surely now he will kill her." I gawked at Titus.

"He rushes over. She jumps up, and one of the crutches, it slip on the wet floor and down she goes. Her skirt flies up. The mean sailor, he stares down at her, at the place where the leg should be. This big bull of a man, he pick her up like the watermelon and set her in the chair."

The wagon wheels ground noisily over stones. I leaned in.

"He asks about that leg. She tells the story. He cannot help, he weeps. After that, he tells her his story—the childhood of beatings, the thieving, the alcohol, the bullying, the women leaving him, the imprisonment. She listens with all her heart and gives good counsel. She tells him that he needs to do the one thing every day to help one person, even the small thing. And to find the work he can do with heart. He listens. Later, she knows she be counseling herself. She returns often, not to drink but to listen. Many people talk to her about the broken lives. Now she has the purpose to live."

I sat quietly for a long time. By now our oxen had skirted the base of Table Mountain, bringing us out onto the plain.

"Titus, I have a confession to make. At first I couldn't

imagine what Effie could teach me. I was so cocksure of my own skills. But she's a genius with the lace, you know. What a little fool I've been."

"Why do you think she have nothing to teach you?" His words were slow, almost jabbing.

"I don't know. I guess because she's from this small outpost."

"Because she be the woman of color, and crippled. Is that not what you think?" Again his words poked.

"Nay, nay. I wasn't looking down on her." He shot me a doubtful look. "Color doesn't matter to me, Titus, nor being lame. I don't think that way." A fine speech, Saskia. But was it absolutely true?

Titus threw back the whip. Its long thongs whistled, then cracked like lightning through the clear air. "You Whites, you *always* be thinking that way." I stared at him. "Europeans always think we have little to offer. We have to work twice as hard to even . . ." He paused, his face screwed up. "You think that way and do not even know you think that way. You wish that we fade into the wallpapers or disappear behind the goats, but still work hard for you. And for what?"

I fell silent. Why was everyone challenging me today? I pulled a blanket from the back and wrapped it around my shoulders. "All right. Maybe I did think no colored woman could teach me much. And maybe I went today just to get away from the manor. But she's so inspiring, Titus! My mind is teeming with all kinds of new ideas."

Titus relaxed his grip on the reins, but his gaze stayed on the road. We rode without speaking over marshlands and out onto sandy plains until the green of vineyards came into view. In the distance a herd of zebra loped across the valley. Then, "I hope we can become friends, Miss Saskia. Even if you do be the girl." The corners of his mouth turned up mischievously. "Even if you *do* be the pinky White Hollander."

"Pinky white?" I grinned, swatting him on the shoulder.

On the ride back to Rustigvallei, I thought of all the unexpected turns my life had taken. Less than a year ago I was living at home in Delft, seeing no way out of a miserable existence. Now I lived at the bottom of the world with a group of new friends on a grand wine estate at the foot of great mountains. Getting paid to make lace. Had a lifetime passed and I hadn't noticed? Life felt as fine and tightly knit as the lace panels sitting in my basket. I looked up at the clouds swirling overhead and smiled.

Close to home, Titus called me out of my reverie. "Let me tell to you the story of Aunt Effie and you will better know who this woman be. One day, before you come, I be in Cape Town with her at the Bo-Kaap market. Before us be the Malay man carrying the large basket of apples on the head, and toward him, down the hill, come the cart loaded so high with the old clothes we could barely see the colored man who steer that thing. These men, they crash, one into the other, the clothes, they spill—"

"Nay, wait!' I cried. "That was you, then—and Effie! She stepped forward and kissed the men's hands!"

"You saw this thing? How strange." I'd thought of that scene many times since, always marveling at the little woman who stopped a fight with a kiss. And the slave who locked eyes with mine. "Then, Miss Saskia, you know well what kind of woman Effie be."

I stared far out over the veldt. What gifts Africa held in its dark and secret wilderness, in the deepest pockets of its human hearts.

Chapter 16

July 1749 (Winter)

"God help him." Cook tucked the white lappets of her cap back under its folds. "Darned if the Master don't feel compromised. He bein a good Calvinist deacon, we know how much he disapproves of musical performances and sumptuous eatin. But ain't he a man of the world too? It's only natural bein curious about foreign ways."

We housegirls stared as she bustled about the kitchen, wondering what she was talking about. Cook always seemed first to know what was going on. She told us that an old friend of the Master's, a Mr. Steenoven, specialty the Java trade, had sailed into Table Bay last week, and to thank the Master for previous hospitality, wanted to come Thursday with his entourage, treating the de Witts to a genuine Asian supper—and rare evening of Javanese performances.

No music, no entertainments—that was the rule at Rustigvallei. So when I passed the dining area at breakfast, I lingered long enough to overhear the Mistress persuade the Master. "Philippe, you have to accept Mr. Steenoven's offer. Any gentleman releases another when he can from feelings of indebtedness. Just this once church rules can take a back seat."

He grunted. The Mistress plumped up folds in her gown, awash with excitement. "We'll invite Adriaan. And how about the Brills? Oh, Saskia, I want you and Johanna to serve Thursday. With Titus and Josiah. You girls wear your brown satins. Tell Cook."

As that poet said, *Welcome, oh sweet and sacred feast!*

What a tizzy we were in—a superbly heathen dinner party! I was glad she chose Josiah to serve, for I knew this young Malay would delight seeing his Javanese kinsmen. I smiled, wondering how Mistress Cingria would feel when the Mistress made no arrangements through her.

Early Thursday morning, Master Steenoven's cook Tiktun and assistant arrived with an immense cartload of brass platters and all manner of Indonesian delicacies that looked quite strange. Among them, a suckling pig, its flesh all smooth and pale, like a giant octopus.

Tiktun was a funny fellow with a flat nose and puffy lips and wore a red-and-black striped silk turban. He came carrying a wonderful oiled paper parasol with painted flowers dancing across it, pink and red and green that disappeared when he collapsed the thing. Tiktun puttered about the kitchen in cotton breeches and an ancient gentleman's brocade coat, scruffy at the wrists. He inspected everything—pantry, hearth, knives, utensils, pots, serving dishes—then took off the coat, revealing a vest of outlandish flowered cotton. They spoke to us in the oddest pidgin Dutch. Titus and I were fascinated.

Earlier, Cook had been flushed with excitement, but when the Asians actually began setting up their native kitchen, her eyebrows arched. She stood in a corner, great arms crossed over her chest, her narrow eyes following Tiktun everywhere. "Now it's foreigners takin over me kitchen," she muttered. "What's the world comin to?"

Pointing his finger imperiously, Tiktun ordered Samuel to remove the parrot and Manassa to scrub the bird's shelf thoroughly. We looked on in wonder as he set up his altar: brocade cloth covered with flowers, rice, salt, and wine in little bowls, and strange idols in gold leaf. He inserted sticks into a red cup packed hard with ashes. When he put fire to them, they gave off a wonderful fragrance, like sweet burnt wood. Then he began chanting.

Cook fell into a chair and fanned her rosy face with a bright green banana leaf she'd pulled out of the cart—overwhelmed, I suppose, at losing her kitchen to an umber-colored infidel. The girls helped the men peel and chop, sautée and sear. Before long, as God-tempting aromas filled the room, Cook mumbled something about at last having a break from cooking. She followed the natives' movements with alert eyes, finally grabbing pencil and paper and scribbling notes.

The Javanese had brought along a mischievous little monkey, Chirinaa—the beast had eyes that darted about and shone like glass marbles. I chased it around the kitchen, laughing as it sailed across the hearth, flying everywhere, upsetting precious pots, pooping. While the Javanese laughed, Cook jabbed at it with her broom. "Tie that beastie down, Saskia," she barked. I chased and caught it, tied a cloth into a whittle and gave it a pretend spanking. Soon it settled down in my arms. "Funny little babe ya gots there, Miss Saskia, isn't it?" Samuel teased.

Early in the evening Johanna and I donned our chocolate brown skirts with their embroidered red bodices, serving-costumes the Mistress had designed, and white ruffled caps—very lovely, very French. We were putting out the best silver and *japanees* porcelain on the table when Titus entered, decked out in a navy suit and white stockings. How handsome he looked in his livery! When he took a couple of awkward steps, I looked down to see his toes squirm under thin black leather.

"If the Master would let you wear boots instead of those pumps," I told him, "you would look every inch the gentleman."

"I hate such shoes!" he whispered. "Like walking in the tight boxes. And this costume makes me feel like the monkey who dance for the copper coin."

"Monkey? Don't you know there's one flying about the kitchen as we speak?"

It was amusing to serve alongside Titus, for I never knew when he was going to mutter something audacious. Not loudly—any bold response would have gotten him a lashing. He carried the trays with precision and elegance, like a good servant, but I caught the twinkle in his eye, as if he knew he were an actor in someone else's play.

Before dark, the Master's nephew Adriaan arrived by horseback from Cape Town. As Lucy let him into the foyer, I smiled. What style he had! A fine lace cravat and riding boots that shone like burnished teak. Anna and Johanna became ridiculously flustered—no surprise there—and even my fingers twitched a bit to see this fine young gallant. Johanna whispered that he was Assistant Councillor for the Compagnie in Cape Town. When his smoke-gray eyes settled on me in the hall, and when he threw me what seemed like an admiring smile, I blushed and hurried to the kitchen.

Soon the Steenovens arrived, their cheeks as plump and pink as the suckling piglet that had been roasting all day. Their dignified entourage of male servants and performers glided in after them, marigolds in their buttonholes. I served the guests glasses of river-chilled wine and perry cider while the Javanese set up their puppet theater, a low stage with a sheet suspended before it. When all the guests were seated, Josiah and Titus extinguished the candles. The Javanese set out oil lamps.

With a banging of gongs and drums, enormous shadow figures, puppets, appeared on the screen, amazing us with shimmering dances. I loved watching the story unfold, a story we could follow without a word being spoken: lovers meeting, courting with lotus blossoms, falling in love. Then soldiers, a clash of swords, and the lovers cruelly separated. They died of heartbreak, then magically sprang back to life in Javanese heaven. We were enchanted.

From my station against the back wall I saw flickers of shadows at the window. Slaves had quietly gathered on the *stoep* to watch, pressing noses against the glass. Mistress Cingria rose and marched out the back door, followed by Cook. I went too. The night was cool and pure.

"Back to your quarters, the lot of you! This instant!" the Housekeeper commanded. Their meek, sad faces turned reluctantly from the window.

Cook stepped in front of her. "Aaw, let them be, Marissa. Ain't doin no harm. Besides, tonight's special."

"Oh, let them watch," I added, then scrambled back inside, afraid of my own boldness, but not before I saw Titus go out to tell them that the Mistress said to let the slaves have their little pleasure. Mistress Cingria strutted back to her seat, indignant. Throughout the evening she glowered at the growing audience outside who fogged up the glass with their rapt breath.

The play over, the puppeteers emerged from the back of the screen, bowing. They revealed their magic by holding up the small, flat puppets of cut leather that had cast such magnificent shadows.

While the guests visited in the front end of the gallery, we girls laid out enormous platters of lobster, crab, turtle, and lamb, and dishes with vegetables unknown to us. Hot sauces of *kerrie* with condiments of strange nuts, chilies, kumin and koriander, coconut and fresh herbs and frightening little black things that may have been insects sitting on decorative leaves—sweet, hot, and pungent tastes Tiktun had devised. All this on a vast tablecloth printed in wavy patterns of blues and siennas—a cloth so wondrous I wished I could steal it and sew it into a petticoat. The moment the guests gathered around the table, Tiktun entered with a flourish, bearing a tray with all the importance of a coronation pillow bearing a crown. His assistant poured liquid spirits over the pork and set light to it. How shocking to see it burst into flame!

"Fire!" the Mistress cried. Titus grabbed a glass of water and threw it at the sacred meal, but Tiktun pivoted just in time, taking the water with his back.

Master Steenoven roared with laughter. "This is part of the meal, dear friends, the food cooking and performing at the same time." With foolish wonder we watched the fire sizzle, then die out, oils hissing and spitting.

Every time Titus and I rushed to the kitchen to refill platters, we grabbed pieces of the foreign meal, gulping down beer when the chilies burned too much. I loved the new, fresh, biting flavors. But Cook's girls puckered their mouths in pain, throwing their food to the monkey. Chirinaa grabbed the scraps with both paws and stuffed them into his face.

Old Samuel grinned. "These foods, they be dancin an singin, they be screamin an fightin in this mouth, isn't it?"

Josiah, who had been captured in Java years ago, gorged like a madman. Grunts of pleasure escaped his mouth, sighs and groans that sounded eerily like pain. These were the dishes of his homeland, he muttered. For a moment he sat quietly, staring out the kitchen window. Light glanced off moisture in his eyes, then mine became teary too. Josiah was the dearest, sweetest man, almost as dear as Samuel. Like many of the slaves, he seemed to carry an unutterable grief he held close, bearing it in deepest silence.

Johanna and I carried final trays to the dining buffet: melons, papayas as orange as sunsets, and a dark blend of my favorite drink, *koffie*, this time from rich Javanese beans. I began plotting how I might steal a cup.

After dinner, the Brills said their thanks and left for home. The children ran upstairs while the women removed themselves to the Mistress's room. Grunting with contentment, the men retired to the study for our best brandy and conversation on weighty matters. I stood outside the door preparing the tray of liquor while Titus offered around tobacco and lights. I entered with the brandy, pretending not to notice Adriaan's gray eyes smiling up at me. Titus and I placed ourselves at the edge of the room, melting into the walls, waiting for our cues.

"What a time we live in, eh, gentlemen?" Mr. Steenoven stretched out his legs. His broad trunk seemed to struggle to stay put on the narrow chair seat. "Exciting—and disturbing. Scholars with their scientific instruments probing every corner of the universe—well, like you here, de Witt." With the stem of his long pipe, he pointed at the Master's brass instruments. "Astrolabes, telescopes. British clocks that tell perfect time. *Ach*, one wonders if we aren't trying to displace God as the center of the universe."

"They say we live in an age of reason," Adriaan mused, leaning in. "Damned if I know what that means. In Europe there's hardly a moment of peace before another war flares up. If our countrymen have to fight one more war, the economy will totally collapse." What a clever fellow, I thought.

"The other night in Stellenbosch," Mr. Steenoven said, "I met some fellows just arrived from Amsterdam. The winds of revolution are kicking up in Europe, they told us. Everywhere you turn, reformers and Abolitionists jumping out of the woodwork. At supper, the fellow next to me had planted in the West Indies—barely escaped with his life. Got caught in that slave uprising. You should have heard his stories—armies of blackies on the rampage, burning down whole sugarcane plantations, killing everyone, their masters and masters' families too. Unspeakable atrocities."

Master de Witt put down his glass, and sucked long on his pipe. Despite my misgivings about him, I had to admit he did cut a fine figure. I took my time filling a silver humidor while Titus stood poised next to the brandy.

"It wasn't just in the Indies, my dear fellow." The Master shifted uncomfortably, then looked his friend full in the face. "Don't you know there was an insurrection here in '12, and another in '38?"

"Heard about the first one because it involved that damned rascal priest Santrij. We threw him out of Java years ago, sent him here. Next I hear he's organized a slave revolt or something. True?"

Adriaan sipped his brandy slowly and leaned back in his chair. I stared at his fine cravat—*Mechelin* pillow lace? *Valenciennes*? "*Ja ja*, all true. Santrij masterminded the whole thing. Twenty-three slaves escaped from Groot Constantia estate. Isn't that right, Uncle? Scoundrels were caught, of course. Cut out Santrij's tongue. Broke him at the wheel. Most others were only flogged. But some had limbs cut off."

Mr. Steenoven's eyes widened. "My God." The men sat quietly. "So what happened in '38?"

"Started in Franschhoek." The Master tucked a thumb into his waistcoat pocket. "Beautiful valley southeast of here settled by French Huguenots. Slaveboy of some widow started the whole mess. He escaped with eleven other slaves owned by a fellow named Cruywagen. They ran east, vowing to kill any Europeans they met on the way. Probably trying to find those other runaways reportedly living in the mountains south of here."

Adriaan sniffed the air sharply. "They murdered Louis Swart and his wife, then some Huguenot. Before they could be captured, they had violated and killed the man's daughter." He stared with grave eyes into his brandy, swirling it in his hand absently. I was shocked.

"An abomination!" Master de Witt muttered, shaking his head.

The men sat in silence. Mr. Steenoven coughed, covered his mouth with an age-flecked hand. I slipped out of the room to prepare embers for their foot warmers. I'd never heard this story, and now I was sorry I had. When I returned, the men were still quietly puffing on their pipes, while Titus looked as if he were trying to compose himself. He must have been desperate to get away.

"Maybe the owners were asking for it." Mr. Steenoven raised a polite hand, refusing the foot warmer. "I heard the Huguenots don't value their slaves nearly as much as their grapepresses." When I offered the foot warmer to the Master, he shoved it aside. But Adriaan smiled and nodded for one, then grazed his cheek ever so slightly against my ear as I placed it under his feet. Did anyone see? Titus shifted from one foot to the other—such uncomfortable shoes.

The Master plunked his glass onto a spindly table and leaned almost rudely toward his guest. "By God, sir, those slaves were property! The masters paid good money for them. Shouldn't matter how they were treated. Besides, all those they murdered, the girl they raped, were not even their owners! It's an abomination, an absolute abomination."

Mr. Steenoven's chair creaked as he moved about uneasily. "My good man, don't you know that many planters in the West

Indies castrated and mutilated their slaves? If they thought them lazy, they'd cut their throats with machetes—without blinking an eye." I blanched, looking at Titus out of the corner of my eyes. His were shut tight. I thought I saw moisture gleam on his brow.

"That's what the estate manager told me, and he was there. Said many of those villains were Hollanders. Revolting, sir, but there you have it." There was an awkward pause. "De Witt, your Frenchmen here can't be as bad as you say. Remember, it was *their* Code Noir that—"

A terrible shouting rang from the other end of the house. The gentlemen rose and walked to the door, looking out with arched eyebrows. Titus and I dashed past them down the gallery. In the kitchen, Josiah knelt in front of two Indonesian puppeteers, who stood shouting and shaking him. When they saw us, they pulled apart, silent—but not before one swung back a fist and punched Josiah smack in the face.

Stern, puffed up, the gentlemen sauntered in, followed by the women. Mr. Steenoven shouted at his men in pidgin, demanding to know, it seemed, what the fracas was about. The Javanese stared at the floor, hands behind their backs, nut-brown faces sullen and dark. The Master scolded Josiah and pointed to the back door. I'd never seen the slave look so devastated. His shoulders slumped as he crept out into the night cupping a bloodied nose. The Mistress walked out after him onto the *stoep*, then, changing her mind, turned to rejoin her guests.

"Let's not let this spoil our evening, gents," Mr. Steenoven said. "Just some squabble among countrymen." Then, drinks still in hand, laughing, everyone walked back to their parties.

"What were you saying, Steenoven?" The Master leaned an elbow on the mantel, puffing out little clouds of smoke. "Before we were so rudely interrupted. Something about the Code Noir."

"Oh, yes." Mr. Steenoven creaked back in his chair, head

turned toward the kitchen—I had the feeling his mind was still on the scuffle. "My apologies, de Witt. As I was saying, that French law specifically forbade unbridled punishment of slaves. A law the planters totally ignored, which was sheer arrogance, if you ask me. Assumed the government would turn a blind eye. Same thing occurred in Asia. Well, officials *did* turn a blind eye, and look what happened—the revolts. I'm not saying for a second, mind you, that the atrocities those slaves committed were justified. But we have to face the fact that terrible things have been going on for years, long before any uprising." He paused, then spoke with more seriousness. "You know, it's the great conceit of bullies to claim *they* are the victims. With the Code Noir—"

"Blast it, sir! Bullies? Code Noir?" Color rose in the Master's face.

I curtsied and darted away with the extra foot warmer, but not before I glanced back at Titus. He stood by the brandy. He seemed to be practicing invisibility. I put the foot warmer on the hall floor and lingered just outside the threshold, dusting a great stinkwood cabinet that didn't need dusting. I could just see the Master push away from the fireplace, gesticulating madly with his pipe.

"Damn the Code Noir! Frenchies wrote that sixty-five years ago! Let them follow their own bloody decrees and leave the rest of us alone!" He took a deep breath and eased himself onto the edge of the desk. "I'm sorry, my dear fellow. I didn't mean to shout. I say, if you can't have control over your slaves, your own property, then what's the point?"

In the room, tension pushed at the walls like a silent, coiled spring. Another chair creaked. "For me, Steenoven, it's a moot argument," the Master said, softening his tone. "I treat my slaves richly. They eat well, they live in decent quarters, they don't work hard—in fact, some hardly work at all, but I still take care of them. They have nothing to complain about. No reason for any uprising here."

"My uncle's right, you know."

"Well, I've heard differently, de Witt." Mr. Steenoven spoke quietly. "I don't mean about you, but about the unrest here. There were grumblings at that dinner in Stellenbosch about an Abolitionist movement spreading its tentacles all over the Cape. Including clandestine meetings. With slaves."

My ears prickled, and hand stopped midair. Leaning dangerously far to my right, I could just see Titus through the doorway. He picked up the etched glass beaker—slow, careful movements—and, with a gloved hand, poured brandy into Mr. Steenoven's outstretched glass.

The room was silent but for the ringing of pipes on silver ashtrays.

"Stuff and nonsense!" the Master cried. "Rumors spread like house-a-fire at the Cape, my friend. I don't believe it for a second. Oh, there have been whispers. Some damn Abolitionists who call themselves philanthropists. Evil-minded agitators, that's what they are. Such meetings are totally forbidden. What did *you* hear, Steenoven?" A scarf of blue smoke wandered out the door.

"That there could be meetings in the mountains around here. Not just slaves, but White agitators too. Don't mean to alarm you, de Witt. Probably nothing to it. Nothing at all, I'm sure."

"Secret meetings? Not here, right, Adriaan? Where do they think they would run to, anyway? Blast it, we're surrounded by mountains, sea, and desert."

I could just see Titus step to the Master's side and pour him brandy too. Then back to the wall, as erect and silent as an iron candlestick.

"Slaves aren't fit for any other way of life. They'd starve if they escaped. Lions would eat them in a fortnight. I've heard about those runaways hiding in the mountains, but they won't last long—haven't a clue how to live off the land. Anyway, no Rustigvallei slaves would ever try to run off. They're too loyal, they love us too much. I'm like a father to them. I've given them everything."

Given them everything?

I headed off Anna as she minced down the gallery with a tray of fruit, cheese, and glazed dates. She bent into my ear, whispering, "That fight in the kitchen? Josiah were asking them men to dress him like one a them and sneak him off the estate when the Steenovens leave tonight. Actually thought he could get to the Netherlands! Ye know—freedom."

For a second I just stared at her. "The fool!" I snatched the tray from her hands and started for the room, leaving her standing there with her mouth open.

I proffered the array of desserts to the gentlemen. Mr. Steenoven took a few grapes, gazing intently at the Master and tilting his head toward Titus, as if asking if it were all right for his slaveman to hear this.

"Oh, my boy here is all right. He's Cape born, a Christian, you know—a tamed *kaffir*." I stiffened. My eyes darted toward Titus. For the smallest second he seemed to bristle.

"We understand each other, don't we, Titus? He knows the way things fall." The Master slipped a box from his pocket and offered his guests snuff. They each took a pinch, inhaling sharply. "This boy of mine and I have an arrangement. He's paying me for his freedom through work, a contract I made with his last owner. Not much more time to go now, isn't that so, Titus?" Eyes ahead, Titus made a small nod. "I shall sorely miss him. Maybe he'll stay on as a servant. I hope he will." He gave Titus a wan smile. "Damned good man, especially with the Arabians."

The bang of a gong. A Javanese stepped into the gallery, announcing that a most wondrous performance was about to begin. The gentlemen rose and refilled their pipes. As they quit the room, brandywine in hand, Adriaan winked at me. Yes, I'm sure he did. I made my way toward the kitchen hall while guests gathered and chattered excitedly in the back foyer.

Titus opened the shuttered double doors halfway down the gallery to make one very long room, which now, in the dark of evening, shone with the soft light of a hundred candles. Slavemen assembled chairs again. I saw Pier brandishing his sword in the front hall. I dashed over and yanked it from his hand. When all were seated, a native clanged the gong again. A small group of men emerged from a side room.

The performers were decked out in yellow silk turbans and sarongs as fanciful as the tablecloth. Marigolds adorned their heads and wrists. The musical instruments sat low on our Persian carpet, pieces of a strange kind of harpsichord with short legs, keys of wood and brass. Titus and I stole places in the kitchen hallway, and the Javanese began—a frenzied banging upon brass tongues with hammers. It jarred my ears, a chaotic, fractious noise. But gradually the music settled inside me. I was whisked away to a lush rainforest where red-blue birds flitted from branch to branch, while green tree frogs opened their eyes each time a ping of golden rain hit their foreheads.

Little Digger and Kupido, barefoot and dressed in livery, stood by the women and fanned them with bouquets of pink flamingo feathers. Their eyes, ears, and mouths were so wide with awe for the musicians that I hoped they could later fit them back into their proper positions. The Mistress sat not far from us, wearing a sacque-back gown and a pained expression.

"What a dreadful noise!" she complained to Mistress

Cingria. “They call that music? The banging of devils! Gives me a headache. Why don’t they just go back to Java?”

Mistress Cingria turned back to the performers, lifting a tight chin and looking uncomfortable. Her hand moved to that chatelaine of keys, which she flung into her lap almost musically. The tension between these two, the thinly veiled antagonism—why couldn’t they put it away for one evening? I was so irritated with my mistress. I thought she was a woman of culture. This performance was grand!

Cook leaned across the others to hand Titus and me cups of strong wine, a special treat for having served tonight. Soon I felt soft and giddy. But the gentlemen’s conversation was eating at me. Adriaan sat at the front of the party, laughing and flirting, to my chagrin, with the Steenoven girl. Titus stood to my side as we took peeks through the doorway, watching and listening to this wild and treacherous performance, while Manassa and Lucy pressed on us from behind.

“So, Titus,” I teased, turning to him slightly, “I guess you know the way things fall. Seeing as you’re a ‘tamed *kaffir*.’ ”

I swear I could feel the heat rise from his pump-shoed toes all the way to his head. “The more he try to tame me, the more I rebel,” he whispered.

This was the Titus few knew. I felt flushed myself from his warm body so close to mine. His solidness, his certainty of who he was, which he seemed to hold inside like a sacrament. His presence comforted me, made me feel safe. His breath smelled like burnt sugar—sweet and hot upon my neck. Safe, yet not so safe.

The mad music raged on, banging our senses into submission. *Bam! Bam!* I felt rapturous, dizzy. In all propriety, perhaps Titus should not have been standing so near. Perhaps we should not have drunk so much. Yet I did not move. *Ching! Ching!* The music shattered me. His breath so warm and close gave me a trembly, excited feeling.

I was frightened by these new sensations and a little angry with Titus for arousing them. But wasn't I to blame too, for perhaps I let myself lean just a little too close, and in sight of the others. Did I have a reckless side that enjoyed seeing what I could get away with?

I felt weak. My knees were wilting. I gripped the doorjamb. I should not have drawn so close to him like this. What made him think he could draw so close to me?

I could not breathe.

Chapter 17

AUGUST 1749 (WINTER/SPRING)

On our fourth trip to Effie's, after picking me up from my lesson, Titus told me I needed to go with Samuel and him to the saddler's. No, I replied, I needed to get to the open-air stalls by Greenmarket.

"Miss Saskia," he said, an edge to his voice, "this town is this day full of the soldiers from England. It is not safe. Come with us to buy the harness. Then we go with you."

"Titus, it's nearly two o'clock half, and the market closes at three. If I can sell my lace, I'll be able to buy a new sunbonnet. If I don't get there today, the hat could be gone. I'll meet you in front of the Groot Kerk, by the Compagnie Gardens. As the bells chime three."

Titus raised a hand in protest. "Miss Saskia, no!"

I gripped my lace basket, picked up my skirts, and sprinted off. When I looked back, his fists were shoved into his hips and his face twisted in annoyance. "I can take care of myself," I shouted over my shoulder. "The Gardens. At three!"

In my basket were two sleeve ruffles, elegant and very fine, which I'd all but completed in Delft. But because I'd finished them at the estate, I told Effie, the Mistress was sure to claim them as her own.

"Nay! You completed these on your own time with your own thread," Effie said. "The ruffles are yours." She wagged a gnarled finger. "Don't let your employers take advantage."

Yes, I decided, in fairness this lace belonged to me. If I could sell it at a fair price, I'd save the money for my future. After one small purchase, that is.

Last time I visited the market, a beautiful straw bonnet literally flew from its perch and landed in front of me on a pile of tablecloths—a *grote halfronde zonnehoed* with yellow and blue ribbons streaming down the sides. I'd gasped—how like the summer bonnets I'd seen in the Mistress's fashion etchings. The ones by her bed that Johanna and I had recently stumbled upon. I found myself weaving dreams around that hat, imagining how elegant I would look in it. I could wear it to church on Sundays and on festival days. Now, if I could only sell these lace *engageantes*. . . I prayed the hat would still be at the stall.

It was a short walk to the open-air market. Titus was right about soldiers—they were everywhere. Some tagged after me, trying to pick me up. I had to keep yelling "Go away!" before they turned back, embarrassed.

I passed canopied stalls draped in Indian textiles glittering with metallic mirrors, bright pink and fuschia, cloth no sane Hollander would dream of wearing—except maybe me. I trotted past brilliantly colored *tika* powders—sacks of red, blue, and purple from Bengal. Further down, I breathed in sharp, musky aromas—cloves, burned sandalwood, cinnamon, *kardemom*.

I stopped to watch a marvelous performance by a troupe of men in turbans and robes. They held owls and falcons, then shot them over the heads of the crowd, thrillingly close. Further on, rough *chinees* agents bartered among mounds of elephant tusks, and others vied for boldly printed African cloth. There were stalls of handmade paper from Japan, and dyes of indigo and cochineal from as far away as the Americas. In open doors of teashops, men squatted on flowered cushions, sipping tobacco from water pipes while boys fanned them with banana leaves, vibrantly green.

Then I spied it: a vendor of European textiles. A British officer, high-ranking it seemed from his red coat laden with honors, stooped to gaze at the trays of lace.

I looked their inventory over carefully but wasn't that impressed. It was the older vendor with whom I wanted to negotiate, apparently a Malay, but he was busy with the officer. I caught the attention of another, his son, perhaps. He wore a long white tunic, and his skin was the color of hulled almonds, and teeth stained red. He was pacing back and forth along rows of textiles, hands behind his back, watching me carefully.

"I would like to sell these, please." I opened my lace basket, slipped on gloves, and drew my *engageantes* from their tissue.

The young man whisked out a tray of black velvet. He stared at my work through a lens, nearly rubbing an oily nose against my precious weaves. "How you get these?"

"I made them! That's how I got them."

His eyes narrowed into slits. He took the tray and studied the ruffles once more. Did he think I'd stolen them? With a *hhhrumphhing* noise he plunked the tray down, as if the goods were worthless. The officer turned to watch. He was dignity personified—a general, I'd wager.

"Here." I opened my basket wide, showing him my small bolster with unfinished lace attached.

"All right. Maybe you made them." He scribbled a number on a scrap of paper and tossed it on the tray in front of me.

I arched my spine. "That's your offer? What a joke!" I knew

how valuable fine lace was. Why, many a person has paid off debts with their best lace. "These ruffles are far superior to anything I see here," I said, looking over his goods. "Such prices!"

He scowled. "We have to add the commission, don't ye know? My offer is good. We vedy vedy busy. You take, you leave." He turned, walking to the back of the booth to greet a Malay woman who'd just arrived. She wore a silk sari shot with gold, and her brown fingers flashed with gems.

That's when the officer stepped quietly to my side. "Good day, my dear young lady." He tipped his wide cocked hat. "Pardon my rudeness, but I couldn't help overhearing. May I take a look?"

Yes, his accent was definitely British, and his manners well bred. He removed a glove and reached for the tray with freshly manicured fingers.

"Perfect for a gentlewoman's sleeves, sir," I said. "*Point de France*. A very difficult pattern, and quite the rage in Europe."

He held the tiers of *engageantes* to the light, placed them carefully against the velvet again, and adjusted his spectacles. His eyes pressed close, no doubt checking for knots or stains. But he would find none. I suddenly realized how much of me was in this lace.

"Italian Renaissance angels, sir. Women love angels. They bring happiness. And grace."

Licking *kerrie* sauce from their fingers, the vendors looked at each other, annoyed.

The officer sniffed. "This lace has a smell to it." I must have looked alarmed. "Acrid, but also sweet. Fruity."

"Oh—I work on a wine estate, sir. Sometimes I weave the lace in the cellar so it will stay supple. The slaves sing as they stir the vats of grapes, and I like to weave the bobbins to their rhythms. The smell will disappear in time."

"Which wine estate?"

"Rustigvallei, sir."

"Rustigvallei? A grand old estate. I know your grapes well." My fingers thrummed against my leg. Did he know the Master? Would he tell him his maid was selling lace? "In fact, we're taking barrels of portwine made from your grapes back to Europe with us. A strange coincidence! Where did you learn to make such lace, young lady, if I may ask?"

"In Delft, sir, the Netherlands. My mother and some lay Sisters taught me."

He sniffed it once more. "Wonderful fragrance. Woven to the rhythm of native music, eh? A charming story." He pulled back his coat sleeve and draped a ruffle over his wrist, imagining the effect on a gown. "Silk?"

"*Chinees* silk, sir. At least three months' work in each tier."

Yes, almost a year's work, every cross of the bobbin marking some journey of my mind: a dream, a fear, a spike of joy. I waited. Finally he said he'd been looking for a special pair of *engageantes* for his wife and that these were more beautiful than anything he'd seen. He pulled out a leather pocketbook, then paused. My heart was in my throat when he plucked up the small piece of paper with the Malay's offer on it. He fished into the jaws of his pocketbook—and dropped several silver coins onto my palm. I was stunned by the sum. So much more than the vendor had offered. Mistaking my silence, he reached into his purse and added yet another. The coins glinted in the sunlight.

"More than enough, sir."

"Well it's a bargain for me—and cuts out these middlemen, what? They'd only turn around and sell it for quadruple the price they offered you." He threw the vendors a sideways glance. They glowered back. "Your work is extraordinary. Well done, young lady, well done."

Well done, indeed! I curtsied, slipped the coins into my needlecase, buttoned it tight, and buried it deep inside my lace basket. No pickpocket could grab it there. I was *so* happy.

"Here, sir." I placed the ruffles in fine linen I'd trimmed with lace, then wrapped them in tissue. "The handkerchief is a gift." He gave me an elegant bow. I watched him walk away, suddenly realizing he would have to smuggle the sleeves in, as foreign lace could not be imported to England. From the back of the stall, the vendors were cursing me with their eyes while my own eyes fluttered with guilt. Well, I *had* cheated them out of a sale.

So—now I was a tradeswoman. Regardless of what people said, I felt no shame in selling what I'd made. For a minute, I almost missed those ruffles. The lay Sisters and I had struggled with the pattern's intricacies, but when I mastered it, they were irked. "It will take you months and months to finish both sleeves, Saskia," they scolded, "and you'll soon give up. God frowns on such ambition, girl."

How I'd smarted from their words! Yes, working two tiers of sleeves in *Point de France* had been ambitious. But I'd done it. What if no one ever challenged themselves? We would be back in the Dark Ages, still paying Rome for indulgences.

I hurried to the stall several rows away. MISTRESS A. GROOTVELD, MILLINER, the sign read. Small and round as a fluffed up robin, she greeted me warmly, for I'd bought many a length of ribbon here. And there it was, the *halfronde zonnehoed*, still perched atop a ceramic head.

"That one be right lovely, don't it, dearie? Like to try it on?" she chirped. I tugged the hat over my cap and turned before the mirror. What a gorgeous wide brim—and that jaunty cutaway in back!

"Finely woven straw. And them ribbons bring out the blue of yer eyes. Very lovely indeed, Miss. You look every inch the lady out fer a day in town, don't ye now."

I told her how I'd sold my lace to a British officer after the vendors had offered almost nothing for it. "Good Lord. Don't deal with those swindlers. Other Malays, yes, but not them. They've more gold than Croesus—and got it real suspicious-like. You sell your lace through me, dearie. I'll see ye gets a fair price."

I pressed a coin into her hand. "I'll wear it. Thanks."

Clever her and clever me! I had a beautiful new bonnet, and sterling too. I rolled up my old hat and stuffed it into my lace basket. From the high street I looked out across the ocean. It curved around the beach like a slice of blue fruit. So much money! Why, I could buy passage back to the Netherlands if I wanted. My spirit swelled with confidence. Or I could lease a shop in town, making lace in the back while I sold textiles, including Effie's lace, up front.

When a breeze kicked up, I tied my hat firmly in the back, pausing to admire myself in a store window. I froze. Who is that? A boy in white was staring at me from a street corner. Wasn't he one of the vendors? I spun around. No, it must have only been that Mussulman selling grilled kabobs to soldiers. Oh, how they loved our antelope!

I ambled down narrow streets, veering toward the water, fascinated by shops I'd never seen. I pawed through outdoor displays of combs and shawls, and fended off vendors who shoved trays of cheap jewelry under my nose. Why, for once in my life I could buy most anything!

Again, the wind played games, nagging at women's skirts and petticoats, trying to steal bonnets and hats. Not this hat. Not today. I wandered aimlessly, peering into *koffie* houses and bakeries, stepping across the street when British soldiers headed my way. Lord, the town swarmed with them! From a street vendor I paused to buy sugared anise seeds and a pungent gingery thing that clung to my teeth. When I came upon a beggar, I pressed a coin into her hand, loving her gasp of astonishment, her prayer for my well-being. What power there is in wealth!

At a small park I stopped to watch Punch and Judy performed on a makeshift stage, happy to think of some people at the estate I'd like to smack. Again, Redcoats everywhere. Two converged and jostled me, chuckling to one another.

I broke off down the street. Cobblestones caught at my wooden clogs, and I stumbled. It was getting late. I had to get to the Gardens. Which direction? Oh, Lord! It *was* that boy vendor, standing in the shade, his eyes climbing all over me. A shiver shot up my spine. Had he been following me all along? I clutched the basket to my chest and broke into a trot.

The afternoon sun was arcing low. Surely it was close to three bells. Or had they already rung? How long would it take to the Gardens? I glanced back. Now the boy was jogging toward me. I picked up my skirts and ran. What did he want? Was this another Claus, or . . . Oh, the money! He'd seen the officer give me those coins. Oh, where were the Redcoats now?

I hurried down the road, but it narrowed into an alleyway. Dark and deserted! I hugged my basket for dear life, my heart in my throat. I looked back, was blinded by the sun's hard glare. Jesus Savior, he was gaining. Guards! Where were the guards? Soldiers? Anyone!

I dashed into a tunnel under a bridge. Suddenly a brick wall rose up out of nowhere, and *bam!* I smashed into it. I wanted to faint, to shout, but the words froze in my throat. I turned. He was so close I could see that unholy look in his eyes. Then, the slamming. My shoulder, my head, rammed against the stone girders of the bridge.

I slumped to the ground, the wind smashed out of me. A foot crashed into my hip. Oh! He wrenched the lace basket from my hands. For a minute I lay there, helpless as a cabbage leaf.

As he ran off, a faint odor of curry and sweat lingered in the air.

~

I lay on the dusty cobbles, breathless. Two slavewomen bearing piles of laundry saw me and scuttled past. I ached all over, ears buzzing at warning pitch. My money! The largest amount I'd ever held—all gone. With all my lace things. I staggered to my feet, head splintering like crystal candy. I dusted myself off. My new sunbonnet lay on the cobbles, squashed. I wanted to cry.

Down the block, raucous sounds of hurdy-gurdies, fiddles, and laughter boiled out of open doors. God in Heaven, what part of town was this? I peeked through a window. By the glow of flickering red lanterns, a woman dressed in a profusion of ostrich feathers pranced before men, her sheer petticoats hiked high. A *bordeel!* So many rough, prematurely aged faces, like those who'd drunk away a lifetime—what my cousin used to call "tore back." The women spotted my nose pressed to the glass, cast hateful looks, and spat.

Further up I collapsed onto a bench that stank of ale and greasy fish. All that money, gone. No more little shop. No financial freedom. Tears threatened to fall. If I'd only gone straight to the Gardens. . . The Master's lace cravat was in the basket too. Oh, what would the de Witts do to me?

I sat in shock. My new hat, its chic brim was now one great crease. I knocked it against the bench. Dust billowed up in little clouds. At least now I wouldn't have to explain how I could afford a new bonnet. It was ready for the bin. I placed it on my head anyway.

The chime of church bells swelled the afternoon air, and the sun was failing. I jumped to my feet. Titus! What hour was it? I had to ask my way. A large sign swung eerily in the breeze: HOUSE OF MIRACLES. Just then the doors flew open, and soldiers spilled out onto the street, laughing. One clearly Dutch, reeling with drink, planted himself in front of me. "Well, looky what we have here." He reached out, and touched my cheek.

A great sob tore up from out of my throat. Fists clenched in pent-up grief, I set on him, beating his chest fiercely, beating with as much might as if he had attacked me.

A woman in a boldly striped dress turned on him. "What you done to this here maid, Geert, you sot?"

"I ain't done *nothin*." He regarded me with unfocused eyes and stepped back. "Meant ye no harm, Creampuff."

"Say, you ain't one of my girls." The woman peered into my face. "Saskia?"

Did I know her? Through the scrim of powder and mascara, familiar features. Why, the girl who had enlightened me about men! "Cornelia?" We grasped each other's hands.

"Come on in, girl. My sweetheart and me owns this here establishment. I'll treat ye to a beer and we can catch up." She scanned my dusty skirt and crushed bonnet. "Something happen to ye?"

The story flew out of my mouth in one torrent. Cornelia's mouth grew hard. "That bastard!" she muttered, almost to herself. "I know who those bloody vendors are, an just what they're capable of. Hey, Kauri!" A towering hulk with hooded eyes, bald head and face covered in tattoos, took up the doorway. I couldn't help but stare. "Can you take over? I'm goin to Greenmarket to help my friend. Come on, Saskia. Let's see what we can get back."

I was wishing she'd brought the hulk with us, but then remembered: this girl had never taken rot from anybody on board the *Windroos*, not the officers, not even the roughest sailors.

Once, I'd happened upon her in the hold. She was pressing a dagger to the throat of a sailor who seemed to be assaulting the cabinboy. "Let that child go, you shit-eating worm," she'd said with stoney authority. "If I ever hears a you touchin a child again, any child, I'll cut you into bite-sized bits and feed ye to the sharks."

~

At Greenmarket, merchants were dismantling their stalls, loading goods onto handcarts and drays. "Is that man your sweetheart?"

"Kauri? He's my insurance policy." Cornelia grabbed a bamboo stake from a pile—one with a sharp point—and marched down the aisle boldly. I only now noticed her blue-striped stockings, the flounces on her tawdry gown.

"Miss Saskia!" A Black man leaped across the water furrow toward me. "Where have you been? The longest time we wait for you!"

"Titus! Thank God! Come! We're going to brazen out some thieving Malays, blackguards who stole my money."

By the time we got to the stall, Cornelia stood berating the vendors, jousting the stake in their direction. She jerked a thumb in my direction. "It were *this* maid one a ye assaulted. If you don't cough up the basket fast—with all the money in it—I'll call the guards to haul you away in irons."

Brava, Cornelia! But what guards would listen to her, a lady of the night? Or, for that matter, a maid?

The elder Malay sniffed. "You talk crazy. I know nothing." With hasty motions he pitched tray upon tray of lace into a cart.

"Liar!" I shouted.

The Malay flashed his eyes at me in warning, but I saw the hesitation. He was complicit.

Titus stiffened, then walked over and spoke to the man in a *taal* unfamiliar to me, first in persuasive tones, then, when the man would not look up, in a tone more insistent. The booth canvas lifted, and the boy who had attacked me stepped into the stall. He took one look at me and started.

"That's him!" I shouted. "*He* stole my basket."

He took off at a run, and Titus sprang after him. Cornelia gave out a loud whistle. Halfway down the street, Titus grabbed the boy's tunic and wrenched him to the ground. I ran to where they lay tussling on the dusty cobbles, punching, choking. I started to panic—it's against the law for a slave to fight, especially to fight a freeman. And we had witnesses.

The boy jumped to his feet, reached into an ankle sheath, and whipped out a knife, its blade flashing in the sun. He swiped at Titus, who jumped. Swiped again. Then all at once there stood the hulk, Kauri. He grabbed the boy's arms and pulled them behind his back. Cornelia whistled again, so sharply, I swear, they must have heard it back at the manor. Titus grabbed the knife and moved in a circle, threatening other men as they closed around us. I grabbed the stave and punched the air with it toward the men. At last someone rang a loud bell.

"Thievin cowards!" Cornelia cast her eyes up and down the street. She whistled again. I held the stave to the boy's throat.

"Where the blazes are those bloody guards!" Cornelia cried, and whistled again.

Two militia, rifles gripped, accompanied by their convict *caffers*, marched around the corner of the square. Cornelia called them toward us.

The Malays shot down the narrow alleys of the Bo-Kaap. Kauri too. Perhaps he'd had dealings with the guards before. Strangely, the boy didn't run but stepped close to me. I felt hairs on the back of my neck stand on end. "Check the Castle guard's office tomorrow for your goddamned basket."

The guards were drawing close now. Titus grabbed the boy's wrist, but he wrung loose and dashed down the alley.

"Run then, you coward," Cornelia shouted. "If I ever set eyes on you again, I'll have your balls for pom-poms."

I shivered like a newborn colt. Titus sucked in a breath, then pressed a handkerchief to his bleeding collarbone. I untied my scarf and started dabbing the bruise on his cheek, but he pushed me away.

Cornelia told the guards—one of whom she seemed to know quite well—how the boy had mugged me, then attacked a defenseless slave, a story close enough to the truth. The guard with a beefy face questioned me. I told him that only a little money was in the basket. If the de Witts ever heard how much I'd lost, they'd question where it came from. If, by some miracle, the money were ever recovered, they'd claim it for themselves. Either way, they'd throttle me. What a mess.

Titus paced up and down nervously. The guard was still writing his report when Titus, one hand clasped to his collarbone, approached. "We must leave now, Miss Saskia." The guard looked him up and down with suspicion. "It is the law, *mynheer*, that I be home before nightfall and we have yet the hours to travel."

The guard frowned and snapped his report book shut.

I wandered over to Cornelia and put a hand on her arm. "Thank you, my brave friend. I'll come see you at your *musicos*. We'll catch up."

She looked away, brushing imaginary dust from her bodice. "No, sweetie. Ye shouldn't be seen with the likes of me."

"I don't care, Cornelia."

"If you don't now, ye will. God be with you. Go well." And she took off down the street.

"Be good now," I shouted after her.

"Good? *Good?*" She flashed me a grin over her shoulder. "Highly overrated, if you asks me."

Titus and I jogged north. I prayed Samuel would be safe at the Gardens and hadn't taken us for dead. The twilight stillness was broken by rowdy music from the drinking houses that drifted across the lanes, fading in and out, following us as we climbed up and down streets. We could just see the gray stone ramparts of the Castle when the enormity of the day overtook me. I trembled, sucked air in deeply. A fierce expression burned in Titus's eyes.

"You're shaking too," I said. "Are you angry?"

"Yes, I be angry. And frightened half to death!" He let out a strange hoot. "Those men, they could have pressed me into breakfast sausage!" Their breath, he said, smelled not only of liquor, but of *dagga*—hashish, maybe mixed with opium and arsenic. "Makes them nasty crazy. They smoke this stuff and think themselves the lion killers."

I laughed. "Titus, you were very brave."

"Brave? I was not so brave. Humiliated. Two young women and the Goliath, they have to save me. That garrison of guards—have you and your lady friend thought to join up?"

I giggled, but it came out funny. Then, from out of nowhere, out of some deep place in my chest, a sob sputtered. "God, I was scared. Men with knives, all liquored up. And that boy . . ." A boy who could have done all manner of things. I thought of Claus, but didn't mention him. No one had to know about Claus.

Suddenly Titus spun around. "Samuel and I, we wait for you at the Gardens for the longest time! You know we must return to the manor before nightfall. We fear something terrible happen to you."

"Something terrible *did* happen to me!" I told him the whole story, a sob curling up once more from deep inside. I turned and started beating Titus on the chest, beating with fists clenched into cannonballs, beating, beating.

He grabbed me by the wrists. "Whoa! What are you doing?" I looked at him in horror. Just what I'd done to the soldier. It hadn't been his fault either.

"I'm sorry, Titus," I stuttered. "So much money. Gone. Enough to buy out my contract—and passage back to Amsterdam too."

"I am sorry you lose this money." He paused. "I did not know you want the passage to your country."

"I'm not sure what I want. But money buys you choices, doesn't it?"

We plodded up the street, drained, a chill breeze whipping at our clothing. "This wind, it be like the drifter who goes off but he return. One day I make friends with this wind."

When we reached a better neighborhood on Strand Street, I felt safer. But people threw us rude stares. Titus stepped dutifully behind.

At Groot Kerk, by the Gardens, Samuel was sitting on the curb chewing his clay pipe. When he saw us, tattered and bruised, he stood up, eyes large and fearful, but asked no questions. On the ride home we related the afternoon's events. He looked from Titus to me, his near toothless mouth ajar. How I loved his kind old face.

Once beyond Table Mountain, I moved up front to sit with Titus. I thought of Cornelia and silently blessed her. So . . . Owner of a *bordeel*. What a fighter! And a tattooed mate. Sundown would find us in another hour or so, and we would have to travel the last miles by lantern and moonlight.

Surely Mistress Cingria would scold us for our bedraggled state. Surely some kind of punishment awaited us for being late, but I didn't care. I would tell everyone how courageous Titus had been, how he had wrestled down the boy who stole my basket—the basket with the Master's lace cravat inside. I hoped I'd save him from a flogging.

All the way home I watched the bright moon smile its crooked smile down upon us, until I lapsed into sleep, falling heavily, unawares, against Titus's warm shoulder.

Chapter 18

AUGUST 1749 (WINTER/SPRING)

When we arrived home that night, tattered and wounded, word got to the Master. He demanded Titus and I appear at his study at once, though the hour was late. I was mostly just shaken, but Titus was truly a sorry sight, his collarbone cut and bloodied, his left eye turning blue and, by now, swollen shut. The Master listened silently to our story, growing more and more furious—but not with us, thank the Lord. I think if my humiliating assault were all that had happened, he could have cared less. But his prize slave, one of his most valued properties, had been neatly chewed up—and he himself robbed of a lace cravat by, as he put it, "some sniveling darkie from the Bo-Kaap."

The following morning Mr. Pesser, the Overseer, rode a horse into Cape Town. Soon the whole estate knew of our adventures—all except the part where I sold my lace and had that small fortune stolen, a secret Titus and Samuel swore to keep.

Word got around that Mr. Pesser had met with Cornelia at the House of Miracles, and she'd corroborated our story. She guided him to the Malay vendors and then he took up the matter with officials at the Castle. True to his word, the boy had dumped my basket at the Castle gates before fleeing. The militia took several of the vendors in for questioning while Mr. Pesser rode back, the basket strapped to his saddle.

The moment he placed the basket in my hands, I flung open the double lid. Thank the Lord—there sat the Master's lace cravat safely on the pillow. Only a few pins anchoring it had fallen out, and some bobbins had unspooled. No great damage. I rifled underneath, feeling for the silver coins I'd buttoned into my needlecase. But there was no needlecase. Not a crooked stuiver anywhere in the basket. I stared into Mr. Pesser's face, but his even and placid expression told me he knew of no money. Of course the vendors had taken it.

~

A few days later the Master's nephew rode from Cape Town to spend a few days at the manor. I was down in the cellar putting to rights the lace cravat when Adriaan snuck up from behind and clapped both hands over my eyes. "Caught you!" he shouted. I must have jumped six inches off the ground. Several bobbins unraveled and clattered to the flagged floor. I grinned, flustered.

Adriaan drew up a stool. He'd heard of my misadventure and wanted to know if I was all right. He ran a sympathetic finger over my bruised brow, which made me tingle all over, then studied the lace I was weaving, complimenting my skill. He talked about his important legal work with the Compagnie, telling me he would use his influence to find the thief and bring him to justice. Somehow he managed to mention his finesse at fencing and prowess in riding and hunting as well. Yes, so he bragged. I was glad to know more about him. And just hoped he hadn't noticed my fingers shake as they rewound the bobbins.

I know a girl is supposed to show indifference, but I couldn't help laughing with him. Adriaan left me confused and flattered. I was not used to the attentions of a fine young gentleman, and he nearly an aristocrat. If his uncle knew, he'd turn apoplectic. Adriaan also sought me out in the yard the next day to talk, and came up to the *kinder*room the night before he left to say goodbye. Thinking of him as sweetly as I did helped me forget all the money I'd lost. Could this be the start of something serious?

~

Early one morning, when spring suddenly exploded, greening the countryside, the Housekeeper told me I was to go on a special errand, one that left me a little nervous. The de Witts had been invited by their neighbor, Madame Remy, to send over someone to select a few volumes for Pier and Catryn's reading pleasure. Madame was a French widow who kept a private library solely for lending books to children. Because Mistress Cingria did not wish to go, the task now fell on me. "But have your wits about you," the Housekeeper warned. For the widow was, well, Roman Catholic.

Mistress Cingria pointed out a farm several miles from us, on the other side of the river. We could see the house from the back of ours: a small stone manor on a hill in a lovely copse of trees. Between our estate and hers, wide meadows with colorful wildflowers spread out like *kilim* carpets.

The Housekeeper sent me off with a note of thanks, a stoneware of wine, and basket of smoked guinea hens. She instructed me to choose only the classics or books on etiquette, geography, and natural history and to return promptly.

What a charming idea! Books especially for young minds that could be borrowed as long as they were returned in reasonable time. Books were scarce in these parts and I was aching to read something myself. The Master had a small library but he would never loan books to servants. I knew, because once I asked. “Impudent girl!” he'd shouted. “If you have time for idle reading, you have time for more work!” I wondered if Madame Remy might exact some payment. Would she force me to kneel before idols and confess my sins? Never!

The day was crisp and beautiful, the sky clear indigo as I set out. I thanked the heavens for the short respite. A chance to be alone and in nature was rare and precious, I thought, closing the iron gate. I followed one of the plantation roads through the fields. Neat rows of vines marched up and down the hills, their green leaves fluttering like banners in the wind.

I passed a field where some forty slaves labored. I waved. Those who dared gave me only a slight nod, for the Foreman Anthonij needed little excuse to ply his cowhide straps. Many slaves were unknown to me, hired from other estates just for this year's planting. They were tilling the red soil to make slots for the saplings and digging furrows for irrigation. The ripened grapes would be harvested in fall, as late in the season as possible for sweetness, then pressed into a dark ruby liquid and stored in barrels underground to mellow.

I thought of the hundreds of barrels now resting in our cellars. Thousands of hours of labor spent making our master richer with every harvest while we, paid the smallest wages imaginable, struggled to buy even a linsey-woolsey garment. And slaves paid nothing at all.

I marched on, the sun making its slow sweep through a fevered sky. The still air teemed with insects. I winced seeing slaves labor without hats. To earn one you had to be, by the Foreman's standards, fluent in Dutch. Mothers stopped in their work to wrench the slings from round their backs and suckle their babes. Sweat poured from their brows and settled in the wrinkles of their dusty faces. The slaves plunged their spades into the hard earth, singing, but a heavy cloud, like condensed desperation, hung over them. Tonight they would stumble home from the fields, bodies bent, one shoulder higher than the other from swinging their spades in one stance day in and day out.

Whenever I felt sorry for myself, I'd think of them and know my life was privileged while theirs were cramped and mean. They took Anthonij's lashings while I sat in comfort at a window weaving lace. Oh, the cost in labor for one small glass of wine! The thought wrapped me up like hog meat in a blanket of depression. If only there were something I could do for our slaves, something to ease their lives a little.

How often the Master would say in a stentorian voice, "There is much dignity and honor to working the fields, maintaining the farm, and cleaning the manor." To which Johanna had once muttered, "If it's honor and dignity he want, the privies could use a good scrubbin."

The Bible says that the meek shall inherit the earth. If that were true, then surely the people before me must inherit the soil they labored upon, this earth under their feet. Surely they were entitled to a corner of their own Africa. That time would come, yes, I felt it in my bones—but not soon. Not soon enough.

I thought of Titus. He was not like other slaves. He'd made much of his life. Perhaps I would pass him on the road today. I was beginning to carry him in my thoughts, as I carried Adriaan, but differently, like a touchstone in my pocket. A comfort for hard days.

As I walked, I watched and listened for wild animals. Samuel had told me workers were frightened of wild beasts and paid a native sorceress, a *sangoma*, to keep them at bay. "Even that tough Portuguese Overseer, he put some money in that pot for that *conjur* woman, isn't it?"

Josiah had carved me a pair of wooden clogs, perfect for cutting across these muddy fields. Only now did I realize they were too large, for my feet were slipping around inside them. In my vanity I had chosen to wear fine white stockings instead of the thick linen ones with long toes that would have filled the extra space. And now, a mile into my journey, my feet felt raw. Too late to go back.

Impulsively, I peeled off the stockings and walked barefoot on the grass alongside the road. How lovely it was to get away from the manor, how lovely to feel the tall weeds tickle my calves. When I heard the jangle of a donkey cart, I quickly stepped into my clogs—oh, no time for the stockings! A wagon of farm workers closed in. I bent my knees and walked low, my skirt covering naked ankles. They looked at me curiously, but I just gave them a little wave. So what if they thought me short and hunched. At least I was friendly.

About a mile from my destination, the air turned cool and dark clouds gathered. A breeze kicked up, and along the road sycamore and protea leaves twirled in the wind. The sky cracked open with a thunderous boom, and as I dashed through Madame Remy's orchards, a torrent of rain poured down. I took the last yards in leaps and bounds, the hard clogs tearing at my toes.

Her house was all gates and gardens. Which door to use? I ran around to the back, the service door, for I was but a maid. The air was thickly fragrant with lemon blossoms and white roses. A maid—so French—with a long face, green eyes close together, and an upturned nose let me into the kitchen. I placed the wine and guinea hens on the table, and she sat me on a bench by the hearthfire. How stylish she was in her blue-and-white-striped skirt and white apron that covered her chest. When she wasn't looking I pulled on my stockings.

The kitchen was small but tasteful—copper tabletops,

bronze-colored tiles, a beautifully carved bread cage on the wall, baroque trim around the hearth. I felt out of place, like some drowned cat. Just another back country Dutch maid, the girl must have thought. A very large Black woman with a flowered headwrap entered, carrying a slab of marble with a giant fish on it. We nodded to one another. Even she looked stylish.

"*Sil vous plait, mademoiselle*," the White maid said. She crouched at my feet, taking a towel to my muddy clogs. "*Merci beaucoup*" was all I could manage, then took the cloth from her to do it myself. When I'd dried out, she took me to the library, kindled the logs, and motioned me to sit on an ottoman before the fire. As I waited for the widow, I remembered Mistress Cingria's cautions: "She's a Papist, you know, as thick a Roman as ever there were, with devilish statuary. Don't let her speak of her religion and you should be safe." Cingria. A Spanish name. The Spanish, once our conquerors. Shouldn't she be Roman herself?

I looked around—how warm and inviting this room was! Books and bouquets of sweet lilies and roses crowded the tables. One wall was painted peach, the others were exposed stone, with wood bookcases. I sat before the fire watching flames warm everything in a soft glow. Through high leaded panes I watched the rain batter pears and peonies. Firelight fell on a carved gilt frame holding a great mirror. "Mirrors are instruments of vanity!" the Master often protested, knowing his wife often primped before a large one.

At the bookcase I sighed with pleasure to see *Tristram Shandy*, *Pamela*, Shakespeare, and our beloved Joost van den Vondel. Books also lined shelves low enough for children. Pier and Catryn would love coming here. Then I saw them: the widow's objects of religious fervor.

A silver heart, life-sized, hung apart on one wall, pitted

black, beautiful, a victim of age. My mind raced—perhaps it had once been a real heart beating in someone's chest until it was found tainted, and so removed. Further along the wall hung a crucifix of carved ivory—Christ nailed to a cross, his head crowned in thorns. Red painted blood coursed down his face and body—such grief and pain. Goodness!

As the rain let up, I heard a muffled voice. Was someone praying? I walked over and cautiously parted a velvet curtain. Fifty or more candles illuminated a small, windowless chapel. The air was thick with the fragrance of beeswax and incense, potent. I squirmed to see a large statue of the Mother, black with smoke, dominating the altar, her palms upturned, beseeching the heavens. And kneeling before her at a *prie-dieu* was a woman in black silks and lace mantle. She whispered words quietly, fervently. Prayer, or incantation? Devotion—or black magic?

"Hail, pure Lady . . . Ladder from earth which raises us all to grace . . ." In her hand she held a rosary, her fingers flicking from one bead to the next. So this was what Papists did! I felt I'd stumbled upon a powerful ritual to conjure some unseen force. To watch seemed an invasion. Maybe dangerous.

I crept back to the shelves, casting a nervous eye at the statuary.

"*Ma petite*, I am sorry to keep you. And you had to come out in this horrid weather."

I jumped. A stately woman with an aureole of gray hair entered—the woman at prayer. Her open, fine-boned face shone as white as the moon. A small musk-apple swung from the rosary around her wrist, and white roses sat pinned at her breast. A terrier padded after her, stepping on her train. Her manner of dress, French-accented speech, the perfume that arrived before she did—all were old-world, feminine, foreign.

I curtsied. "Saskia Klaassens, madame." This woman held a presence, a power. Was she saint—or witch? I giggled nervously as I leaned down to stroke the dog's ears, which stuck straight out from the sides of its head.

The widow smiled. "You look curiously at these religious arts, *mademoiselle, non*? Perhaps you think them fantastical." Madame Remy reached out a hand as pale and crumpled as her corsage of roses. She took my arm and guided me along the gallery wall, telling me about each piece. Oh, this was what Mistress Cingria warned me against! A veil of light seemed to trail behind her as she walked. I would make no judgment. Yet.

"The saints are God's intermediaries, *non*? Not everyone believes as I do that God can everywhere be—at once!" She laughed, her voice light and clear as a bell.

I stopped in front of one painting that particularly attracted me: a small, crude rendering of a Black man. "Spanish folk art?" I guessed, then felt ashamed. What did I know about religious art? When her terrier jumped at my leg, I picked him up.

"Mexican, actually," she said, a curious tilt to her had. "But *très bien*! That's close."

Mexicans often copied Spanish art, she told me, such as this Black saint, San Benito de Palermo, also called "The Black Moor." Son of devout African Christian slaves, when freed he joined a monastery of hermits—and amazed the Inquisition with his knowledge of scripture, despite his being illiterate. And he could read minds. "Now he is the patron saint of slaves." She flashed a brilliant smile.

A patron saint of slaves! I could hardly wait to tell Titus. Even if he scoffed, saying this was just another White man's trick to glorify slavery.

She led me to the shelves. I put her dog down, pulling out one beautiful leather-bound volume after another, telling her how pleased I was that she lent books to children. I chose a book about African animals, a picturebook of Bible stories, and *The*

Odyssey. The Mistress would approve.

"Oh, thank you, madame," I curtsied when the widow said to choose one for myself. "Any book that will improve my mind."

"Oh, *pffffftt*!" She pulled out a slim blue volume. "You're young and have eyes that carry the dreams in them. I think you this prefer, *non*?" She smiled, placing the volume in my hands. I laughed. She'd chosen a book of poetry—I was so happy! Then I began worrying. Would she now make me kneel and say confession? Instead, she led me to the front door where she wrapped the books in muslin and slipped them into my basket.

Her maid approached. "Sorry to interrupt, madame, but the ragman is at the back. Should I let him have the clothing?"

She was going to give away old clothing? I felt emboldened.

"Madame Remy, you've been so generous. Forgive me, but could I look through the items first? Our slaves are so in need. If your slaves don't need them, that is."

"My dear girl, no slaves have we here. We free them long before."

Freed their slaves—the wonder! I pulled out many lovely items from the pile—a white shirt for Titus, a waistcoat for Samuel, kerchiefs and frocks for the girls. Madame asked me if the de Witts would not be offended. Not intending to ask them, I blithely said, "Oh, absolutely not. It's only your religion that offends them." My cheeks turned hot. I looked down, ashamed of my indiscretion. "I'm so sorry, Madame Remy." For a moment we were silent.

"Many here do not approve, for I am what you call *paapsgezind*, Popish, *non*? Beliefs intolerable to them. Well, I choose to live among Calvinists, do I not?" She laughed, stroking the terrier now curled in her arms. "So that is my work then." She put the dog down. It ran out into the garden. "I just bless everyone. Blessing makes us queens and kings of heaven. And we're blessed in return."

I bundled up the clothing and walked to the door. Madame Remy snapped off a rose and worked it into a buttonhole of my jacket. "Before they die, flowers send out the most intense perfume. Did you know Jesus is 'The Rose'? That is why so many I grow in my garden. Sacred flowers. I place them everywhere. The thorns are like harsh thoughts. When I start to judge someone, they remind to me my own failings.

"We live in a world of right and wrong, do we not, Mademoiselle Saskia? You must love God this way, not that. To this person you may speak but not that other. So tiring. The world is as it is." She sighed. "But it can also be the miracle, *non*?"

I noticed a painting of a ship at sea. Someone was throwing a line to someone washed overboard. I stared. Memories rushed forth and hit me between the eyes.

"Why, you turn white, child. Come sit."

She led me back, and I slumped into a corner of the sofa. I told her about the Jewish boy falling into the ocean, his mother's frantic attempts to throw him a line and free the lifeboats, how she screamed for the men to get out there. Much too dangerous, they'd said. So we watched him drown.

"It shattered me to the core, madame. Children shouldn't die." I looked far into the fire. Flames crackled and spit, tearing apart the embers. She put a hand on mine. "How brittle life is! I used to meet life as it came, Madame Remy. Now I fear it. Sometimes I think death is more powerful than life." She lowered her eyes, and the silence enfolded us. Finally I rose. "I'm sorry to have bothered you so."

"Death, she has touched you deeply, *ma fille*. That is hard, but not always bad. Let it remind us to embrace the life we have, not fear it."

At the front door she smiled brightly. "So go and enjoy your poems. And please come visit to me again soon, yes?" She pulled me close and kissed each cheek, her skin fragrant with rose oil. I blushed with pleasure. "And thank your dear mistress for the wine and guinea hens. So kind of her. Wait. I want to give to her some token." She drifted out of the room, and when she returned she filled my basket with French soaps. The smell of lavender sparked my senses. "God be with you, and all of you over there. Go well."

The rain had stopped, and the garden smelled fresh from its morning bath. A rainbow etched an arc across the valley. I stood with feet planted in the wet grass, inhaling flowered air, allowing the intense and glorious beauty of Africa to settle inside. I stood as still as time itself, glad I'd emptied my heart to Madame Remy. I hadn't realized until now that some important vein in me had gone numb. Now it pulsed with life again.

Running down the hill, I thought of the Mother of God. She was a stranger to me, a mystery, in our church a minor character in the Jesus story. Why did we never talk about the nurturing one, the sweet Mother? At Rustigvallei they mocked Madame Remy because of her faith. But I wanted to be in her company again, soon. As I passed beyond the gates of her farm, I found myself wondering if Mary had had eyes like hers.

In a meadow just beyond the manor, I climbed onto the low branch of a wild pear. My feet! Once again they were throbbing. I let my clogs fall, then wiped my book free of rain that dripped from leaves above. I opened to a love poem. Adriaan's face flashed before me and when the flowering pears sent their fragrance out on the wind, I felt deeply content.

But something was jumping up and down on my hat. A chameleon? I unloosed the ribbons and set the bonnet on my lap. It was a little weaverbird, the kind that spins deep, hanging nests. Black, with spots of green, like unripe lemons. I marveled as it picked at the ribbon around the bonnet's crown, as if to steal it. Ah, for its nest. When it chirped and tilted its head at me, I laughed.

Slowly I guided my hands forward, encircled the wings—and snatched hold. The bird's heart beat fast against my thumbs. The little head! The bright black eyes! I released my grip, and, to my surprise, it didn't fly away but fluttered into my lap. Did it want to adopt me?

Oh, I suddenly thought, it's late! If I don't get back soon I'll be punished. But the weaverbird would not go. I wrapped it in a handkerchief, slipped it into my apron pocket, picked up my things and ran down the hill, not even minding the blisters rubbing against my shoes. The little bulk knocked and squirmed against my thigh.

Just before I reached the first field of home, I caught sight of Titus walking toward me. My heart skipped a beat. His hat of reeds covered his headscarf and he wore it at a funny angle. Two grape saplings straddled one shoulder and on the other rested a dirt-encrusted spade. I would ask him if his wounds were healing, tell him about the Black saint, my new books, show him my weaverbird and give him that shirt.

But as he drew close I saw it was not Titus, but Isaiah. I greeted him but did not stop. This slave had a reputation for stealing food from the pantry and wine from the cellars. Considering the slaves' poverty, that didn't seem such sins. But his eyes bothered me—they were furtive, like a wild dog's, and did not inspire trust.

I hurried across the stone bridge toward the yard, composing excuses in my head for my tardiness. The last mile home I began wondering why mistaking another man for Titus had disappointed me. After all, there was gallant Adriaan to think about. Certainly not some slaveman.

Chapter 19

SEPTEMBER 1749 (SPRING)

In the dark hours of the morning I stumbled into the cottage to fetch Johanna—she was still in bed. "Changed my mind, Saski." She pulled the covers over her head. "Sleepin in today."

"But I was counting on your company."

"Well, *un*-count it!"

Last night Titus told us that if we wanted to use our day off to go into town, we'd have to be ready early, for he had a stop to make to arrange the siring of a blooded horse. Before daybreak we loaded the wagon and Titus tethered the thoroughbred to the back. I was happy to see him wearing the crisp white shirt I'd picked from Madame Remy's ragpile and patched the tears. How pleased he was! Samuel was looking proud in his newly acquired waistcoat, so I was distressed when, just as we rumbled through the pilaster gates, he vomited over the sideboards. I gently wiped his mouth, then Titus walked him back to the Quarters.

"He be all right," he said, taking the reins. "Too much beer last night."

Barely a mile into the trip, I realized this was the first time Titus and I had traveled together alone. Employers frown on it, a female servant traveling alone with a slaveman of a certain age. But we hadn't considered that. Or didn't want to. Once I realized what we'd done, my mouth grew dry as cotton.

Just as the sun pushed its tangerine crown up over the horizon, we arrived at the Brill farm. I was ready to spend some time helping Jaco's wife, a seamstress there, while Titus finalized the details of the siring. But Master Brill was not at home. "Suddenly called to Stellenbosch," his Stable Master apologized. "Emergency Drostdy meeting." Titus pondered for a moment. Because Master Brill was a trustworthy neighbor, he decided we'd leave the horse rather than take it all the way to Cape Town. So Titus and I took off, glad of the free time. A nervousness sparked the air, or so it seemed. He is only a friend, I kept telling myself. We were exceptionally quiet.

Toward noon, we stopped at a fine patch of grass near a creek. Under the shade of a blossoming thorntree, we spread out our blanket, unpacking bread, fresh berries, pickled harderfish, cheese, and diluted wine. While Titus scrambled for water, I looked up at a canopy of yellow flowers, inhaling the sweet-sourness of dying blossoms.

Titus returned with a wet cloth. I whispered thanks and wiped the mask of grit from my face. He took off his hat and headband and shook his dusty hair. I studied the black coils at the nape of his neck, imagined pushing at them, then peeled off my bonnet and cap. Locks of hair fell across my eyes, and as I raised my arms to pin them back, I caught him watching, looking away, then watching again. Hastily I put the cap back on.

How awkward this was! I made Titus a napkin of food, snatching glimpses. He squatted at the edge of the blanket as if unsure whether to join me there. That head would be interesting to draw, I thought—round, high cheekbones, the hollow space running to his chin, the deep slant of his forehead. Could I capture it on paper, the face that would flush with temper, then suddenly quicken the air with a smile? Who was he?

"Titus, how are you able let go of your anger so swiftly?" I pushed the food into his hands.

He poked at the fishbones. "Do I?"

"Remember when that vendor cut you? That must have bridled, but you never mentioned it again."

"Why should I mention that thing? Slaves know many bullies. For me, once this wrath is out, it is used up. The wind, she takes it."

My feet hurt. I wriggled out of my clogs, wincing, picking stocking from my toes.

"What has happened to those feet of yours, Miss Saskia? Why the blood?"

"Blisters. I hiked to the Remy farm the other day, and my feet slipped and slid in these new clogs. Pretty, don't you think?" I arranged the shoes neatly on the grass. "Josiah carved them for me."

"You could have stuffed the shoes with grass, you know." I looked at him and blinked. Not something a lady would do—but then, I wasn't exactly a lady, was I? "It be dangerous to walk the veldt alone. Why did you not ask me to drive you?" His tone was annoyed. "At least I could saddle for you the horse."

"You were busy. You're always busy. You'd have had to get permission. I don't feel it's dangerous." I took a bite of cheese—sweet and tangy. The girls had churned the curds last month from goatmilk. "I like to walk. It gives me time to think. And, to tell the truth, I don't ride very well."

Titus looked up. "How can you live here and not know how to ride? I will teach you. I will ask the Master if I can saddle the horse for you and lead you around the paddock."

I leaned back, my eyes resting on the horizon. "I wish we

could just ride out into the countryside, Titus, ride and ride over the savanna, until the estate were only a memory." As soon as the words were out, I regretted them. How forward!

"You know I cannot ride out of the estate just like that." Titus had freedoms few other slaves had, like traveling the countryside on business. But pleasure rides? In his dreams.

"Let me see those toes, Miss Saskia. They be wounded."

"Take off my stockings? Nay!" I laughed, biting into a hunk of bread and fish.

He shot me a stern look. "You bleed. This be not the time to be stupidly proper." Then, more softly, "Miss Saskia, I just want to see if those feet, they need the doctoring."

"So now you're a *toverman*, are you? A witch doctor?"

"Do not make fun of the medicine people."

"Oh, Titus, you're too smart and too educated to believe such nonsense!"

He scowled. "You do not know of what you speak."

A silence fell, thick and heavy. "What are you then—a Christian or a heathen?"

"Do I have to choose?"

"*Ja*, of course."

He wandered over to a sycamore by the water. "Those stockings, Miss Saskia."

I took another bite of food, chewing slowly. My feet were feverish, throbbing. How was I going to walk across town in such pain? From behind the thorntree, I hiked up my skirt, loosening the ribbons holding up my stockings. I glanced back over my shoulder.

"Don't you dare peek, now. *Ach!* They're stuck to the blisters." My toes and footpads were swollen with red, tender bubbles.

Titus was sitting leaning against the sycamore, long legs stretched out in front of him. "Go wet them in the creek, then."

"*Ja, baas!*" I muttered, "Anything you says, *baas*!" I bowed and scraped backward. Titus's mouth twisted in a sardonic grin. "Is this the extent of your doctoring, then, Titus—having me soak my feet in water?" I walked on heels, gingerly, past where he sat, white stockings rolled down around my ankles. "*Toverman,*" I whispered, and plunked down onto the banks of the stream. The water was bracing. "Oh, Lord! This is colder than a frigid canal." Feet jerked out, then plunged back in again. The stockings were loosening from the wounds. I pulled at them cautiously. "I've skated on ice warmer than this!"

"Let me see those feet." My feet rose from the water, but I didn't stir from the banks. "I mean up close."

"Are you joking? Show me yours first."

He bent his right leg back, grimaced, examined the bottom of one foot, then the other. "There be nothing to see, my sister, just the leather of skin from wearing not the shoes."

"Why don't they give you shoes?"

"Not allowed. Only when we have the heavy work to do, then they give us *veldshoen*. A lot of good those do." He shifted uncomfortably under the tree. "What does it mean when you say 'skate on ice'?"

"Show me the soles of those black feet." Still sitting, I twirled to face him, bare feet hovering above the grass. "Come on. You've seen mine. Now show me yours."

"What be the 'skate on ice'? You tell me, Miss Saskia, then maybe I will show you these feet." His white teeth flashed a sudden smile.

I stood up and trotted gingerly on heels to pick a purple wildflower. I spun it under my chin, walking over to Titus.

"Hand me my wine first," I grinned. "*Slave.*" He scowled, handing me the horn cup. My eyes lingered on his fingertips, callused and shiny, with a pearly underbloom. I took a deep drink. "All right. Ice-skating is a way of walking on ice. Ice, you know, frozen water? Haven't you ever seen ice? It's like the snow you see from the highest peaks, but compressed."

"I have seen that snow. It dusts the mountains white, like sugar on the Easter cake."

"The Netherlands are much colder than here, you know. In winter the canals freeze over, and we strap metal blades to our shoes and dance on the water." I slid over the grass, mimicking the striding gait of skaters.

Titus watched, brows knitted. "Hah! Do you think this I believe?"

"But we do. The water gets so hard you can walk on it, even push others around in carts. In a really cold winter, horses and carriages can ride on the ice. God's truth. It's easy to fall, though, and that hurts. Ice is very slippery."

Titus arched an eyebrow. "Maybe it is your stories that be slippery. You miss your Dutch country, is it not so?"

I looked up. The sky burned with a blue more intense than any I'd seen in the Netherlands, and beyond the spiky branches, a lacery of clouds spread like sheets of voile. I reached and pulled down a blossom. "When I was there I only wanted to get away. Now I dream of it sometimes. We're funny creatures, aren't we, always wanting what we can't have."

Titus said nothing, only looked toward the green hills and distant mountains. Now a pensive mood enveloped us. We had wandered into some strange backwater, not sure of the way out.

Suddenly he raised his legs and flashed the soles of his feet—callused soles, scuffed and dark, with tender pink edging up the sides. I'd often noticed those long, finely formed toes, but the bottoms were, as he said, like leather. I laughed. "Let me see those up close." I peered at them. "Absolutely disgusting. They look like burnt pancakes."

"They do not!"

"*Do!*" I snatched his hat from the grass and twirled the bowl in my fist. "What kind of hat is this, anyway? Looks like the roof of a Hottentot hut. Or a little mountain with a knob on top."

He put out an arm. "Give me that, Miss Saskia."

"A slave has to learn Dutch just for the right to wear a greasy old thing like this?"

Titus jumped up and lunged for the hat, but I pulled it behind my back, running a few steps around the tree. He hesitated.

"Pancake feet!" I taunted. "Ouch!" My blisters dashed onto pebbles in the grass, making me wince. "Pancake feet, burnt pancake feet," I chanted like a child. "Titus has burnt *pannenkoek* feet." I put on his hat, so large it slipped down over my ears.

"They be more pretty than the feet of you, you pale, plucked Holland chicken," he countered. He lurched toward me. "Skin so white. Like the belly of a fish."

"Oh!"

"And with those ugly red balloons of blisters!" he teased. "Now my feet, they be *fine*."

"My God, you're arrogant."

"The hat, please."

I extended it to him, then just as he touched it, jerked it back. He chased me around the tree as I laughed, holding it out of reach. Squeals of pain, then laughter, until he caught me by the arm, and I stumbled. He reached out to break my fall, and we both fell onto the grass. We were panting, his arm under my elbow. I didn't move. I didn't want to move. Excitement shot through my body. My heart pounded so loudly, I could almost hear it.

Everything was spinning—our breath, the droning insects, the fragrance of crushed grass and petals. Yellow blossoms swam across the sky like stars. I didn't dare look at him, hardly dared breathe, his face so close. I turned and for an alarming moment let his eyes rest in mine.

He pulled away with a jerk, frowned, and sat up. I rose to fetch my sewing basket from the wagon, then sank down in front of him, handed him a needle, and thrust an ankle across his leg.

"Here. If you be such a great medicine man, then lance these blisters."

He stared at me, finally grabbing my ankle. His Black fingers flicked bark and petals from my pink foot as he inspected the wounds. "Titus, how do you see me? Be honest."

He did not look up. Brow screwed in concentration, he plunged the needle into bubbles of skin, and squeezed. I felt little pangs. Clear fluid trickled out. He was gripping my ankle quite firmly now.

"I see you as . . . the shameless flirt."

I started, and pulled my foot back. "Am not!" But he grabbed it, tightly.

"I see you . . ." He hesitated. "I see the maid who, before most people, be very, very quiet. All reined in and polite, like the lady, but inside, there be the filly who champs strong at the bit." Thrusting the ankle aside, he picked up the other, held the needle precisely, and pierced each blister. He looked at me a moment, his long fingers clasped around my heel. My heart was beating like a hummingbird's. Pleasure raced up my leg.

"The fillies, they start out wild and spirited, you know. Then we must break them. When you break the horses, then you can use them. But you break also the edge of the wildness. And the wildness—well, that be the real beauty of a thing. You," he said, tilting his head back and leveling his eyes at me, "it be still there in you, I think. Maybe you just be wanting someone to take off the harness and let you run loose."

I stared at him. A flutter of danger shadowed my breath. He ripped a blade of grass from the earth and tickled my sole. I cried out, yanking my foot back under my skirt, then jumped up. I blushed. Had I invited this?

He turned and looked out across the gleaming water. "Maybe you are wanting the wild run in the pasture in the green, green grass under the blue, blue sky." He smiled—white teeth against blue lips. What do I say now? He pointed to the locket that fell between my breasts. "So tell me, what lover's face be hidden there?" I fingered the gold pendant, hot now from the sun, hesitating. Then sprung the lock open. I handed it to him. "She died."

His face clouded over. "My mother, she also die too young. I am sorry."

Afterward, when we had climbed back into the wagon, I glanced at those dark fingers that wove themselves through the reins. Fingers that had held and cradled my ankles. I felt lightheaded, trembly, and guilty. Somehow, by our words, by this innocent touching, a knowing had passed between us. And the knowing said we could never go back to how we'd been before.

~

Titus and I arrived home from Cape Town just before sunset. Johanna ran toward us from the ox *kraal*, frowning, swinging a bucket, smoothing her apron in agitation. "I have to talk to ye, Saski." As soon as Titus helped me alight, she grabbed my hand and pulled me down the yard.

"Saski, how could you?" We stood in the shadow of the well. Johanna's voice was hushed, brimming with irritation. She hooked the bucket to the rope, tossed it over the stone edge, and hauled water up. "Running off to town today alone with Titus." I blinked, then glanced over to him as he outspanned the oxen. "Now there be all kinds of gossip goin round. They sayin you two poisoned Samuel so's ye could go off and make love in the woods."

The muscles in my face tightened. "*What?*"

Johanna looked around, then crunched the bucket against her hip with such force that water splashed over her skirt. "It don't be true, do it? I told them it was lies. You woulda told me if you be doin the nasties with Titus, wouldn't ye?"

"Who says such things?"

"Anna overheard someone tell Mistress Cingria, but she couldn't see who. Said it sounded like a slavegirl, though. Course Anna said you'll both burn in hell."

I felt nauseous. Perhaps Titus and I did cross a line today, but not *that* line. How dare people ruin our lives with such talk! There was only one slavegirl who would try.

"If it be true, Saski, stop it! I don't know bout you, but I value my employment here. Every day my stomach is full and every night a dry roof lie over my head. If the Master ever found out you be doin it with a slave. . . Listen, I can understand havin feelings, but don't do nothin with him . . . it's too dangerous."

"Titus and I have done nothing!" The words felt false. She hadn't heard them anyway.

"Ye'd be out in a heartbeat, no references neither, ya hear? Dropped from Rustigvallei quicker than a turd from a short sow. Ye couldn't find no decent work nowhere. No money. No passage home. Thrown onto the streets of Cape Town, a wanderin woman prey to any man's fancy, if you know what I mean." This felt a bit rich, coming from Johanna. "As for Titus . . . Remember that slave at Groot Constantia who did it with a White woman? Castrated him. Tied him up, stuffed his privates in his mouth. Left him to bleed to death."

I stared at her, aghast. "Johanna, I'm trying to tell you. *We are not lovers.* I've never had a lover, understand?" I stormed down the grassy yard to the house. Johanna's speech had scared me, more for Titus than myself. She was right about one thing though—Titus and I had been foolhardy.

In the kitchen, Cook and her girls were murmuring. They stared at me, exchanging knowing glances. I glared back, then ran up the steps to my room.

I could never be alone with Titus again. Ever.

Chapter 20

Zounds, ye whore! Is black so base a hue?
—Shakespeare, Titus Andronicus

October 1749 (Spring)

"Here, Miss Saskia." Samuel turned in his seat and offered me a callused hand. "You come up front here now an sit next ta Titus, for this young Black gent, he want your very, very nice conversation plenty more mine, isn't it? I move back sit dose sacks, cause I wants the small small nap."

On these trips to Cape Town, the Master entrusted Titus with delivering barrels of wine and negotiating other estate affairs, including the trading of horses. He entrusted Oom Samuel with collecting the mail and buying provisions. And I always had a place in the wagon, for the Master entrusted me with creating lace, an employment he felt sure would, like other slave labor, fatten his coffers.

Once we traveled past sight of the estate, Samuel always offered me his seat up front, but only when there were just the three of us. When other workers rode along, he didn't offer, for they would read too much into it. Everyone, it seemed, had been reading altogether too much into my friendship with Titus. Only Samuel understood. I seemed to beam at our budding friendship. But after Johanna's warning, I hesitated, even though traveling to see Effie with just these two men were the days I treasured most. Especially when I could talk to Titus.

We'd left early that morning, as we always did, around sunrise. Fog stole over the countryside and wrapped us in its gray shawl. We rattled down the dirt road past fields where men were already out irrigating vines under the watch of moon-silvered mountains. Now, two hours later, the sun had burned away the mist, casting sharp shadows from trees and mountain walls, revealing a crisp spring morning. Lupins and wild lilies littered the earth with blue. I recognized so many flowers now: the showy birds of paradise, flame red lilies, tuberoses, jeranums, crocuses, and the jutting proteas.

On our last trip, we were caught in a deluge. With no time to secure the bamboo ribs and mount the canvases, Johanna and I pulled an oiled tarp over ourselves. But water gushed down the folds, streaming out onto the boards where it flooded our feet and soiled the hems of our skirts. As driver, Titus had the worst of it, for he took the rain head on. There were places we had to get out and push the wagon—wheels mired in mud so deep it sucked at our clogs. All that day and the next, and the next, we sneezed and blew stuffy noses. It's a wonder we haven't all died yet of colds.

Whenever we passed Europeans on the road and they saw me sitting with Titus, they would glare. I could almost hear the tongues clucking. What did I care what people thought? True, word might get back to our master, but it was worth the risk, for we always had so much to discuss. And on this day Titus let loose a secret.

"We slaves have the way of talking about you Whites, did you know?" I looked at him blankly. "When we say, 'Big Rooster, he be squawking mad today' or 'Gray Ass, he be kicking people bad'—can you not guess what we be saying?"

"You really talk like that?"

"Big Rooster squawking mad . . . Can you guess who?"

My brain scrambled to understand. "When you say 'rooster,' do you mean the Master?" Titus grinned. "But gray ass . . . Just a minute."

"Who be the most biggest ass at Rustigvallei?"

"Anthonij! His gray hair. He's the nastiest for sure."

Titus chuckled. "Can you guess who the women call 'The Adder'?"

"Mistress Cingria! Who else?" We laughed.

Samuel had been lying curled in the back on a sack of aged grapes. Now he stirred. "Titus, son, doan you be spoilin tellin everything this maid. Men finds out, little while be plenty plenty trouble—lotta lotta thrashing good. Then slave talk be already finished, isn't it?"

I grinned. "Don't worry, Uncle, I won't tell. You chaps are too funny."

Often on these journeys Titus would tease me. But he also taught me about Africa. One day he pointed out a baboon dragging her dead babe behind her. "To keep it from the vultures." Oh! And he told me about the honeybirds that actually lead people to honeycombs, which helped them get at the grubs underneath. And to always leave a little honey for the birds as thanks. Today we passed a great flock of green and yellow weaverbirds singing noisily in a thorn tree. "Just like my Tulip!" I exclaimed.

Titus told me the weavers had a way of picking off thorns

without hurting themselves and weaving them into sac-like nests. Snakes and goshawks would attack the nests for their eggs, but more often than not the thorns won the day.

"*Dis kamma so*. I think those nests dream of being Hottentot huts when they grow up." I sighed. We chuckled. "Thank you again, Titus, for the perch you made for Tulip." To keep my bird from flying away, he took a string, nailed one end to a shelf, and tied the other around its leg.

"Now it is my slave," I'd teased.

"Cept that it do no work."

As our conversations deepened, so did our trust and friendship. But even when we did not speak, even when we rode along for long stretches in silence, we took comfort in each other's company. We felt for each other's plight. I chafed at exhausting, menial work and unreasonable authority. Titus, of course, chafed under a much heavier yoke.

Sometimes we discussed books we read, for I had become a kind of thief, borrowing books from Madame Remy but sharing them with Titus. I hated being devious in any way with her, but I couldn't ask her to lend a book to a slave. To Titus, books were pure gold. He comprehended well, for the Moravian missionary who taught him to read taught him to think too. From time to time I helped explain a phrase in Dutch or a cultural reference. Soon he'll read better than I.

On the journey into town this morning, Titus recited poetry. It's uncanny how many poems he has committed to memory. I only wished I liked them more.

"Here be the great line from the English poet Marvell," Titus said, clearing his throat. " 'O who shall from this dungeon raise / A soul enslaved so many ways? / With bolts of bones, that fettered stands / In feet; and manacled in hands.' "

"Titus," I said playing with the ribbons on my bonnet, "when there are so many beautiful lines of poetry in the world, why do you always memorize those about slavery?" When I turned to him, his face was severe.

"Why slavery? Miss Saskia, never be the minute I do not bear the burden of belonging to another." His brow clouded over. "The degradation."

I rocked back and forth on the bench, acutely uncomfortable. Then my devilish twin rose up. "The Master says that God has ordained that you of heathen descent were born to be our slaves and we to be your betters. Your betters and your masters."

Samuel stirred restlessly on his sacks, groaning. Titus's eyes were wild. "How can you say such a thing? Do you believe that?"

"I'm not sure what I believe." I looked down, fidgeting with buttons now, avoiding his gaze. "I never liked the idea of slavery," I said in a defensive tone, "even when I was little. No one taught me—I just felt it. The Netherlands have no slaves that I know of. But here everyone has slaves, and the *predikant* in church last Sunday told us God has ordained that we show you the way to Him. People wiser than I say that your ancestor, Ham, committed many sins, and now your people must atone for them. God has ordained it."

As soon as the words were out, they seemed to turn and bite the walls of my mouth. I glanced to the back of the wagon. Old Samuel lay crouched on the sacks, a kerchief lowered over his ears. Did I believe that? Or did I say it just to provoke?

The knuckles of Titus's hands clenched the reins, turning pale. " 'People wiser than I'—what elephant shit! Again the White man, he try to justify the bondage of our people. 'God has ordained it.' God has ordained nothing! Does God ordain that some men treat other men like the beasts? That we forever atone for the story in the Bible? How can you, Miss Saskia, someone I thought intelligent—how can you believe this thing?"

Titus's body shuddered, as if releasing something toxic. My gaze fell to my lap, wet palms pressing into my skirt. "You speak as if *I* am the one who enslaved you."

"You enslave me every second when you speak like that, my sister." He threw the reins from one hand to the other, picked up his whip, and cracked it.

We rode along in silence. I knew in my bones he was right. What Titus didn't know was how many times back home I'd been called heretic, arguing with my parents about many a *predikant's* sermon.

When we reached a river, Titus pulled the team over. I stretched, unable to shake off my discomfort. Titus and Samuel watered the oxen while I found a cool spot under the branches of a wild mulberry and set out our food. Soon the men joined me.

"Look, Oom Samuel. Now I've gone and got Titus angry." I cut slices of cheese and bread and handed it to the men. Samuel shook his head, chuckled, and wandered off toward the river.

"I'm just telling you what I've been told since childhood, Titus, and especially since coming to the Cape. It doesn't mean I believe it." I leaned back against the trunk. "I want to understand the truth of things. I don't know who speaks the truth."

For the longest time, Titus said nothing, just fanned himself with his hat. "I cannot blame you what they tell you, Miss Saskia. I just want you to open the eyes. Any man's hatred, even mine, it be like drinking from the poisoned river. At first it satisfies, but then it kills the one who drinks. My life, it be not so bad as the others. But you have seen my brothers and my sisters, barely able to walk the last paces to the Quarters after the day in the fields. They have not the smallest thing to give their children." He stared at his napkin of food, then put it on the grass. "Separated from the ones we love. Punished. Whipped. You have seen our lives. You know."

He picked up a twig and snapped it between his fingers. His voice grew high pitched. "If we don't die from exhaustion, we die because our souls, they be lost to us." He lifted his chin haughtily and stared me in the eye. "And you ask, my sister, why I speak of slavery?"

He reached up and pulled a clump of ripe mulberries from the tree, crushing them in his palm, letting the wine-colored juice dribble down his arm. "Is our blood not the same red as yours when we bleed? Do we not grieve, love, suffer—die—just as you? Are we not also human? Or do we not be human enough?"

The bread caught in my throat. I put down my food. I had never seen Titus so impassioned. "I see you've read your Shakespeare. You use him well."

An awkward silence fell between us. I looked up through the branches heavy with dark berries, feeling deeply uncertain about everything. I'd been raised to believe that people of color are of another order than us. Lesser. But Titus had such integrity and presence. Samuel such forbearance.

I cleared my throat, for something close to tears was collecting there. "I've often wondered what it must be like to be a person of color, and a slave. Just to be born a woman in a world run by men is a kind of slavery. But I know the yoke your kinsmen bear is a hundred times heavier. Heavier a thousand times." I pulled mulberries from the tree. They fell apart in my fingers.

We sat for a minute in silence. "You know you must never repeat any this talk. The Master, he would flog me close to death."

"Of course not. On my life. I respect you too much. Let us be friends again, Titus." He said nothing, only gazed over at Samuel, who was chattering to himself by the water. "But Titus, the slaves aren't always miserable. You jest and tease, you laugh. You love your horses. I've even heard you sing. You slaves *seem* happy." I cut off a slice of cheese, offering it to Titus, but he pushed it away.

" 'You slaves'—see how you talk? I decide long ago God do love the Black man. But my happiness be what I make. See Samuel there—what the fine old brother. Dignity. Peace. I think this peace come from the courage of the heart of him. This be the hardest courage of all."

Samuel sat propped up against a willow, half hidden behind long green branches. "I love that man," I said. "He's so humble."

Titus turned and held me in his gaze. "We *all* be humble." I looked at him dubiously. "We slaves, we *perfect* the humble. It is the virtue we cultivate to stay alive."

Samuel was laughing, talking, and singing to something in some native tongue. We strained to hear. "Why, he be talking to the fishes in the water," Titus said. "With the affection, in the silly way, as to little babes."

Back on the road, I sat reflecting. Titus's speeches were daring. His wild moods frightened me, but how grand that he trusted me with them. I'd never known a man so fine and yet so . . . *perilous*. Once, Manassa told me, while Anthonij was lashing her mercilessly for stepping on his cat's tail, Titus strode over, snatched the *sjambok* from his hand, and crumpled him with his gaze. Anthonij, slight, feisty, shook in his boots, then threatened that one day he'd crush Titus.

Later, back on the road, the wagon lurched and threw my body against his. I grabbed his arm. Touching him—oh, so forbidden! A thrill ripped through me. He had a pleasant earthy smell, of dust and tobacco. I looked at my fingers stained with mulberries. I'd have to scrub them well at Effie's before they touched the threads. Then, before I knew it, the broad wall of Table Mountain loomed before us.

Titus chewed on a piece of bark, the kind that freshens the breath. He was looking straight ahead, turning it with his tongue. "Africa was the virgin until the White man came and raped her."

I shot him a look, sucked air in sharply. "*What did you say?*" My mind scrambled to understand—could a continent be raped, ravaged as a woman might be? I frowned, shading my eyes from a sun that beat down fiercely.

"It be in the world, my sister. You Europeans, you never want to speak of it. You do it, but never speak of it. It be too close with us."

I stared at him. Was he referring to the White sailors who visited the Slave Lodge in town? Some slavewoman he knew? Or had he heard something about Claus? "I don't know what you're talking about." Ox hooves kicked up small stones that went *ping* on the sides of the wagon. When we turned a corner in the road, I saw the rim of ocean spread out on the horizon. Soon we would be in Cape Town.

"I love to read the Dutch Bible. I read the words of the teacher Jesus, and they be sweet—like the walk in the river on the hot summer day. Like the moon that glitters in the winter sky. So kind, these words; so much truth. Then the Christian man, he injure that *swarte jongen*." His voice resembled gravel. "I do not understand this. They tell us we be godless heathens, then they go and do that thing. You tell me why."

The wagon axles creaked and complained and the oxen moaned softly as we crested a high hill, forcing us deep into our seats. "*What's this?*"

He snorted with contempt. "Have you not heard?" I shook my head. Titus shifted in his seat, gripping the reins tighter. "Then I cannot tell you."

A strong breeze picked up, blowing at the brim of my hat. "Tell me."

"You do not want to know."

"Of course I want to know! *Tell me!*"

"Some White man rape the slaveboy at Rustigvallei. That is all I can say."

I inhaled a lungful of air. "What! Who, Titus? It wasn't Digger, was it?"

"No, not your Digger. So much shame!"

My mind reeled, a wave of nausea ripped through my stomach. Rape. I hated that word. Rape was when a man forced a woman to lie with him against her will. But . . . a boy . . .?

"Does the Master know? You must tell the Master."

"He know." Titus shot me a look of rage. "He *allow*." He drove on, his fists clenched as tight as cannonballs.

My mind was spinning. A slaveboy. Raped at our estate. And the Master . . . Was this the night I'd seen a boy taken from the Quarters?

"Makes me so mad I could hang someone." Titus lifted his long bamboo whip, reached out as if to lash the oxen, then, at the last moment, struck and crackled the air above their backs.

I said nothing. There was nothing I could say. I was ashamed of being White.

~

Just outside Cape Town, as Titus outspanned the oxen, I watched him. Every time he removed the yokes and harnesses here, his demeanor changed. Breathing came faster, a stiffening through the chest. Every time we entered town, he braced himself, for soon he would walk among European youths who would taunt and bully him. Aunt Effie said that some men did whatever they could to strip a slaveman of his manhood, as apparently they had so little of their own. Once I shouted back at some such idiots, but Titus made me to stop.

An hour into my lace lesson, Widow Huyskens asked why I was so quiet. I took a deep breath.

"Aunt Effie, how can a man rape a boy?" When she told me, I was stunned. "But why? Why would a man do such a thing?"

"Twisted desire. Power over someone helpless. The need to steal some child's purity. I don't know, Saskia."

"Oh, Auntie. Titus told me this happened at Rustigvallei. By a White man. And the Master let him. What can we do?"

She bowed her head, working the bobbins with trembly hands. "Nothing, Saskia. Nothing. Except wait for our moment."

"What do you mean?" But she fell dourly silent.

On the drive home, a dark, troubled mood descended over us, a silent tension the air could barely contain. For me it lingered far into the night.

From my attic window I watched a crescent moon rise out of the forest only to be swallowed up by clouds. Oh, the mess and grief that is the world! Everywhere, innocence lost. I pulled out my journal.

When Mama died, we fell into a kind of darkness. We had each other in our grief, Papa and I. That should have been enough. But a family friend, a widow, dropped by the house with soups and cakes "to bring solace to you in your sorrow." She stayed too long, quite ignoring me. Her smiles and solicitations were flimsy as paper. Mama had been so wonderful—how could Papa let this other woman into our lives?

I was bad, I know. I told Papa the widow was into her cups, that she often took the name of the Lord in vain. But when my lies were discovered, I was the one he turned against. Then Papa married that woman. To lose Mama was already beyond bearing—then to lose him also, to a woman who would have me out of the way. After a while, when Papa was gone, she took the belt and came at me. He never saw it. No one ever saw it but Bertje, who dared not speak of it. I tried to tell him, but he accused me of lying. For ever so long I endured her lashings, never speaking of them again. I was angry with everyone, even God. Then, they had a babe.

They doted on that boy. As if all Papa's dreams of what he had wanted to become fell upon that child. Dreams he never had for me. I was left to my own devices, living in their house like an unwanted tenant. When Papa returned from his travels, he was too tired to pay me heed, but went to see the babe. That woman would take Papa in her arms, away from me. How my heart hurt. For solace I would lock myself in my room and weave lace.

If only Mama were alive to comfort me, Papa here to lend good counsel. I was bereft. I'd sent so many letters to Papa from the Cape, but received only one in return. Gertruyd wrote that they had visited the farm, that Papa seemed well, that the child never stopped chattering, and Papa's wife—not so new now—managed her family like a dock boss. Was that why he hadn't written?

I slipped from the house whenever I could, walking the brick roads and alleyways of the city. Sometimes I took the canal boat to cousin Gertruyd's farm, and the family welcomed me. Sometimes I visited the Sisters of Mercy and Charity to help them sort clothing and linens for the poor. Often they taught me new lace patterns, praising my skills. I gave them much of the lace I made, even teaching the craft to orphans and women at the poorhouse.

That's when I put my anger in my apron pocket, taking it out only when the neighborhood boys teased me: "Sassy Saski, Hornet Angry." I chased them through windmill towers and under bridges. When I caught them, I didn't really know what to do with them, so I pushed them down, even into the canals, or kicked them. When they told on me, I got into trouble. I don't know why I did it. I didn't really want to hurt them. It's just that my insides were churning at being left to bring myself up without the closeness and love my parents once showered on me. And left to such a stepmother.

Mostly, below the heavy blanket of anger, I was sad. Less and less I sought others out. Would I always and forever be an outsider, a child at the window scratching through the frost, watching the happiness of others? My loneliness cramped me in, kept me as frigid as the icy canals in winter. When I saw the butcher strip hide from a cow, I felt it was my skin. When the blacksmith hammered an iron pot in his red-hot fire, I thought it must be my heart. And when the crippled street people petitioned me for a coin, I wanted to tear my clothes and join them—for my soul had become a beggar in disguise.

Chapter 21

NOVEMBER 1749 (SUMMER)

Oh, summer was hot! Another day of sun burning down like a smithy's anvil. I was grateful to be settled on a stool in a small, cool room under the house, working lace for the de Witts, stripped to my chemise, shutters opened just enough for one strong beam of light to illuminate my lace pillow. There were moments when I loved being in the thick of things—and moments like these when I loved being quietly alone.

More rumors! Titus and I lovers? What sausage! We'd barely touched. Now people were watching my belly. "Nothing but a common whore, and a slave's whore at that." "Despicable! She should be whipped and dismissed!" The 'gossip spiders,' Johanna called them. They liked to catch you in their webs, spinning juicy stories to chew upon.

What could I say? *I am not with child.* Time would prove me innocent. Meanwhile, all I could do was work hard—sweep and scrub and tend the children—to prove my virtue, to win back my good name. But once stigma falls upon you, what can you do? Sometimes I felt like a moth locked away in a drawer, beating furious wings, watching them turn to dust.

I suppose I went a little crazy, for I got into another kind of trouble.

Yesterday started out well enough. In the afternoon, when I came into the *kinder*room, Catryn was clomping about in her mother's green satin mules, her small feet quite lost in them. She looked so funny and dear that I burst out laughing. That's when I decided we were all going to get decked out.

"I'll be a general, then," Pier declared. "I'll only dress up if I can be the general."

"I'll see what we can come up with—sir!" and saluted him. "All right, children. Follow me."

In my room, I parted the curtain in the back and opened the heavy lids of trunks. What treasure-troves of strange clothing they held! At least three generations old, divinely vintage. Artistic Catryn chose a silk lounging dress to slip into, and I pinned up the long train. Pier pulled out a heavily embroidered red *chinees* tunic which I lowered over his head, then topped it with a stiff white neckruff. Catryn giggled.

"This is no general's uniform!" he complained.

"It is in China," I fudged. "Use your imagination. Anyway, it's the most marvelous thing here, and you get to wear it."

Pier unraveled a magnificent green obi, and Catryn and I spun him round until it cinched his waist. He looked at it and laughed—a warm, genuine laugh. Pier's next find was a man's wig of auburn curls, at least seventy-five years out of fashion and quite outrageous. We coughed as dust and little insects flew out. When the long spirals spilled over his eyes and tickled his mouth, Catryn and I just about fell over laughing. Even Pier let out a few guffaws.

In the second trunk, I discovered a great overwide black military hat, and let out a yelp. "Mine!" I opened the doors of my wardrobe and studied the hat's effect in the looking glass, chuckling, turning the creased brims front to back, then sideways. Grand beyond words!

Catryn minced to my side in her long dress. "Mirrors like that are not allowed servants." Then she stepped in front of me to look at herself.

"Well, dearest, if you don't tell, I'll let you use it sometimes."

From my wardrobe I pulled out the blue silk dress the Mistress had given me, shorn of its ruffles and lace, but with good bones. I started to undress. Through the looking glass I saw Pier staring at me in my chemise and stays. I hastily dressed. He was that age where a bit of manhood begins to poke through, something I hadn't considered. Too late now. Under my sleeves I tied another excavation, some moth-eaten lace.

A shallow tray at the top of one trunk held skeins of ribbon, brass chains, and necklaces of paste pearls—we hung every one round Catryn's neck. In mysterious tins was thick white foundation that we smeared over our faces until we looked as pale as death. Then rouged our lips and cheeks unmercifully. When Pier found sticky black beauty patches cut into stars and moons, we stuck them onto our foreheads, cheeks, and chins, giggling.

I pinned Catryn's long curls high, stuffed them with unspun wool, and powdered the coiffure with crushed chalk. "Madame de Pompadour! At your service!"

With soot from my oil lamp, I smudged a grand mustache under Pier's nose. He ran to his room, returning with his Javanese *kris*. I secured the wavy sword under his sash.

"Let's see how we look together." We preened and giggled. "Absolutely, deliciously fantastic, don't you think? Like a troupe of theater actors."

"Or painted dolls from Paris," Catryn exclaimed. "Let's go downstairs and show everyone."

"Wait!" Pier dashed off, returning twirling his walking stick. "Brandish it like a baton," he said, handing it to Catryn. "And *I've* got *this*!" He held up his small brass trumpet, then whipped his prized *kris* from out of his sash. "You carry this, Miss Saskia."

"An honor, sir." I saluted.

Down the steps we marched, Pier at the helm. The corners of my hat stuck out so widely, I had to turn sideways. In the kitchen Cook and the girls gaped at us. I grabbed a copper pot. Then it was out into the yard, under the old oak, and along the stables, Pier blasting noisily on his horn, Catryn stumbling over her long skirt and trying to twirl the stick while I pounded on my pot with my *kris*. How caught up in the moment we were! Maybe I was secretly hoping Titus would hear us and leave his horses to come look.

The Black laundresses paused as they reached to hang up the sheets, craning their necks to gawk. Workers poured from outbuildings, resting their saws and planes to shout and whistle. "Hey, you raggedy-taggers! Are ye lost?" One yelled out, "I think some streetwalkers in Cape Town be missing some outfits!" Johanna came running out of the milking barn and Manassa the Slave Kitchen, guffawing, cheering us on. Gardeners, carpenters, everyone we strutted past—and we did strut—shouted out. How we loved it! I took the lead from Pier, proudly guiding my young brood through the garden and around the house, a mother duck escorting her chicks.

Just as we turned the corner to the front, I spotted him. Titus was in the drive holding a horse hitched to a carriage, and when he saw us, his lips parted in astonishment. I straightened my back and flashed him a regal smile. We marched toward him onto the pebble drive with the utmost dignity, blasting our instruments. That's when we saw them.

On the front *stoep* the Mistress was giving a sendoff to

a woman who, by her grand sweep of gown, looked very important indeed. Her footman was holding open the carriage door. Dressed in the plainest brown satin gowns, the women stared at us—we might have just fallen from the sky, refugees from a distant star. Their jaws dropped so far open you could have stuck buns in them.

I spun on my heels, shouted "Aboooouut turn!" and steered my motley patrol back again, down the yard and into the kitchen past Cook and her girls. We marched upstairs, all the time my heart beating like drums in my chest. We had hardly put down our wigs and instruments when we heard Johanna shout that the Mistress wanted to speak to us in her room. All of us. *Now!*

She stood in front of her writing table gripping a bamboo switch. The children and I assembled before her, still in costume, faces thick with powder. I tore off my beauty spots and spoke fast. "The children are innocent, Mistress. Please, this was all my doing."

"Miss Klaassens, do you realize who that was? Mistress Swellengrebel, the High Governor's wife! My own children and servant, tarted up like cheap street performers, marching in front of us. Let me tell you," she said, her voice strident, "we were not amused!" And threw me a look that would shrivel a turnip. "Saskia, you are a master at upsetting the peace of this household! Our family's good standing at the Cape depends upon the behavior of us all."

Such a caning I got! Not from her—she would not soil her hands with such work—but from Mistress Cingria, who was all too glad to do it. She splintered the bamboo rod across the backs of my hands until it drew blood. "Not the fingers," the Mistress instructed. "I'm not about to ruin my lacemaking investment by bruising her fingers." As if my hands weren't crippled now anyway.

I was given no dinner that night, nor breakfast the next morning. As for the children, they were not allowed to play racquets for two weeks, nor ride their pony, nor go outside at all—none of which they wanted to do anyway in this heat.

The next day, in the *kinder*room, Catryn was in a mood but would not blame me—she was too kind for that. But Pier seemed to forget all our fun and vented his ire from his bed in language too foul to repeat. I was *so* tempted to march into his room and give him a good *klop*. When I finally sat down to work the lace, I could not—my knuckles were numb.

Later, when I passed through the foyer, Jezza strutted from the kitchen, banging her shoulder against mine. "You always showin off," she whispered. "Always tryin to gets the attentions." And rushed off down the gallery. My face burned, as though a viper had bitten it. Trouble was, there was truth in what she said. But I resented her saying it.

That afternoon Johanna and I changed linens in the Master's bedroom. "What hypocrisy, Johanna!" I punched a pillow into its case, then winced with pain. "Other people have fun, don't they? Not Calvinists. Only rules, rules, and no mercy. Never, ever mercy." We pulled a sheet taut, wrapped it tightly around the mattress.

"I don't know, Saski. When I saw the bunch a ye paradin down the yard in that getup, I thought, Lordy, this estate become one huge looney bin, and some residents just got loose." We laughed as we threw the comforter across the bed and smoothed it with our palms. "Made me merry just to see ye. But, oh, Saski, you act so bold sometimes. One day you're gonna get yourself into real trouble."

I stood up straight and pulled a long face. " 'All silliness indulged at one's own risk.' " I threw forward my wounded hands. "So call out the guards and arrest me. Hang me from the rafters and burn me at the stake. Charges preferred: playing dress-up." We giggled as we gathered up the dirty linens. "You know, we Calvinists are like abandoned houses—boarded up, blankets thrown over every urge to whimsy. And for one brief hour, I opened the windows and aired mine out."

Johanna pulled me into the small room adjoining the Master's, a room I'd never been in. She lowered her voice. "Ye know, Saski, the Mistress may have thought you be mockin her. Don't you know not to mock your employers?"

"Well, not to their faces!" We looked around, tittering behind our hands.

Johanna checked the door, then smiled like someone about to reveal a delicious secret. "Didn't ye hear what happen to the Mistress, just afore your little parade trooped by?" she whispered. "The Master being aways, the Mistress went and got all kitted out. Yellow silk gown, lace flounces, ribbons, makeup, everything. She was in the Master's front office when who come callin? The High Governor's wife, and no one expectin her. You and the children musta been upstairs getting kitted out yourselves."

Apparently Johanna had entered the office to announce our illustrious and very Calvinist guest, but the Mistress was caught in the most inappropriate attire. And the path to her bedroom blocked, for Mistress Swellengrebel and her companion were sitting in the foyer, just between the two doors.

"I had to help the Mistress crawl out the side window in her fancy gown, would you believe it? She almost didn't make it through the opening with them wide pannier skirts and whalebone hoops. Well, she tore down the side lawn like a frightened rheebok, around the kitchen, through the garden, running all the way to the east courtyard and through her bedroom window to change into her sedate browns—just so she could come out and greet her guest proper-like." Johanna and I roared as we pulled sheets from the guest bed.

She sat down, her face serious. "Ye know the Mistress may also be skittish from the gossip going around—that the Master sleeps with some slavewoman. Haven't ye noticed that the Housekeeper and her staff of Black women be under the Master's special protection? So our Mistress takes her frustration out on the rest of us. Please, dearie, take caution. What you do affect all of us."

I stood up and leaned against a cupboard, regarding her. My elbow must have hit the latch, for suddenly the door fell open. A cavelike space yawned before us. This was no cupboard—it opened to a short hallway. Johanna and I stepped in cautiously, gaping up over a banister onto a narrow, spiral staircase. What was this? A secret stair to the second floor?

We heard footsteps moving purposefully down the gallery, and that familiar rattle of keys. We shut the door and rushed back to the Master's bedroom, hands fumbling with linens, feigning innocence. Mistress Cingria walked past slowly and stiffly, but didn't stop.

For a long time that hidden stairway haunted me.

~

About a week later, in the afternoon, I was in the kitchen setting trays for the children's tea when I glanced out the top half of the door. Pier was playing near the paddock, flashing his riding stick like a rapier at the Master's hounds. They whimpered. "Pier, let those dogs be!" Then, from way down the yard, I heard a persistent rapping. Four men stumbled out of the vines toward the back gate in tattered, dusty breeches and capes of antelope hide. Red kerchiefs rode high on their necks. One hobbled forward on a rough-hewn crutch. What poor wraiths were these?

One leaned against the gate as if exhausted. And again began rapping, spoons on metal pans. Begging for food is not unusual in this land, and to refuse the hungry is unthinkable. But these beggars looked different. I called out, then hurried to pile a tray with bread, cheese, broken rusks, fruit, and a jug of thin beer, and strolled across the yard to meet them.

Two had skin the color of charred wood. The others looked of mixed blood. I suddenly stopped, for their kerchiefs were not around their necks, but their mouths. I stepped closer, cautiously, seeing now the decaying flesh. Then the stench—loathsome, overly sweet yet sour. My thoughts tumbled about, the tray rattled in my hands. I paused, felt my stomach turn. Forced myself to keep walking toward them.

They offered up their tin pans, and one, an open palm. Some of his fingers had rotted to the knuckles. The oldest peered at me from the shadows of his hood—nostrils and much of his lips were eaten away. Horror filled my heart. I sucked in a breath. His eyes were set deep in his skull and radiated something. My mind swirled. I felt a field of silence. My heart was breaking, as when I'd spotted Effie's missing leg.

Just then the Master's hounds streaked around the corner, barking viciously, saliva streaking from their mouths, crashing against the iron gate. Something whizzed past my ear. Pier was pelting rocks at the lepers. "*Vootsek!* Go on, get out of here, you goddamned lepers! Get your stinking carcasses off my property or I'll horsewhip you!"

Thirteen years old—his property indeed! Workers scurried from barns and stables. Titus stood at the tack room door, then ran forward, thrusting himself between Pier and the men. He pushed a threatening finger into the boy's face. "I would not talk like that, Master Pier. These people, they have the right to the food and the drink just as you and I."

In truth, these lepers should not have been here. It was against Compagnie law for them to roam the countryside begging. But what choice did they have? Life on Robben Island with criminals? Exile to inland caves? Left to battle wild beasts, I'd been told—or starve as they watched their bodies disintegrate, waiting for death. People go crazy when lepers approach. I too felt anxious—leprosy here was dangerous. Contagious.

Titus was calm. I rested the tray on a ledge while he tied up the dogs. I tried to fill the beggars' gourds, but my fingers shook too much. Titus fed them for me. "Here, my brothers. Take the refreshment. Sit in the shade and rest awhile," he said, opening the gate. "There be more food and beer when you have this finished."

They did not enter, glancing cautiously at the dogs, at Pier, pocketed some food, and blessed us before they stumbled back down the fields.

"You worthless monkey face!" Pier yelled at Titus. "You're only a slave! What right have you to invite those diseased animals onto our property! They're lepers, you *kaffir.* And you're nothing but a useless tarboy, a stinking *schepselen*!" This last cut was the worst. *Schepselen.* Creature.

Titus marched to Pier and raised an arm, as if to strike him. My heart stopped. Would he dare? He grabbed Pier by the waistband and thrust him over his shoulders. Pier sputtered and screamed as Titus locked arms around him, sauntered past the winery building, down the broad wall of the barn. The workers and I followed. Titus stopped before the piggery, lifted Pier high over his head, dangled him over the fence—then tossed him in. And calmly walked to where I stood.

From the piggery came a snort, then a beastly shriek. With

dismay, I watched the black sow bare her incisors and charge Pier. He ducked, cursed, and slipped about in the muck. Finally he mounted the fence and fell out, covered head to foot in black pig shit. Workers turned their backs and sniggered.

"Who," I murmured to Titus, "is the tar monkey now?"

Pier staggered to the well, frozen with rage, swatting madly at the muck that coated him—as if it were alive and eating him. He glared around until his eyes fell on me. "Well, bitch, are you going to clean me off, or what?"

"You're on your own this time, little man." I crossed my arms, turned, and marched toward the house. Titus, with a barely seen grin, slipped through the stable door. Sladie, who must have been watching the whole time, muttered to Manassa, "That weren't yust lepers. That were *persons*."

Yes, persons. Behind us old Samuel poured buckets of well water over a shivering Pier.

My Lord, the boy was angry! He had it coming, but I worried about Titus. Later we heard how sorely vexed the de Witts were, and the only thing that saved Titus, Cook told us, was the Master's great need for him and his lack of respect for Pier. Titus did get a lashing, but a mild one. From this moment forward, I believe, the Master started watching Titus.

When the children and I finally settled down in the *kinder*room to have our tea, a newly bathed Pier shouted, "Damn that stupid slave. Damn every Black creature in this damn Black country!"

"Shut up, Pier!" Never before was I so close to thrashing him.

I grabbed Catryn by the arm and pulled her downstairs.

~

That night I sat by sputtering candlelight and opened my journal. So many thoughts rattled about in my head, I had to free them.

Pier is like an ill wind—he unleashes storms everywhere he goes. I must work to change his ways soon, or he will become the death of us.

To make matters worse, now Jezza has told all who will listen that I am lazy. I'm not lazy. They don't usually see me when I work weaving the lace. Except for the lacemaking and a few friends, this isn't the life I dreamed of.

Tonight I thought about my early childhood. There was such good laughter and freedom. And we talked about things, even feelings, at least when Mama was alive.

But later, the hard memories. Grandfather told me girls are worthless encumbrances and that I must live to serve, and be thankful for whatever life hands me. And what life handed me was Stepmother. When others disliked me so, how could I like myself? Self-loathing is like turning over a log only to find creepy little things underneath: vipers, worms, and bones rotting in the moist earth. I was angry at everything then, and it seems anger has followed me to the Cape. It just has new faces.

Sometimes at night I sit at my lace pillow and

think of someone with whom I'm upset. I make the little nooses of thread, picturing their faces on the heads of pins, whip the thread around their necks and tug, cinching the knots tight. And so I execute anyone who galls me, at least in my imagination. Anxiety abates. I feel better, at least for the moment. Then I wonder who has read my evil thoughts. Surely God has.

Sometimes I worry about this dark and vengeful heart. I must work to purify it, for there seems to be a devil inside me. But don't most of us have a devil within?

Then I remember the look in the eyes of that leper. The silence. Silence that wanted nothing from me, that fed me. Eyes so steady, so full, so shining . . . like planets. Dark roads leading into deepest space. Yes, yes, I'm sure of it. In those leprous eyes, God was present.

Chapter 22

DECEMBER 1749 (SUMMER)

Lord it was hot again! One day, after a pelting rain, the sun bore down like a fireball, baking the land and sucking the life out of us. Night after night we were wakened from sleep by the buzzing of that African flea they call *mosquito*—and spent the next two weeks scratching the itchy wounds with our fingernails.

Then fires raged for a month, mostly in the bush, but we were all on edge. For days clouds of pink and yellow smoke filled the sky, spuming ash, making breathing difficult. One fire was too close for comfort. It started in the hills surrounding Stellenbosch, and all the farms for miles around sent slaves and workers to put it out. Rumor was that a servant forgot to extinguish his night candle, and the farmhouse thatch caught flame. Thankfully everyone, and most of the animals, escaped, but by morning all the family's belongings had melted into hot embers, and the buildings were flattened. Wildfires could ruin us all, just as armories could, exploding with magazines of gunpowder.

Despite such terrors, life at the estate could be sweet. New

Year holidays were nigh, and we'd just celebrated everyone's favorite, Sinterklaasfeest. The eve before, Johanna, the Mistress, and I loaded the children's clogs with little toys, napkins of sweet *speculaas* and gingerbread. The de Witts had arranged for a neighbor to dress up in St. Nick's red greatcoat. He rode grandly up our drive on a white horse, a slave on a donkey at his side playing Black Piet. Black Piet chased the "bad" little slavechildren across the yard, frightening them half to death, before he let them escape. I felt Pier the one who needed a scare.

If my respect for Pier was weakening, my fondness for Johanna, Samuel, and Titus was growing. One morning Johanna and I were sitting at the dining table dipping split lemon into salt, rubbing the copper pots to a high polish. Suddenly she tilted her head and pointed to a painting over the console, a fine copy of a Vermeer.

"Now why d'ya think that maid be all dressed up like that, Saski, and asleep at the kitchen table?"

I rested my hands on the samovar. "Vermeer is probably telling a moral tale, as painters often do. Look at her. Not only is that servant wearing all her finery to work, which you know is forbidden, but she's asleep on the job. Could be a poke at lazy, disobedient servants. The family probably put this where we workers are likely to see it. Reminder, I suppose."

"Well crimey—how d'ya like that? As if we don't get enough lecturin. Say, how comes ye knows so much about art?"

"My father is an art and antiquities broker. A family business for generations. Art was all anyone ever talked about in our house. After the Bible, that is."

"Art dealers, ye say?"

I told her how Papa had linked artists with patrons, as had many generations of Klaassens. My forebears had worked with the best painters of their day: Vermeer, Cuypers, Rembrandt, ter Borch. Names she probably wouldn't know. "Papa says the art world is nothing like it was a century ago—no more patrons for young geniuses. It's sad, but in the past few years Papa has hardly made any money at all. He keeps hoping Dutch art will return to its former glory once the economy improves. Seems like nothing is certain or stable in the Netherlands these days."

"Ain't that the truth. Better to be here, at the bottom of nowhere, where things are boomin, than strugglin to make ends meet back home."

Samuel traipsed in, bringing us more tarnished copper.

"Saskia here say the maid in this painting is lazy."

"I seen you sleep sleep at the table yust like that, Miss Johanna, isn't it?" He grinned.

Johanna swatted his arm. "You have not, you old rooster. Well, maybe once."

"Vermeer, you see," I continued, "is also doing something extraordinary with light. See the little white prisms sparkling on the Persian rug on the tabletop?" No response. "I was named after Rembrandt's first wife, you know. Their son was named Titus."

They giggled. "He doan look none like your son, isn't it, Miss Saskia?" My mouth curled into a half smile.

"Rembrandt ended up bankrupt—one of those fools who invested in tulips. He also bought too many old artifacts for props."

"Sold to him by your great-grandfather, were they?" Johanna teased.

I grinned. "Who knows?"

"Ladies, I gots to tell the story about me an paintings." We looked at the old slave, surprised. "When I first be brought this land, everything so new new, isn't it? First time I come the Massa's house, I see mens and womens looking down at me from holes in the walls, not movin, all angry like. Wherever I step, they follows me wit' the eyes. I's so spooked, hairs on my neck crawl crawl. I wonders, what kinda magic, what kinda White man's *tover* do this be? Couldn't wait get outta there, isn't it?" Johanna and I threw back our heads and roared.

Summer evenings came and went. Some could be especially sweet, the sun taking a long time to lie down for the night, a cool breeze moving in. One such evening, Johanna, Samuel, Titus, and I sat relaxing on the grass under our favorite oak. Titus lit his clay pipe. I pulled some crochet work out of my pocket.

"How come you ain't married, Saski?" Johanna suddenly asked. She pushed a stray curl under her cap, popping a date into her mouth. "You musta had mobs of suitors." Titus was leaning against the tree, knees bent, looking out over lilac mountains. I watched him from the corner of my eye, watched his lips blow blue smoke languorously above our heads. I thought his ears might have pricked up.

Truth was, I only seemed to know stern, tightlipped, stuffy Dutchmen. The church turned them out like gingermen from wooden cookie molds. One minute they were piously quoting scripture to you, the next they were into their cups and thrusting fingers down your bodice.

"Maybe one or two. But I didn't care for them. And I didn't have much of a dowry. Men are always looking for a good dowry. A closetful of paintings was all my father had to offer." I sighed, putting down my crochet work. "There was one young man—Dirck van der Velde. He wanted to marry me despite no dowry. He was to inherit a considerable sum of money one day, and a grand house too, along a beautiful canal. Decent enough fellow, but condescending. When I refused him, Papa nearly threw me out of the house. Later, when I told Papa I was going to work for the de Witts, he said, 'You think marriage is slavery, do you? What do you think a life in service is then? A day at the fair?' "

Johanna looked at me hard, her hands flying to her hips. "And he was right. Are ye crazy, Saski, or just pullin this here leg?"

I laughed, again taking up thread and hook. "It's all true. Guess I like my freedom too much. There's no freedom married to that kind of man—or that much money."

"Well *I* wouldn't mind bein bound to pots and pots of gold, let me tell ye. If that be slavery, well, let me have it! Hand over my yoke now!" The men grinned, exchanging glances, while Johanna and I giggled.

Johanna turned to Titus. "What about you, dearie. Think you'll ever marry?"

Titus sucked hard on his pipe, trying to rekindle the embers, looking suddenly awkward. "Marry? Me? I do not think so. You know, Miss Johanna, when the slave marries, it not be like you Whites. No *predikant* to speak the words over you. Even when I'm freed, the marriage will be different." He looked down, brooding it seemed, tearing up handfuls of grass. I felt sad.

"In his village, he woulda been chief like the father, if parents not been taken for the slave, isn't it, Titus?" Samuel was whittling a point on a twig and now picked his few teeth with it. "Probably woulda sailed the ocean wit his tribesmen, visitin foreign places, hostin importan men, not bein slave to them. Woulda had his pick a pretty girls, isn't it, Titus? Woulda had riches." Samuel's voice tapered off into sadness. "If he not been the slave . . ."

I looked at Titus with interest. I knew nothing of this. He shifted uncomfortably, and for a second I thought he would stand up and leave. "What good is there thinking what would have been?" He knocked his pipe against the tree, loosening the old tobacco until it spilled onto the grass. "Fact be, here we are.

None of us be the person of the rank. Anything we be only come through us making it so. It is that way we become strong."

I said nothing. We all sat in silence, watching the first white crust of moon climb over the mountains. Johanna poked Titus with a twig. "Say, do it be true you Africans don't kiss?"

"You mean that thing you Europeans do with your mouths?" He sniffed. "Never do we do this thing."

Johanna and I gawked at him, as if we'd just seen a fish fall out of the tree. Strange creatures, these Africans.

Johanna tapped Samuel's shoulder, a teasing grin on her face. "And you, Samuel? How is it you never wed, you old bachelor?"

All at once our friend looked bereft. He stared into the grass, moisture filling his eyes. "Rather not talks about it, Miss Johanna, you doan mind." He rose on unsteady feet and shuffled off toward the Quarters.

"Oh, dear. What did I say now?"

Titus hesitated. "Don't you know? He *was* married. Snatched from the bush. No chance to say fare-thee-well to the wife, the babes."

Later that night I sat at my casement window and looked up at the night sky. I thought of Oom Samuel—how he would never see his family again. What if I hadn't been allowed to say goodbye to Papa? If I'd just disappeared into the ethers? If Titus's parents had not been captured, he would now be a young warrior in Mosambiek. We would never have met. I took out my journal.

Perhaps I should have married Dirck and borne his condescension along with his children. I would have had security, social standing. Am I better off now? For all my hard work, maids are not respected. I chose my freedom over marriage. But what kind of freedom?

Women are not taken seriously in our country. Men say we're foggy-headed, vain, and frivolous creatures. I say, give us education and responsibility and we'll show what we can do. But even when we excel at an art, men don't want us to be more than accomplished amateurs. They want us as pretty ornaments, not creative rivals.

I hear of societies in the world where women are strong and their opinions heeded. At the French court, women already have an important voice in the political affairs of the nation, and so of the world. Even in Africa there are tribes where women set down the law. Not White women at the Cape. We're only valued here because we are scarce.

Whether maid or aristocrat, we are never expected to contribute anything of greatness. It's the same with the slaves. Titus longs to make his mark on the world, as do I. He works so hard to master his many skills. And he's garnered much respect. But for us to expect greater lives is, well, fantasy.

I think about Titus's energy, how large it is. I've heard him snap with impatience at stupid workers. But his vexation is clean—it expends itself quickly, like the blast of a pistol, then is gone. My own vexation is another matter. I often hide it inside, let it fester and seethe. Then it bursts through the seams that were supposed to hold it in, and explodes on people. I wish I could be more like Titus.

But in important ways Titus and I are alike. We hate hypocrisy and those who disdain skin a different color than their own. He has helped me decry the enslavement of any human anywhere, and we both decry the enslavement of women to men everywhere. In town we've seen men mount the sidewalk crates and rail against slavery. Then watched the guards carry the poor reformer off.

By moon's light I gazed out over the frozen ocean of mountains. They looked menacing tonight, like a great walled city. I once felt they protected me. Now they hemmed me in.

Even in this tiny backwater at the bottom of the world, I feel the same stirrings of revolt of which Mr. Steenoven spoke. The hushed excitement when the slaves hear of others trying to escape, though most attempts fail. Like Josiah's at our feast from Java. Still, some keep the flame of hope alive, flickering though it be. A few owners are as naïve as the Master, telling themselves that their human possessions are content, loyal, even grateful. But I wouldn't be surprised if revolution isn't taking shape right now, in this very land.

A few days later Titus said something that made me feel I might just be right.

Every few months, several of us had the wonder of a day

off that fell on the same day. Thursday was such a day, and the wagon into Cape Town was packed. Titus drove, and I made an excuse to sit up front with him. Johanna and Jaco, Anna and Josiah rode in the back. We girls were decked out in our crisp red holiday bodices, the men sporting clean shirts and kerchiefs. The moment we were out of sight of Rustigvallei, Johanna coyly lifted the hems of her petticoats and pulled out two small casks of beer. Everyone cheered. The clever girl had smuggled them from the cellar, tying them from her waist where they banged her knees but eluded detection.

Anna objected, of course, saying we were all going to hell. But we cajoled her, and when Jaco spoke sweet words in her ear, she gave in. Now the crew poured cup after cup for one another. Beer spilled freely onto the wagon boards as they bantered, sang, and drank. It spilled over breeches and skirts as they toasted each other, toasted the birds in the trees, the clouds in the sky, anything. As for Titus and me, they paid us no heed. We'd only had one drink each. We were boring.

Titus turned to me. "It seem the slave owner, he control his slave, does he not?" He flashed me a mischievous smile.

I was wary. "Well . . . yes."

"Do the owner not be bound in need to the slave as much as the slave be bound to him?" I nodded, not sure I liked where this was going. "Then who has the power, slave or master? The slave lives with the rebellion, and in his gut the Master this he knows. Know that fury burns like hot oil in the slave. And the fear and the guilt, they burn the holes in his own White soul. He know one day the slave, he may burn down the house, or poison the irrigation furrows, or powder with glass the soup he eats."

I looked at him intently. Sometimes he was such a chameleon—eyes red with passion or black with rage. "Titus, stop talking like that. Gives me the creeps to think of such a thing." Johanna and Jaco were roaring with laughter behind us. I glanced around to see if they'd heard. "Sometimes you scare me, you know? How hot your blood is! But surely you'd never harm the de Witts." When he was silent I stared at him. "You wouldn't, would you?"

His eyebrow arched with cunning. "Perhaps you do not know me."

"What does that mean?"

He loosened the reins from where they caught in the harnesses. "It mean nothing, Miss Saskia. Forget it. Perhaps I like to tease."

We rode along in silence for some time. The party behind us started to quiet down, some nodding off. I felt off balance. Titus was right about one thing. Hatred binds us to those we despise as surely as caring does to those we love. Threads around lace pins. Either way, we are bound.

"What will you do when you are freed?"

The sun was hot and high in the sky now. Sweat ran down Titus's neck and stained his shirt. "I have thought much about that thing. Perhaps I will go to the place of my ancestors, Mosambiek, though there still be the danger of capture there. The Master, he has asked me to stay at Rustigvallei, paying me the wage. I have also thought to work for Master Houtman near Paarl. He has seen me with the horses, and offered me to train his. I like him and his Arabians. I think it is this last thing I do."

I felt sad. If Titus leaves, I suddenly realized, Rustigvallei will hold little for me. "What is it about horses that you love so much?"

"*Ach*, they have so much the dignity. Curiosity. They listen to you. They speak to you, if you take the time to learn that. They speak with the tilt of the head, the movement of the ear, with the snort or the stomp or the swish of the tail. If you learn their language, if they trust you, they do what you ask. The horses, they be noble. Spirited. I love the spirit of the wild thing."

We passed a marshy river. A flurry of waterfowl suddenly flew out of the thicket, startling us. There was a subtle shift in Titus's mood. "You know, Miss Saskia, never before have I the talk with the woman the way we talk. Never spoken out of this heart."

I drew my breath in deeply and smiled. His words felt intimate—a slip worn next to the skin. I wanted to touch him lightly on the arm, but burrowed my hands deep into my lap instead. For the rest of the trip we rode in easy silence. For some time afterward, I pondered what he'd said.

Late in the afternoon, toward the end of my lesson, I was packing up my lace things when Effie and I heard a knock at the door. I jumped to greet Titus. But the man who stood before me was a gentleman. Adriaan de Witt bowed, tricorn hat in hand, his smile as wide as the sea. "I'll wager you're surprised to see me here, Miss Klaassens."

I stared at him, confused, then pleased. I gave a slight curtsy. "Come in, sir."

In the sitting room I introduced Adriaan and Effie. I was still in wonderment, unable to grasp his world and mine converging here. "Won't you sit down, *mynheer*?" Effie asked.

"No thank you, Mistress." He turned to me. "I heard you were in town, Miss Klaassens, and, with some sleuthing, found out where exactly." My eyes sparkled, pleased with his cleverness. "I wanted to know if you'd like a ride back to Rustigvallei. I'm headed there myself and have a carriage waiting. I thought it might be a more pleasant trip than by ox wagon."

There was a confident knock on the door, a song of greeting, and Titus entered. When he saw the Master's nephew, he started, bowed, then stepped back against the wall. Adriaan barely glanced his way. But that is how gentlemen treat slaves. My fingers must have been fluttering. With whom should I ride? Effie seemed to sense my predicament. "Would you care for some tea, *mynheer*?"

"No, no thank you," he said coolly, and strutted toward the window. When his eyes settled on the *hindoo* statue of Shiva and the elephant god, he seemed to stiffen. *Hurry up, Saskia. Make up your mind.*

"Titus, Master de Witt has very kindly offered to take me back to Rustigvallei in his carriage." For just a moment, something passed almost imperceptibly over Titus's face, a look like a shamed dog. "I'm sorry you walked all this way for nothing." He grunted, nodded to Effie, and started for the door. At the threshold he paused, shot me a sullen look, then at Adriaan's back.

As our carriage rumbled through town, Adriaan was lighthearted. He leaned forward every now and then to touch me briefly on the arm. I laughed as he regaled me with story after story about card gambling with elders of the Compagnie, stories he commanded me to keep absolutely secret from his uncle. He told me ironic tales of dealings with his servants and slaves, whom he portrayed with such humor—what fools they all seemed!

Our carriage rumbled around Sugar Loaf, the sun slanted low over the ocean, and the buildings of Cape Town became faint toys asleep in the lap of the mountain. After about an hour, I fell quiet. All this talk about parties and the trials of the upper class was beginning to wear. My polite laughs came fewer and farther between, my mouth tired from smiles. Seeming to sense my withdrawal, Adriaan told tales even more bizarre—months he'd spent living with the San Bushmen in the Karoo desert, whale fishing at the tip of South America. Were these stories even true? I shrank back in my seat, remembering what Titus and I had shared.

"You seem to spend much time with slaves and mulattos, Miss Klaassens." An amused smirk.

"Yes, Mr. de Witt, I do. I'm much thrown into their company." *Much thrown into their company?* What fine words! Who did I think I was?

He asked if I enjoyed that company, and I hedged. "Sometimes." I fiddled with the ribbons on my bodice, feeling uneasy. Surely he could not approve of such constant associations. Surely he was testing me. *Look at you, Saskia, betraying your dearest friendships before this person of high birth.* Something suddenly flipped inside, a gear I'd forgotten. I would play with this fellow a little. Flush him out too.

"I'm getting to know Effie Huyskens very well." I leaned forward, a gleam in my eye. "She's one of the most amazing women I've ever known, so wise, so pure of heart. You know the old slave Samuel? Well he's a dear, and I love him to death. And Titus and I have wonderfully deep discussions on our travels into town."

"The Black boy at the house?" Almost imperceptibly Adriaan's back arched. "Do you indeed."

"Titus is quite intelligent, you know. Do you read literature, Master de Witt?"

"Not if I can help it."

"I borrow books from our neighbor and lend them to him."

"Your slave friend reads? I heartily disapprove. Surely he can't read well."

"Quite well. Sometimes we discuss books Madame Remy lends us."

He had pulled out his snuffbox. Now his hand froze in its movement toward his nose. "Do you mean the *Papist*?" So he too used that word.

"Yes, Roman Catholic. Another incredible woman I'm proud to call friend. Mentor, even. Along with Effie Huyskens."

Outside, the high mountains shimmered in the heat of twilight. Across the distant veldt, the wind was tunneling into the dry red dust of summer, swirling the sandy earth into mighty dust-devils. "Well, well. Papists. Slaves. Mulattos. You *do* keep interesting company, Miss Klaassens."

He sniffed at the white powder in his fingers. Oh dear. His new puppy runs with a pack of strays—in his eyes, rabid strays. Why, Adriaan de Witt was even more of a snob than his uncle. At least the Master showed respect for Titus. Something that had been hopeful in me, some bright flower of affection that had been budding for this *gallant*, now shriveled. But I couldn't completely squelch my grin.

We traveled the rest of the miles in tense silence. Oh, why hadn't I chosen to journey home with the others? Vanity had blinded me. When we finally arrived at the estate, I thanked him courteously, then ran to find my friends.

Chapter 23

JANUARY 1750 (SUMMER)

How excited I was! For after our lesson today, Effie packed a bag and rode with us in the wagon back to the estate. Goodness knows she'd heard enough about Rustigvallei from my chattering about it, but this would be her first time to see it for herself. Titus and I had cooked up the idea, and I'd petitioned the Mistress. She not only granted permission, she suggested—to my utter delight—that Effie spend a few nights.

I fairly glowed as our wagon rumbled around Table Mountain. What an honor it was having Effie with us, what a pleasure to acquaint this woman I loved so much to my other life. But I also worried how those at the estate would receive her. Effie was a freewoman of color who owned a house and even had a profession of sorts. To many, she was a curious bird indeed.

The children and staff were in the kitchen when we arrived. Pier gave Effie a peremptory nod, then ran off to play by the river with the slavechildren, but Catryn followed wherever Effie's crutches went, even upstairs to my room, a place I gave her for the duration of her stay. Effie insisted she could manage the steps, but I followed close behind in case she fell. She did fine.

Aunt Effie seemed interested in everything here, especially the odd treasures in my room—the Rembrandt etching, the embroidered blue *chinees* curtain, the worn Persian rug, the coffins I used as window seats—and, sitting on my lace pillow, my first few inches of Bruges flower lace. She eased down at my table, pulled out her own lace pillow and taught Catryn a few lacemaking weaves. I used the moment to take some sleep things over to the cottage, for I would be staying with Anna and Johanna.

Titus too was pleased as punch to have Effie here. At supper he led us down the yard to the long trestle table under the oaks where we joined the others. A warm breeze flowed down from the hills, holding us in its palm. Titus tried to seat Effie at the head of the table, but she demurred, settling between Titus and me.

Jezza was clearly turning a strange shade of envy—that's the only way I can put it. "I don't see what all the fuss be over one crippled old mulatto," she murmured a little too loudly.

A hush fell over the table. Effie remained very still. I was about to leap to my feet, take the girl by the shoulders, and shake her good. How dare she talk like that—and she herself a mulatto!

"Jezza," Titus barked, "you seem to be ignorant of the fact that some people truly be your betters. Apologize to Mistress Huyskens." The slavegirl scowled, muttered "Sorry!" as if unduly put out, and strutted off.

After the meal, Titus set out chairs by the camphor tree for Effie and Cook, while Johanna, Samuel and I climbed into the toe-like roots. We lit our clay pipes, enjoying the fragrant smoke that floated about our heads like summer clouds. A feeling of warmth and belonging expanded into the night air, holding us in deep contentment.

When Titus was free the next morning, he lifted Effie into a donkey cart and drove her about the grounds, Catryn in the back. Later I took Catryn by the hand, finally coaxing her away from Effie with the promise of a slice of milktart, so that Effie could visit with Titus while he groomed the horses.

In the afternoon Effie was at the kitchen table helping me prepare a tray for the children. She had just arranged an orchid blossom in a small porcelain vase when the Master sauntered in from the hall. "Who are *you*, then?" he said, staring at her rudely. "Bring me a beaker of beer, and bread and cheese too—to my study now, if you please."

I scurried forward. "*Mynheer*, this is not a servant. This is Mistress Huyskens, my lace teacher. She's visiting for a few days." Effie half lifted herself from the bench and, arms braced on the table, curtsied the best she could.

For a second, the Master looked abashed. "Oh. Then *you* bring a tray to my office, Miss Klaassens." And marched off. I clenched a fist. Show her some respect!

Most of the day I had to work stripping beds, but Effie and I squeezed in some private time midafternoon, working the lace together. We climbed down to my lacemaking spot in the cellar, escaping the heat. We talked of many things, but I was particularly grateful when she suggested ways I could use my lace skills to make money in coming years, and thus wean myself from life as a servant.

That night at supper, Jezza ate in the Quarters while the rest of us dined outdoors again in warm camaraderie. After supper, gathering up the dishes, I watched Effie sit quietly under the trees, lace pillow on her knee, working her signature brown lace. Several female workers drifted to her side, watching her palm the bobbins. Manassa came, then Black Lucy, and Johanna. Even Jaco sat on the grass and talked to her. I watched them in snatches from the window as I dried dishes. Effie was listening to them long and well before she spoke. I could not hear what they said, but invariably my friends would nod gravely, or smile. I knew she was offering good counsel. Effie's presence here seemed to have a grounding effect on us all.

So I shouldn't have been surprised when Mistress de Witt, on the last day of Effie's visit, invited her to her room for tea. The Mistress had asked me to prepare a tray of the best porcelain cups, to fill the *japanees* teapot with our special Darjeeling, and arrange a plate of cakes. Entering with the tray, I found the Mistress had blanketed her bed with mounds of lace. In all my life, I've never seen such a wealth of it! The Mistress stood next to Effie, asking her which pieces were the best and how much she thought they were worth. Effie leaned over crutches, helping sort sleeve ruffles, cravats, caps, curtains, and shawls into piles, telling the Mistress which dealer in Cape Town would buy them at fair price, telling her it was worth more here than in Europe, as so little was available. Effie counseled the Mistress to wrap the lace in tissue, and which pieces to keep as insurance against hard times.

To my delight, the Mistress asked me to fetch my lacemaking things and join them. When I returned, she was pouring Effie a cup of tea, asking her the proper thing to do when slaves insisted on burying their own. She listened attentively and nodded as Effie explained that Africans have strong taboos surrounding death and burial, and that the Dutch, when at all possible, would do well to respect their rituals.

The Mistress cast me a sly look. "Let me tell you, Mistress Huyskens, of the day Saskia played dress-up with the children." I couldn't believe my ears! She began to tell the story of the surprise visit by the High Governor's wife and how she had to run around the house and climb in and out of windows in pannier skirts. And how our troupe of costumed players nearly gave her guest a heart attack. Effie laughed from the tips of her toes, and by the time the Mistress had finished, tears of laughter were running down both their faces. I rolled my eyes. Events that had brought me punishment were now an inside joke.

"What a romp, Mistress de Witt," Effie said. "A story to savor and share. I'll wager the children had a great time dressing up." I turned away, hiding my crooked grin. "Although our dear Saskia here," she added, "occasionally enjoys making a spectacle of herself. Don't you, my dear?" *Touché!*

Effie's grasped a piece of lace from the bed, splaying the scarf over her arm. "Why, this looks like something Saskia might have woven."

Indeed! It was the very *fichu* scarf the Mistress had "appropriated" the day she caught me making lace. Now she looked flustered. "Saskia did make this. She loaned it to me some time ago, and I've been meaning to return it." Mistress de Witt folded the *fichu* gently and placed it on the chair next to me. "Here you are, Saskia dear. Thank you."

You could have knocked me over with an ostrich feather.

Effie rose. "Now I must take my afternoon nap, Mistress. Feeling my age, I'm afraid."

"You're not old, Mistress Huyskens."

"Oh, yes I am. I'm continually stumbling over little pieces of myself. I put them in a drawer, thinking one day I'll try to glue them back on again."

There was a moment of silence. Effie giggled, then the Mistress and I too.

"I'll be returning early tomorrow, Mistress de Witt. Thank you from the bottom of my heart for your family's kind hospitality."

"I'm sending you home with a cask of our best Rustigvallei

red," the Mistress said. "And a second cask for your slaves."

Effie paused. "I thank you humbly, Mistress. I will gladly accept a cask, but not a second, for I have no slaves." She paused, then held my mistress with an even gaze. "With all respect, *mevrouw*, even if I could afford slaves, I would not have them." Silence. The Mistress looked at her in wonder, then away. "I'm afraid I've tired you out, Mistress de Witt." I took my cue, grabbed my things, and curtsied out of the room.

"On the contrary, my dear Mistress Huyskens. You've helped me in ways you cannot know."

From the hall I heard the Mistress ask Effie if she might visit her in Cape Town some day. Effie replied that she had only a humble cottage in the infamous Bo-Kaap, but she would be honored to receive her any time.

~

It was the dead of night when a persistent clang of the alarm startled us out of sleep. Was there fire? Johanna sprang out of bed, ripped the blanket from me, and ran outside. I rummaged for my clogs while Anna grabbed our shawls. The cold night slammed into us like a wall. By moonlight we could just glimpse a man slip out of the barn and run for the groves. Cook, in nightdress, was yanking at the bell rope like there was no tomorrow. Slaves poured from the Quarters, Titus among them. Workers gathered. Half-dressed, the Master emerged from the house, yelling at Cook to stop.

"I tell you, *mynheer*," Cook said, "I seen someone trying to steal a slavechild. Or so it seem."

The Master stared at her. "Who did you see? Where? How many?"

"Just the one, sir."

He took out his handkerchief, and though the air was cold, mopped his brow. As groggy from sleep as I was, something didn't make sense. I pointed toward the barn, and was about to speak of the man we'd seen when something stern in Cook's eyes made me check myself. I glanced up to my room. Effie stood there in the window, looking down.

"I tell ye, a noise musta woke me. When I looked out the window, I seen a man come outta the Quarters carryin little Eli." Cook's voice was strong with defiance. "I know ye don't want no one messin with yer slaves, sir. So I ran out and rung the bell."

"Where did the thief go?" Anthonij demanded.

"Over theres somewhere," she murmured, pointing toward the cow barn.

Titus, Anthonij, and Josiah raced down the yard. A minute later Anthonij held Eli aloft by the waistband—as if he were the criminal. The Master paced in circles, dabbing at his forehead. He looked strange.

"Are you all right, boy?" Cook called. "Anyone harm ye?"

Eli looked at the ground in shame, tucking in his shirt. His small body was trembling. Manassa tripped through the crowd, took her son in her arms, and held him close.

"All right, all right, everyone go back to bed," the Master shouted.

Mr. Pesser glared from the Master to the boy, then away. He was strangely silent, his mouth working. Why wasn't anyone going after the thief? A sick feeling stole over me.

"*Mynheer*," I finally said, "Anna and I saw a White man run into the groves."

"Well it's too late to catch him now, isn't it?" he shouted. "The boy is safe. No one has been harmed. Now everyone, go back to bed."

The Mistress stood stiffly on the *stoep*, her arms around Catryn and Pier. Mistress Cingria watched from behind, clenching her keys. "Nothing to distress yourself about, Annetje," the Master said, strolling to his wife's side. He patted her back as if to soothe her, but she was already calm. "Someone may have tried to steal Eli. But he's all right. Everything's all right now. All of you, go back to bed!" At the window Effie looked down, still as a statue.

"Take him into the house," the Mistress instructed Manassa. "You can sleep with Eli tonight, in the room off mine," she said. "Philippe, aren't you sending anyone out to find this man?"

"I can go, *mynheer*," Titus said, stepping forward. "I will take the men and flush him out."

"A bloody waste of time," the Master shouted. "The man's long gone. It's over. For God's sake, everyone just go back to bed!" And he stormed into the house.

I turned to Cook. She was leaning against the belltower, still holding the rope, brow set in a strangely knowing look. Titus was watching her too. He seemed to be thanking her with his eyes.

Back in the cottage, Anna sat on the edge of her bed. "Why didn't the Master send the men out after the thief?"

Why indeed. The scene tonight suddenly felt familiar. "Because the Master was complicit, Anna. Mr. Pesser too, perhaps against his will." I whispered now, for Cook was in the next room. "That has to be it. Cook saw them kidnapping Eli. And stopped the worst of it."

"The worst of what?"

Johanna crawled into bed. "Anna, figure it out for yerself. And once ye do, forget it."

I lay in bed for a long time, thinking about what had happened. I must have witnessed the same thing several months ago but hadn't understood it then—the Master helping some friend of his steal Eli from the Quarters. To take to the barn for some depraved use. I bet Cook saw the whole thing—and when the Master returned to the house, she dashed outside and rang the alarm. Exposed their little intrigue, she had—without exposing the Master. What a blackguard the Master is! Poor Eli. I decided to be extra kind to him.

For a long time I couldn't sleep, sure the man was still on the property, hiding among the vines. Finally—stealthy footsteps padding across the yard from the groves, the creaking of stable doors. I ran outside only to see the last of a man galloping down the lane. We'd probably never learn who he was. He'd probably get away with it again. High-powered men always do. But not at this estate.

In the early hours of the morning, after little sleep, I rose to see off Effie. I kissed her cheeks, Titus packed her into the wagon, and Jaco mounted the driver's seat. I watched them disappear through the line of oaks that stood blue in the morning light, wondering how much of the story she had witnessed, or heard, or guessed. Knowing Effie, she'd understood it all.

Later I praised Cook for her bravery. She said she must owe it to Effie. That talking to the widow the past few days had somehow inspired in her an uncommon courage—not to mention a wise sort of cunning.

Chapter 24

JANUARY 1750 (SUMMER)

The evening was sticky from recent rains, and my room stifling, so around eight o'clock I stepped outside to breathe in some coolness. Cook was sitting alone under the camphors in Samuel's old rattan chair munching melons and quinces. She motioned me to pull up a chair. Most everyone had retired for the night. Only a couple of slaves lingered in the yard, returning from their river baths.

Cook made it her business to know everything about everyone at the manor, and tonight, to my surprise, she began talking about our employers. I was all ears. Apparently the Master was a man of secrets, one rumor being he bedded some unknown woman—and now this last despicable act. Of those I didn't dare ask. But perhaps Cook would tell me why the de Witts decided to leave the homeland.

"Seems everyone at this outpost is running from something or other, don't it? What you running from, Saskia?" I hesitated, silent under her knowing smile, then relieved when she laughed and talked on. "Master de Witt, you see, hadn't much money, not for his style of life, though he come from one of them really important families back home." Cook leaned so far back, I worried the spindly chair would break beneath her. "I thinks his grandfather were Governor of most of the provinces, or something like that. But there was political trouble."

She set her plate of melon rinds on the grass, pressed tobacco into her pipe, then pulled another from her pocket, offering it to me. In respect to this deepening friendship, I took it. Would she notice I hadn't yet learned how to inhale?

She struck a flint. "It was the year known as *Rampjaar*—Year of Disaster. Seems that this same grandfather, Johan de Witt, and the grandfather's brother be accused of hatchin some plot or other against the prince. One brother were put in prison, tortured and everything, but wouldn't confess." She smacked her lips, relishing this. "When his brother Johan came to visit, the guards were mysteriously sent away. The brothers were set upon by an angry mob. Murdered em both, that mob did—in cold blood. Lynched and cut into pieces." Cook leaned toward me, lowering her voice. "Rumor was, parts of em were *eaten* by that mob."

"Good Lord! And they call the natives *here* barbaric." I gave Cook a wry look. "I suppose that's as close as most of them ever got to being part of the upper class."

Cook stared at me, then howled. "Not a stew *I'd* like to brew. Some says the mob be put up to it by the prince and his henchmen. So, even though that be years and years ago, it's like the Master gots this history hangin over his head. Maybe there be some family shame. Maybe thinks he got something to prove out here."

Goodness, this was juicy stuff! I'd never heard any of it. Papa might have known something though, because he'd looked startled when I told him the name of my new employers. Yet he said nothing.

"The Master, he be married once before." This too I'd never heard. "*Ja.* Her and the babe both die in childbed, they did. Sad. Then he marry the Mistress and have Pier and Catryn."

"Cook, why do you think Pier is so difficult?"

"I dunno. The Master, he subscribe to some funny ideas. You know, don't let the son take away your authority or some such nonsense. Hear he used the switch on the poor lad afore he barely be out of the crib." We shook our heads. "They says the Master married money before too, but it be less than he thought and was gone quick enough. Our Mistress be much wealthier."

"I *wondered* if the Mistress had money of her own." Once when I was serving afternoon coffee to them, the Mistress snapped at the Master, insisting she'd purchased a certain gown with her own money, so he had nothing to complain about.

"Born into wealth she were. Old patrician money. Landowners. Used to havin nice things. Our mistress do like her silk gowns and ornaments, don't she? Only the best for m'lady, mind you. Real pearls, furs, lace. You seen it too, Saskia.

"Only the good Lord know how much that must irk the poor Master, bein the strict Calvinistic he is, careful with every stuiver. But it be her money." Cook lifted her thick legs onto a root of the camphor, letting her shoes drop, undoing the worn ribbons holding up her stockings. "That's better," she sighed.

"Course everyone at Rustigvallei know what happens when he go away, her dressin up and all. That be the best time to ask her for somethin, after she's all fancied up. After Black Lucy is done dressing her hair and powdering it, that's when she's in the best of moods. 'Goodness, milady, don't ye look smart.' That's what ye say. Once the Master come home unexpected and give her bloody hell for it, though he do lets her get away with it from time to time, mind you—that and the amber liquid in the decanter. And he should, cause he gots his own little secrets, he do. We all knows that." Cook shot me a look loaded with meaning.

I looked up at the sky. The stars were out. They glowed like fireflies flickering over the night veldt and a light breeze made the leaves above us tremble. "I think the Mistress displays great wit at times," I offered.

"Deed she do, deed she do. One day she told me to prepare a special meal for some guests. Said she didn't much like one of em—that he look so slippery, 'twas if God had taken him at birth and dipped him in olive oil."

A laugh burst from my throat. "Serving at dinner once, I overheard them talk about Louis XV. The Mistress said: 'The French court can be a dangerous place, sir. Humans sacrificed daily on the altar of wit.' Later, one of the guests had praised her, saying she was as refreshing as a jar of cherries. She'd beamed, replying, 'And twice as marinated!' Her guests laughed at that."

I leaned back, reflecting. The Master didn't seem to appreciate her humor, nor sensibilities, for that matter. Her drinking embarrassed him, and sometimes he spoke to her with contempt. Perhaps she drank because she simply could not abide the coarseness of life here. Or, if she knew, her husband's betrayal. She was like a piece of delicate porcelain, but bisqueware—decorated with glaze but not yet fired into strength and resiliency. In another land with another husband, the Mistress might have blossomed into her best self. An elegant feather in a more feeling man's hat.

Cook knocked pipe ashes to the grass. "A lady in her situation won't likely take it sittin down for long, mark my words. Women like her can take only so much afore they get sick or go mad or rebel. Why do ye think the Mistress brought you out here as Nursemaid, girl? Yust to get Mistress Cingria's goat, I thinks."

I stared at Cook. Oh, that explained so much! If my presence was an affront to the Housekeeper, she had to resent me—and keep me down. Had I been nothing but a pawn in a power play between these women? Suddenly I felt as heavy as a bucket of tar.

I trudged up to my room, and as I unlaced my bodice, felt a flood of sadness. I pulled out my writing kit.

So many secrets! Secrets will make you ill, Mama used to say. Beneath the tension, a raw underbelly of hidden things. But then I have my own secret.

The sailor Claus and I had been such good friends. Maybe I was infatuated. Perhaps that's why his betrayal hurt so much. He seemed so sensitive—had me read poetry to him while he swabbed the deck. Once I shouted out half a book of Shakespearean sonnets to him, the hems of my skirts trailing behind in wash water. It was he who took up a collection for the Jewess Rechel Haas when she lost her son overboard. He'd even rescued me from a sailor who cornered me in the hall and jerked his knife up and down in obscene motions. What a kind soul, I thought. Then came the night Mistress Haas, distraught, threw herself into the sea. I was shattered, for she'd become a friend. I hid in a closet of nets to grieve, but Claus found me. He was drunk. He wouldn't listen to my protests, didn't care that I fought him tooth and nail. Was it all my fault? Did my friendliness only lead him on?

I could write no more. If only one could sever the nerve connecting us to hard memories.

The buzz of mosquitoes! Legions could keep me awake with buzzing and biting. I slammed the shutters shut.

Once again I picked up my quill.

Effie says we know when someone judges us, and it's a rare person who can remain herself before it. I need to forgive the Mistress. She's an exotic bird brought to a distant land, requiring a special kind of air not available here. She simply cannot breathe.

Not being able to breathe is something I understand. Sometimes the tension at the estate feels as thick as the humidity, and just as heavy with oppression. At Rustigvallei one cannot escape being judged. It's only when I ride into Cape Town that I seem to be able to breathe as I talk and laugh with Titus, Johanna, and Samuel. Or when I'm with Aunt Effie or Madame Remy. Or when I work the bobbins alone in my attic.

My head kept nodding. I awakened to find my cheek fallen on the journal. Bleary-eyed, I corked the inkwell. It was done, then. The thoughts too difficult to hold were now part of the page. I stumbled to bed, falling in without fully undressing, a soft, unnamed anxiety swirling close, pervading my being.

~

The next evening, as I loaded up my bowl with stew, Cook clapped a hand on my arm. "Ye be servin supper to the family tonight, dearie," she said, pointing to our best *amari* platters. "The good Dr. Buehl, he be joinin us. Manassa be with her Eli, who gots a cough. So eat fast, missy, then tidy that cap. I been cookin all day and don't want no hairs fallin into my *bobotie*."

I grumbled under my breath. I'd been looking forward to spending time with my friends at supper. In fact, I'd just persuaded Titus to let me sketch his portrait. No chance now.

"Mistress Cingria not be joinin em." Cook turned away, adding with a faint sigh, "And probably won't be again."

What? More tension between her and the Mistress?

The good doctor arrived, looked in on Eli, then joined the Master in the cool of the *stoep* where they sipped portwine and smoked while Johanna and I dressed the dining table. When dinner was announced, Mistress de Witt glided down the gallery, happy and daringly festive in her new sacque-back robe. Fountains of lace, a great cinch of satin trailing behind. Diamonds and pearls. Master de Witt followed Dr. Buehl to the table, who limped in on a stinkwood cane.

"I know it's my overindulging," he told the Master. "Too much good meat and wine." He laughed. "Can't seem to give it up, even when it causes such trouble."

"My good man," the Master said, "who *can* give up those wonderful things?"

Generously said, I thought, for a man who made a high art of self-discipline. In truth the Master's disdain for the doctor's gout and careless dress was barely veiled. To me, Dr. Buehl was like someone's dear and slightly absent-minded uncle. Many was the time I'd seen him stumble painfully up the front steps of the manor to attend the Mistress in her lapses. Black Lucy told me he often requested a large tray of food and portwine after examining and treating the Mistress for "nerves." Then he'd stumble into the backyard until the slavechildren caught sight of him. He'd reach into that charred pocket and pull out sweetmeats and coins for them all. They adored him.

The Master spoke of crops and the marketing of wine. I stood erect before the console. Dr. Buehl smiled and gave a slight nod my way—not many guests would acknowledge a servant so. Pier swaggered in, bored and fidgety in a velvet suit, then Catryn in a blue satin dress with tight red sash, her mother in miniature.

"You'll never be able to eat in that," Pier grumbled. "You look ridiculous."

She squirmed. "Oh, shut up, Pier."

"Children!" the Master snapped. "We have a guest. Put on your manners, or you can eat outside with the laborers."

Master de Witt carved the roast antelope while Dr. Buehl lent an attentive ear to both the Mistress and children. She related, between gulps of wine, a long tale of how she was finally able to obtain the gown she now wore from a firm in Paris, a gown identical to one owned by a celebrated mistress of the French king. The Master flushed crimson, apologizing for the tough meat.

"My dears," the doctor announced, "the *rheebok* is divine. And the *bobotie* a triumph, a culinary triumph! Compliments to Cook."

"A rather common supper, Doctor," the Mistress demurred. "Now, if we'd served you peacock or suckling pig . . ."

"I prefer this stew, Mistress de Witt." He motioned me for more. Throughout the dinner, I watched him also consume quantities of turtle soup, guinea fowl, stewed cauliflower, beets, milktart, and jeranum pudding, all washed down with the Master's best red. When the Mistress started talking about her noble family in the Netherlands, the Master interrupted.

"My friend, have you heard about that Huguenot group in Franschhoek that came up with some newfangled device for sorting grapes? I admire inventive minds. Speaking of which—you know my boy Titus? The blackie from Mosambiek?" Pier frowned.

"You mean your Stable Master?" With his napkin, Dr. Buehl took swipes at soup dripping from his cravat. "Good man."

"Yes, indeed." The Master pulled gristle from his mouth. "About a month ago I asked the boy to my office. The field manager and I were wondering how in thunder we were going to irrigate the new vines we hope to plant up the foothills. I'd just purchased a couple of new varietals from a Franschhoek grower, you see, but had no more land. No one's been able to irrigate vines with much success before on such high slopes. Well, damned if that boy Titus didn't come back the next day with an irrigation plan, and a fantastic one. Said he talked to the Malays, asked how they laid out the crops on hillsides in their country. In terraces, it seems. Titus came up with a scheme that would pump water through furrows from the river by waterwheel and mule power. Brilliant, absolutely brilliant. Even my field manager was impressed."

I leaned down to offer Pier a platter of fruit, and saw his eyelid spasm. He shoved the platter away.

"I'll tell you how clever that boy is, Buehl," the Master continued. "I was having a problem with a horse last fall. New Arabian, beautiful animal, a real athlete, but not yet broken, too spirited. Damned if any of the men could tame it, even Titus. But he had an idea. Maybe the horse would respond to being handled by only one groom. Curried by that groom, fed by him, walked—just one man it could come to trust. I told him to give it a try. Damned if he wasn't saddling and riding the bloody thing in less than three weeks. Now he's one of my best racers. I'd almost sold the animal at a loss. Damned good man, that Titus."

I beamed inside, proud.

Pier sat up rigidly. "That pompous, good-for-nothing *kaffir*?" He stole a glance at his father.

"What did you say, Pier de Witt?" The muscles tightened around the Master's mouth. He flung his knife onto his plate, making a resounding ring. "How dare you belittle those more competent than yourself. I know what's eating you. You're still angry at Titus for throwing you in with the sows."

The doctor looked from Pier to the Master with a bemused look while the Mistress gulped at her wine.

"The minute I see you've one ounce of that slaveboy's ingenuity, son, I'll build you a house right here on the estate, a real *jonkershuis*," he said, jabbing a finger repeatedly at him. "But all I see in you is arrogance, laziness, and disobedience."

Pier slumped forward. It was all too true—and reflected badly on me, his nursemaid. But these words were harsh.

"Look at you, you can't even sit up straight. When you can show me you're half the man Titus is, that's the day I'll celebrate."

Pier glared into his plate, fighting back tears.

"Philippe, that's not fair," the Mistress said. "Why would you compare Pier to a slave? To a grown man? He's just a boy. Give him time."

"Time? Time? I know boys half his age who've crewed on ships to China. Hell, they've gone to war! How much time would you have me give him, Annetje? Maybe if you'd stop indulging him, I could get him out of his baptismal gown long enough to make a man out of him. Look at him, his face as long as the table. He's nothing but a milksop."

Pier's face flamed scarlet. He pushed back his chair and stood up, as if threatening to leave. Dr. Buehl looked down, embarrassed. I was torn. Lord knows the boy deserved a comeuppance, but in front of a guest? Catryn's face turned blotchy. She looked from her brother to her father, tears already forming.

"Don't leave the table until I give you permission, boy," the Master bellowed, slamming his fist down so hard the plates jumped. Pier glared back, hatred flashing in his eyes, then bolted from the room. The Mistress rose. "Annetje, don't you dare go after him." He turned to his guest. "My apologies, Doctor."

The Mistress settled back into her chair. You could see her frustration—son or husband? Catryn let out a sob. "Saskia, take Catryn upstairs, will you?" she sighed. From the kitchen we could heard Dr. Buehl laughing, breaking the tension with a story about responding to an emergency call astride a recalcitrant mule. From the top of the stairs we heard the de Witts roar with laughter.

Upstairs I knocked on his bedroom door. "Pier? Are you all right?"

"Go away!"

I undressed Catryn and tucked her into bed. Oh, why didn't the Master stop subscribing to all these fancy theories, and give his son some encouragement for a change? Poor Pier. It was as if he were turning into glass: surface hard, but hit a certain point and it all shattered. If someone didn't act soon, what was left of him would reassemble into a pile of shards.

I opened Pier's door a crack. He lay in his bed, wheezing, breathing wildly. I entered, sat at the edge of the mattress, and reached out for him. Chin trembling, he sat up, flung his head onto my shoulder, and sobbed.

Chapter 25

February 1750 (Summer)

When Sunday arrived, I was secretly overjoyed, for at seven half in the morning all at the farm but me had readied themselves for the journey to church. And they wouldn't be back for hours. Once a month and on sacred days the slaves hitched horses to the family carriage, and oxen and mules to all the wagons, for the two-hour trek. Everyone would get smartened up in their best finery, only to be covered shortly thereafter in a fine layer of dust, or blown apart by wind, or soaked with rain as they rode over dunes and marshland to the lovely little chapel in Stellenbosch. No one of the dark races was allowed inside the church, unless they attended children. The slaves and coloreds had their own tents set up in the Braak's open fields where they sang and prayed and made a great deal of noise, having a lot more fun of it than we Europeans.

Most of us looked forward to this chance to get out, to see and be seen. After church we would lay our midday meal on blankets on the lawn and socialize. Perhaps we were even inspired to act holier the following week, if the sermon was eloquent enough. We servants usually met those from other estates, and occasionally a new romance would blossom. Church was mandatory, except for the sick. But someone had to stay behind to keep watch over the manor, and on this Sunday that duty was mine. It hardly seemed possible that the de Witts would leave me in charge, but today they did. Wonders never ceased!

For me, being home alone was a delight, for there was no work and no watchful eyes boring down. I felt as carefree as days growing up when Mama and Papa would take the rare evening out and leave me at home with Bertje, who would then sneak her sweetheart in through the back. I would extort a pastry out of her, read a forbidden book, perhaps take a few puffs on Papa's pipe—that being the extent of my criminality. Now I harbored a similar plan, but only after sneaking a peek at some lace.

Mistress Cingria barked her last instructions on what to do in case an emergency struck—such as a leopard striding into the yard and making for the livestock, or the house catching fire. "*Ja, ja.*" I nodded, barely listening, impatient for everyone to go. When all finally packed themselves into the conveyances, I flew to my spy station at the front and watched until I saw the calico skirt of the last serving girl billowing out of the last wagon that trundled down the lane.

I floated up and down the gallery, humming, dancing, feeling deliciously criminal, peeking out the front window now and then to be sure no one suddenly returned for a forgotten glove. It was such a beautiful day, for a moment I almost regretted being alone. But this was a rare opportunity.

I poked my head into the Mistress's bedroom. Her great bounty of lace—I knew it lay tucked away in her great cabinet, locked from prying eyes and sticky fingers, the gorgeous treasure I wanted so to touch and see and smell once again. I rifled through the little enameled boxes on her dressing table—ah, the key! I threw open the drawers. The middle one was stuffed with an arsenal of fans—*chinees* fans with delicate paintings, sandalwood fans inlaid with ivory, gilt-edged fans from Germany. She must have more than the Crown Princess of Saxony! Then, in the bottom drawer, old lace neatly rolled in scrolls, interleaved with fragrant skins of lavender tissue that hid it from the light. A king's ransom, asleep in its mausoleum.

Carefully I unrolled them on the bed. Edging. Neck borders. Sleeves. Cravats. Gloves. *Fichu*. Bed curtains. Most made of silk, all of the finest weave, as radiant as ice crystals, glittering like snowflakes. I floated a mantua over my head, letting it spill over my shoulders like folds of rain. I placed black lace against the window panes. Through the dark prism the world looked grim indeed, so I changed it for white. Finally, when I'd had my fill, when I'd studied the patterns well, when my hunger for beauty was sated, I put it all away.

In the kitchen I stirred cocoa, honey, cinnamon, and almond paste in a bowl and, brewing hot milk, whipped up some hot chocolate. Poured the frothy drink into a porcelain cup on a silver tray and helped myself to an apple turnover. This was my day off. I'd worked hard this year, and deserved this.

Then to the Master's study, that cozy, olive-colored room I loved so much, walls bordered with painted oak leaves. A glass cabinet housed a fine collection of books. Perfumed oranges and sweet brandied tobacco cut the odor of must.

Sitting at the Master's long desk, lounging back in his chair, my tray of delectables before me, looking out the front drive, I felt what he must feel: wealthy, powerful, and master of all I surveyed. Paintings, maps, racks of pistols, and rifles adorned the walls. I examined a globe of the world, stared through a microscope and telescope, toyed with his astrolabe. This day I claimed the room as my own. This day I would snub my nose at church laws. After all that austerity, I needed a feast of the senses.

I took a bite of turnover, sipped my cocoa, then pulled out a volume: *The Tragedies of Shakespeare.* I drew adjacent books out an inch to show myself where to replace it. The Master must never know I'd been here.

Tossing cushions to the floor, about to settle down to serious reading, I spotted it: the tray with etched carafe and glasses. Portwine from Rustigvallei's finest grapes. Oh, the jeweled color, the sweet, sharp fragrance! In all my life, the only portwine I'd had was a sip or two left in some guest's glass at cleanup. The Master and Mistress adored their portwine. He called it "burnt honey dripping from the hives of heaven." No, the Mistress said, it was "moonlight singing to the night ocean." Do I dare? Just a taste. Not enough to be missed.

The syrupy fluid sparkled as it trickled into the glass—liquid rubies! I swirled it in the bowl, as the de Witts did, then took a sip. Oh, how it burned, then soothed, warming my belly with its fire. I took another sip, coughing, then another. Delicious! I could form a serious attachment to this juice!

I sank deeply into a cushion. Opening a portfolio, I unfolded maps, tracing with my finger the journey I'd made by sea from the Netherlands along the African coast. I found India and Asia, the Celebes, Malacca and even Mosambiek—why, I knew slaves from these lands. Then I dove into the Shakespeare, laughing out loud when I saw a play called *Titus.* I pored over it, skipping what I didn't understand to get to the good parts.

Mysteriously, the carafe had moved next to me on the floor. I sipped, then sipped some more, gratefully, reverently, feeling a pleasant lightness in the head. All right—I'd just replenish it later from a barrel in the cellar. I drank as I read, filling my glass several times. My head began to reel, the edges of thoughts felt fuzzy, words on the page became harder and harder to comprehend. I lay back, arms and legs akimbo, thinking of all sorts of delightful things, letting out little explosions of glee. Everything seemed so terribly funny. This liquor worked!

That's when I heard rhythmic beating issue from the yard. So—slaves too ill to go to church had recovered enough to play their drums. The family would surely have denied them that pleasure, especially on the Sabbath. I staggered up, knocking some wine over. Oops! I'd clean that later. I sailed down the gallery and into the kitchen, opening the top of the door, and listened to the music pouring from the Quarters. Thunderous drumming. Hypnotic. Compelling. The portwine had loosened something, compelled me to move. I stomped one foot, the other, loving the way my clogs hit the tiles with a *clack clack*. Just as the slaves moved! I fashioned my neckscarf into a turban, and loosened my stays.

The drums beat harder and faster now, almost in frenzy. I was wild with the thrumming, on fire with the rhythms of Africa, as if I'd been born from the clay of this earth, dangerously primitive. I leapt onto the bench, onto the table, jerking my shoulders about, lifting knees, humming. My turban fell off, and hair whipped about me like boughs of willow. Throbbing blood rushed to my head. I was a disembodied spirit wailing into the storm, lost to the world. It was all so brilliant!

Then, from the other end of the table, smoke circled toward me in a blue haze, the smell of tobacco filled my nostrils. I stopped cold—someone was sitting in the shadow of the door. Oh Lord—they must have seen everything—my dance, my banshee cries.

"Who goes there?" I hiccuped. Deep laughter trickled from the corner, and the door slammed shut. Startled, I slipped onto the hard table. "Ow!" I tried to focus, but there was a fuzzy edge around everything. Then, in the bare light of smoke, I saw the dark complexion. The familiar white neckerchief.

"Titus!" I cried. "Oh, Titus, I'm glad it's you!" An unexpected hiccup, then a giggle from my throat. "Have you been watching me?" Speech was coming out funny now. I pressed two fingers to my tongue—yes, it was still there. More hiccups, a staccato of little laughs. I stared at him, my body as loose as a rag doll—and everything so deliciously funny.

Titus rose, strolled to where I lay sprawled, hands on his hips. He frowned down at me.

"Don't look at me in that tone of voice!" I scolded. A smile crept across his face. "Do I look like a suckling pig?" I giggled, kicking my foot. A clog clattered to the tile. I scrutinized the floor, trying to locate the shoe.

A corner of his mouth twisted into a smile. "What the devil you been getting yourself into, Miss Saskia?" He sniffed at me, then jerked back. "Smells like you crawl into the bottle of port."

"No, silly man," I giggled. "That port crawled into *me*! Master's best!"

Titus shook his head. "I did enjoy the dance, my sister. We get you to the bed to sleep this off before the family, they come home. Miss Saskia, you be more African than White sometimes. These eyes be glad you do know how to move."

I hiccuped and took his hand. "Titus, my friend. You have to have some. It's sooo delicious! Makes your head all soft and fuzzy."

"I don't really drink."

"I do. I just learned how. I'll teach you. Let me get you some." I scrambled down from the table and slipped. He grabbed my arm.

"We be putting you up to the bed."

"Oooh," I pouted. "Just when we're having a good time."

"This good time, it be over."

"Wait. I have something to show something. A play. S'about you. Well, not you, silly. Your namesake."

I stumbled down the gallery, pulling a reluctant Titus by the wrist. When he saw the messy study, his eyes grew wide. I placed the volume in his hands. "What's this? *The Most Lamentable Romain Tragedie of Titus Andronicus.* Ach! My name." He flipped rapidly through the pages. "What do this play be about?"

"Oh, you know. Rape. Mutilation. People eating pies of human meat. The ushual." I flung my hand out, faltered, but caught myself on the desk.

"Wonderful." He slammed the book shut. "We take you to the bed to sleep now, Miss Saskia. You have way too much drink."

He grasped me by the arm and walked me toward the kitchen. I was limp, kept stumbling. He bent down and threw me over his shoulder. My stomach lurched. I fumbled, grabbed the bottom of his buttocks. He yelped and slapped my hand. My fingers clutched the waistband of his breeches. I was enjoying this. In the kitchen I thrust my arm backward, pointing toward the flight of steps, forgetting he already knew where my bedroom was—he'd once built a fan there. "Thatta way, my noble prince."

He squatted down to pick up my cap and shoe. " 'We take you to the bed.' 'We'?" I mimicked, " 'We'? Do you speak in the royal plural, sire? Ah, I knew you were a royal."

Titus paused at the base of the staircase, trying to hold me upright, but my legs were rubber. He lifted me into his arms. "Your body be like the boiled cabbage leaves—but much more heavier."

I threw my arms around his neck and looked him in the eyes, and for a long second he looked back. I thought I'd never seen such eyes before—soft, yet burning. At my room, he lowered me gently onto my bed.

"Be careful, young man. For you are pure as the driven

snow, and I must leave you such." I hooked my fingers into the pocket of his vest and pulled him close. "Did you know you have the most resplendent eyes of any man I've ever known?" And hiccuped. He drew away.

My lids were as heavy as Persian carpets. The last thing I remembered before passing out was footsteps descending the staircase, and Titus chuckling under his breath.

~

Late in the afternoon, light from the window seeped under my eyelids. Oh, my head.

The sound of hooves pounding gravel, wheels grinding along the drive. The family! I put a hand to my brow. Oh! Had a door slammed on it? Suddenly I remembered the liqueur. I leapt to my feet, nearly falling over. I must have slept for hours! Then it all came back: the Master's study, books strewn over the floor, the empty carafe of port . . . They will crucify me! I slapped on my cap, slipped into shoes, and rushed downstairs, tidying my skirts as I flew down the gallery. Just as my hand touched the iron latch on the study door, he stepped into the house. I turned and dropped a curtsy.

"Well, Miss Klaassens." The Master set his hat and gloves on the hall table. "How is everything? Any elephants trample down the Quarters and destroy my vines? Or was it a slow, dull Sunday, hmm?"

How upright and Calvinist he looked. The Mistress straggled in with Catryn and Pier, all looking tired. Without a word, she handed me her bonnet, and wandered into her bedroom, the children padding behind.

"Just a dull Sunday, sir." Lord help me, I had to get into that room before he did.

He crossed in front of me, hand on the door. "Good, good. Now fetch me a tankard of beer, will you? That's a good maid."

I curtsied. How could I fetch him beer when I didn't really expect to live that much longer? As he entered his study, I stood outside, unable to breathe. Surely my employment would soon be a smudge of a footnote in the history of this manor. I braced and waited for his bellow. But none came. I dashed for the beer.

When I returned with the tray, the Master was at his desk, calmly reading. I stole a glance around. Extraordinary! Everything was in order—books back on the shelves, sparkling glasses on their tray, a clean and orderly floor, and the carafe full of port. I breathed with relief. Only one thing was amiss: two books jutted out from the shelves. Just an inch. When the Mistress called out, I curtsied and closed the door behind me.

Who cleaned the study? Who saved me from a sacking? Titus. Noble friend, I am in your debt. Hugely! Then I groaned inside, remembering some of what I'd said. Would he remind me? Or be gallant enough to forget?

~

When I rose the next morning, my body throbbed and ached. How idiotic to drink so much! I dressed, thinking how I needed to thank Titus. In truth, I was embarrassed to face him. I heard Digger's voice in the kitchen and hastily penned Titus a note.

I paused on the steps to watch the boy and smiled. He sat at the table holding Squabble, a parrot Cook had purchased from a sailor. It lived on a perch next to the hearth. Digger pushed pumpkin seeds into its beak and nuzzled its feathers.

I looked around—only the boy was about. "Digger, would

you like to earn a coin? Take this to Titus. He's probably in the stables. Don't show it to anyone else, do you hear?"

Digger nodded, tore the note from my hand and rushed out. Later, as I prepared a tray for the children, he stumbled back in, breathless. "I done as you asks, Miss Saskia. Here." He placed a folded paper in my hand and beamed when I tucked a bright copper coin into his fingers. I put a finger to my lips—our secret! Cook burst through the back door carrying an armload of brass serving pots, so Digger and I rushed to help. Then Digger crouched on the tile floor, pushing around a little oxcart he'd carved himself. How precocious this slaveboy was!

"Now don't you gets under me foot none, Digger," Cook cautioned, "or I'll throw ye outside."

"Digger, would you like paper and charcoal? Sit at the table here, and we can draw again, if you like."

I dashed up to my room and opened Titus's note. Printed in his careful hand: WHEN YOU MOVE, YOUR HIPS THEY SING. And: WHAT DOES RESPLENDANT MEAN? My forehead flushed hot. Now, was that gentlemanly?

In the kitchen I spread a half sheet and stub of charcoal before Digger, and soon he was bent over, as I'd shown him before, drawing. Cook and I watched the line of a beak emerge, then the awkward bulk of a bird. He drew slowly, using every inch of space, finishing with careful marks for talons. Paper was precious, and rarely came his way. With a few grunts and "*Ja, goed,*" Cook and I went about our tasks. From time to time I helped, showing him how to smudge the line, then ran upstairs to wake the children. When I returned, he called out to me, excited.

"Look what I drew, Miss Saskia, Mistress Cook."

We leaned over. He'd made a second drawing on the reverse, two prone figures, a dark couple. Cook and I stared at one another. The man and woman were naked on a bed, the man on top of the woman. I grabbed the sheet. The charcoal dropped to the tile floor, shattering.

"Where did you see such a thing, Digger?"

"The Quarters." He pulled the drawing from my hand and pointed. "This one be Titus and that one be Miss Jezza."

I sank into a chair, feeling the blood drain from my face. Cook gave Digger a sudden *klop* on the ear. He cried out.

"What are ye drawing, boy? This be downright nasty!" She snatched the sheet, crumpled it in her fist, and hurled it into the burning hearth.

A shadow crossed Digger's face and moisture gathered in his dark eyes. "It's not the boy's fault, you know!" I shouted. He dashed from the house, door slamming behind him.

I ran upstairs, collapsed onto the bed, and held my face. My heart was splintering into a thousand pieces. How foolish I'd been! Knowing Cook, she'd soon tell everyone how I felt about Titus. And everyone would also know this: that he bedded someone else.

Chapter 26

February 1750 (Summer)

This morning as I helped the slavemen load the wagon with willow baskets, Jezza shimmied down the yard. My heart sank. So she would ride into town with us. I was still in shock from Digger's drawing. Was it true they were lovers?

When Titus smiled at me, my face froze. How bold I'd been when drunk, flirtatious! And all the time, he enthralled with another. The shame. Perhaps it was best she came along today, for I felt too stunned to talk to him.

Jezza climbed up front next to Titus, her worn pink dress covered with a shawl bright with orange flowers and little embroidered mirrors. Tacky! I sat in the rear of the wagon with Samuel, curled up in a corner, which suited me just fine. Neither Jezza nor I regarded each other, and it was annoying to watch her titter and giggle. Soon as we were beyond the manor, she laughed loudly, teasing Titus in the *taal*, cuddling up against him. Sometimes he talked to her, returning her smile. Other times he remained silent, even impatient. Oom Samuel would watch them too, then nestled into a sleep. When I imagined them in bed, like Digger's drawing, I felt ill.

Jezza tilted her head coyly. "When you gonna teach me read an write, Titus?" He stared straight ahead. "You promise ta teach me," she pouted.

"I do no such thing."

We rode along quietly for a long time, then Jezza grasped his arm. "You still goin ta them meetins in the mountains?"

"*Jezza!*" Titus whispered. He half turned, eyes darting at me. What meetings in the mountains? I shook Oom Samuel by the elbow, pretending I hadn't heard.

Samuel stirred from his doze. "Well, Miss Saskia. You be lookin more more like the colored miss every day, isn't it? You keep sittin this here sun and gets dark dark, they gonna put you that slave block Cape Town, sell you from highest payer! Then you be already finished."

I laughed, then grew sad. "Oh, Samuel! Right now even slavery would feel better than this." The old slave shook his head.

We rode in silence for some time. Samuel had just begun to tell me about an encounter with a *toverman* when Titus turned around.

"Miss Saskia, I—"

"Look! Look!" Jezza shrieked. "Above!"

We arched our necks just as a great undulating wave of pink filled the sky. The shattering flight of flamingos was always lovely, but common enough. Jezza put her hands on Titus's arm, then laid her chin upon them. I looked at Samuel. He glanced from them to me, understanding crossing his face. "Things doan always be like they seems, my daughter."

My daughter. His African mode of address always touched me. Now I wondered. He would know if they were lovers, wouldn't he? When I looked back, Titus's arm was free of her. Samuel took his cloth parcel and, rapping the walls of the wagon for attention, unveiled a bounty: almonds, yellow quince, and shiny red apples, all perfect. He offered them to us.

"Hey, Samuel," I said loudly, "I thought you weren't allowed to pluck from estate trees. This fruit looks too good to be falls."

"These *be* the falls, Miss Saskia, these *be* the falls. We do only pick from the groun. Course, no one tol we couldn't shake them trees hard hard, isn't it?"

We laughed, and I reached for a quince. Apples made me cringe these days—they reminded me of warthogs. Titus chose an apple, then Jezza took one too. "Stolen fruits *do* be sweeter!" he chuckled.

Our wagon plodded along for hours, Jezza asleep and leaning against Titus, Samuel dozing on a pile of empty hemp sacks, wheezing in his slumbers. We passed field after field of green and purple vineyards, and I reflected how, season upon season, our lives ebbed and flowed with the life of the vines. Right now, grapes were bitter.

Finally our wagon rumbled around Table Mountain, and we stopped to outspan the oxen in the foothills. Today Titus would search for a white pony for Pier, Samuel would fetch the mail and rent a cart to buy Cook's long list of provisions, and I would walk to the Bo-Kaap for a lace lesson with Aunt Effie. I didn't ask Jezza what tasks she was assigned, but I was certain she'd tag along after Titus if she could. He climbed from his seat and reached to help me out of the wagon, when Jezza, in a flash, jumped between us and grabbed his hand. Startled, he eased her to the ground. I leapt down before he could offer his hand again and took off at a run. I should have pushed her out of the wagon back at Duiker River.

At Effie's I forced my attention on the lesson. She was excited to show me a new pattern she'd designed, leopards lounging under palm trees. It was splendid. Soon we settled into the work, and again, I found peace weaving the lace. Effie began singing a Natal Bushman song we'd sing to brighten the hours, but this time I didn't join in. Then we worked side by side in silence.

I wound the linen thread onto bobbins, my mind drifting to Madame Remy. When I'd ridden out to see her a few days before, she'd upset me by saying she had a fancy to sell her farm, house, fields, everything, and return to France. For years, she said, she'd dreamed of entering a retreat house close to a chapel somewhere in Provence and wanted to go before she was too old to make the journey. I asked her why, since she had a married daughter, grandchild, and a wonderful home here—everything a woman her age could want.

"Oh, I'll probably never get around to actually going, *ma petit*," she said, patting my hand. "But it has long been a dream to seclude myself in a gardened cloister and devote to God the ending of this life. I dearly love my family and my home, but to be closer to God—well, it would mean at last putting nothing between Him and me."

"Madame Remy," I'd argued, "haven't you told me that everything is God? How would giving up everything that is God, then, bring you closer to Him?"

She regarded me with curious eyes. "Saskia, sometimes you astonish. Perhaps you are the theologian at heart, *non*? What I mean is that no longer do things of the world hold me. Like this handkerchief I embroider. What a mistake it would be to stitch myself to it." I asked if what she really wanted was more time to pray. "*Oui*," she'd said, "but already I always pray. I pray as we sit here now." Before I could ask what she meant, something had interrupted us.

Now Titus crept back into my thoughts, and melancholy pressed in.

"You know, Saskia," Effie said, "when Titus gains his freedom, I think he will go far. I'm sure you've seen his special talents, his intelligence. They value him quite highly at Rustigvallei, I hear."

My shoulders tensed. I yanked at the threads. "Don't speak his name to me, Auntie. He's a-a blackguard! A scoundrel!"

Effie put down her bobbins. "Well, well, now. Whatever has happened to the two of *you*? I thought you were thick as thieves."

Just then I heard a sharp noise. My eyes darted to the kitchen, then back to Effie. She looked down, fingers flustering with her bobbins. "Pay no mind, my dear. That's just a girl helping me out." She grabbed her crutches, hobbled into the kitchen, and spoke to her in sharp tones before returning.

"I'm glad you found some help, Auntie, for sometimes I worry about you living alone like this. Who is she?"

"Someone temporary." She leaned across to inspect my work, traced the pattern in the air above the pins with her finger. "So what's come between you and Titus?"

"Not what—who. Never mind. Titus is his own man. He can do whatever he pleases with whomever. I don't want to talk about it."

Blessedly, she asked no more questions, only pointed out where I'd twisted several threads in the wrong direction. I sighed, pulled the weave apart and started over again. Clearly my mind wasn't on lacemaking. She sat back in her chair, telling me about a new milliner's shop downtown with lace supplies, ribbons, fabrics, and cage dolls decked out in the latest European fashions. For a time I forgot all else.

When the clock struck two, I pushed my lace pillow aside, stood up, and stretched. "I'll make us some tea."

In the kitchen, a child-woman cringed in the corner. Swathed in yards of red, skin like oil-roasted nuts, with heavy eyebrows that glided above her eyes like wings of a blackbird. I was caught up short, as if a gust of wind had blown some rare tropical bird through the door. Was she from Ceylon?

Effie barked out some command. I followed the girl as she ran to Effie's bedroom. But where was she? The bookcase stood ajar, like a door. I pulled it open. A secret room! The girl sat on a cot, fear blazing her eyes.

When I returned to the sitting room with the tray of tea things, Effie was quiet. She held the pot, fingers fumbling on the lid.

"What an enchanting helpmate you have, Aunt Effie. I followed her to . . . that other room."

Effie sighed, offering me a plate of rusks. "That foolish girl! Saskia, you must not tell anyone of any of this. It's terribly important. Promise me!"

"What is this all about?"

Effie plunked the plate down on the table. Behind her spectacles her eyes were almost fierce. "I'm going to have to trust you with this, Saskia. She is not my servant. She's in hiding. A group of us snatched her from a procurer who'd bought her from her Indian family. She's a virgin and could fetch a high price, you see. Promise me you won't say a thing about this. Her life depends on it. Maybe mine too."

I blinked at my teacher. Only a few weeks before, Titus had told me in strictest confidence that Effie and her husband had once helped runaway slaves find passage to other parts of the globe. So—she continued the work.

"Effie Huyskens, you are one remarkable woman! Of course I'll say nothing. God's oath."

A stomping of synchronized feet on stone, shadows moving past the window made us start. Militia! They pressed on down the street. "Effie, please, take care."

"My dear, I've been taking care for over thirty years."

For the next hour we worked our lace in silence. The girl's family had sold her! How precarious life was for us women.

What if I'd been sold to strangers to use any way they liked? The thought was too frightening to contemplate.

~

Just before bed I sat in the yard nestled among the camphor roots, running my fingers along the gray bark. By special permission the slavemen had brought their drums outside and set them up along the winery wall, Titus among them. They sat on barrels, tapping softly, gradually pounding harder, like gathering thunder. It had been a long day. I was glad for the energy that now thrummed in my veins. Beyond, over the ragged mountains, the sun flared into bright streaks as orange as mango flesh.

Johanna ran across the yard to me, breathless, falling onto the grass. "I asked around, Saski, discretely. I fear it's true. They be lovers."

I glanced at her briefly. "What are you talking about, Johanna?" All at once I understood why Calvinists hated this music: drumming was too powerful, too primitive, too . . . sensual.

"Titus. Titus and Jezza, who d'ya think?" Johanna shouted against the noise. "Josiah just told me. He says everyone in the Quarters knows. Began two years ago."

I grew still. A kind of sickness began to churn deep in my stomach. I bent my forehead and rested it on my knees.

"What's wrong, Saski? Oh, no. I'm so sorry. Ye really cares, don't ye?"

For a minute the drums rang louder, then pulled back, muffled and distant. I couldn't be upset. What happened between Titus and another woman had nothing to do with me.

Johanna put a gentle hand on my shoulder. "You're in love with him, aren't ye? Oh, don't love him, Saski. Don't even think of loving a slave. It'll be the ruin of ye. The ruin of ye both."

~

A month of summer passed, some days the heat so stifling it was hard to breathe. We shuttered the entire house as best we could from the fierce sun. Thank the Lord for the fan Titus made me! At night I would sit at the dormer window upon my seat of stacked coffins and tug at the sash, flooding my room with breeze as I looked out over the fields.

This night was fine and glorious. I sat back, thinking of Titus. I thought of him all the time now. A kind of poem was forming in my head: *There is a man I think of in the morning when I'm alone, when light from the sun first penetrates my room.* His face floated before me at the most inconvenient times: while Mistress Cingria gave me instructions, while reciting prayers with the household before supper, while counting bobbins for my lace. *I have watched him in the yard below, mutely, through lace I hold against panes of glass.* When I would run into him, as I did crossing the river the other day, my heart would light up like a chandelier—until I remembered that he loved another. Then I could not even reply to his cheerful "hallo." No longer would I sit up front with him in the wagon. *I carry this man close, like a song, like a wound.* If he sat down next to me at supper, I would move away. He rarely attempted it now. I was torn up. He was ever in my thoughts, yet I had to forget him.

Of course, the more I tried to forget Titus, the more I thought of him. Surely it was a sin to think of him as I sometimes did. At night, as I lay alone, I called up his form, feeling waves of pleasure surge through me. Sinful longings. I would be feverish, unable to sleep for thinking of him, for wanting him close, wanting his touch—wanting and fearing. Then my whole body would become one knot of longing, and I only wanted him next to me. Is that how it feels when you lie with a man in the heat of passion?

In the secret silences of my bed I would caress myself—oh, I can hardly admit it, so forbidden it is. But the pleasure made me short of breath, and faint. I made up stories in which my fingers became his strong fine fingers . . . Then I'd stop, twisting and turning in my sheets, knowing this had to be a sin. Is God really so cruel as to make such pleasure sinful? If anyone in the house knew the desire in my heart, there would be hell to pay. Hell may need paying anyway.

I wasn't even sure I was still a virgin. After Claus had forced himself on me in the closet of nets, before Midshipman Soolmans pulled him off, what had happened? I'd sought out Cornelia, for here at last was a friend with experience. I'd looked around to be sure we were alone. "Cornelia, if a man . . ." I'd paused, flushing full red and whispering what had happened. "Does that mean I've been deflowered?"

She'd laughed, showing a set of crooked teeth. "Is that what that jackass did to ye? Blackguard! A nasty business—unless you be wantin it. Ye may still be a virgin. By my standards, anyway." I left, more confused than ever. And what exactly *were* Cornelia's standards?

I lit a tallow, even as the night breeze bent the flame. After the longcase clock struck eleven, something stirred below.

A large moon rose and hung over the cloud-shrouded mountains like silver fruit. Below, in the clearing by the slave garden, I spotted Titus. He was just standing there, looking up at the stars. Moonlight fell like water on his face, sculpting the edges, illuminating them. It shimmered in the whites of his eyes, on his teeth, on the shoulders of his shirt. Something deep was moving in my chest, growing and blooming with night flowers.

I shuddered, trying to push away the enchantment. How impossible it all was—a Black slave, a White maid, all the powers lined up against us. It was just as well he loved another. This very night he might take her to his bed. But I couldn't help myself. Some ancient part of me cleaved to him still. *Wanted* to love him.

Suddenly Titus looked up and saw me. Too late to retreat. Our eyes met and hung there. Something moved silently between us, I thought, something more potent than words. I stopped breathing. Time sped backward, forward, inward, imploding. The moon rushed through all its phases and raced across the sky. Cords were sent and received, pulling us to harbor.

Then I knew what I had not known before: Titus loved me too.

Chapter 27

MARCH 1750 (LATE SUMMER)

One sultry afternoon, walking from the Slave Kitchen, I saw Josiah and Titus enter the barn. I stopped near the window to adjust freshly baked loaves of bread under my arms when I overheard Josiah tell Titus that, since the moon was waning, they must listen for the drums. What drums? They spoke in whispery tones, not realizing I was close.

That night I tossed and turned in my bed. What were the slavemen up to? The longcase clock downstairs had barely chimed eleven half when a distant rumble of drums drifted through the night air.

A sliver of moon, cloud-muffled, rose over the mountains, lending barely enough light by which to see. Beyond the estate lay shadowy savannas where beasts slumbered under thorn trees, while others prowled the night for prey. Jezza had talked of meetings in the mountains. I dressed quickly, donned my cape, and placed a taper in a hooded lantern. With a tinderbox in my pocket, I would be ready. I sat at my window seat, hiding in darkness, watching to see if the men would make a move. If they did, I'd follow them.

I must have nodded off, for I awoke with a start. The night was silent. Then once again I heard a faint drumming from the eastern hills. The only other noise was the braying of the mules, and an occasional screech of guinea fowl.

Light of the moon glinted on something below, and a slight movement broke the stillness. Two Black men, barely visible in the pale light, crept across the slaveyard, looking right and left. I could just make out Titus's profile—the other might be Josiah. They were setting a wooden barrel along the fence closest to the forest, climbing it, then lowering a second barrel down the other side with ropes. They mounted the fence. I hardly dared breathe. A third slave darted out of the shadows and disappeared with the first barrel. How clever! For the Overseers blocked the gatehouse doors with their beds.

I lit my lantern and, shoes in hand, scurried downstairs. Manassa! Sleeping unexpectedly by the hearth this temperate night. I tiptoed around her and, silent as a mouse, slipped out the kitchen door. I had to hurry, or I'd lose them.

The drums were silent now, and the moon dim. I stole down the yard toward the opening in the arches. The metal gate screeched unexpectedly, and just as I thought I was exposed, a guinea fowl cried out. Silently I gave thanks for the cover. When I'd last seen them, the men were jogging along the edge of the forest, almost completely under shadow. I would have to run slightly behind and parallel, through the vines, keeping my head down, then double back to the forest's edge. I blew out the lantern's flame.

All my skills of stealth, all my childhood stalking games, would be put to the test tonight, for no one must see or hear me. A bad idea, probably, but I needed to know what Titus was up to. Shivers rattled through me as the bitter air crept under my cape.

Something scurried through the underbrush right by my feet—only rock rabbits, I told myself. I chanted silent prayers that I wouldn't come upon a warthog or wild dogs or . . . a leopard. Were the men involved in something dangerous? They could be risking their lives. I might be too.

A strange howl, high and unearthly, issued from somewhere in the shadows. I froze. These forests were haunted by the angry spirits of dead slaves, Samuel told me, spirits as predatory as night beasts. *Spoeks* eager to stalk a Hollander. Lord, what was I doing out here in the dead of night?

I kept to the shaded trees at the forest's edge, finally spotting the men as they crossed the fields. Then I lost them. I scanned the terrain, confused. There, far down the veldt! Cutting across a row of grapevines, I scrambled to make up the quarter mile that lay between us before they disappeared once more into the shrubs. They were heading east, toward the mountains.

I crept low, making for an oak tree flanking the vineyard, and slunk behind it. I listened for them. Only cold silence and the moaning wind. Suddenly, from branches above, two guinea hens pierced the air with cries, making me jump. When they flapped their wings and flew off, I fell against the tree, heart thumping.

For a long time there was silence. Had I lost them? There was a rustling through the thicket some good distance up the mountain, and Titus's silhouette appeared, barely visible against the light green of the *fynbos*. If I could keep pace, catching sight of them every few minutes, yet stay hidden, I might succeed in tracking them. I prayed the noisy birds would give me cover.

I hurried along the narrow goat path to where the foothills started their upward slope, avoiding the tangle of succulents. Dry protea flowers, though they kept stabbing me, were beautiful tonight, glinting silver in the light of the moon. The mountain cliffs loomed high above and I prayed the men weren't heading for them. Then a dead tree branch cracked underfoot. Bloody hell!

"What be that?" Titus's voice sounded muffled, wary. I was shocked he was so close.

I squatted in the brush, draping my cape over my face, stifling the sound of breathing and the wild beating of my heart, which surely the men could hear. Small animals scurried underfoot. I trembled. What would be worse—wild beasts discovering me, or the men? I should have thought this through more carefully, should have considered the consequences of stalking anyone. If they discovered me, they would be furious. But I was too far along to go back. For endless minutes there was nothing but silence, broken from time to time by the sudden scream of a guinea fowl, the purr of a nightjar. Should I dump this useless lantern?

The men scrambled over rocks, clearly making for the pass between mountains—the low saddle, the *kloof* to the east. So they *would* cross the mountain. I'd heard rumor of an abandoned shepherd hut just beyond, out of sight of the estate. I moved more slowly now. For the next fifteen minutes or so, I stumbled up the rocky escarpment, losing and finding the path. So steep! I stopped to catch my breath,

But where was the hut? Just when I was thinking what a huge mistake this had been, hauling myself up this tangled mountain for nothing, I saw Titus and Josiah crest the mountain and disappear over the other side.

I reached the dip in the saddle, paused to catch my breath, watched and listened. Below me, the forest gave way to flat, grassy openings. The moon with its ghostly smile was lower in the sky now, and when I stepped over the other side of mountain, my heart stopped. Not far down the slope a fire crackled before a tall, narrow mud hut—and in front of the hut, men. Oh, my God! We were far, far from the manor. I took a deep breath and stepped into forest shadows.

In the clearing, figures moved about easily, backlit by burnt orange flames. They greeted one another in pidgin Dutch and Malay. Voices muffled, then clear again, as they entered and left the dwelling. What an inspired place for covert meetings! No one but distant Hottentots would hear the talk or spot the fire, and they wouldn't care.

I screwed up my courage. Under cover of the forest, mindful of how my clogs crunched and slipped on needles, I wove between trees closer to the clearing, still yards and yards distant. This hovel with its thatched roof was longer than others I'd seen, with a hole at the back for window. Two men fed the fire while others wandered in and out, lit their pipes with an ember, then disappeared inside again. Titus and Josiah mingled and talked with Africans, Malays, and colored men, and, to my astonishment, two Europeans, one dressed like a laborer and the other a missionary. At least twelve men, probably from surrounding farms. What were they up to?

I broke out in a sweat, shivered. Clandestine meetings were utterly forbidden. If discovered, the punishment would be swift and, for the slaves, dire.

I crouched in the dark behind a thick tree, my fingers gripping sap-sticky bark. I would be as glass, yes, I'd heard of this trick. Think oneself a pillar of glass, clear, invisible to eyes, as solid as light. A cool breeze blew, drugging the air with smells of sweet resin. Someone threw open the shutters at the hut's rear, and I heard snatches of argument. Some questioned while others persuaded, implored, but the only full sentence I heard was: "Better to be the jackal in the forest than the greyhound on the golden leash."

Abolitionists!

Soon my legs crawled with ants, but I needed to hear more. With utmost stealth, I tiptoed on dry, crusted fir needles to the back window and, still some paces distant, tried to peer into the hut. Light from a small fire spilled out the back window, along with a veil of tobacco smoke, but the opening was so high I could not see in. I stepped on a nearby rock. Titus and Josiah were squatting with others on the floor, smoking pipes, arguing.

An irrational surge of longing, even resentment, overtook me. I wanted to be part of this. As a White maid, I could be of help to them. Yet, here were rebels, outcasts—criminals! The hunted.

Cutting the air abruptly with his pipe, a thin, dark-skinned man, eyes blazing, spoke of the same slave uprising Mr. Steenoven mentioned at our Javanese dinner. "They nearly got away wit it. They not organized. Shoulda got every slave on the Cape ta join em fust, stole many the weapons, then struck hard. When we rise up, we kill every Hollanders gets in our way."

Waves of cold rushed up my back, and I broke into a sweat.

A slave jumped to his feet. "We kill those White bastards for what they done ta us! Well, not you, my White brothers."

What a terrible mistake it was coming here! Then Titus raised a powerful arm. "No, brothers, no." He shook his head ferociously. "We do not kill the one European. We must not do them the harm, no matter what they have done."

Suddenly I cried out—someone was wrenching my arm behind my back. Sharp cold metal pushed at the flesh under my jaw while a rancid smell, like curry, rose to my nostrils.

"Don't you move! *Ach*, my brothers," my captor barked. "Come. Come! I catch the spy!"

Bloody hell! From the corner of my eye, I could see he was huge, a human lemur with dusky circles under his eyes. "You're breaking my arm!" I shouted.

Men rushed from the hut. When they saw me, their mouths set into hard, grim lines. "White woman! Who she be?"

"Spy!" another shouted. "She be the spy! Kill her!"

The rusty machete pressed deeper against my skin. A trickle of blood fell warmly upon my collarbone. The lemur held me tighter, forcing me to bend forward until my legs buckled under. My eyes reached up, saw Josiah standing by the fire, gaping at me. I looked around desperately for Titus.

He sauntered up the incline, fists clenched and tight to his side. His face was exploding in fury.

Sweet Jesus!

Chapter 28

March 1750 (Late Summer)

"I know this woman. I deal with her." Titus's voice was tight and high pitched. "Please, my brothers, go back. I will soon come."

They skulked away, looking back over their shoulders, faces wrenched in distrust. My heart worked madly in my chest.

Titus pushed the machete from my throat with the heel of his hand, then grabbed my arm and jerked me a few yards from the guard. He shook me hard. For the first time, just a little, I feared him.

"Why do you follow us? How dare you! All of us you put in such danger!" A shadow fell over his face, then he pushed me away with disgust. "Or do you draw me close only to betray me?" He looked far into my eyes, scanning their depths.

Blood was draining inside me, and I felt faint. He thought I was just one more deceitful European, this one sent by the Master. "Titus, I would ne-never," I stammered. "I would never betray you. Don't you know that? I was afraid you might be involved in something dangerous—and you are!"

"Here, you keep her," he cried, pushing me toward the guard.

"Do not the harm, but do not let her go." To me, pointing an angry finger, "I deal with you after."

I waited, hunched on the cold ground. Lord, what trouble had I got myself into now? The lemur man stood close, gnawing on a wad and watching me, his machete poised at his side. What a rough character he was. Did he chew tobacco—or iron filings? I didn't recognize him. Had he lived at Rustigvallei, he would have known Titus and I were friends. But this night even Titus seemed to doubt that.

The guard jerked in alarm every time I moved, so I stopped. Loud arguing issued from the hut. Were they deciding my fate? I hoped to God Titus still trusted me. When a bitter wind blew through the trees, I didn't even dare pull up my cape.

Finally, men spilled out into the clearing, threw me hard glances, then scattered through the forest and down the mountain. I recognized one of them, a slave from the Brill estate. Josiah and Titus stood silently warming their hands by the fire. With a nod from Titus, my guard lowered his machete, glowered at me, and tramped down the mountain. I sighed with relief. Titus kept standing at the fire, his arms tight across his chest, angry. Firelight cast copper shadows on his face. Finally I got up and walked down. I searched his eyes. Didn't he know how I felt about him?

"Titus, no one sent me." My throat was raw. Moisture gathered in my eyes. I couldn't stand that he might distrust me. "No one even knows I'm gone. I heard you and Josiah talking about meetings, drums. Lord knows what those at the estate will do if they ever find out." My eyes softened. "You're so close to earning your freedom, Titus. Why do you take risks like this?"

He breathed deeply, filling a defiant chest. "Don't you know what happen to the men who betray their masters?" His voice was even. "They take them to the Castle and hang them upside down from the high high dome by the chain. The prisoner, he cries for mercy. When he can take the pain no more, they loose the chain and the man, he falls. Onto the stony ground."

"Don't tell me this!"

"If they live, if the head of him does not crack open like the melon, do you know what then they do? The guards, they take him to the stone room that has no window. So dark, like the moonless night. The airless cave."

"Stop!" I crushed my hands over ears.

"I hear of this room. It is by the sea, and has the large hole cut into the middle of the floor. There be more hole than floor here. The prisoners, they have hardly the place to stand. Then they hear the ocean rush in at the high tide. First wet upon the ankles. Then the water, it rushes higher, higher. Do you know there are the marks of the fingers cut high into the stone, where the prisoners, they try to escape?"

My head shook violently. "I would never betray you, Titus, never! You of all men should know my heart by now."

He stared at me fiercely for what seemed eons. "The heart of you—I think that be the great mystery."

I stared into the dark of his eyes, watched the firelight dance in them. Slowly, something hard there seemed to yield. "You frighten me to death attending these meetings." I was almost whispering now. "But I would never betray this secret. How could I ever harm you, Titus? To harm you would be to harm myself. I'd die first." My words shocked even me. I trembled.

Titus scanned my face. "Come here," he said, stepping close and wiping my tears with the back of his fingers. Somewhere above us an owl hooted into the night, then swooped out of a tree, rushing close. Josiah went into the hut and returned with a *banjah*, a gourd with long neck and strings. He leaned against the door and started plucking. A gentle sound floated through the trees and out over the clearing.

"Something more tuneful, my brother," Titus commanded.

The slave picked faster, singing some African song that was both strange and joyful, bobbing his head in time to the music. I had to chuckle when Titus tapped a foot on the hard dirt, then twisted, bobbed, swinging about in the clearing. He stopped to stretch out a hand, smiling. How glad I was for that smile.

"Will you . . .?"

"Nay!" I threw up my hands and stepped back.

A shadow crossed his face. "Why not?"

I lowered my eyes, pressing damp palms on my skirt. "I've wanted to dance, like the farmers do. But . . . it's just that . . ." I blurted it out. "Well, it's not proper!" I clamped my hands under my arms.

"Except when you be drunk."

I must have blushed, but by firelight, who could see? "It's forbidden to dance that way. It's forbidden to dance with *you*. It's late, Titus. We shouldn't even be here." My voice was high, and quivering, but I made no motion to leave. The fire seemed to dim for a minute. Shadows of overarching firs enveloped us in their darkness.

"Yes, it be forbidden," he frowned. "Forbidden we be on the mountain tonight." His voice rose in strength, and he made a grand sweep with his arm. "The meetings, they be forbidden. So be you and I and Josiah, here together, alone. So be the touching your hair, the white of that your skin. All forbidden!" He snorted, fierce eyes staring at me. He was frightening. Exciting.

He swung his arms, swayed, rolled shoulders, moved sensually to the rhythms. " 'Not allowed, brother Titus,' " he sang, mocking. Held his arms out, moved slowly toward me, smiled a come-hither smile. "But I am the man." He thrust an arm around my waist, pulling me close, so close I thought he might kiss me. I shut my eyes and held my breath. "You be so . . ."

And suddenly he swept me into a reel, and we were dancing to the beat of Josiah's music. My cape flew into the brush, my petticoats swirled high, and something lurched in my throat. *No, no, this is wrong.* But how could something so thrilling be wrong?

"Why, God be dancing and singing in the heavens right now, Miss Saskia!"

And then, at once, the dark verdant green of the forest, in all its beauty, enfolded me in its arms. I let out a yelp.

Around we twirled, stumbling about in the darkening light, me trying to follow Titus's violent leaps, leaping myself, laughing. Only the last flickers of dying fire and the moon's faint light illuminated our steps.

"God would have us joyful. God would have us passionate!" he shouted. "He cause the thunder to break with His heels and the lightning to spark when He strike the clouds with His feet. What kind of God He be, who does not allow the dance, does not allow the song and the laugh?" Titus twirled me round and round. "Where the joy in your religion? You Dutch, you are the crazy people!"

"Praise the Lord!" I cried, and we tore around the clearing, blood surging through our limbs, fingers clasping shoulders. How excited, how incredibly happy I was! When I stepped on his toes, I shouted an apology.

"Do not worry, my sister—if these feet they be in the way, I take them off."

I screamed with excitement. Titus lifted me by the waist and swirled me in circles across the forest floor. Pine needles crushed into the earth, heady aromas rose up to meet us, air thick with the scent of evergreen.

Josiah played on, the forest, moon, and sky our witness. My skirts billowed like sails, hair streamed behind in banners. I loved the grip of Titus's fingers on my shoulder, his hand at my waist. I had never loved being alive so much in my life.

He looked at me intently, and our eyes smiled. I damn *would* dance with this Black man on a mountain in the middle of the night! How bold we were! My heart soared into space . . .

Josiah stopped, and our dance came to an abrupt halt. "I return now, my brother," he said. "Do you not come?"

Titus's eyes sought mine, as if for direction, but I looked away. By now the moon was low in the sky. Soon it would completely drop behind the mountain.

"We come soon, my friend. Go well."

Josiah nodded. "Go well, then, my brother, my sister." We watched him climb up the slope toward home.

"You are my damnation, Titus." I laughed, shivering, rubbing my arms for warmth.

"You mean I be your *salvation*." He took my elbow and steered my back against a tree, enclosing my hands in his. His eyes traveled my face, like a map he was trying to read. "The other day I saw you walk through the fields. Your white dress, it catch on the wind, and the wind fills it. You look like the little cloud hurrying across the veldt. I thought this my heart would explode."

I was struck dumb.

"I have seen that strange thing you Europeans do with your mouths. Do you like to do that thing?" He took me by the chin and drew my face to his. I felt the pounding of his heart, smelled the musk and smoke and spice of his breath.

I pushed away, letting out a nervous laugh. "I'm not going to kiss you."

"I don't want to do that thing anyway. It be so unclean!" He snorted with disgust.

"Unclean? Do you really think so?"

I looked far into the forest. Memories surfaced—a drunken Claus demanding love at the end of a knife. That was unclean. But sweet, guilty memories flooded me too: the miller's son when I was fourteen, kissing me hard and long under the steps of the windmill.

"If you Africans don't kiss, then what do you do?"

"This I will show." He grasped my shoulders and drew my face to within a hand's breadth. "Do to me what I do to you."

My heart seemed to stop, leaving me faint. "Only in the interests of scientific investigation, you understand."

Titus threw his head back and laughed. Gingerly he put fingers to my neck, nervous fingers, and drew my face to his. Breath from his nostrils beating soft against my nostrils. Sharply he inhaled and exhaled, as if inhaling my skin. I tried to relax, but . . . Titters of laughter welled up and trickled out. I pulled away.

"Do you . . .?" I was giggling too hard to speak. "Do you mean I'm supposed to do that? Is that what Africans do? Breathe into each other's noses?" Titus turned away, hands on his hips, pouting. "I'm sorry," I said. "I don't mean to laugh. But it's so funny."

"*Ja?* So funny. You have not tried, yet you make the joke of it. Do you not know that what you Hollanders do to each other with your mouths—well, how stupid it look."

"But you have not tried it. You're trying to trick me into kissing you, aren't you?"

He leaned down and put his face on my cheek. "Do you tell me you don't even do this?" he whispered.

"We do this." I closed my eyes and parted my lips, curling them slightly, then pressed my mouth against his, then around it, exploring. As the miller's son had done.

"Oh," he murmured.

Holding me by the waist, he kissed me softly, awkwardly, ardently. My months of desire. I melted into the kiss. His fingers played with my hair. "Young tendrils of the grapevine," he whispered, stepping back. "Come." He took me by the hand and pulled me toward the hut. I stood there like stone, all at once overcome with dread, but with longing too. "Come," he said, his tone urgent. By the last embers of fire, his eyes flickered like stars. My knees weakened.

"Nay, Titus," I said gently, letting go his hand.

His face grew cold. "It is because I be Black. That be the truth of it then."

"That's not it." I paused. "I've had some unhappy experiences with men. And you already have a lover." I could not speak her name.

"Who tells you so? Not for the long time now. Well, will you come?" And once again he took up my hand.

I searched his face. "I cannot." I stared through the darkness of forest to the hills beyond. Something troubling flooded my consciousness. "I'm not ready."

Then everything shifted. "It be late. We must go." His voice had an edge. Was he angry? He found my cape and placed it over my shoulders, fingers lingering there. "You ask why I come to the mountains for the meetings." His voice was steady and solemn. "I come for my brothers and my sisters. I come for my people. How can I take the freedom knowing they are still enslaved?" His gaze seemed to pierce the mountainside, drifting away toward the estate. "I would give my life for them."

I could not speak. He lit the lanterns and we clambered up through the trees. When we reached the saddle, he snuffed out the flames. I grasped his shoulder from behind, letting him guide us down the mountain. As we picked our way over boulders, through prickly agave, I wondered what it would have been like had I given in to the longings that rose inside me tonight like gathering storms. Lain with him as men and women do.

Further down the rocky slope, walking side by side, I took his hand. Oh, why, why was the forbidden life, the dangerous life, the one worth living? When we reached the fields, we stopped to gaze at the expanse of sky that blazed above with a thousand lights. "I think the stars, they be the windows in the walls of night," he said. "And from these windows the ancestors of us look down, blessing and smiling upon us."

We walked in silence, keeping to the narrow roads between the vines. I thought of Mama. Was she looking down on us from her star window? Like others, would she judge this man by the color of his skin? Or by his heart?

Close to the manor, our gait slackened. We were loath to part. When we reached the arches, we stopped and listened, letting the stillness of the night fall upon and hold us. Titus turned to me. "My dear sister, the life we be given—it be short. It be uncertain." He held my eyes with an intensity I both loved and feared. "Too uncertain not to take the sweetness when life give you the gift of it." He kissed me on the forehead, lips lingering there.

My eyes followed him as he walked through the forest to the Quarters. Oh, Titus, I know, I know—know well how brittle life is. I waited to be sure no commotion followed, no discovery. He was safe.

I unlatched the kitchen door, removed my clogs, and slunk through the kitchen, stepping around Manassa as she slept, then tiptoed up the steps. On the landing, I paused. If only I could make it down the short hall with its squeaky wooden floor without waking anyone, then up the last steps to my attic.

I was almost there when I heard the cold grating of door hinges. I froze, stared down the hall, panic rising to my throat. A figure holding a lit candle glided silently out of Mistress Cingria's room, its light illuminating the passageway. Oh, Lord! There was nowhere to hide. I braced for her ire.

Then, to my shock, I saw not her, but the Master, dressed in a long night banyan and slippers. A woman's hand reached out and drew in his neck, the lace of her chemise floating across the threshold. A murmur, a kiss. So the rumors were true. It wasn't some slavewoman, it was her! Mistress Cingria! The secret staircase.

The Master turned, and for moments we stood staring at one another, like thieves catching each other in the same act in the same house on the same night. Then, without a word, he turned to his stairwell and I to my attic door—conspirators of silence.

Never in days to come would one word be spoken between us about that night, nor mentioned to another. For as far as the world was concerned, that night never happened.

Chapter 29

MARCH 1750 (SUMMER/AUTUMN)

My dearest Gertruyd,

Only recently did I receive your last letter—written five and a half months ago. I'm so glad that all of you are well, Aunt Hendrika and Uncle Henk. Congratulations to Gerrit for landing a job in the mayor's office, and kisses to Lijsbeth and Guus. Kiss your new piglets for me too. I'm in good health, although low in spirits from the loss of a couple of slaves here at the estate, one tragically. I'll tell you what happened.

But first, know I particularly loved what you wrote of your beloved Simon, and the romantic ways he comes to court. Did he actually bring you a muleload of hothouse peonies and tulips? He sounds perfection. Stash him in your hope chest and marry him quickly, while your parents still approve. I, who have avoided marriage like the pox, envy your sweet, easy love.

I envy you in other ways too, my dear Cousin, for you're approaching winter. How I miss skating house to house with you and your brothers on the canals, warming our noses by fires we visited and stomachs with hot apple cider and gingerbread. Reading books with you by firelight. Did I tell you there is a Frenchwoman here, a neighbor, who lets me borrow her books? I go whenever I can. She is a special woman, and we have amazing talks.

The last three days here have felt like winter. Seas of rain have beaten down with such violence, dripping from the eaves and forming lakes of mud in the yard. There are holes in the thatched roof above my attic room, and today, as yesterday, I rushed about placing pails under the drips. My bed has not escaped the gush, and for days I've had to sleep in a dry corner in a nest of clothes and blankets.

But it's more than a leaky roof that upsets me. Events at Rustigvallei have plunged many of us into depression. The first episode started a month ago, and involved a wee, dear, wild thing, a foundling. Titus, a slaveman, had traveled with the Master and others for ten days to hunt big game. They returned with two wagons loaded with birds, hartebeest, springbok, eland, even a spotted leopard. I noticed my friend Titus wearing a sling across his chest, and something small squirming inside. We marveled at the young meerkat, which had lost its mother in the Little Karoo and wandered into camp looking for food. Titus fed the beastie, which then followed him everywhere.

A meerkat, dear Gertruyd, is a kind of squirrel standing no higher than your knee, with lovely golden fur and black rings around shiny eyes. Everyone at the estate came to be so fond of it. It let you pet it, but only when Titus held it. Sometimes it even stood on Titus's head, grasping his scalp with its hind legs and standing up straight as a rule, looking this way and that. But the beastie annoyed the Master. His hounds would lunge at it, threatening to shred it to pieces.

After several weeks of nursing his pet, one day Titus was riding a horse in the paddock, the little beastie, as usual, nestled in the sling. The Master must have been in a rotten mood, for he marched over and yanked that meerkat out by the tail. The animal yelped, bit the Master's hand, and fell to the ground. Master de Witt was furious. He whacked it mercilously with his riding crop, then told Titus to take it away and finish killing it. Well, Gertruyd, you might as well tell a man to kill his own babe. Titus told me he carried the wounded thing into the bush and set it free. But it found its way back to the Slave Quarters and hid under a bed. No one knew until the odor got real bad. Had that poor little meerkat died from the beating, or did some wild beast get to it? This was the only time, someone told me, he ever saw Titus cry.

A few weeks passed when another act tested our endurance to the max. I was already furious with my master, Gertruyd, but after what they did to Cato . . . Cato was a brash and rebellious slave. Once again he'd talked back to the cruel Foreman, Anthonij. Cato called him a "fuckin Black pig" and "sonofabitch kaffir." Cato must have been contemplating suicide.

With the Master's permission, Anthonij gave Cato "the honey treatment." They tied the naked slave to an unshaded post in the center of the yard. Slaves were forced to slather his body with sticky honey, and he was left to stand all day in the fierce African sun. Flies, wasps, poisonous ants all soon found him and bit, stung, tortured that poor slave. He bore it bravely, but slowly his body began to bloat and swell. How we wanted to bring him water, to cover him, but dared not. Late in the afternoon he cried out for us to kill him. Some of us were in tears. Anthonij and the Master sat on the back stoep that afternoon, drinking beer and gloating as they watched Cato writhe, congratulating each other on how "the creature" had surely learned its lesson. The Mistress, though, was begging the Master to stop. No way.

Finally, the Mistress marched down the yard with some slaves, who cut him loose and carried him down to the river. There they placed him on shallow rocks, letting the waters cool and cleanse his wounds. Cato was sick for a long time after that. This is how they *break the spirit of these people, Gertruyd. I'm sure you now have a sense of the character of the man for whom I work. But that was last week. There's more.*

Yesterday the slaves discovered one of their own dead in his hut at the Quarters, hanging from a beam by a noose of his own making. He'd been carrying a grief too hard to bear, and so took his life. We know because he left a sign. His wife, Sara, had gone missing—and yours truly had a lot to do with it.

Sara was a beautiful maiden our age accompanying a shipment from East Africa. Cook told me that the Master was smiling ear to ear when he brought her home from the Cape Town Slave Market, having outbid many other planters for her. Our Housekeeper trained her to be a serving girl, and she was a good one.

Sara was from Mosambiek, with delicate features and a soft ball of hair, graceful in her walk with its little sway, and dancer-like in the movements of her hands. The family stripped her of her ox skins and clothed her in a sad little homespun dress. Except on special serving occasions when they put her in finer attire, she always wore that one dress. Its print of faded flowers reminded me of the passing of summer. But she wore a lime green headwrap that set off the bronze of her skin. The Mistress was so charmed by Sara that she presented her a silver earring that had lost its gems. The slavegirl hung tiny shells from it, which tinkled when she moved her head.

Sara had a fetching way about her, touching you softly for your attention. She loved to watch the lace being woven, so I showed her how to weave a few stitches. She was innocent and sweet and everyone loved her. But the one who loved her most ardently was Abraham.

Abraham was a big hulk of a slave, black as a starless night, with a heart as large as a beech. He worked in the smithy. Not as bright as Titus, nor as resourceful, but eager to please. He had a commanding head and fine, white teeth. Truly, when he flashed his smile it was as if the clouds had parted.

Abraham courted Sara with a passion, Gertruyd, the kind of passion every woman longs for. Titus told me he helped him invent sweet phrases to whisper into her ear after supper, although I heard he was mostly too shy to ever speak them. He picked wildflowers for her and worked overtime at neighboring estates to buy her trifles: a brass ring, bracelets. And he learned to play the gourd banjah so that he could sing to her in his deep, sonorous voice. He even bought amulets with love potions from the toverman to ensure her love.

In the end, of course, she adored him. I think it was his sincere ardor that made her turn her heart to him, a flower to the sun. The couple with perfect biblical names "married" in a small slave ceremony just three months ago. That day I had them stand in their best clothing while I drew their portrait in charcoal, a celebratory gift. In a moment of uncharacteristic sentiment, the Master let them build their own hut in the Quarters. They were so happy in their love—until ten days ago, when everything unraveled.

Sara and I were both waiting table, she kitted out in a fine blue dress, for the family had important guests visiting. Former Governor and Mistress van Aelst and their rather old son Govert were traveling back to the Netherlands when their ship made a stop in Cape Town. Master van Aelst was retired from many years governing one of the principal islands in the Celebes.

Gertruyd, they were the strangest looking wealthy folk you'll ever see, each one in a bizarre wig. Mistress van Aelst's rose high and wide, grizzled with gray powder. Often she wore a turban on top of the wig with ostrich feathers sticking out so high they tickled the brass chandeliers, and whenever she turned her head we feared her head would catch fire.

Govert's wig was of, get this, hedgehog fur. Thick tufts stood up from his head in spikes, as if a cold wind had frozen them midair, giving him a startled look. He would lounge on the settee like an obese cat, scratching beneath the wig, displacing it.

His mother had a toy dog from the Orient, small enough to fit into her valise. It had ugly, protruding eyes, and its bark was like fine china breaking on tiles.

Mistress van Aelst would stroke both the dog in her lap, then her son's neck. Govert bragged of his many female conquests, which made all of us, including the de Witts, squirm. He also boasted of his fine German education. I muttered to Johanna, "In any case, well read in petticoats."

The van Aelsts had left behind a favorite female slave, and became taken with Sara. She shouldn't have served with such gentility, for their minds were soon made up: they had to have her. "Would you consider selling this girl, de Witt?" Mr. van Aelst coaxed, opening up his pocketbook. "Name your price, my good man. We will treat her well."

We could all see how embarrassed the Master was, how uncomfortably he shifted in his chair. In the kitchen, Cook told me she was sure the family wanted Sara as a nyai, a concubine, for that scrofulous Govert. When he pinched Sara's behind one evening as she ladled out crab soup, even the Master was offended.

But there was more. One afternoon I heard whimpering in the hallway to the kitchen. Govert had pinned Sara up against the wall, one hand down her bodice and the other up her skirt. Abraham had just come out of the kitchen, and he began shaking hard. As mere slave he could do nothing. Suddenly I became a lioness seeing someone mistreat her cub—I punched Govert's hands and yanked Sara away. When I told

Cook, she swore she would stew that lecher's potatoes in poisoned herbs. I wished I'd taken a hot poker to his groin.

Now, the Master didn't want to sell Sara. I actually think he was touched by Abraham and Sara's love. Besides, she was his discovery. But the van Aelsts badgered him for a week. Unfortunately, Master van Aelst was still an influential person at the Dutch East India Compagnie, and one could refuse him only with repercussions. Eventually the Master gave in, stipulating he would let her go if they purchased her husband too. But the family did not want Abraham.

In the end the Master and Mistress sold Sara without Abraham. They locked her in a small room in the cellar for fear she might run. From my casement window that night I saw Abraham kneeling on the grass under the open sky, tears streaming from his eyes, negotiating with God. He even refused to work. Anthonij whipped him, to no avail. When he asked the Master if he could give Abraham the honey treatment, the Master said no, to let him be. We would see the slave wandering about day and night, trying to get to Sara in the cellar.

All of us were beside ourselves. Then Titus approached me quietly with an idea. Somehow we would smuggle Sara and Abraham across the river to Madame Remy, a sympathetic neighbor, who might help them escape. After the midday meal, with the excuse of returning books to Madame Remy, I rode out to her farm. She listened to my story, thought long, then said she would help, but only if we had a good, tight plan. If she could get the slaves to Effie's cottage in Cape Town, I said, I knew my teacher would find them passage somewhere, probably in a voortrekker's wagon bound for the interior. We had to act fast, though, for the van Aelsts were planning to leave the next day—with Sara. Then Madame Remy had an idea. She sat at her desk and wrote out an order for five barrels of Rustigvallei wine which needed to be delivered immediately for an impromptu party. Only a select few of us would know that not all the barrels arriving would contain wine.

When I delivered Madame Remy's order to the Master, he instructed slaves to back a wagon up to the cellar door and start loading five barrels of his estate red. Now I had to steal the key to Sara's door, and quickly. Anna, who brought Sara's meals, told me where it was. I planted myself by the merchant chest at the back foyer and began organizing silverware, or pretended to. My jittery fingers plunked the spoons about, making a mess. But from there I could watch the Housekeeper's office. Finally she marched out and down the gallery. This was my moment. I dashed into her office, fumbled around in the drawer until I found the key, and fled.

In the cellar, my slave friends Josiah and Samuel, bless them, were sitting on two large, empty wine barrels. But where was Titus? "Gone to find Abraham," Samuel blustered. The men had told Sara the plan through the crack in her door, but no one knew where Abraham was. Lord, Gertruyd, it was nerve-racking! "This plan has to go perfectly," I cried to the slavemen, flailing my hands in frustration. And that wasn't happening.

When I unlocked Sara's door, she was ready with her little bag of belongings. "Where's Abraham?" she asked. "He's coming. Quick, into your barrel." We poked the lid with a gimlet for breath holes, then shut her in. The Master would be watching any minute now for a loaded wagon to head down the road toward Madame Remy's. But where were Titus and Abraham? We poked holes in another barrel, praying he would fit. Josiah and Samuel loaded three barrels of real wine onto the wagon, while we stalled for time. At that point I was too nervous to think straight. The moment Abraham entered the cellar, we would have to stash him into a barrel next to Sara and load them onto the wagon.

Samuel, Josiah, and I were pacing back and forth, foreheads beading with sweat, when the Overseer marched down the steps. "Master wants to know what's taking so long! Where's Titus?" he thundered. "He's supposed to be organizing this! Looks like I'm going to have to do it myself." He turned to me. "What the hell are you doing here?"

"Making lace, sir, what do you think?" I answered in an aggressive voice, sidling over to my lace pillow. Just then Sara coughed. We all tried not to stare toward her. Samuel, dear resourceful Samuel, stumbled in front of Sara's barrel and wheezed loudly. Mr. Pesser looked at him blankly and stepped outside.

We had hardly caught our breath when the Overseer barked for Sara's barrel to be lifted onto the wagon. I held my breath as they placed Sara's barrel safely on the boards. Josiah was tying the barrels down with ropes, the Overseer complaining about Titus's absence, when the man frightened us all to death by shouting, "Wait! This barrel says white! That's not what Madame Remy ordered." The Overseer rapped his stick on an end barrel, ordering the men to roll it off. Sweating like beakers of beer, Samuel and Josiah picked it up, then looked relieved. It was not Sara.

Finally Titus ran up, alone. "Where the hell have you been?" Mr. Pesser demanded. "Searching for a lost horse," Titus lied, then looked at us with troubled eyes. What a blessing he had not brought Abraham just then. Finally we could no longer stall, so they loaded the fifth barrel—of real wine. Titus and Josiah hitched up the mules and started out for Madame

Remy's. Shaking like the last leaf of autumn, I hurried to the house and replaced the key. What if someone found Sara missing and realized what we'd done? Rode after the wagon and found Sara? What would our horrible punishment be?

By the time the men returned, Gertruyd, I was a royal wreck. I ran to the stables. Titus told me all went well, praising Madame Remy's courage. Meanwhile, Abraham was nowhere to be found. "Damn!" I murmured. And slept piteously that night, praying Sara would make it to Cape Town safely. Somehow, Titus and I agreed, we'd find a way to get Abraham to her.

The next morning, as the van Aelsts prepared to leave, they found Sara missing. The Master was irate and sent out a search party. They found, caught in river rocks, Sara's torn dress and headscarf. Samuel had done his part well, planting her clothing to make it look as if she had flung herself into the current and drowned.

But later in the morning the slaves found something quite disturbing—Abraham hanging by his neck in his hut. He'd pinned a "message" to his shirt—my portrait of Sara and him. And at his feet was Sara's damp dress. How my whole being ached hearing this! He had not returned that night and so never learned of her escape. The slaves gave him her dress that morning, for all but a few thought her drowned. Oh, what folly!

Tomorrow the slaves will bury him in their cemetery in the forest. Oh Sara!

Meanwhile, Mr. Pesser raged into the Master's office, saying he was sure some of us had smuggled Sara out in a wine barrel. Oh, did my hair stand on end when Cook told me that! But Abraham's suicide had somehow persuaded the Master that Sara had really drowned. I think the Master was sick to death with the whole debacle and had no heart to pursue the matter further. The van Aelsts left in a whirlwind of anger, even with their money returned, convinced the Master had botched the whole affair on purpose.

Now the manor is buzzing with grief at Abraham's death and, for those who know, excitement at Sara's escape. The slaves whisper about wanting out more than ever. I wish I could help them all, for their lives are unspeakable, as the church and governing bodies, in their greed, constantly turn blind eyes to the cruelties of slavery. At my lace lesson today, Effie assured me that Sara is on her way back to Mosambiek. How glad I am for that!

Pray, do not repeat these confidences to anyone, Cousin. Our lives here depend on it. And never ever tell Papa. He will say, "I told you not to go to Africa." But as you see, my allegiances have altered. After everything my master has done, all loyalty is gone.

I do have one piece of good news. Do you remember my writing you about Carra and her beloved Purser Jan Graaf from the Windroos? How they fell in love onboard—while Carra was betrothed to a burgher in Cape Town she'd never met? I went to visit Cornelia, a friend from the ship. Over a tankard of beer, she told me a story. Carra broke her contract with the burgher before marriage could take place, seeking Cornelia's help. Cornelia contacted Jan Graaf, and they escaped on a ship bound for Macao. As a matter of honor, Jan repaid the burgher Carra's passage from Amsterdam. I pray for the couple's well-being at the same time I applaud their courage. Would that I, in the face of true love, have as much pluck.

I have been composing something in words. Certain lines keep rattling round in my head, repeating themselves like cadences of a poem. I guess they are telling me something. A very special man inspired them, but right now I can tell you no more. You may be shocked. But can one help whom one loves?

Write me soon of your own life, for I'm longing for some glad news.

My kindest regards to your family and any of my old friends back home. And pray, destroy this letter. Swear you'll take my secrets with you to the grave.

Yours affectionately,
Your Cousin, Saskia

My stomach clutched. This missive was too dangerous to keep around until my next trip to Cape Town to mail. Pier and Mistress Cingria had been known to go through my things. I sat for a long time, contemplating, then grasped each page and crumpled them, dropping them into the ceramic basin, flames biting at the words, blackening them beyond recognition. And so burned for all time our saga of rescue and escape.

But we were not out of danger yet. The Master seemed to be watching me. Our ploy could still be discovered, and if it was, he'd roast us alive.

Chapter 30

March 1750 (Autumn)

I was working the lace in my room when I looked out over the blazing ocean of vineyards, burned russet by the sun, the mountains at their backs. A warm breeze brushed up against me as gently as a hearth cat. It had been weeks since the tragedy of Abraham and Sara, and only now was I allowing any happiness to return. I'd finished a beautiful *fichu* of silk lace, and when I presented it to the Master and Mistress, they were so pleased they pressed a sterling coin into my palm. When they sell it, my lace will fetch quite a bit more, but no matter. I was in their good graces—at least for now.

The air at Rustigvallei was crackling with excitement: the Harvest Festival was nigh! Soon there'd be an even larger one in Stellenbosch, with booths selling everything from ginger candy to winter hosiery to the finest portwines. All of us looked forward to these celebrations, and no one more than the Master. From the *kinder*room window I watched him walk the fields and orchards for hours with his Foreman, pleased as punch with the year's labors, the magnificent bounty of pumpkins, melons, pears, apricots, peaches, quinces, almonds, corn for the animals, even tobacco. Not to mention the grapes. The Wine Master had praised the year's yield, the sweet perfection of grape flesh, the fine balance in the finished wine. Celebrations were rare, and now we could truly look forward to something. God knows we all needed the chance to cut loose a bit.

In the days leading up to the festivities, we began roasting geese, antelope, and all manner of vegetables, baking tarts and puddings, polishing brass and silver, scrubbing floors, washing linens, and preparing table. Our labors exhausted us, but we gained energy knowing that soon we'd have a few days off, with only the lightest of duties. How we looked forward to revelry, music, and games for once, guests, grand food, and a few extra pints of beer.

I spent the early part of the days attending to Pier and Catryn, trying to keep them neatly pressed and out of trouble. Manassa and Sladie took over while I stole some time in the cellar to work the lace, but that was when the slavewomen were apt to lose the children. Pier and Catryn took advantage of the slow gentleness of their *ajahs*, sending them on fool's errands to fetch cider, or something from the laundry, meanwhile sneaking out to meet Digger or little Kupido down by the river. They would return muddied, wet, and disheveled, and it was the *ajahs* who had to clean them.

Moreover, Pier was doing his best to try my patience. Neglected, with too much time on his hands, he devised mischievous pranks to see how much I could endure without strangling him. One day in the *kinder*room I reached into my lacemaking basket only to feel a cold snake wriggle beneath my fingertips. I let out a scream so earth-curdling I'm sure they heard it in Cape Town. Pier loved it.

Today I fell victim to another. I'd taken a long time hemming a skirt I'd been making especially for the festivities, a beautiful piece of Indian calico from Madame Remy with red flowers and green leaves on ivory ground. When I returned to my room, I reached to pluck the skirt from its hook only to find it mysteriously heavy. It slumped to the floor, ringing as musically as Christmas harnesses. That rascal Pier had sewn masses of small bells into the hem, and it took me twenty precious minutes to cut them off. If he would spend half the time he put into jokes into doing good for others, he'd certainly be canonized by the Pope. I hid the bells away—next year I'll get back at him by hiding a few inside his Christmas cake. *Crunch.*

Despite pranks, I'd had fun making the skirt and helped Johanna and Anna sew theirs. The three of us had had a great time weeks before scouring the Bo-Kaap for bargain cloth, finding a damaged coverlet of white *matelasse* for Johanna's, and for Anna's, an old pink damask tablecloth. I guided them in the construction and sewing. We'd match these marvelous skirts to our best bodices and jackets—heat be damned—adding our reddest ribbons and most beautifully embroidered scarves, for we were determined to look dazzling. This was my first harvest festival, a rare chance to dress up, look my best and, well, do a little mad flirting.

~

The first morning of the festival, the girls and I were up in my room dressing. We'd bathed, washed our hair in rosewater until it shone, run lemons under our armpits to sweeten them. We'd sewn and starched winged linen caps like the country girls. Now we stood in front of my looking glass. These were the first new outfits we'd had in years, and we cried out in wonder—how fine we looked! What a thrill it would be to watch the men fill their eyes with us!

The first bit of fun to open with—the blanket toss! I'd watched them in the past, but had never taken part. Butterflies swarmed in my stomach at the thought of being thrown high into the air—and, for a few minutes, being the center of attention. I told Johanna I'd join the circle as observer only. "Not if I have anything to do about it," she replied.

In the afternoon we gathered in the grass on the side lawn, while the Master and Mistress arranged themselves in rattan chairs to watch from the shade. Little Eli and Digger hovered close, fanning them with great palm leaves. Of course Pier and Catryn had run off. Mistress Cingria sat a little distance apart, looking uncomfortable, her five and a half fingers playing nervously with that chatelaine. Her gaze was fixed beyond the Mistress, and the Mistress stared stiffly away. I almost felt sorry for our Housekeeper, for she would have no part to play in the activities. But then, I thought, she could always play the part of shunned, eleven-fingered pariah mistress.

Our Wine Master and men from the estates laid a red wool blanket, reinforced with canvas, upon the grass. We women—me, the girls, Cook, our neighbors—held hands and formed a circle around the blanket. The men made a larger circle and began strutting clockwise around us. We women had to walk counterclockwise, the men teased, because women were "perverse." The men sang the "Blanket Song," prompting the women forward, and we sang back our response. A bevy of slaves stood under a stand of oaks, faces blank or morose, excluded once again. Without thinking, my eyes looked for Titus. He stood leaning against a trunk, hands in his pockets, wearing a bemused smile and the shirt from Madame Remy.

"I'll be first!" Johanna exclaimed.

"Not you! You're too heavy. You'll split the blanket!"

"Oh, shove it, Egbert! I'll have all your hides if you drop me!"

"If you're still alive," one laughed back.

"Say, Johanna," taunted Mr. Pesser. "Who you waitin for to join ye?"

"Not you!" Everyone roared.

All the men—Jaco bright and muscular in his best waistcoat, Egbert grinning like an eel—grabbed hold of the hems and lifted. They rolled Johanna around, making tentative tosses. She soared into the air, skirts and petticoats flying up, dropped down again, shrieked in excitement, her body once dipping awfully close to the ground. "Keep it taut, fellas," Jaco cried. I was thrilled to the bone, then unnerved when Egbert, cracking jokes and looking away, stumbled, losing his grip. Johanna rolled swiftly toward him, in peril of falling off, when Jaco rushed forward and slipped his big arms beneath her, lowering her to the ground. We laughed, pushed Jaco down and rolled the two into a tight cocoon. Jaco grinned, Johanna giggled, halfheartedly fighting their way out. I laughed too, but couldn't help wondering about Jaco's wife. But she worked on another estate.

Before I knew it, Anna and Egbert had pushed me onto the blanket. "Nay! Nay!" I screamed, and hardly had time to pull down my skirts when I felt myself rising upward. "Give it up, Saski," Cook shouted. "You're in it and you're lovin it!"

High, higher, ascending into the air, I gazed down at Titus. He watched with a guarded look. I was bursting with excitement, flung so toward the heavens. "Don't you dare . . . drop. . . me!" I yelled.

Up toward the clouds, roofs, trees, mountains flashing past. For the fleetest moment, oh, the filigree of branches! My stomach lurched, for I'd left it midair, and my body was plunging back to earth. Then suddenly I was flat against the blanket, rolling rapidly toward a man. Oh, no! Egbert! He'd lowered his edge on purpose. Before I could escape, they'd rolled us up together. Oh, poo! I punched my way out and stood brushing him from my clothing. But how thrilling to be airborne, soaring like a kestrel toward the sun. I looked for Titus, but he was gone.

For days the tables groaned with food—*bobotie* stew, pumpkin *kerries*, roasted antelope, clove cakes. Neighbors like the Brills and Bestbiers dropped by each day to partake, bringing gifts from their own harvests to share. To our great surprise, the Master asked the slaves to sing for the guests, to play their drums, gourd *banjah*s, and fiddles. How happy that made everyone! We clapped and stomped our feet, asking if we'd be allowed to dance. Nay. Oh, to dance again like Titus and I had that night in the forest!

Horse races were set up in the paddock and foot races down the yard. The Master himself took part in an archery competition, then in a sack race with all the children, the slavechildren included, much to everyone's delight. And the tug-of-war, with estate families grappling rope, pitted against their male servants. I loved it when the servants sent the gentlemen toppling! Master de Witt seemed glad to show off his athletic skills—and more than a little *noblesse oblige*. The Mistress looked on from the *stoep*, fanning and mingling with her guests, offering them food, sherry, pear cider. Mistress Cingria had moved to an outdoor table with Cook. I played with all the children, then joined the servants. One young man, not unattractive, followed me around, bringing me plates of food, daring me, rather boldly I must say, to take off my cap and show my hair. And the whole time I was looking around for someone else.

The slaves were allowed to eat all they wanted, to gather at the edge of the river, swim and play their games. I noticed some slavemen squatting under the canopy of the wild holly, drinking beer, throwing knucklebones, grabbing their women and pulling them down under cover of ferns. Where was Titus?

Later Cook, Johanna, and I sat in the kitchen, escaping the afternoon heat with mugs of river-chilled cider. Suddenly a slave poked his head through the top of the double door, eyes popping, flailed his arms about, roared a few bars of song, then stumbled back into the yard again. We looked at one another and laughed.

"Drunk as a skunk! Maybe smoking a little *dagga* too," Johanna mused. I raised an eyebrow.

"Oh, the Master knows, lass," Cook said. "Knows about the drinkin and the *dagga* and the gamblin and all the other carryings ons. He's smart enough to see the slaves need a little wickedness now and then." She grinned. "Keeps em from revoltin completely, or going mad. Yust so's they don't destroy each other. And the farm."

"I wish I were allowed a little wickedness."

Johanna gave a sardonic laugh. "Dearie, I think ye gets yer kicks in."

"But I always get caught!"

~

Night fell. It was one of those wonderful autumn nights, soft and warm and languid with a silky breeze that caressed. A few hours after twilight the heat had died away, pulling many outside. We moved slowly, tired and content, but sad too, for our celebrations were all but over.

We supped on leftovers, at least those still hungry. The slaves joined us at the table under the oaks, something I'd missed the last few days. Slaves and servants in rickety chairs, on benches, or under the camphor trees, resting from exertions and indulgence, yawning and basking in familiar company, content. Too full of holiday food to eat, I walked about, looking for I know not what. Couples seemed drawn together by the sweetness of the night. I looked for Titus, realizing I'd been doing that all day.

I carried a few sheets of paper, vine charcoal, and a board in hopes of finding someone to draw. Then, as I sat down, I saw him. His taut curls were wet from bathing in the river. He lounged in a rattan chair at the end of the table, smoking his pipe, watching me. He wore the shirt I'd saved him and the red-checkered bandanna I'd bought him at market. How handsome he looked! A smile tugged at my mouth as I arranged my art materials on the table. I stole another glance—he was smiling back, as if to say, "Caught you!"

A vase of tulips sat before me, their white petals on fire with flames of scarlet. I plucked one and held it before my face. When Titus looked up again—well, I don't know what devil got into me, but suddenly I was twirling the stem in my fingers, pressing petals against my cheek, staring at him, lips parted. The petals quivered. Two fell onto the table. Titus rose, walked over to me—my heart began thumping. He bent to my ear, whispering, "You brazen flirt! You shameless, brazen temptress!"

I blushed to the roots of my hair. That was what Claus had called me—temptress! I opened my palm. The tulip dropped. But Titus did not pull away. His mouth lingered by my cheek.

"Now do not be riled, my sister." His breath was heady with tobacco, his voice gentle. Torchlight blazed in his eyes. He picked up the flower and crushed it against my arm. The petals opened and fell apart like petticoats. "*You* be the one true flower here tonight," he whispered. "The beautiful tulip. Two lips." He touched his fingers to his mouth. A delicious shudder ran through me. Titus had never been so bold with me before others. Everyone was staring.

I sat up straight, clearing my throat. "Sit over there and let me draw you. I need the practice." I moved closer to a rush torch and propped up the drawing board. "This light will do. Further back, please."

Titus hesitated. "I should not allow the drawing, Miss Saskia," he said, finally easing himself down. "I think you try to steal this my soul." He grinned.

"Absolutely. My absolute intention. Hold your head higher, please." I leaned forward and adjusted his chin, then blocked in the shape of head. "So hard to render a dark complexion," I muttered, crumpling and throwing my first attempt on the ground. I was startled when a slave rushed to grab it. But paper was precious to them.

His eyes were gazing at me intently. How could I focus? "I love to watch the hands of you, the way you use them," he whispered.

"From behind this board? You can't even see them."

"The fingers of you, they seem to know the way around the paper."

An odd compliment, but it pleased me. And made me think about *his* fingers. "Don't talk! I can't draw you if you're going to talk."

"Yes, *mejuffrouw*," he said in mock servility.

Now his eyes threatened to undo me. I focused harder. The portrait was starting to pull together. I darkened the hair, the shadow along his nose, smudged some edges. I was about to show him the drawing when Jezza sallied down the yard, hips sashaying in neat little movements, hands rustling the folds of her satiny skirts. Where did she get such a dress?

"Titus!" she called out.

Damn her eyes! She was ruining the only time I'd had with

him in days.

"Titus, my brother, I have desperate need ta talk." Her lashes fluttered like insect wings. "Mos' dreadful thing happen and I do have desperate need your wise counsel. Take me for a turn and I tell you all bout it."

And she pulled him down the yard. Over his shoulder, he cast me a helpless look before they disappeared into the orchard. My face burned, my chest grew tight. Men! A pretty woman in distress—ambushed every time.

Johanna bustled over, sitting where Titus had been. "I saw that. What a piss-stocking! Maybe you should try some of her little tricks yourself. They seems to work." I said nothing. "She's shameless! Believe me, Saski, I'd kill a woman who snatched my man from me like that."

"Titus is not my man."

Johanna raised her chin. "*Ja*, like you don't take a fancy to Titus. Sure, sweetie." She threw her legs over the bench and took off.

I waited some time for Titus to return. Then a sick feeling began to well in my stomach. Had they wandered back to the Quarters to make love? If I waited any longer, I'd be his fool. I swept the tulip petals off the table—just another ruined thing. Sharp points of darkness needled my heart. I was spiraling downward . . . *Don't go there, Saskia. Get up and leave!*

Samuel sat crouched in his chair next to the kitchen, mouth ajar, nodding off, his ragged cat on his lap. Light from the open door blanketed his shoulders in yellow. Dearest Samuel. How bedraggled he looked—a hard life for a man his age. I hurried to the house, returning with a tray of water, soap, towel, comb, razor, and scissors. "Say, Samuel, are you awake?" I shook his thin shoulders.

He roused fretfully. "Well, I is *now*."

"How would it be if I cut your hair? And that stubble you've got for a beard looks like it could use a trim."

"Nay, Miss Saskia," he said, waving me away gently, "don't you bother bout this old slave. No." I wrapped the towel around his shoulders, feeling the spare bones, and tugged a comb through frizzled hair. "No bother, Uncle. I like playing gardener, pruning your old hedge like this."

He slapped a hand on his thigh, chuckled, and leaned back. As I clipped the wild growths around his ears, he let out a sigh. "Doan know why everybody so sweet sweet ta me these days, isn't it?"

"Everybody?"

He'd fallen asleep last night in his cot, he told me, while mending a pair of breeches, and awakened to find Titus sitting next to him, needle and thread in hand. He watched out of the corner of his eye as Titus finished sewing on the patch.

"I's such a lazy cuss, I yust keep pretendin ta sleep, and yust let him finish that patchin. And when he through, that Titus, darned if he don't yust put them breeches back in my hand, give old Samuel a kiss on the head, and go." I paused, holding the scissors midair. "He sure be a fine one, isn't it, Miss Saskia?"

Soon two other slaves gathered around, asking me to cut their hair too. "All right, all right. But only you two."

Manassa settled in first, and with every row I clipped, I pulled out a louse. Then Sladie slid her sturdy body into the chair. Just as I started clipping, Titus walked into the yard. I stiffened. Returning from a trip under Jezza's petticoats? He sat on the edge of the table, picked up his portrait, studied it, and looked our way. I kept my eyes on Sladie, who chattered gaily as I tugged a comb through her gray locks.

"Is this hair, Sladie, or what?"

"This ain't no hair. This be thatch. Roofin thatch. Gots

insects an all."

We giggled. From the corner of my eye, I saw Titus smile with pleasure. I clipped away, molding Sladie's tight curls into a ball, feeling glad to play barber. Titus could have returned to find me flirting with one of the laborers. Or just gone. Instead, I chose to cut the slaves' hair. *You see, Titus? I do very well without you.*

As Sladie rose, he touched her affectionately, we wished her goodnight, and he dropped down into the cutting chair. The last of the evening stragglers were easing back toward their quarters.

"The portrait, it is good," he proclaimed. "Very good. All right, I be ready." He whipped off his headscarf and arranged the towel around his shoulders. "You may now cut this fine head."

"Too late. Barber's closed for the night." I snapped the towel from his shoulders, nipping him in the neck. Hastily I gathered up my tools.

Titus frowned. "What's wrong?" He reached for my arm, but I drew back.

"Nothing!"

"Women always say that when they're angry."

"You seem to know a lot about women."

"You be jealous because I walk off with Jezza. Is that it?"

"Jealous! Of you two? I don't give a damn about either one of you!" Something had taken me over now. My ire had a life of its own. "You and Jezza are just a couple of stupid, savage blackies, two ignorant *kaffirs* who don't know which end is up! And you can both go to hell, together, for all I care!" I snatched the portrait from his fingers, crushed it in my fists, and hurled it into his face. There!

I was astonished at my tirade. Already part of me was ashamed, sorry even, but another part glad. He deserved that!

Titus stared at the ground, unmoving. Blood seemed to

rush to his face, turning it strangely purple. His eyes rimmed with moisture. Then a wild animal appeared to arise in him. He clenched a fist, slammed it hard against the chair. He took a few deep breaths, picked up the crumpled drawing, and stormed off.

My mouth went dry. Oh, Lord in heaven, I'd done it now. I stomped into the house, shaking, banging the door behind me. Upstairs, I sat on my bed, sniffing back tears, trying to sort through what had just happened. Titus had never really loved me at all. It had all been a game. I was just a piece of prey to hunt, capture, then abandon. And a free White girl too—oh, how he would brag about that.

There were footfalls on the steps, and Johanna burst into my room, dashing to the window. "Look, Saski. Look, I tell ye!"

Reluctantly I rose. In a far corner of the vineyard, a coral glow lit up the dark. Smoke billowed up, blotting out the stars. For a moment, in my self-absorption, I wondered if Titus had done something foolish. "Is the mill on fire?"

"Naw. But some of the men have got into some mischief. Let's go." She grabbed me by the hand. I jerked it away. "What's wrong with *you*?"

"I'm not in the mood." Still, I could not wrench my gaze from the fire, from the smoke that already spiked the air with incandescent cinders. "What's happening?"

"You and your moods. Come *on*."

I stumbled into my shoes, and we flew down the yard and out the winery arches toward the mill. Huge windblades of the gantry groaned in the wind. The mill had never worked very well, but its presence comforted me, reminding me of home. The closer we got to the flames, the more acridly thick the smoke. It clotted the horizon.

"What's happening?"

"They're burning a witch," Johanna grinned. I looked at her

askance. "Come on, hurry, or it'll be over afore we gets there."

Wind was scattering cinders over our shoulders and caps, and my throat and eyes felt dry. We stepped carefully over large rocks to the other side of the river. In a clearing about forty feet away, colored women I'd didn't know circled a bonfire, while White laborers stoked the blaze with faggots, pitch, and straw. They stumbled about, screeching with laughter and drink. That's when I saw the witch.

Looming above, hovering and trembling over the flames was a tall, slender young fir shorn of its branches, tied high on its pinnacle. An awkwardly formed figure, bodice and tattered skirts bundled into the shape of a woman and stuffed with straw. A crudely painted gourd served as a head, and twigs for limbs. Why? As she hung from her burning crucifix, I thought of every pathetic, poignant, suffering woman I'd ever known.

The fire had just begun traveling up the pole when the dancers took hold of each other's hands and reeled wildly in a circle. I could hardly believe my eyes. My mind flashed back years ago to a ceremony I'd witnessed on the outskirts of Delft: field workers burning the effigy of a witch. "To celebrate the threshing of the last sheaves of harvest," my uncle had explained. Were these people mad? They dared perform a pagan ritual on the Master's land!

Johanna and I watched transfixed as tongues of flame licked at the witchy skirts, eating their way up her body. The wind shifted, pricking our eyes and lungs with smoke. In ghostly glow, the effigy shivered its last breath. A glittering torch piercing the dark. Then, piece by charred piece, her shriveled body fell to earth.

As the flames died back, men jumped across the fiery embers, singing, "O Lady, we shake on you our fleas and lice, and all the illnesses of our hearts and bones. We pass through you new as we pass through all the years to come."

It was only an old harvest ritual, but . . . Not long ago the Inquisition had burned real women, alive. This week, at the stake, Castle guards might burn a woman. And now, even symbolically, men dropped their vermin on a woman's ashes to purify themselves. To take on her strength. I shuddered. Men were always stealing women's strength.

"Does the Master know of this?" Just then I turned to see men marching toward us, brandishing torches, fury on their brows.

"Speak of the devil," Johanna whispered. "Mr. Pesser too."

I grabbed Johanna's arm and pulled her into a copse, then across the river and down rows of vines until the Master's raging voice faded from our ears. I couldn't afford to get in trouble one more time. We stumbled back to the house, giggling behind our hands like little girls.

In my room, I told Johanna what I'd said to Titus.

"Crimey, Saskia. What's wrong with ye? Weren't nothin coulda hurt him more." I cocked my head, looking away in shame. "Ye didn't mean it, did you? Do Titus be a *kaffir* to you?"

My eyes grew red and hot.

After Johanna left, I opened the wardrobe and stood before the looking glass, staring and staring at what I saw. I was White, that was sure. Why did we feel White was better? Superior? Did I disdain the natives, like most Dutch? I studied the pink of my hands. Did these fingers cut vegetables more sweetly than Black fingers? Hold children with more love? Weave better lace?

What I'd said was cruel! Violent words. Dirty words, words that wanted to cut. Could he ever forgive me? But could I forgive his betrayal?

I checked the sleeping children, then crawled into bed. The ritual I'd witnessed this night—we still clung to our pagan past. No matter what we said about ourselves as enlightened Christians, we were still people of the land, steeped in earth lore, corded to the soil. Just like Africans.

I closed my eyes. I'd always thought Titus and I were denizens of another world, a world more luminous. Finally I drifted off to sleep, dreaming of roots, great webs of them, Dutch colonial roots, that burrowed deeper and deeper into the red soil, snaking beneath the heathen floor of Africa—until they'd fractured the clay of an entire continent.

Chapter 31

March 1750 (Autumn)

At midday I leaned against the wall outside the kitchen with my plate of cabbage and *snoek*, thinking how dreary life had become. With my heavy workload today, I wouldn't have time to make lace. And I was upset about Titus. My insults had been nothing more than what other Europeans called him, yet I was terribly ashamed. I'd struck him in the worst possible way. Even though I was still angry with him, I knew I must apologize. Perhaps I was afraid of this love. Perhaps I was trying to push him away.

These were my thoughts when, to my astonishment, the man himself staggered around the corner of the carriagehouse, Pier in his arms. I hurried to where they slumped against the *stoep*. Dripping wet shirts and breeches clung to muscle and thigh, damp curls plastered their foreheads, and I could smell the must of river on them.

"What happened?"

Titus lowered Pier before the steps, then collapsed. They looked at one another, panting, coughing. Pier wobbled to his feet and pushed past me, making for the house. By now other workers had gathered.

"The young master," Titus said, wheezing to Mr. Pesser, "he fell into the river. I was setting the traps of eel. The current, it take him so fast."

My heart was in my throat, knowing Pier probably fought. He could have brought Titus down with him.

"Go to the Quarters and rest, Titus," Mr. Pesser said. "I'll inform the Master and Mistress."

Josiah helped Titus to his feet. I also took an arm, whispering, "Titus, I'm so sor—"

"Miss Klaassens," Mistress Cingria barked from the door. "Your duty is to Pier, not the slaves. Run up and get him out of those wet clothes." I flashed Titus a concerned look before I turned for the house.

Upstairs Pier was peeling off his breeches. I laid out his nightshirt. He sputtered coughs, shambling into bed like an old man. "Are you all right?" I helped him in, and he eased into the pillows, shivering. "Shall I bring you a hot drink?" I placed the back of my hand on his forehead, then untangled wet locks with my fingers. "So. Titus saved your life."

"He didn't save my life. I saved his. Stupid slave."

I toweled his hair with vigor. "Is that so?"

"I saved his life, that's what happened. Stupid *kaffir* doesn't even know how to swim."

"I told you not to use that word, Pier!" Then caught myself short—I had used the word myself recently. "Your pride's hurt, that's all." I tucked him under the sheets. "I happen to know Titus can swim very well. You swim about as well as a pig." Oh, that was a bad association. "You should be deeply grateful when someone snatches you from the jaws of death."

"I don't want to talk about it," he said, and turned his face to the wall.

"You need to learn to tell the truth, young man. Now get some sleep."

Just as I rose to leave, the Mistress burst into the room, Catryn in tow. "I'll take over, Miss Klaassens." She sat on the edge of the bed. "How are you, my boy?"

In the kitchen I chopped the turnips so hard I nicked my finger. Blood seeped into the white root, spreading its pink stain like a bloom. I wrapped my finger in a kitchen cloth. That boy is heading down a treacherous path if he can't even acknowledge a debt to his deliverer.

Titus was doing well, Cook told me. The Master and Mistress were sending over a special hot supper.

The next afternoon the de Witts invited Titus to the Master's office. I was envious when they sent Jezza, not me, to the cellars for wine. The Master sat Titus before the fire, gave him a glass of fine port, and pulled out volume after precious volume to show him, which pleased them both. Master de Witt demonstrated the use of his telescope and astrolabe, showed off his spinning globe, and let him hold his gold pocketwatch. Then, with great ceremony, the de Witts presented him with a beautiful little silver box. I know all this because I peered in from the gallery, making excuses to wander past the door. The three of them drank and talked for over an hour. Titus must have felt well honored indeed for rescuing his employers' only son.

~

Several mornings later the family rumbled out the drive in the carriage to Cape Town, taking Pier to Dr. Buehl's surgery to check his recovery, but also for a day in town. Before leaving, they instructed Mistress Cingria to entrust several of us with a special chore. With winter soon upon us, the Mistress had decided the family comforters needed feathers more than our poor birds did.

So, despite last night's heavy downpour, despite water sopping the yard and turning it to mud, Mistress Cingria ordered Isaiah, Luther, Samuel, and little Digger to gather all the ducks and geese and bring them to the barn. At two o'clock half, Johanna and I made a dash through the pelting rain. We were cranky because this was supposed to be our rest period. Jezza swaggered in late.

Feather-gathering from live animals is a hateful task, for the birds will not hesitate to protest. Of course their feathers will grow back, but how can one blame the birds for wanting their bodies left intact?

We organized a bench against the barn wall where the pluckers would sit. The men would chase down the birds, bind their beaks and legs with leather thongs, and pass them along to us girls, who would grip the flailing animals under one arm as we pulled out fluffy down. Young Digger had the easiest task, to wipe blood from the feathers, gather them in his arms, and drop them into linen cases.

Rainwater dripped from above through holes in the thatch, turning the ash, dung, and oxblood floor slick. "Mistress Cingria," I protested, "this is absolutely the wrong day to de-feather birds. We'll make a royal mess."

"Then you'll just have to be careful, won't you, Miss Klaassens?" She swung around before she reached the door. "That's why I'm leaving *you* in charge. Use your God-given brains," she called over her shoulder, threw up the hood of her cape, and was gone.

Why had I opened my big mouth? What an impossible undertaking! Some sixty birds ran about the pen honking and squawking—they knew something was up. I scanned the barn, eyes resting on piles of straw and oilcloth tarps.

"Luther, Isaiah," I commanded, "move the benches away from those leaks. All of you, help me put straw over the puddles and cover them with those tarps."

Soon everyone joined in, scattering armfuls of straw over the floor. Everyone, that is, except Jezza, who stood tightly, arms across her chest. "Who done say we needs obey *you*?"

"Mistress Cingria say—or didn't you hear? Now snap to, and no more backtalk!"

As others draped the tarps, she stood motionless, finally flinging herself onto the bench. Lord—this girl was going to be trouble.

Rain poured down hard now. White geese and brown ducks the size of pigs screeched, flapping their clipped wings wildly. Isaiah and Luther lunged at them, often falling down empty-handed. Finally Isaiah caught a small duck that flailed under his arm until Luther could grab a thong and bind it. What a racket the birds made! This was madness! Samuel snatched a goose and sat down next to Jezza, who stared into space, a portrait of boredom. Rain dripped onto us. I clenched my teeth. We were cold, and wet too.

"You're the expert, Samuel. What do we do next?"

"Just got to wing it. Until then, stay plucky," Johanna punned. Titters and groans.

"You gots to hold the bird like this, isn't it, Miss Saskia?" The duck squirmed under his arm. "You puts the belly up in front you, and yust starts pullin. All we needs is the soft ones, the ones they line their nests wit, isn't it?"

The bird jerked and let out muffled cries as Samuel plucked its bottom. The first few feathers of down drifted through the air, landing on the tarp. Digger sprang forward, dragged the comforter case over and, grabbing an armload of feathers, shoved them in. Many escaped, flying into the air before slowly drifting everywhere.

"Well, that went well. Don't look none too hard to me, do it, people?" Johanna giggled.

"Digger, wipe your feet." I handed him a rag. "I'll bring the comforters to you. Can't have you dragging them through the dirt. And stay on the tarp, or you'll get mud all over them again. And don't forget to wipe the blood off each feather."

Jezza shook her head, muttering under her breath, "Digger, do this. Digger, do that."

I glared at her through slits of eyes. "What did you say, Jezza?"

"Me? I hain't say nothin." She began plucking.

I sighed and brushed the dirt from the comforter. Why hadn't Mistress Cingria given us sacks? We could have transferred the down to the comforter covers later, in a clean, dry place. How unfair to be in charge of a task I didn't know how to perform. I think that woman set me up for failure.

Soon we had a little system going. Luther and Isaiah caught and bound the birds, handing them to us girls, who ripped out feathers and threw them on the clean tarp. Samuel stationed himself by the barn door, and when we finished with a duck or goose, we handed it to Digger, who handed it to Samuel, who untethered it and tossed it out into the rain. Then Digger would fill his arms with the fluff, and smash it into comforter covers—sometimes only remembering to wipe the blood off afterward. Yes. A kind of controlled chaos.

When we filled our first comforter, I was elated. But the cushy mound was too much for the boy. He took a flying leap, squealed, and plopped on top, landing with a thud. Feathers burst out, floating on the air like summer clouds, scattering everywhere, undoing in a moment what we'd spent the better part of an hour putting together. Everyone shouted.

"Digger!" Luther walloped him on the behind. "This be no game!" Digger cried out and ran to me, taking hold of my skirt. Was that comforter his first soft thing?

"Digger, put those feathers back into the covers." I got up to help.

Our work went on. Sighs rose and fell like church hymns. The barn was cold and wet, we were cold and wet, birds were running madly about the pen, screeching. Occasionally one of the men bound a bird too tightly, or slipped and fell on one, and it let out a shriek to wake the dead.

"Don't you go breakin no bones a them birds," Samuel shouted. "The *baas*, he gonna break *your* bones then, isn't it?"

"Yow!" Johanna cried. "It bit me! You need to tie those beaks tighter, boys." She pulled out a handful of down. "Why don't they use ostrich feathers? Big feathers gotta go faster than this."

"Well, who gonna hold that big bird down, Miss Johanna?" Samuel asked. "Not me, that for sure. Ain't me gonna catch no big old ostrich, no suh. Those birds kick like nobody's business. Kick and break yer leg, isn't it? I ain't catchin no ostrich. Ain't gonna bind none, nor pluck none neither."

We worked on and on, binding and plucking, fingers so cold they could hardly move. Meanwhile the rain beat down, leaks through the thatch pooling into mud. Then I breathed a sigh of relief. We'd filled almost three comforters. One more to go.

"What I wouldn't give to be sittin in front of the kitchen hearth right now, all warm and cozy-like," Johanna said, rubbing her hands under her armpits. She jerked loose a long goose feather, wiping it on her apron. "Bloody birds!"

"Cup of hot perry in hand," I cooed.

What a miserable task, this. Johanna and I compared arms, which were covered in welts. "And all those bites in places that don't show," Johanna sighed, "so we can't even brag how hard we had it. Hey, I think one ate a piece of my arm!"

I sat squeezed between Johanna and Jezza. Until now, the slavegirl had worked quietly. She rose and sauntered to the door, ignoring Samuel, and untied a bird herself, throwing it out the open doorway where it flapped its wings and honked. "I hain't doin this no more."

I could have guessed. Without the Housekeeper here, that girl was as reckless as mercury in the palm. "Shut up and get back to work, Jezza. And wipe those filthy feet before you step onto the tarp again."

She spun around, hands on hips, and leered. "I *said* I hain't doin this no more!" She massaged the wounds on her arms. We glared at one another. "Gettin bitten and kicked half ta death."

"Well, who isn't? Just sit down and stop your whining."

Even in the dim light, Jezza's eyes looked dark and fierce. "Says who? You not my *baas*!" There was a puddle by the tarp, and she slammed her foot into it. Droplets of mud splashed on the comforter and across our skirts. Johanna and I gawked in disbelief.

I jumped to my feet, dropping my trussed duck. "How dare you!"

"I dares!"

So she wanted war, did she?

I stomped a foot toward her. Fast as lightning, she grabbed the collar of my jacket and yanked me forward. My feet slipped, I stumbled backward, falling on wet dirt. Is this really happening? "Damn you, Jezza!"

She stood her ground, looking down at me, a smirk curling the sides of her lips. *I'll kill her.*

It all happened so fast. My ankle hooked under hers and yanked, she buckled, crashed into the cold, wet mud—mud now mingling with the floor's oxblood, earth, manure, and straw. Pungent odors of animal rose up. The slavemen looked from her to me, eyes bulging.

Johanna jumped from the bench. "What are you two doing?" Then, "You get her, Saski!"

I started to rise, but Jezza jumped, pushing me into the puddle. A cold wetness sucked rapidly through my skirts and petticoats. I pounced. We thrashed around in the mud, tearing at each other's caps and hair, mashing handfuls of muck into each other's faces. It was cold and rank on my face. Jezza's headwrap fell off, and my own hair spilled over my shoulders.

"Stop, Jezza!" the slaves shouted. We must have been screaming, for now laborers were standing in the doorway, cheering us on. How men loved to see women tear into each other!

One of my oversleeves split open, my arm razed with bloody tracks from Jezza's nails. It was then that I saw my beloved red cap, the one I'd embroidered so beautifully, floating in a pool of mud. Suddenly a rage like I'd never known came to a head. The beast was unleashed.

I grabbed the neckline of her dress and yanked—the sound of cloth ripping, an exposed breast. Digger screamed and ran from the barn. I stared at the frail patch of fabric in my hand.

"My only dress!" she sobbed. Her only dress, my precious cap. I wanted to cry.

The workers were pounding on the walls like drums, calling for more. Luther had Jezza in his grip, but she pulled loose and made for my ear. I cried out. Warm blood trickled down my neck. She'd ripped the earring through the lobe! Before I knew it, my fingers had circled her neck, squeezing, squeezing. She coughed, trying to pull free.

"Saskia, no!" Johanna shouted, and a multitude of hands reached out.

The next thing I knew, Samuel had jumped between us, and Isaiah was dragging Jezza across the tarp. She cursed me in

Malay pidgin. I pressed my apron to my ear.

Then Titus was at the barn door, a pail in each hand. His eyes took us in, silently. I looked at us too, slathered in wet dirt, prickly with feather tufts, hair thick with mud. Two giant, mucked up goslings.

Titus's face broke into a grin. He laughed. I shook my head. Then they were all laughing, all except Jezza and me. Then I was laughing too, laughing and crying.

Titus walked to where she sat and, holding a wood bucket high, poured water slowly over her head. "Damn you, Titus!" Jezza gasped. Death throes of a wet duck.

He strolled to where I sat in the mud and gave me a warm smile. Just when I thought he'd offer me a hand, he lifted the second bucket—cold water tumbled over me in a shock. I cried out, shuddering. Feathers slid off, floating now in the mud. By the time Titus marched out of the barn, Jezza was whimpering.

What a mess! Fortunately the first three comforters lay in a dry corner, safely stacked. But the other was filthy, the feathers we had so painstakingly collected, drenched with mud. I rose and wiped away muck. This project had been my responsibility. How had my anger gotten the best of me—again?

Then Mistress Cingria and Cook were at the barn door. Mistress Cingria shrieked, buried her face in her hands, chest heaving hysterically. Cook held her in her great arms as she surveyed the scene, shaking her head.

Shame-faced, angry, Jezza and I started cleaning up. I yanked my earring from Jezza's grasp and trawled the puddle for my cap and clogs. My body ached, my right eye throbbed. Mistress Cingria poked our backs with a rake and marched us out across the rainy yard to the laundry, filthy case in hand. We stood shivering before barrels of water, heads bowed.

"You two are not to leave this room until you've washed

everything you've soiled, and I mean thoroughly." Her thin lips were so tight, I thought they would snap. "Wash the case, Miss Klaassens, then hang it to dry. Both of you, wash each and every feather and lay them one by one on the table. You can thank your friends for cleaning up the rest. You will then go to your quarters without supper and pray for your salvation. In the morning, when Master de Witt returns, you'll go to him and humbly beg his forgiveness. Never in all my life have I known such wicked, wicked girls!"

I knew I'd acted stupidly, but . . . I hated her scolding. I looked the Housekeeper in the eyes. "And will the Master also beg the Mistress's forgiveness," I said, chin jutting in defiance, "for his nightly perambulations?"

Oh God in heaven! The words had just popped out.

"I'm sure I don't know what you're talking about," Mistress Cingria snapped. "But if you can't hold that impertinent tongue, I'll take the whip to you myself." She hustled away. Did I imagine it, or had the hand that reached for her keys just trembled?

Jezza and I stood as far from each other as possible. We stripped to our chemises and poured water over ourselves, bare feet on icy floor, bitterly cold, not speaking, shivering. She wore only the thinnest, dingiest chemise, quite patched. I almost felt sorry for her.

Johanna snuck in, bringing us towels. "You maids picked just the wrong time to get Mistress Cingria's back up." She looked at us ruefully. "She and the Mistress had a big row yesterday over who's to run the household. Oh, Lordy. Made me fear the family'd be lookin for a new Housekeeper. Gotta go."

I barely had time to digest her words when Egbert, in a newly pressed shirt and breeches, poked his head through the door. He munched on an apple, surveying us in our scant coverings. Patches of mud and feathers still stuck here and there to legs and hair.

"You're both pathetic! Two drowned pigeons! When the de Witts get home and hear what you've done, oh, will you two be in trouble."

I crossed my eyes and thrust my tongue out. Jezza cocked him a *snook*. He left, but not before giving my body another scan, winking. I threw a wet cloth at him. Now my throat ached; I'd better not catch the ague. My face felt tender and swollen, and I, foolish—though secretly glad I got in a few punches. What punishment awaited us? Surely I'd be sacked.

~

How humiliating, that Titus caught me fighting with Jezza. Well, he got me back. Just when I was about to apologize. Perhaps it would be best if I just caught cold and died.

I trundled back to my room, clothes dripping, face and ear stinging, remembering how he'd left with Jezza that night. And wondered whether I could ever face him again.

Chapter 32

I have passed from the outermost portal
To the shrine where a sin is a prayer.
—A.G. Swinburne

April 1750 (Autumn)

A faint, pearly sun had just sent shafts of light over the mountains when we set out for Cape Town, this time in a smaller wagon drawn by six draft horses. We were hoping to make the trip in under three hours, rather than the usual four, because Titus had to meet a man about an Arabian. Samuel sat up front while I sat in the back with Johanna, Jaco, and two baskets of rags for the ragman. We'd flipped back the canvas top, exposing ourselves to an increasingly warm sun.

I was too embarrassed to talk to Titus, or even regard him. We hadn't had a proper conversation since I'd drawn his portrait and called him terrible names. And then there was that little scuffle with Jezza. What a mess.

It was a miracle, but Mistress Cingria never told the Master and Mistress what had happened in the barn that day. Had I actually frightened her into silence? Me, so young and already a blackmailer! Egbert had the nerve to try to snitch on us and threw a fit later in the kitchen when the Master wouldn't believe him. Cook, bless her heart, not wishing us any more suffering, had already told the de Witts my bruises were from falling off a horse, and Jezza's from a beating by a jilted lover. He believed her. Employers always love juicy stories about the lives of their underlings.

I couldn't stop touching my swollen eye. Titus turned back to look, then cracked the whip, urging the horses on, expressionless. What he must think of me.

My fight with Jezza was over him, the servants gossiped. Actually she's always shown me contempt. But a knockdown fight over a man? Couldn't be. Couldn't.

This morning, as if in denial, I'd powdered my bruises and put on—along with a fine blue skirt, red bodice, and a lace-edged petticoat—a proud attitude. I held my head high, and with studied nonchalance watched white clouds clot the sky. I wanted to forget all of it.

"Hey, Saskia, we didn't know you had such a powerful left jab," Jaco shouted for all to hear. Jaco had been a boxer back home, fought for prize money, even had noble patrons. He was basically kind but a little rough around the edges. He knew a lot about life. "You'd have pulverized *me* into *mieliepap*. If it was you against the stowmen at the harbor, I'd put my money on you."

Johanna burst into laughter, as did Jaco. Samuel chuckled into his hand. I looked away, trying to hide a grin, then saw that Titus too was smiling.

"You flattened her, Saski," said Johanna. We passed under the shade of wild figs, and the wind blew great frizzled locks out of her cap. "Good Lord knows she had it comin. Someone shoulda knocked the feathers out of that ostrich long ago."

I turned, looking pointedly at the back of Titus's head, saying, "Somebody here already has—time and time again, from what I've heard."

"Whoooa!" Titters of laughter. Titus, face forward, mumbled something under his breath.

"What did you say, Titus?"

Jaco grinned. "He said, some mares like many the mountings."

Jaco and Johanna roared with laughter while Samuel buried his.

"If that's the way you think about women," I countered, "don't expect any decent maid to have anything to do with you!"

There. My dignity demanded that. He looked back, glowering. Everyone shifted about in discomfort. We rode on in silence.

"Hey, Samuel," Jaco called out abruptly, tapping the old man's shoulder. "When was the last time you did it with a woman? A hundred years ago?" Johanna giggled.

"More like one hundert twenty. No, Massa Jaco, I wants you ta know I still gots lead in dis here pencil, isn't it?"

Titus grinned while the rest of us hooted with laughter. "Yes, my uncle, maybe you do have the lead, but maybe you forget how to write." Gales of laughter, for Samuel was illiterate. Titus smiled happily.

"S'not bout forgettin, son," Samuel retorted. "I yust got no body to write *to*!"

We exploded. How quickly this talk had turned bawdy! Johanna and Jaco chimed in with a sewing song: *"Let my needle pierce your little hole, let me ply in and out, sewing you up so neatly . . .*" I grinned and shook my head.

Just then, a farm wagon clambered over the hill at full speed. Our horses bolted and Titus pulled them to the right, calming them. We recognized the Portuguese foreman from a neighboring estate. "Men attacked!" he shouted. "Leopard! Men bleeding bad! Can't get em on wagon by myself. Please help."

Sweet Jesus! Laborers were clearing land when the beast leapt out of the forest.

Titus said, "We follow in this wagon."

"No, Titus!" Johanna cried. "You *have to* buy that Arabian *today*! And Saskia has her lesson. Jaco can go. Uncle and me knows how to care for wounds, don't we, Sammie?" She reached into one of the baskets and pulled out torn sheets. "Ragman won't miss these. Cape Town will just have to wait."

"Hurry, *please*," the foreman begged, turning his team around. The three of them clambered into his wagon, and they disappeared over the hill.

Titus and I sat for a minute, me still in the back. We scanned the fields. A leopard mauling field workers, still loose in the countryside. "Damn rogue leopard," I mumbled.

"All leopards be rogue leopards." Titus's voice was flat. "I surely would like to see that cat." He knotted the reins and stuck a leg through them, pulling out a hide bundle no larger than an egg. He rolled it in his palm, as if it were precious.

"What's that?"

"Just the *muti*. Protection." After some urging, he poured the contents onto his hand. I moved closer—small pieces of stone, bone, dried herbs, and other strange matter. I pointed to a yellowed object. "The toenail of the leopard."

"Claw. It's called a claw."

"Claw, then. I go nowhere without this." He looked over the veldt. "The leopard, he be the night hunter, cautious. For the longest time never we see him, but the hunters and the trekkers drive the leopard back onto the estates. Then this thing happen." He held the talisman to his belly, muttered some words, then wrapped it up and pushed it back into his pocket. So Titus was superstitious.

As we rode, we scanned the bush nervously. When something crashed out of the trees, the horses reared, neighing, and we jumped. It was a kudu with enormous, spiraled horns, and when it saw us, tore back through the brush.

Titus whipped harder on the horses' backs, and we trotted furiously along the road. How I wished we had a musket! Jaco had taken it with him. The only weapon Titus had was his bamboo-and-leather whip. Could we beat off a leopard with it? After crossing sand dunes, then through a valley of farms and small estates, we started to relax a little.

Suddenly it struck me that traveling alone like this with Titus was strictly forbidden, even if we hadn't arranged it. What rumors it spawned last time! Since then, so many feelings had passed between us, yet . . . A jittery excitement filled me.

"Come, Saskia. Come sit up front with me."

How nakedly he used my name! So familiar, without the polite "Miss." I obeyed.

We didn't speak. He stared straight ahead, his gaze threatening to burn a hole through the horse's collar. There was a large, unspoken thing between us, swelling with weight. "Oh, God, Titus, I'm mortified at what I said the other—"

"I thought you understand me," he said with controlled anger. "I thought I understand you."

"After our time on the mountain, I felt . . . You flirted with me at the festival, too, damn it! Outrageously! Then padded after Jezza like a lost pup. Made love in the Quarters, no doubt." I drew in a sharp breath, unable to look at him.

"What are you talking about?"

"You know what you did. Bewitched me, then, then—I felt so dishonored! Perhaps I shouldn't expect any more from-

from—"

"The savage blackie? The ignorant *kaffir* slave?" His eyes tore at me like darts. Beneath his dark skin, a blush of purple.

"Titus, I'm so ashamed. I guess I just wanted to hurt you."

"How good you are at that. You find the best words for that."

We rode in silence for some time. "I suppose," I said, "you're used to taking women. Eating the melon when ripe, then tossing aside the rind."

"What is this talk? Nothing do you know. How you tear the ground from these feet! This *juffrouw* Saskia, she be above that. So I did think."

I felt raw. Moisture gathered in my lashes. I looked out into the sky, following the movements of an eagle soaring at the edge of bluffs. "I thought I was above that too. Maybe I'm just as bad as the rest of them." Now tears fell.

Titus found his handkerchief. "Dry those eyes, those eyes the color of the rain. The tears, they make those whites red. And the face of yours already be black and blue. Too much color for one face in one day."

I laughed, dabbing at my lashes.

"I do not do you the dishonor, Saskia. It be true that once I knew Jezza like that. Then I tell her very long time ago, nothing happen between us again. She does not let go. In the orchard I scold her. When I return, you be cutting the hair, and you do not let me speak."

I drew in a deep breath. I wanted to believe him.

The rough road knocked the wagon about, and his shoulder brushed against mine. "Why is it, when I sit next to you like this, I go so very crazy? Do you not know what you mean to me?" We drove under the shadows of wide thorntrees. "Something happen ever since these eyes, they fill themselves with you. But you be White, I be Black and the slave. How could you love me too?"

"But Jezza . . ."

Titus breathed impatiently. "Very pretty. And holds the spite and the guile. The more I drift from her, the more she fasten to me."

Titus went on to tell me she had not been faithful to him. That she was taken when very young, by her first master, then his sons. And that was the life of the slavewoman. Lilies plucked before their time, left to wither in the dust. He said that to be a person of color was bad, but to be a woman and a slave—well, to Whites that was . . . unforgivable. "You be different. You have the bright spirit. The good heart. You speak true. When you not be angry, that is."

A twisted smile. "I don't always speak truly, Titus. But I do to those who are honest with me. What does that make me then?"

"The slave, he cannot always be honest, even if he wish it. You also be the slave." He looked at me mischievously. "But the dangerous kind."

"Dangerous? Because I challenge my masters? A foolish slave then," I grinned. "Though very intelligent. Don't forget intelligent. And talented."

"*Ja, ja*, also those things. Pretty too. Pretty crazy." I laughed. "When I meet you, I see the woman who treat me like the man and not the slave. Tender, fresh, like the blossom."

"Did you know I used to fear you, Titus? Even then, I couldn't put you out of my mind. But I thought you must prefer an African woman. You know—a tribal thing."

"Nay." He turned toward me, and an exquisite warmth descended through my chest. "I do not know how, but I *know* you. You come to the estate, and . . . this head fight it, but . . . this heart . . ."

I hesitated, then placed my hand on his—white skin on

black. We laced our fingers together tightly. We rode along like that for some time, the sun beating on our backs. My heart was flooding its banks while the lilies on the hillside burned red with new life. Then, for no reason, he reined in the horses and awkwardly folded me in his arms. "Let me take you to the hidden place."

A great rush, a wave of surrender and fear. And that rumbling of inner thunder. We drove perhaps a mile until he abruptly turned the team down a road nearly obscured by forest. I was shivering like willow leaves. The sky was more incandescently blue. The earth slipped beneath our wheels. From the distance a deep hum traveled on the air toward us then grew into a booming sound—the rush of water. All at once the trees opened onto a grassy clearing, and beyond the clearing, a waterfall.

"I show this only to you."

"Oh! Oh!" And what a waterfall it was, magnificent, as tall and narrow as a three-story canal house. It gushed in torrents over rocks, descending into a great pool. Churned-up foam splayed into lacey filaments and prisms of broken colors bridged to land. Beyond that, orchids, feather ferns, and lush moss greened the shadowed cliffs.

We ran to the pond, splashed faces and mouths. Titus watered the horses, took my hand, and led me along the pond's edge to the wall of cascade.

"This way," he shouted over the roar. He pointed to a web spanning the space between two bushes. The water spider paused, silky filaments stirred in the breeze. Beads of water caught in its lace, glinting like silver in the sun. "Ariadne. You are *my* Ariadne."

I breathed in sharply, strangely pleased. Ariadne, Princess of Crete, who saved Theseus from the confounding labyrinth by offering him a ball of thread.

I looked away as he peeled off waistcoat and breeches. Then he stood before me in his long white shirt, legs hard and shiny in the long grass. He offered me a palm. I hesitated, took it, my heart thrumming like a coming storm. This beautiful and terrible mystery.

My skirts billowed in the breeze. A shiver coursed through my body, and I clasped my arms across my chest.

"How like the exotic bird you look!" he said. When his toes pried at one of my shoes, I lifted my foot, then sat in the deep grass and unloosened the ribbons holding up stockings. He knelt next to me."Let me do it." His Black fingers slid down my legs, pressing into the skin as if he were playing the keys of a virginal—but they trembled.

"I thought you do this all the time," I laughed, hoping my nervousness would not show.

"Not all the time. Never with you."

I untied my hat and lace-edged cap. He helped me with more: jacket, petticoats, each unwrapped like sheets of tissue, until I was in only my chemise and stays. Pleasure, such pleasure, pleasure and heat, exquisite, demanding heat. I loosened the pins, and my hair fell about my shoulders. He buried his dark face in it. "When I see you like this, when this way I touch you, this blood, it floods this heart."

My head was reeling, my senses drunk. Was I really going to give myself this day to this man, this Black slaveman I loved so much? I felt myself being sucked into some dark, redeeming maelstrom, afraid, yet longing to fall in. There was a fleeting vision that death was stalking us. The cessation of breath, a soft enveloping darkness. If death was stalking us, so was life.

My eyes must have shown fear, because Titus took my hand and led me over rocks to the edge of the waterfall, past kingfishers and wild white orchids, then down a narrow passage behind the torrent. Dank and fusty smells rose up. We leaned back, letting the spray batter and sting us. If for one moment I could freeze that spume, what pattern of lace would be revealed? I lost myself in water that rushed by like an upended river—floating, floating out of my body, merging with mist. For one long moment, the light, the water, the two of us—all wove neatly into some timeless tapestry I cannot explain.

Something caught my eye, something in the hollow of rock behind us, like a pile of bleached twigs.

"Bones," Titus said. "This be where the beasts come to die."

I stared at the great mound that now took on shapes: legbones, ribs, skulls of antelope, spiraled horns, tangled piles of them, like old ivory, smelling of must.

"A wild animal cemetery?"

"Do not touch. These bones, they be sacred."

He stepped forward into the rush of water, letting it wash over him, and gasped at the cold. His shirt clung to his body so completely I saw every living muscle. Suddenly I wanted to run out into the sun again. Instead I plunged into the cascade, let out a shocked cry, jumped back. I looked down at my wet chemise. In the dim light of the tunnel, Titus and I regarded one another. I started to shiver, slowly at first, then violently. I was on the verge of tears.

"Come." He frowned. "It is wrong I do this to you."

He grasped my hand and we edged our way cautiously along the tunnel's slippery rocks, out into the warmth. He dove into the pool, his head, moments later, cresting some distance away. I was confused. I settled on an outcropping of flat boulder, my head on knees, rocking back and forth. Heat from the sun pulled steam from my chemise, and I shook. My stomach felt queasy.

Titus burst out of the pool, returning with a blanket from the wagon, which he lowered over my hunched shoulders. "I am so sorry, Saskia. I am such the fool. We will dress and go."

I watched as he brushed water from his body. How I loved him! I rose, letting the blanket slip away, and pulled him toward me. I kissed him, kissed again. The sun was high. Above the roar of the waterfall, insects thrummed in the grass. I wanted to be close to him, so close that the eagles overhead would read us as one tree rooted deep into the earth. This is it, I told myself. This. Now.

"I don't want to go." The wind whipped at my damp hair, snapping it about like ropes. I laid the blanket under an old wide-spreading fig and knelt. He came and knelt close. "I want you to make love to me," I said, playing with his fingers. "But first I must tell you something. You may not want me then."

He sat back on his haunches. "What be that?"

I hesitated, slipped my hands from his. "It's so hard to speak it." My eyes were brimming. The hem of my chemise fluttered in the breeze. Then his hands were on my shoulders.

"Do not worry. Whatever it be, it is all right. Have you been with another?"

I breathed in deeply. "No. Yes. Not by choice." I breathed in and out slowly, gathering courage. "A man broke into me. I didn't want him to, but he did." Yes, broke in, as if I were a precious casket, and he had torn the latch.

"What do you mean?"

Again, I hesitated. "On board ship, coming here. A sailor. He caught me alone and thrust his . . . his fingers into me." Chattering leaves made conversation in the wind. Through their shadows, the sun dappled light on our skin, over our blanket. "His seed spilled out. Over my thigh."

"My precious Saskia, I be so sorry. But I do not care about that. Think no more on it."

"The shame!"

"Nay. All people, they carry some shame. And they cannot speak of it." He rocked me in his arms for a long time. His tenderness took me unawares. Such a hard memory I'd been carrying, and now it broke open like a shell.

Titus reached for his breeches and took out his leather talisman. I watched in wonder as he placed a leaf upon a boulder, tapped out herbs and, striking a flint, set light to them. White smoke curled skyward, a sweet odor permeating the air. He uttered some kind of prayer, then, "I ask the ancestors of us for the blessing," he said, "that what we are about to do be sacred in every way."

I waited for him to show me. He drew my face to his, kissed my eyelids, my wounded ear, the bones of my cheeks, the neck's hollow. Pressed a hand to my breast. "I have so many wounds," I said, touching my face. "So imperfect for you!"

"Hush."

Breathless. Thinking stopped. I shuddered, a rush of sensation, emotion, pleasure. Pulsing. He kissed me so hard it hurt. "Do you be afraid?"

"No. Yes."

He lay me gently back. Through his taut curls, through patches of leaves, I watched the sky—brilliant sky, riotous sky, sky bluer than cobalt glass. I could only bear to look at the curve of his Black shoulder. My hands found their way around his back, into furrowed places, into scars of whips.

Then only earth and sky were witness. Earth, sky, sun, and all our ancestors. His urgency, the hurt, the hurt all mixed up with the pleasure, and bits of blood. The droning of the wind. Skin like dark ponds, and buried bones. Black wings beating hard against the air. Somewhere, in a distant meadow, I was climbing a hill of wildflowers, higher, higher still. Bliss so raw it felt like pain, or fear.

~

Afterward, he held me, and I thought I felt the breathing of the earth. I watched him in his nap—a sleeping lion, breath falling in little tremors. Cape Town, the manor, all seemed far, far away. Places I dreamed of once.

When he turned, I flinched—whip scars covered his back. I had felt them as we lay together. Now, to see, actually see them . . . When I asked, he said they were from an early master. And that they were his eternal shame. "Why shame? You did nothing wrong."

"*Ja*, I did the wrong. One day I tell you."

Before we left, I looked long at the waterfall. A hundred thousand droplets frozen midair, all dashing back to merge into the waters again. All coming home.

~

We were late to my appointment with Effie, very late. Titus walked me to her door, squeezing my hand behind my skirt.

"Will you have time to purchase your mare?"

"Just enough. Do not worry." He smelled his palm. "The dust of your gold be still on my hand."

"I am a scarlet woman now," I whispered. "You made me so."

"You look more the pink than the scarlet, as always you do. Except for those wounds."

I apologized to Effie. She didn't ask why I was late, only sank into her tattered yellow chair. "Well, how much can we do in an hour, hmmm?"

I took out the lace I'd been working on and tried to compose myself, as if nothing extraordinary had happened. Finally my hands stopped and rested on the pillow.

"Aunt Effie, can people of color be bigots too?" I suddenly realized how much I loved her.

"We're all bigots, Saskia, every last one of us. That's what I've observed." She sighed, put down her bobbins and tried telling me a story about her husband once mediating two cases that looked similar, one involving a White burgher beating his slave, while the other beater was a Malay woman beating her worker. The man got twice the prison time. I think that was the story, but I found myself remembering the curve of Titus's arm. I felt him still, exquisitely, as if he were still inside of me. *You're going to rot in hell,* Anna would tell me, if she knew.

"Of course my husband had pointed out—Saskia, dear, have you listened to one word I've said?"

She cocked her head toward my lace. I'd been working the bobbins, not even noticing that several had fallen over the chair, and that I'd been tying all kinds of strange knots. All the lace I'd made since arriving was a mess, a royal mess. A web spun by a drunken spider.

I gazed up helplessly. "Auntie, I'm sorry. Now I'll have to undo the whole thing! Damnation!" I plunked my lace pillow onto the table. "Oh, I can't face reworking all this now." Titus would be coming for me soon—how I longed to see him again.

Effie gazed at me thoughtfully as afternoon light sifted low through the window. She asked if my bruises hurt, and before I knew it I was telling her all about the fight with Jezza. "Tell me, Effie. Do you think it horribly sinful for a Black man and a White woman to love one another? I mean to *really* love one another?"

She put down her bobbins and eyed me with surprise. "How could I possibly think it a sin? My parents had a mixed race marriage. So did my husband and I. How could the good Lord object to races mixing when he put us all on this earth together? It's just some humans who get all worked up." She pushed aside her pillow. "Do you love Titus so very much then?"

"What? Oh, no, no. I'm talking about a maid at the estate."

She regarded me with dancing eyes. "Are you, now?"

I looked at her in alarm. Did she know? Did it show that, just a few hours before, I'd given myself to him? Did I look different? Smell different? Was I bleeding through my skirt? For the last hour I'd been living in a country of Titus. We were of the same earth now, and nothing on this African continent, nothing anywhere, could come between us.

I heard his familiar knock, ran, and opened the door, beaming. Effie pulled herself up, and Titus gave her a hug. I gathered up my lace things, grasped Effie's shoulders, and crushed her cheeks with kisses. When I looked at Titus, his whole body seemed to smile.

"Go well, my children," Effie called out as we hurried down the street.

"Stay well," we shouted back.

"And be careful!"

But how can love be careful? Or how could we expect, that from this day forward, that things would go well at all?

Chapter 33

April 1750 (Autumn)

I awoke early, before the horn, even before the sun rose, for I was bitter cold. I reached down and pulled up another blanket, and lay thinking. I'd tossed and turned last night, obsessing that the most beautiful thing I'd ever felt, lying with Titus, was the worst of sins. I somehow had to purify myself or give up all hope of heaven. But lying with Titus *was* heaven. If the Master or the *predikant* ever found out, they would crucify me. My mind swam in treacherous eddies: what is good, what is evil?

Good, evil—the words spooled out of me again, like floss from a spider, weaving webs across my mind.

There is a man I think of in the morning when I'm alone, when light from the sun first penetrates my room. I have watched him in the yard below, mutely, through lace I hold against panes of glass. I carry this man close, like a song, like a wound. There is a man I think of who is like darkest earth. He warms me like mist rising from the soil of Africa.

There is a man I speak to in my thoughts. I think of him as I write the whiteness of lace. He floats up to me, a poem rising like water from the filaments. There is a dark-skinned man who swims to me in my dreams, dreams that hover like birds of desire.

I rose as the cocks screeched and opened my shutters to the bare light of dawn. Dogs yapped, donkeys bawled, a distant jackal called back, and in the thicket a rock pigeon cooed the morning into awakening.

So many emotions were boiling inside—I could explode with them. I looked out over the hills to Madame Remy's farm, so happy I'd have the chance to talk to her today, for the family had asked me to go again to return and pick up books. Her blessing for Titus and me would make all the difference, but would she give it? Could I dare tell her?

I splashed water onto my face. I wouldn't tell my friends what had passed between Titus and me. I loved him so much, and that terrified me. In the past, it had always spelled loss. Titus hadn't said it, but he too had to be afraid. But our course was set. No longer could we dam the river, even if the waters sucked us down into their undertow and drowned us.

Late morning, I wrapped the borrowed volumes in cloth. I would ask for *The Life and Adventures of Robinson Crusoe*, a book the children and I were eager to read. At the kitchen door, Cook tucked two ceramic jugs into my arms. "Give these to the widow with thanks from the Mistress, Saskia. Rustigvallei's best portwine."

As I entered the stables, morning sun filtered in through narrow slits of windows. Motes of dust floated on the air like dry mist. Smells of horses filled my nostrils, friendly smells. Titus was already saddling a great Friesian for me named "Snowball." Such light shone from Titus's eyes, I feared I'd disintegrate. "Go fetch water from the well and fill the trough," he instructed the stableboy. He tightened the leather cinch under the mare's belly, hardly looking up.

I was glad he sent the boy away. One careless word from a slavechild could be our ruin. Titus packed the jugs and books into the saddlebags, looked around, then stepped behind me, wrapping his great arms around my waist, rocking me. How sweet he smelled—*kardemom* and groomed mares. Perhaps I never had to eat again; just to touch him was such nourishment. He rested two fingers on the area around my eye, my wounds still black and blue, and laughed.

"How you mock me," I said.

"Here, I have something for you." He reached into a pocket and handed me a folded piece of paper, its wrinkles smoothed. "I want you to have this to remember me by, ever we be parted."

Be parted? It was the portrait I made of him the night of the harvest festival. I was pleased to have it back. It *was* a good likeness.

"Thank you, Titus." I parted my cape, feeling for the pocket beneath my skirt.

"Wait. Do you not see the poem I write for you on the back?"

"You wrote me a poem? No one has ever done that for me. What a lovely thing!"

"It not be the Shakespeare. But it come from the heart of me. Please, read it later." The mare stomped, whinnied impatiently.

"I only wish I had something for you."

"You do." He selected a large pair of shears from the wall, the kind used to trim manes. He circled me, inspecting my head, snapping the blades.

Cautiously I removed my cap, then recoiled in exaggeration, arms protecting my head. "You aren't going to chop off *all* of it, are you?"

He laughed. "I will make the whip out of it and use it to keep you obedient! Hold still." A glint of metal flashed frighteningly close to my head, and I felt a tug. A lock of hair dropped into his callused palm. "The band of the sunlight." He smiled.

"Give me those." I held the shears to his neck and snipped off a few curls. "The wool of the lamb." I pulled the drawing from my pocket, tore off two corners, and we folded each other's locks into the paper. "Titus, I want to read your poem *now*!"

"Nay," he said, folding the paper up again. "Later, when you all alone be." Then his voice dropped to a whisper. "Saskia, I have the plan of escape."

I cocked my head playfully. "Are you going away with me or without me, then?"

He arched an eyebrow. "Do you wish to be with me, Saskia, to marry and live with this poor Black man?"

A chill ran up my spine. I was silent. Snowball stomped her foot impatiently. Did I have the courage to run away and be with this Black man forever? My fingers played with the horse's mane, then I turned and looked straight into his eyes. "I'd spend my life in a trekker's wagon to be with you, Titus—or a Bushman's hut. I'd swim with the penguins to Antarctica, if that's where you'd be."

He let out a long breath. "Then to the ends of the earth it be. I have been thinking about the land of China. I have listened when the travelers, they talk of it. In that land there be no Calvinists with the slaves and the heavy laws. I can tend the horses. You can make the lace. We will be free to love in openness."

"China," I mused, my voice trailing away. My gaze wandered,

trying to imagine that land. Papa once brokered paintings of people with small, oriental eyes scurrying about in sedan chairs. Mystic mountains, flying monks, nobles in great embroidered robes. *Chinees* women sometimes traversed the streets of Cape Town, carried on the backs of slaves or tottering painfully on the arms of servants. Blood drained from my face. "Will they bind my feet?"

Titus laughed. "I will not let them do that thing."

China. And marriage!

"But we must go soon."

A seriousness descended on me. "I need time to think about this, Titus."

The stableboy stepped back inside. Titus cupped his fingers against the horse's belly. I slipped my foot in, and he hoisted me astride the old horse. "Will you be all right? Do you want my boy to ride with you?" Titus adjusted the stirrups, grasping my ankle when the boy was not looking. "Wait." He returned from the tack room with a long whip, positioning it in the saddlebag.

"I don't know how to use that."

"There be the many dangerous animals about. You have watched me use it."

He held the horse's bridle and led us out into the sun, giving Snowball's rump a slap. My sleepy steed broke into a half-trot. I reached back and touched the handle of the whip as I passed under the winery arches, turned in the saddle and cast Titus a lingering glance. He stood leaning against the stable door, arms folded across his long leather apron, watching me. What a fine figure my Black man cut!

Snowball and I followed the vine roads, passing fields where laborers bent and stretched, picking grapes baked into raisins by a late autumn sun. At last beyond the manor, I reined in my mare under the shade of a yellowwood and reached for

Titus's poem.

The rain was courting the spider.
He came in the morning with the dew,
Catching on her web, courting her.
She touched the rain, and
The web shimmered,
Wet in the rising sun.

When she touched the rain
He turned to mist; he
Enveloped her fragrance
With his mist.

The rain came to court the
Spider maiden.
He came in the morning by the
Waterfall,
Catching on her web,
Courting her, turning
Lush the grass.

~

In front of Madame Remy's house stood a horse trap and a fine carriage. So I was not her only visitor. Her groom took Snowball, and I walked the well-laid stones past pruned rosebushes. Would there be roses in China?

Bulky Apolline let me into the hall, her expression grim. Stooping against his cane in the parlor was Dr. Buehl, and next to him a very elegant woman in a dark traveling suit, her linen-colored hair swept high. She had removed her bonnet and placed it on the table in the foyer, something only a family member would do.

The two had not seen me. They talked in soft, concerned tones. I hesitated. From scraps of conversation, I gathered that Madame Remy had collapsed but was recovering. The young woman glanced into the hallway, then hastened out to greet me, taking my hands. She looked startled as she surveyed my face, and for a moment seemed to lose her composure. I had forgotten the bruises on my face. I blushed.

"Dearest girl, you must be Saskia. I am Adele Servier, madame's daughter," she said in slightly accented Dutch. "My mother has mentioned how fond of you she is." How gracious! For I was but a servant from another manor. I curtsied. "We're trying not to worry about her. She's resting. Her heart was in considerable pain, but she seems all right now, God willing." Tendrils of fear like a thorny rose pierced my heart. I could not speak. "The good doctor tells me he detects no permanent damage. Is that not so, Doctor?"

"She'll most likely be on her feet again soon, and outlive all of us," Dr. Buehl said, stepping forward, his cane rapping on the yellowwood floor. "How are you, young lady? You're Saskia, the young maid from Rustigvallei, are you not?"

"I am indeed, sir," I curtsied, glad to see him. If anyone at the Cape could heal, it would be him.

From the sitting room, Madame Remy's wavering voice. "Let the girl in! I want to speak to her. The rest of you, you've been here fretting over me long enough. Now go home!"

I looked at the two, feeling both flattered and embarrassed.

In the great room, the widow sat on a settee, bundled with her terrier in a thick paisley shawl. The draperies were partly closed, and light from the fire illuminated one side of her face. How ashen her skin—and a blush of blue in the lips.

"Madame needs her rest," Apolline commanded, staring at me pointedly before ambling toward the door.

"Rest I do not need. Tea I need, with my friend Saskia," Madame Remy said, coughing. "Bring us a tray, would you? I should never have freed you, Apolline." She shook a bony finger at her maid. "You've been bossing me about ever since!"

"Well, guess who done taught me that!" the maid retorted. We were all chuckling as she closed the door behind her.

I stood awkwardly just inside the room, not knowing what to say. I curtsied. "Madame, I'm so deeply sorry you are ill."

"*Comment vas-tu, ma fille?*" She scanned my face with that keen look. "What happen? Were you stampeded by the elephant?"

My hand flew to my wounds. "More of a fight with a big cat, I'm afraid. But how are *you*, madame, and your heart? I'm distressed for you."

"A big cat, eh? We two are the living wounded, *non, ma petite*?" She tapped her breast. "The gears in this old timepiece have been meshing strangely." She coughed. "But God does not up there want me raising Cain and pruning just yet his roses. Anyway, I am sorry you come all this way for nothing. Forgive me if we do not exchange books today."

"Books don't seem very important right now, madame. But thank you so for these." I placed the borrowed volumes on a table and sat down before her on an ottoman, glad to see more color rise in her cheeks. "I brought you a small gift."

"What's this?" When she unwrapped the tissue, rapture filled her face. All over a length of simple lace edging.

"*Ma cherie*, did you make this? How lovely! How great the skill you have. Thank you, dear Saskia." I beamed, telling her it wasn't much, but enough to trim a neckline.

"And what is news about the slave Sara?" she whispered. I pulled back as her maid walked through the door with cakes and Ceylon tea. "Oh, Apolline knows."

Of course. She must have helped. "Safely in Mosambiek." I smiled. "And she wouldn't have made it without your help, Madame Remy. And you, Apolline."

The terrier Stubble jumped to the floor. I surveyed the room, again admiring its beauty, the pantheon of saints and madonnas who breathed out blessings. On the table sat orchids as white as river-bleached handkerchiefs, and in spring the room would be filled once again with tulips and roses. I was at peace in this room.

She poured tea, a triumphant smile on her lips, asking how my lacemaking was going and if my dear crippled teacher was well. Again, I began opening my heart to her. I told her how ungodly I felt, how I was tempted to do rebellious things, even strike Pier when he spoke against the Blacks. I told her how angry I got when people said I was lazy when I sat at the window making lace. How I felt vindictive when they spread untrue rumors about me. "Madame Remy, you are my Mother Confessor." Except for that one thing I could not yet confess.

"You do get into situations, do you not, *ma cherie*? From where does all this anger come?"

"I don't know, madame. The world can be so unjust . . . Grandfather said Calvin fought the devil daily, and that I should too." I put down my cup, lowered my voice, and leaned toward her. "I feel I *do* fight the devil, madame. But I fear he's winning."

She laughed, then realizing it was not a joke, looked at me reflectively. How calm her eyes were! "Perhaps what your grandfather and Calvin meant was that every second of the day, we must be brutally honest with ourselves about our motivations. And when we see ourselves about to do or say anything hurtful or self-indulgent, we must stop and ask what would please God."

I reached down and stroked Stubble. Though she was Roman Catholic, she would not condemn Calvin but sought the truth in his teachings. As for my asking what God wished me to do, that was not so easy, for when I'm angry I want to stay angry, even to hurt someone. I know that is not pretty, but it is honest.

"What does God want for our lives, Madame Remy? Is it to be good?"

She puckered her mouth as if she had just sucked a lemon. I wanted to laugh. "Good? Good? What is good? Everyone has the different thought what is good."

"Goodness is to love and help people, isn't it?"

"Yes. But mostly we love and help with the motive of our own. We do what we think others *should* need—not what their soul needs. Which we cannot know. Too much doing good, we may do harm."

I sat and pondered her words, not really knowing what she meant. "What is God, Madame Remy?"

"I know not how to answer that, *ma fille.*" She sipped her tea. "I only know there is nothing God is not."

For some minutes we sat in silence. I wanted to tell her all my confusing emotions. Longed to tell someone with an understanding heart that Titus and I had touched and loved and known as wedded people do. "Madame, do I look different to you?"

"Well, now." She turned my face to the fire. "Despite the wounds, I think you do look the little bit different. Your eyes, *oui*, they sparkle, like *petite* fireflies. Saskia, are you in love?"

I lowered my gaze, but did not answer. Oh, what had I started here? I dared not tell her the truth. How could she possibly understand?

"You *are* in love, aren't you, my Saskia? *Ah, la!* He did not hit you, did he? I hope that wound is not from the man you love!"

"Oh, no, madame, no!" I put my hand to my eye. "It was a fight with a slavegirl." I lowered my eyelids. "I'm so ashamed."

"Do you fight over this man? Tsk, tsk. Not to do! But you may tell me about him, unless you feel this old woman, she pry . . ." By firelight her eyes blazed, and in a flash I felt she had dipped into the interior of me. "Perhaps you are even a bit mad with love, *non*?" She struck the arm of the settee again, startling me. "Well, it is about time! He is fortunate to have you—if you can learn to curb this your anger. Is he the fine man?"

"The finest. But I don't think my father would be happy with my choice." I stared far into the flames. Nor the Master, nor the Mistress, I thought. Nor you, Madame Remy. Probably not even Titus's aunt, Sladie. Certainly not Calvin, for that matter.

"Saskia, dear, let me tell you a secret: the passion and the object are one. The source of love and what is loved are one. Do you understand, *ma cherie*? One and the same." I wrinkled my brow, stretching to understand. She took two fingers and tapped them lightly on my chest. "Women have the beautiful pearl at the core of their being, Saskia. Once you uncover your pearl, you will find all the beauty and purity that waits within. Then, *ma cherie*, when you love a man by the light of that pearl, you have loved rightly. That is the secret, dear Saskia. And one more secret there is yet: shine your pearl on the world, share your pearl, but do not give it away. Hold it close. It is who you are. All men search for the light of that pearl—for it shows them who *they* are." Her cool white fingers fell gently on mine. "If you only knew, *ma petite cherie*, the beauty I see within you."

I stared into Madame Remy's face, then gazed out the window. Everywhere, raindrops sparkled on barren twigs. Her words struck some chord deep within, and I worked to set them to memory. I inhaled deeply and clasped my hands to my lap. "Thank you, Madame Remy, with all my heart. But what if the man I love is . . . is . . . *Black*?"

There was a catch in her breath. She turned and stared into the fire. I felt her pull from me. My heart dropped. I watched the log sputter in the fireplace as my hands flew together, as in prayer. "Dear madame, I hope I have not offended you."

"You have not offended me, *ma fille*. I was remembering something." She rested her soft eyes on me. "I also love once the man of color—the beautiful gentleman, from India. What you said made me think of him."

"When, Madame Remy?"

"Before you were born. He was the diplomat, you see. We met in Paris at a dinner . . ." Her voice trailed away. "We fall mad in love the first time our eyes, they catch. How dashing he was! And each of us married to another. He had the marriage of arrangement, and well, I think you could say I as well."

She paused. "We met when we could, but we thought our situation *très tragique*! Five months together, the happiest of my life, *ma cherie*. Then he was called back to Bombay." She focused on me now, as if awaking from a dream. "But I'm sorry, Saskia dear. Tell me about this man of yours, this man of color."

"He is a slave."

"Oh, *mon Dieu*!" The dog, startled, woke from its sleep and growled.

"But soon he's to have his freedom. It's all written in a contract. And he is a Christian."

"*Très bien*. Now—is he worthy of you, my dear?"

I leaned forward eagerly. "Oh, yes, madame, he is the very best of men."

She gave me a cautious eye. "But this liaison be against your

Dutch law, no?"

"Not only against civil law." I cast my eyes down, shame flushing my face. "The Bible too commands against it."

"Where in the Bible it says such a thing?"

"Deuteronomy 7. So says the *predikant*."

"Well, my dear, let us see for ourselves." She pointed to a large Bible sitting on its own table. I staggered under the weight, placing it on the cushion next to her. "*Merci*. Deuteronomy. Deuter . . . Here it is. Ah la! 'Hittites . . . Canaanites . . . seven nations . . . Neither shalt thou make marriages with them; Thy daughter shalt not give unto his son . . .' But this speaks of a people not to marry their enemies. *C'est de l'histoire ancienne.* Not about you at all."

I sighed with relief. On impulse, I grabbed her wan hand and kissed it.

"But why do you choose to love this . . . *Éthiop*?"

"I never chose it, madame. I tried hard *not* to love him. It is forbidden. And he so proud! But in my thoughts and in my dreams, there he was and is, always. Always Titus is with me. I cannot help it." I looked down at hands that sat upturned on my lap—how powerless they seemed. "He is a truly exceptional man, Madame Remy. And when I'm with him . . ." I stared into flames that licked greedily at the logs. "When I'm with him . . . I feel ignited . . . like that fire. All lit up inside. As if constellations of stars are swirling around inside me and flying out to him and to the world."

Laughter rang from Madame Remy like a tinkling bell. "Ah, *that's* the important thing, *ma cherie*. That's what people like these priests do not understand." As she leaned back into the pillows, her terrier jumped back into her lap. She tickled his chin.

"My dear, it is not the color of the man, but the quality in him that counts. And how much you love one another. You know, I choose my husband for the style, the wealth, the position, as my family wanted. He was not a bad man. But, *mon Dieu*, how often he kill my spirit, not put light to it. And though never do I want for anything, something inside nearly dies. In the end, I had to thank him." Her eyes were soft. "He pushed me into the arms of the Infinite.

"Listen to me, Saskia. These dark races have a fire to them, a ferocity." Her voice grew deep. "They are of the primal substance, are they not? If their souls have not been stolen by the White race." She sighed. "Sometimes I think we Europeans live in the beautiful walled garden, caught under the great upside-down champagne glass, breathing and rebreathing our own thin air, pushing away *real* life. If I could live my life over again, Saskia, I would do whatever it took to be with my Indian, even if only to be his mistress."

I leaned back, shocked. Yet I could understand feeling so strongly about a man that you might resign to being only his lover. Besides—madame was *French*.

When Stubble padded to the door and scratched, I let him out, allowing time for her words to settle in me. Madame Remy coughed as I sat down again, then turned to me with earnestness.

"I do not talk about the passion, my dear, that which the man and the woman have, for that does not remain forever. It may change into something deeper. Or into nothing at all. But please, *ma cherie*, choose the man who knows the value of the pearl that is *you*. That is the thing, dear Saskia. That is the thing!"

With an unsteady finger, she pointed to an oval table at the far end of her settee. "Bring me that black lace handkerchief, would you, Saskia? There's something inside it I have been wanting to give you for some time—if you will have it. It has been with my family many years, the precious thing I have held most days. It carries the devotion of many women loving God."

Then I was holding a rosary that glittered in the firelight. Tiny beads of coral—for each, a prayer to the Mother. Swinging from the chain were a medal of the Virgin crowned with stars and a crucifix. Christ in delicately carved ivory, fastened to his cross with miniature gold nails. I watched as flames cast a red shimmer over the figures, making them tremble.

Something in me was still cautious about this Roman religion, yet . . . it held a mystery and devotion I had not found in the only church I knew. I gazed at it—all the passion, all the pain of Christ's sufferings, his dying, the sadness in the Mother's eyes—all flooded over me. It was the most exquisite object anyone had ever given me, and dear to a woman I held dear. I reached out to hold it. One more precious object so terribly, terribly forbidden me. One more secret to hide. I had become a harbinger of secrets.

"Will you have it, *ma cherie*?"

"Already I cherish it."

"Keep this rosary safe. Perhaps one day you will understand the love of the Mother. She contains all, endures all, holds all." Like threads of lace, I thought. She grasped my wrist. "Do you know, *ma petite*, what you will be facing if you marry this *Éthiop*? Perhaps you do not know the depth of hatred in the hearts of some when they see love between the White woman with the Black man. Do you know this?"

"I know this, madame." I sighed. "We know the way the world is. We are ready for it."

Her shawl had slipped, exposing a patch of frail shoulder. I helped her wrap it more tightly across her chest. Dark circles swam under her eyes like mist. "Do you really know this? Are you truly so prepared? I will pray for the two of you."

"And I will pray for your complete and speedy recovery."

I turned to her with bashful eyes. "I don't want anything to happen to you."

"*Merci*, Saskia." She paused. "You know, I do not mind it, to die. This little play we call life, perhaps it is but a thought flashing through the mind of God. And all we must do is be truly present on stage."

She slumped back, her face paler than when I'd first come. Now I'd exhausted her. Still, I didn't want our time together to end. She reached for my hand. Her fingers were bent and frail, white flowers wilted at the stem.

"Who knows," she muttered in a thinning voice. "Perhaps we wrote the play ourselves. Please excuse me now, my dear. I am a little tired."

As I left, her head was falling back onto the cushions and a small wheeze whistled from out of her mouth.

~

A week after I'd visited Madame Remy, our conversation still lingered in my mind. Her crucifix now lived in the hollow leg of my footstool, wrapped securely in a muslin cloth where no one would find it.

I was making my bed in the attic that morning, dreaming of a life with Titus, when I suddenly smelled, out of nowhere, the scent of roses. Sweet! So fragrant! As I pulled the sheet taut and wrapped it under the mattress, I suddenly realized how strange that was. I owned no perfumes. It was too late in the year for flowers.

I plumped the pillow and smoothed the blankets, and smelled the scent again, this time intensely. The air was thick with it, as if a bottle of rose essence had fallen to the floor and shattered. I thought of Madame Remy and the beautiful bouquets of white roses she always had about her house. From my eastern window, I watched the sun just rising over coralline hills.

Shortly before midday, the children and I arrived home from a walk. I was taking off Catryn's jacket in the back foyer when Black Lucy answered a knock at the front door. Through the open gallery I saw the good Dr. Buehl, leaning weakly on his cane. I told the children to go upstairs, then hurried down the gallery.

"Lucy," he said, "fetch Mistress de Witt for me, would you please?" The doctor removed his dusty black hat and, refusing Lucy's offer to take it, folded it respectfully under his arm. "I won't be staying."

He took a few steps toward me, his brow creased in deep furrows. To my surprise, he grasped my hand for a moment, but said nothing. I fetched him a chair, starting to feel anxious.

Finally Mistress de Witt stood at her threshold in a long morning gown.

"Excuse the intrusion, Mistress. I came to tell you that . . ." His voice was brittle, faltering. "It's about your neighbor, Madame Remy." The doctor shifted his eyes from the Mistress to me. She had never met this neighbor of ours. "She died in her bed this morning."

I gasped.

"I'd been attending her since last night, when she suffered another seizure of the heart. Her family and servants were by her side." He raised his spectacles and blotted at moisture around his eyes. "Forgive me," he mumbled. "She was a dear friend."

The Mistress stood absolutely still. I turned away, my body tightening, and gazed all the way down the gallery, out the back door, to the bare oaks.

"She seemed to be waiting for her brother before she felt

ready to go. He galloped all the way from Cape Town. He'd been a priest in France, you see, and laid out the cloths and oils to give her Last Rites. I suppose it is the custom, because he asked her, 'Have you made your peace with God, dear sister?'

"It was difficult for her to talk, but she answered him clearly. 'Dear brother. I was not aware He and I had been quarreling.' Then she requested a white silk rose, patting the lace on her bed jacket. Her daughter pinned one on, saying, 'Mother, this is not a real rose. It has no perfume.' None of us could believe what happened next. Suddenly the fragrance of roses was everywhere, intense, strong, filling the room. She died the very moment the sun came up over the mountains."

I grabbed my skirts and tore down the gallery, through the back door and out into the yard. I ran and ran, stumbling on roots of the old camphor, finally falling in a heap on the grass, sobbing. She was dead. My beloved Madame Remy, dead.

She was the fragrance. She the flower. For as long as I'd known her, she had opened her petals wide, so wide, to everyone, as if to take in, and give back in blessing, all the light of the sun.

Now those petals could do only this: fall back to the soil and mingle with the gentle earth.

Chapter 34

May 1750 (Autumn/Winter)

Today the sky opened up and let loose heaven's rains—not only heaven's, but mine, tears no one at Rustigvallei wanted to see.

The day Madame Remy died, I felt a pain in my chest so powerful, I might have walked into the sails of a windmill. I began taking the rosary she'd given me from the leg of my footstool, wrapping it around my wrist, and reaching up to stroke Tulip's feathers. For some reason that soothed me.

One bright morning I went about the house collecting dirty linens, only to bury my face in them. In the kitchen Mistress Cingria and Cook were sitting drinking tea.

"Why are your eyes so red, girl?" the Housekeeper snapped. "You look terrible." I looked down, sorry she'd caught me so. "You're crying for that Madame Remy, aren't you? Crying at the death of a Papist. What wasted tears!" She lifted her head contemptuously and started for the hall.

"Are not all souls lovely in the sight of God, including Catholics?" I cried.

She spun around, eyes cold enough to frighten an ice bear.

"Watch your tongue, girl! I suppose it was that wretched French widow who taught you to be so brash!"

Wretched French widow? My cheeks burned beetroot red. Within two weeks I'd had two cannonades explode on me: my time with Titus and Madame Remy's death. One moment I'd be ecstatic, the next, in deep grief.

That afternoon I worked the lace in my attic, gazing out across Madame Remy's farm. I could almost see the widow just as I'd found her one spring morning, standing regally in a long flowing morning gown in her garden, as still and white as a Greek statue. Each visit with her was a gift. She'd seen something fine and good in me, showed me a path to myself. Helped me become a better woman.

Now her death stirred up memories of my mother's death, all the old grief and loneliness welling up. Would everyone I came to love soon die? Madame Remy would have said, "Rubbish, *ma petite*!" Love given is never lost, she would say. And love expressed never brought death, only more life.

What brought me life, glowing life, was thinking of Titus. My heart leaped just hearing the sound of his voice. Now, wherever I was, I looked for him, seeking like one addicted for that jolt to rip through me when he was close.

All my life, I mused, I'd been a silkworm spinning her threads at breakneck pace, trying to attain who knows what, only to be captive in my own shell. Titus broke through. Soon we would soar free of this place—once I learned to hold my tongue and keep out of trouble. For it was not yet time.

This morning Cook instructed me to take breakfast to the Mistress, but at her bedroom door, about to knock, I heard shouting. I paused, then put my ear to the crack.

"Annetje," the Master implored.

"Choose, Philippe," the Mistress shrieked. "Either she goes, or I take the next ship back to Amsterdam, the children with me. This whole household knows. How could you humiliate me so? And with a servant! Under my own roof!"

"Annetje, be reasonable."

"*You* be reasonable! I bought this house, and most everything else at Rustigvallei, or have you forgotten? Without my money, this estate would collapse."

I put the tray on the chest outside her door and tiptoed back to the kitchen. So the Mistress had at last stood up to the Master. Well, good for her! But if the estate were sold, what would become of the rest of us?

I wandered outside and into the stables. Pungent smells of horses, sounds of whinnying and stomping legs. The stables were a powerful world, and the man I loved master there. The light was dim. Softly, I called out Titus's name. Suddenly someone grabbed my arm and jerked me into a stall.

Around Titus's neck was the red-checkered bandanna I'd bought him the same afternoon we lay together by the waterfall. For a second he held me to him with such force, I thought all the air would be squeezed from me. My face against his shirt—a scent of straw and stable dust. He had been currying the tall black Arabian. "Did I tell you how much I love your poem?"

"You did. But that you can tell me every time again." He stepped back, his face almost grim. "I am so sorry you lose your friend the Madame Remy. How sad! I know you value her much."

"Thank you, Titus." I paused. "I have something for you." From my pocket I pulled a small bundle of muslin. He wiped his hands. "Oh!" Then he held the lace-edged handkerchief to the light. "I'm trying to read the message. The lace, it has a message, doesn't it?"

A laugh rippled from my throat. "Probably. As Madame

Remy said, 'God has sewn love into the cloth of the universe.' "

Titus traced a finger along the lace. " 'T & S.' Ah!" He smiled broadly, eyes softening. "This gift be too much for this slave. Perhaps people wonder how I get so fine this thing."

I folded his fingers over it, telling him to hide it. "I will treasure this thing you make to celebrate us," he said, tucking it away. Then he reached into a cubbyhole in the stable wall. Inside a rag were twelve pairs of ivory bobbins, beautifully carved, with ridges at the top to hold the thread.

"Oooooooohhhh. Did you make these?" I weighed each in my palm. Ah, perfectly balanced.

Then he was nuzzling my neck. My blood jumped, a delicious richness pulsing through my fingertips. "Titus, let's talk. Your freedom comes in a few months. After that we can sail to Asia."

The stallion snorted. Titus picked up a grooming brush and brushed at the coat. It gleamed like a river. "Yes. But we cannot wait. Too many guess the truth of us. We must run soon."

"It's too dangerous." Then I told him about the argument, the Mistress's ultimatum. "I wonder if the estate will even be here in a few months."

He leaned against the stall, scratching his forehead. "Sell the estate? What will become of the promise of freedom? Nay," he said, "all the more reason to flee now." He brushed the stallion's flanks vigorously, then rested his hand there and gazed at me.

Distress was mounting in my face. "It's too soon. We don't have money for passage."

"They will discover the secret of us, Saskia! They will send you from here, and no good reference. You will not be able to find the work. It will be very bad for you. As for me, well . . ." His voice trailed off. "Can we take the chance?"

Titus ducked under the stallion's neck to stand by my side. I frowned, silent, as he ran fingers through my hair. Perhaps I was just scared. "But where can we go?"

"Nowhere," he said. "Not west, not south—the great ocean. Not north, not east. The Great Karoo to bleach these bones. Or the mountains, with many the lions, and rivers of crocodiles."

I shivered. I'd heard stories of people on riverbanks suddenly snapped up by long jaws with terrible teeth, dragged down into the waters. "Shall we swim to China, then?"

He looked at me askance, then saw my smile. "We will be hunted. We leave by ship from Cape Town. Aunt Effie will help, like she help Sara." He pressed two fingers against my lips. "This be the big secret."

"I know. I know."

The Master, he reminded me, had let him earn some money, but not yet enough. He did have the little silver box the de Witts gave him for saving Pier. "This I could sell."

"I'm ashamed, Titus. That money stolen from me. It would have been enough for China. If we can wait til the end of the year, I'll have my wages. And enough time to make more lace. So we might as well wait until you're free."

"And hope the estate does not sell before. Perhaps that is better," he relented. "I have the more work to do yet for my brothers and sisters."

"You mean those meetings in the mountains? No, Titus! No more!"

And we argued. I not wanting him to go back, he insisting he must. Why? Why? I pressed him.

"Because of that thing I did when young." And he told me that when he was a boy on another estate, a slaveman escaped, running to a safe house in the hills that he knew about. He was questioned and finally whipped so badly that he told. The safe house was discovered and burned to the ground, and the slaveman captured, along with others. They were also whipped severely. Titus blamed himself.

"I give in, and many suffer, even die. This be my great shame. I have sought the redemption with my work in the mountains. This be not yet finished."

I was silent. I wanted to cry for him. Now I understood.

And so we decided to wait. Meanwhile, we had to alter how people saw us. "How will I be able to resist the touching of you?" he whispered. I looked at him with such petulance that he cocked his head and pouted, mimicking me. I smiled. His fingers brushed against my cheek. "When you make the smile like that, the heavens, they do open."

Stumbling out into sunlight, I nearly knocked into Jezza. She slid her almond eyes from me to Titus. He stood just inside the stable door, staring out from the shadows. Damnation! She knew about us. But then, she'd always known.

I hurried to the house, counting the times Titus and I had been openly bold. Clearly we had to start publicly destroying what we'd spent the last year creating. We set our strategy in motion, telling stories to fellow workers of a huge argument that had devastated our friendship, refusing details. At meals, we no longer sat together. When we did allow ourselves the momentary pleasure of standing close in a group, we barely glanced at one another, and if we did, we were certain to scowl. For people can read silent messages between lovers.

Then, happily, we began hearing people say such things as, "Shame. Saskia and Titus used to be such friends." Only Johanna and Samuel knew of our love, and they were sworn to secrecy, knowing how high the stakes were. I began to sense something heavy and final descend, as if Fate were pressing its hand upon us.

Of course, I missed the small intimacies: sitting up front with him in the wagon, discussing life and books, lolling on the grass after dinner with our friends, smoking our pipes. Standing next to him in the kitchen, feeling the strength of his presence. And of course, there was the larger intimacy. Sometimes I felt a ferocious hunger for him, but quelled it. For surely we would have our day . . .

~

One afternoon we did encounter each other, and in the yard, for all to see. After delivering a bundle of newly arrived tools, I came out of the winery to see little Eva running about on the grass. Eva was the honey-colored daughter of Manassa and some unnamed White man, a little beauty with a heart-shaped face and radiant smile. The toddler was chasing Samuel's mangey old cat. I set out after her, but Titus dashed from the tack room and scooped her up. I walked over and took her, squirming, from his arms. "You little rascal. Who's been watching you? How did you get loose?"

Titus stepped back and regarded us, checking that we were out of earshot. "You know, she have the skin of the children of you and me, when we have them."

I turned terribly still and gazed at Eva. I had never imagined my children would be any color but White. Then I seemed to snap out of an old dream into a new one. Our children would look like the man I loved and me, merged into a wonderful new being. I pushed my face into her curls, and she giggled. "What a beautiful color you are. Like the sun setting on applewood. You know, I think every shade of skin is beautiful."

Titus leaned to my ear."I miss you. Like parched earth, it miss the rain." I couldn't speak.

Just then, Hannah, the field slave with the bent wing of an arm, stumbled through the garden gates, calling for Eva. There was something about this woman I couldn't understand. She never looked me in the eye, never smiled when I inquired about her. I handed her the little girl, and as casually as I could, ambled back to Titus's side. "How ironic," I whispered. "When we were barely friends, there were such wild rumors flying around about us. Now that we're together, the rumors have stopped. I guess our ruse has worked."

Without warning, the sky rumbled with thunder. We squinted up at clouds gathering over the mountains, rolling fast on the wind. "Perhaps not entirely," he said, an unfamiliar sharpness in his voice. "Jezza be up to something. This I can feel."

When Cook shouted my name, Titus disappeared into the stables. A blustery cold whipped down from the foothills, snapping my skirts like flags while the sky loomed low and foreboding. Suddenly Mr. Pesser dashed down the yard and banged the copper bell hard, over and over. Panic rose in my throat.

Then noises were issuing from the girls' lodging, crashing noises, like furniture being overturned. I paused, confused, made for the cottage, until again Cook called me to the house, this time more urgently.

I opened the kitchen door, only to find pandemonium.

Chapter 35

May 1750 (Autumn/Winter)

Household staff crowded the kitchen: Anna, Johanna, Samuel, Jezza, Manassa, Black Lucy, and Cook. They stood mute, faces frozen, feet shuffling. Overhead, the sound of objects smashing.

"What in heaven's name is going on?" I pushed past everyone and mounted the first steps before Johanna caught me by the arm.

"They're goin through our things, what ye think?" she bleated.

Anna's eyes grew large. "Some wickedness goin on. Someone's gonna burn in hell, that's for sure."

I wrested from Johanna's grasp and took the steps in leaps. Upstairs, the Master was cursing. Petticoats, jacket, bed linens, footstool, hairbrush—my belongings lay slumped in the hallway like slaughtered chickens. I watched in shock as my lace pillow sailed through the air and landed at my feet. Pins spilled out of the newly made lace, bobbins unspooling.

"Stay downstairs, Miss Klaassens," Mistress Cingria barked from my room.

I glowered at her, fists tightening in the folds of my skirt, and made a reluctant retreat. In the kitchen, Manassa was trembling.

She mumbled something about the Overseers turning out the contents of the Slave Quarters while Mr. Pesser ripped apart cots and bunks.

Cook climbed several steps, looking down on us, and clapped her hands. "Listen up, all of ye! The Master instructs we gather in the gallery right after afternoon prayer. Every one of you. Ye got that?" Murmurs rippled through those gathered.

Egbert skipped down the steps looking almost jubilant. Damn! Had he been in my room too?

"Something's been stolen, hasn't it, Egbert?" Johanna cried. "The Master was cursing. They wouldn't be trawling through our things something not been stolen."

"Something's been stolen all right."

"Quiet!" Cook raised her thick hand. "Simmer down, will ye? The Master's pocketwatch, the one from England that he value so much—been stolen, it has!"

There was a low gasp. We looked around, trying to gauge if the person next to us looked guilty. "Someone's going to burn," Anna murmured. "*Burn.*"

Egbert wore a smug expression. "Hush! The Master saw it several nights ago, in the top drawer of his desk, where he always puts it. And now it's gone. Twenty-two karat gold it is. We've had no visitors. Someone at the estate stole it."

"What pocketwatch?" Anna asked, wide-eyed.

"The gold one, girl, edged in blue enamel." Johanna nudged her with an elbow. "We seen it peekin from the Master's desk while we was dusting a few weeks ago, remember?"

Johanna frowned, pacing. Anna sucked on a corner of her apron. These girls were too honest to steal. So was Samuel. I looked for Jezza. She was leaning against the hearth wall, rubbing the side of her nose, mouth twitching. If she knew something, she wasn't saying.

Suddenly fear ripped through me. What if the hunting party upstairs found my crucifix? I was sure I'd crammed it deep into the footstool leg, but . . .

Mistress Cingria clambered down the stairs, her black eyes small and hard. We stared at her, trying to look innocent, even when we were. Her chatelaine in one hand, she raised a threatening finger. "If any one of you has stolen the Master's watch, turn it over now. No one leaves the estate or eats until the watch is found. Now get back to your work, and if you don't have work, find some. Cook, I want every piece of silver and brass, every spoon and every candlestick counted. And you, Samuel, ask the Foreman for work. No one's to return to their lodgings until they've been searched."

I spent my free hour upstairs salvaging my scattered possessions and putting them back where they belonged. I wanted to cry. Pins had dropped from my lace pillow, and all the lace I'd kept so pristine was mottled with dirt. My petticoats were wrinkled, my red bodice creased with dust.

Throughout the afternoon we worked at our tasks, but in hunger. At tea with the children, I looked longingly at the blue plate filled with honey rusks, until I could stand it no longer, and fast as lightning, snatched one up. Pier grabbed my wrist. "If you eat that, I'll tell, and you'll really get it!" And stuffed it into his mouth.

"Heartless monster. I think you were born in a thorn tree."

For the rest of the day, they ransacked our rooms, and the Overseers the slave dwellings. But no pocketwatch. When there were rumors about body searches, we got upset, whispering that Master de Witt had probably misplaced the precious item, forgetting it in some vest pocket or other, and now we had to suffer for it. Meanwhile, the Mistress retired to her room with a carafe of sherry.

In the back foyer, the longcase clock stood guard like an upended coffin, marking time. When it struck five, we assembled for prayer. I was starved, lightheaded. Stomachs growled and voices quavered as we sang psalms. If they didn't find that damnable watch soon, there would also be no supper.

After prayers, the Master bellowed, "No one eats until I have my watch! If it doesn't appear on my desk in the next hour, I will interrogate every last one of you! The guilty shall stand to account!"

I winced. Soon we would be roasting like ox meat on his spit of an Inquisition. At seven o'clock, Josiah opened the folding doors of the gallery into one long room, and the Housekeeper directed us servants to file against a wall. The slaves shambled in, shaking like poplar leaves. Even Digger, Eli, and Kupido attended. Where was Titus?

The long dining table dominated one end of the room and Mistress Cingria sat there, stiffly, in a ladder-back chair, ceremoniously settling her skirts. Her eyes pinned us down like insects to an entomologist's drawer. Isaiah had been right when he said that damnable woman had no blood running through her veins, only vipers.

The Master stood facing the room from behind the table, with a low interrogation stool opposite. No one was allowed to leave until all the interviews were over, he said—or until the watch was recovered. What a sad lot we were, feeling like naughty children. Egbert placed himself behind the Master, arms crossed, glaring at us with a righteous expression. I wanted to walk over and kick him.

The Housekeeper rose solemnly. "Manassa!"

Egbert stepped forward and called out the name again, louder. "Manassa!"

"Shut it, Egbert!" the Master barked. "You're not immune

from interrogation yourself." The valet stepped back, flushing.

One by one the slaves were called, brought to the rocky stool, and questioned. Some babbled on and on incoherently. As interview after interview proved fruitless, they shuttled back against the wall. I happened to be standing close to the table, able to see all the wretched faces.

My stomach ached. When the longcase clock struck eight, I feared this would go on forever. What an exercise in futility! Who would admit to such a crime, or snitch on another? Some slaves thoroughly disliked each other, but under the gun they stuck together with ferocious solidarity.

Jezza was the exception. "Why, I distinctly members seein the Masta show Titus his watch the day after the young Masta nearly drown in the river. Don't the Masta member, *mynheer*, sir?" When she fluttered her lashes, he stared at her narrowly. "My, how Titus did admire it. Don't the Masta member? I was servin the portwine. How Titus did hold that gold watch of yours up to the sunlight, Masta, then cradle it like a chick, sayin he never seen nothing so beautiful all his life. Member, *mynheer*? That's what Titus did. *Ja*, suh."

What was her little game? Titus would never steal. Certainly nothing as valuable as a gold pocketwatch.

Master de Witt rose suddenly and kicked back his chair, looking at Jezza with suspicion. Finally he sat close on the edge of the table and fixed his eyes on her. "Egbert," he snapped, "fetch me some portwine." His eyes found Samuel. "Tell Mr. Pesser," he said in a more subdued voice, "to look through Titus's things once more." Jezza cast her eyes to the floor. Was she suppressing a smile?

The old slave shuffled off, feet moving heavily as if shackled. I stared at Jezza, my eyes burning into her face. She seemed to sense it, for she looked at me for a second, then squirmed. Was she taking vengeance on Titus for spurning her? Well, her ploy would only backfire. Titus was innocent. Besides, the Master trusted Titus. Nobody trusted Jezza.

The waiting was unbearable. The Master paced back and forth in agitation while Mistress Cingria glared coldly at the lot of us. When Egbert returned with wine, Master de Witt downed a glass in one gulp. All of us shifted about, listening as the longcase clock struck once more.

Finally Samuel shambled back. We all looked up. "Mr. Pesser, he lookin for the watch in Titus's hut now, Masta." Samuel's voice was shaky.

Master de Witt returned to his chair, tapped on the tray for Egbert to pour another glass, and fixed us with caustic eyes. We looked down. "All the slaves will get whippings, and all the workers punished, if you don't each tell everything you know! Hold back nothing, do you hear? Who's next?"

"Hannah of Madagascar," Mistress Cingria called out. Like Titus, Hannah was working to buy her freedom but didn't look likely to win it. More than any slave I'd known, this field worker with the flat face and badly mangled arm looked as if she'd barely survived a trampling. She took a seat before the Master, trembling hard. She'd probably never spoken to him in her life and surely wanted to please.

"I don't know nothing bout that watch, *mynheer*. Don know nothing bout dat gold watch." Her left eye twitched as she rocked back and forth on the stool. "But I do knows somethin . . . I knows somethin the Masta, he do surely wants to know."

Master de Witt leaned back in his chair. He tapped his spectacles on the table, looking skeptical. "And what would that be, Hannah?"

I stared, transfixed. She couldn't know about the meetings. And if she did, she wouldn't dare betray her brothers. It had to be something else.

"I knows there be slavemen from this here estate who goes ta meetins." She cast her eyes down, then shifted them to the Master again. A look of hope seemed to break across her face. "Forbidden meetins, *mynheer*."

The room had already been tense. Now gasps broke the silence. Mistress Cingria rose from her chair, her eyes searing into Hannah. Master de Witt turned rigid. Suddenly I saw the toxic power of these two: with a turn of the screw, they could crush us like grapes, instantly, lees, dregs, juice, and all.

"Just . . . what . . . *kind* . . .of . . . forbidden . . . meetings?"

Hannah's eyes fluttered, beads of sweat broke out on her forehead. In her lap, she twisted a section of her dress with her fists.

I could not breathe. *No, Hannah. Don't say it! For God's sake, don't say it!*

"Some of the slavemen, *mynheer*, they been goin up ta them meetins in the mountains. Ye know, to talk bout things." Her fingers had now squeezed the cloth as tightly as a corkscrew. Slaves fidgeted. Their mouths hardened, eyes blinked helplessly and darted about the room.

Color crept up the Master's neck, and his hand tugged at his cravat. "What kind of things do they talk about in these meetings, Hannah?"

"I doan know, *mynheer*. Doan know them things. I never goes myself."

"What kind of things do you *think* they talk about?" The Master's voice cracked. "What have you *heard people say* they talk about? Come on, Hannah. I won't punish you for telling me. In fact, I'll reward you." He fished into his waistcoat pocket, examined coins in his hand, then flicked a large silver one on the table before her. It spun on its edge, ringing, before it fell. By candlelight, for a second, it shone like a small full moon. "Well, Hannah. I'm waiting. Maybe you're the one person here whom I can trust. What do you think they talk about at these meetings?"

Hannah stared at the coin with large bloodshot eyes, looked to her side, hesitated. It had to have been the largest amount of money ever offered her. "Oh, maybe they talks about gettin their freedoms and such." Her voice dropped to a whisper. "Those kindsa things."

Silence reigned. I pressed my hands hard against my thighs. *Hannah, how could you reveal such an important secret?* I wanted to tear at my hair, to run up and choke her.

The Master's face was scarlet now, his jaw hard. His words came out strangely, as if squeezed through a tube. "Freedom and such. You mean they talk of escape. Is that what you mean?"

Hannah! If you dare tell one more thing . . . Out of the corner of my eye I glanced at Josiah, who looked ready to faint. Hannah reached for the coin, then changed her mind, drawing back the gnarled fist. Her mahogany skin turned strangely ashen.

"Just who goes to these meetings, Hannah? Tell me. Tell me and the coin is yours."

She kept staring at her feet. Did she know she'd gone too far? When one of the slaves wheezed, Hannah's eyes flickered around the room, as if searching for an exit. Then her body quivered, and she began to weep. "I don't know who, *mynheer*."

At that moment, Mr. Pesser burst through the back door and lumbered down the gallery, White laborers at his heels. With dramatic flourish, he opened his hand. Folded into white cloth, a gold object shone in the candlelight. "Beggin yer pardon, Master de Witt, but is this the missing piece?" There it was—the gold watch nested in the lace-edged handkerchief I'd given Titus. All the blood drained from my face.

The Master plucked them up. "Where did you find this?"

Mr. Pesser shifted from one foot to the other. "Well, sir, I hates to tell ye. I can hardly believe it meself."

"Out with it, man!"

He coughed. "In the box under Titus's bed."

A low moan rippled through the room, and my hands fluttered to my face. *No! No!* The walls began to close in on me. I could not breathe.

I looked at Jezza. A strange half smile curled the corners of her mouth, which she bit back. I don't know what came over me, but all at once I stood in front of the Master and slammed my fist on the table. "Titus would never do such a thing, sir! He's not a thief, and you know it. Someone else stole the watch and planted it among his things, I'm certain!"

The Master hesitated. From his look, I think he wanted to believe me. "How would you know, Miss Klaassens? And how is it your concern?"

"He has enemies." I glared at Jezza. Her eyes spat hatred at me, then looked down. "I'm not accusing anyone, sir, for I have no evidence, but there are those here who wish to destroy Titus. Other slaves."

The Master held his forehead. "Stop it!" he boomed. "I'm sick of all these accusations! Thieving slaves, secret meetings, plots! It's an abomination! And you, Miss Klaassens." His eyes flashed. In front of my face he swished the lace handkerchief, initialed "T & S." Held it by the corner with fingertips, as if it were foul. I lowered my lashes, flustered. "I'd say you have a very personal interest in protecting Titus."

Mr. Pesser reached into his pocket and, in another extraordinary gesture, placed a small silvery box on the table. "Found this in Titus's things too, sir. A little too fancy an ornament for a slave, I thinks."

The Master stared at the sterling box. It was the one he

himself had bestowed on Titus the day Titus pulled Pier from the river. His face turned pale. "That belongs to Titus," he said quietly. His eyes commandeered the assembled. "Fetch him at once, Mr. Pesser. Where the hell is he, anyway? Jezza, you stay here. Now all the rest of you, get out! I'm going to get to the bottom of this, even if it brings down every man and woman on the estate!" And poured himself another glass of portwine.

I melted into the crowd that stumbled down the gallery. In the back foyer, Titus was entering the house. We exchanged looks, his of puzzlement, mine of dread. When the folding doors banged shut behind him, I leaned as close to the crack as I could, listening, despite Cook motioning me to leave. Titus was denying ever taking the watch while Jezza, gushing, pleaded her ignorance.

I hurried out into the cold night, shivering and pacing under the winter-padded trees, scanning the sky for moon and stars that were not there. *Lord, Lord.* Hunger was gone now. There was only a deep aching hollow in my stomach. The mountains seemed to close in like prison walls.

Titus would never trade his freedom for a pocketwatch. I think he wanted to be free even more than he wanted me. Oh, Hannah! The slaves will beat you tonight within an inch of your life. And the Master knows I wove those initials into that handkerchief. I was scared, very scared.

I walked into the stables to wait for Titus. In the dim light, I noticed a couple embracing, whispering *seuntjie*, sweetie to each other. As my eyes adjusted to the dark, I saw Johanna pull away from Jaco. Burly *married* Jaco. "Who's there?" he called out sharply.

"Just what kind of trouble are you two getting into?"

Johanna stroked her lover's cheek, then turned to me with a bold smirk. "Trouble? Us, dearie? Looky who's courtin trouble.

You, who be none too proud to cock a leg for a slaveman."

My face turned hot. I ran to grab her and pull her into a corner. "That's a fine thing to say to a friend!" My voice dropped to a hush. "Have you told Jaco anything?"

"Nothin he ain't already guessed." Johanna sighed, placing a plump hand on my shoulder. "Oh, Saski. Seems the lot of us are bent on makin our private pilgrimage to hell. Well, if I'm goin, and you're goin, so is the rest of this damned estate."

I left them falling into an empty stall. How could they, when everything was falling apart? Outside, a great trembling overtook me. How I wanted the comfort of Titus's arms. Catryn dashed out the kitchen door and tugged at my apron. "Mistress Cingria says you're to come inside and take care of us, Miss Saskia."

Just then Titus was coming down the back *stoep* with Mr. Pesser at his heels. Before our paths crossed, I stopped, searching his face for a sign. He looked pale and grim, shot me a look full with meaning. The Foreman made for the well where he drew water, bending to wash his face and hands. Maybe he was giving us a gift, a moment to talk.

Titus stepped close, paused, stooped down to remove a *veldshoen*, and pretended to knock a stone from it. "Oh, Saskia," he whispered. "The smell of blood. I fear it be upon me."

My lips trembled. "Let's run now, Titus. Tonight!"

"Not tonight. Tonight they watch me close." As the Foreman turned and strode toward us, I picked up my skirts and ran for the kitchen. My soul was burning, burning cold as ice.

~

That night I tossed and turned in bed, thoughts of the day gnawing at me. Then, from a deep sleep, a nightmare, one I'd dreamed before.

The children and I are onboard the Windroos, sailing dangerously close to shore. A storm throws our vessel skyward, crashing upon African shoals, splintering like kindling on the ax. Although I cannot swim, in my dream I make my way round and round the ship, scooping up Catryn and Pier who are floundering in the swells, their lungs half-filled with water. With great effort I secure their hold on a mast that floats by, then grab hold myself.

Pier is wearing the dogskin gloves of a nobleman's son. We are all gripping the mast for dear life, but Pier's gloves slip and he goes under. I gasp for breath, then dive after him. That's when I see the heavy weight hanging from his neck—the huge face of a clock. He grabs me tightly, pulling us down, further down into the icy depths. "Release the weight!" I mouth, but the water swallows my voice. Desperately I tug at the black rope. "Let it go, Pier!" But he cannot hear. Then the rope coils around my neck too as it grows and grows into giant black lace. The more we fight, the more we are gripped in its net. Down we go, inhaling lungfuls of water with every breath, sinking deeper and deeper into the inky sea.

And then I know as well as I know anything: we are going to die.

Chapter 36

Alexander the Great, seeing Diogenes looking attentively at a parcel of human bones, asked the philosopher what he was looking for. "That which I cannot find," was the reply. "The difference between your father's bones and those of his slaves."
—Plutarch

May 1750 (Autumn/Winter)

I opened my garret shutters. The sky was dark and threatening as I sat at the window seat, pillow on my lap, working the lace. I lit the taper candles next to the globes for more light. Words that had been rumbling around in my brain now spilled out, in final lyrics.

> *There is a man I speak to in my thoughts. I think of him as I write the whiteness of lace. He floats up to me, a poem rising like water from the filaments. There is a dark-skinned man who swims to me in my dreams,*

dreams that hover like birds of desire.

There is a man I think of in the morning when alone, when light from the sun first penetrates my room. I have watched him in the yard below, mutely, through lace I hold to panes of glass. I carry this man close, like a song, like a wound. There is a man who is darkest earth. He warms me like mist rising from the soil of Africa.

There is a man I think of in the depths of night. I wear him close, like moonlight on my face, like a thread spinning its web upon my lacemaking pillow. In my dreams I swim to him, like the moon falling into the river's throat at night.

There is a man I think of when I walk the vines and grasslands. Skin of my skin, bone of my bones; a man I belong to as I belong to this land, whose wildness has entered me.

Then, carelessly, I pricked my thumb on a lace pin. A drop of blood fell in one bright red circle onto the paper pattern. Quickly I swiped it away with a finger. A bad omen.

Where are my scissors? I clattered downstairs. There, on the chest in the rear vestibule where I last wove the lace. Just as my fingers touched the handles, I heard the Mistress through the cracked door of the Master's bedroom. I inched closer and peeked in. She was on her knees, clinging to his leg, pleading with him. "I have no choice!" he shouted, wrenching the leg away. Suddenly the door slammed shut. I snatched the scissors. Was this about Mistress Cingria? Was the Mistress finally going to leave him? Would they sell the estate after all? If they sold Titus, would his new owners honor the freedom promised him? From the window I saw Pier trot his pony around the paddock, prodding it with a riding stick, while Digger and Kupido, astride the old mule, struggled to keep up.

The next day, in the gray of the afternoon, I sat in the *kinder*room mending a lace ruffle. Pier readied his lead soldiers for battle while Catryn scolded two naughty dolls and put them to bed without supper. Then something outside startled us, a sound like tittering laughter, but which soon broke into a chorus of frantic yelps. Hyenas! Then the *bang bang* of clogs on steps, and Johanna burst through the doorway. She stammered something, exploding in sobs.

I put down my needle. "For heaven's sake, Johanna, what's wrong? You're not frightened by those wild dogs, are you?"

"It's Titus and Josiah!" she choked. "Sladie said they cut them bad!"

The children dropped their toys. I sat motionless, my mind refusing to work. Somewhere within, a darkness descended, my breath slowly leaking away. "Cut them? How? Who cut them?"

"I don't know who." Johanna cried. "The Master musta ordered it. Someone told on them, Saski. And they. . . they cut them something horrible, Sladie said." Johanna slumped into a chair and covered her face with her hands. Catryn grabbed me by the skirt, chin trembling. Pier slipped through the door into his bedroom.

I jumped up. "They wouldn't. No one would hurt Titus. Where are they?"

"I don't know. In the woods, where the slaves bury their dead. Oh, Saskia, they're cut so bad!"

"Nay!" I shouted, pulling my shawl close and hurrying past her. "Nay, nay."

My head felt hot. My body broke into a sweat, then a chill. I took the steps in leaps, dashed past the girls and out the door where cold air hit me like a fist. I ran back inside and snatched some cloths.

"They'll be needin somethin for the pain," Cook said, her voice tender. She shoved a crock of brandy into my hands. She knew. Anna, Luther, and little Digger, all huddled around the table, stared at me, dread pulling at their faces. They all knew. Was I the last to be told?

I raced down the yard but my clogs sank into wet earth. A shadow began to fall over my brain. Stars flashed behind my eyes, then darkness, like shutters closing. *Don't faint.* I looked beyond rows of vines to the smoky blur of hills, the sun obscured by thick clouds. Lightning crackled across the distant mountains, and over the valley came the bellow of thunder. A light rain began to fall.

I tore through the arches of the winery. Johanna always exaggerated. It could not be that bad. A few of the Black field workers stood leaning against the wall, bodies heavy, ghostly, as if embalmed in ice.

"Where's Titus?"

One pointed toward the forest. The rain now fell in hard pellets. "Yust past the millhouse. But them ladies won't let no European in, Miss Saskia. They guardin that place like a fort."

I snatched a lantern from the wall and took off at a run. Energy pumped through me, ebbed away, then surged again. I slipped and stumbled on newly wet grass and mud, took the wooden bridge in leaps, clogs clattering and slipping on the mossy wood. Was what I feared most coming to pass?

The milling house stood north of the riverbanks, close to where the men had burned a witch in effigy, and beyond that the forest. As I ran past wind-torn sails, a faint light from distant torches glowed in the mist. A chorus of strange singing curled toward me on the air until I understood. That was not singing. It was moaning. *Oh, God!*

In the woods I paused at the slave cemetery with its crooked branch markers and sun-bleached ribbons. The rains fell harder. Tall firs and wild oaks rose up in walls of darkness that obscured the clearing, and a fence of protea roots formed an impenetrable barrier. I pulled my shawl over my head.

"Who goes there?" A woman's voice. Black Lucy stood defiantly, arms across her chest. This timid slavewoman, now a colossus of strength. Other women too, territorial, stepped forward to block my path. Beyond, groves of Blacks and coloreds stood watch over two prone figures. The air was charged with some strange, sad current.

Rain beat down hard now. If he were here, I *would* get in. "Lucy, is Titus hurt? You must let me in!" I held up the crock of brandy. "Lucy, for pity's sake!"

She peered under the shadows of my shawl. "Oh, it be you, Miss Saskia."

Some yards away a waxed tarp floated tentlike on stakes, protecting someone from the downpour. As I made my way closer I saw a man beneath, hunched against the trunk of a tree. Over his shoulders was the red-checkered kerchief I had given Titus. But this man looked half dead.

I approached slowly. Sharp odors hit my senses—bitter herbs in wine, turpentine antiseptic—and the burnt smell of cauterized flesh. Blood was everywhere—in a pool on the ground where he lay, blanketing his legs, his hands, on the clothes of slavewomen who attended him. Sladie knelt at his side, one hand on his brow, while Manassa held a horn cup to his mouth. "Come, my son, drink."

I lifted the lantern and stared into his face. It was Titus.

How ancient and pale he looked. Eyes round, dazed, slightly vacant, as if not sure what had happened. Terrible little groans sputtered from his lips. As I handed the women the brandy, my eyes traveled the length of his body, which lay partly in shadow, looking for cuts. Then I saw them. The bottoms of his legs were bandaged, dark with crusted blood.

"Don't let her see!" a man whispered. I wheeled around. Light from the lantern spilled across the grass. Several yards away, two slaves were shoveling soil into a small pit, burying something. I blinked. Blinked again. Hastily, they threw fistfuls of dirt over dark-skinned toes, toes with a pink bloom curling up from the sole. A foot. My fingers started to convulse. I swung back toward Titus and ran my eyes down his legs—legs I could now see were stumps. Blood thudded through my temples. *Nay! Nay!*

Lightning crashed across the mountains. A weaverbird drifted out of a tree, its movements incredibly plodding, taking forever to cross the expanse of sky. I walked away, as if in a dream, started to retch, but held it in, swallowed, walked back to him. Every step I took was slow and labored, as if I were walking under the ocean.

The roof of Titus's tarp glowed eerily from candles, and rain slashed at the canvas. I crawled to his side and reached for his hands. They were clammy and limp.

"Titus." He turned slowly and studied me, eyes heavy as boulders. But he did not know me. He twisted his head back and forth, mumbling something in some tribal tongue.

Sladie approached, grief etched into her face. We sat there for a long time, silent. "Devil's fever," she finally said. "That head, it be in the nother world. He beggin all afternoon ta go see his mama. Say she be dyin."

I gazed from Sladie to Manassa. "But his mother has been

dead for years."

They lowered their eyes. Sladie tilted back Titus's head and poured brandy into his mouth, then turned to me. "He been tryin to get up and go to her. He doan know he ain't got no mama. Doan even know he ain't got no feet."

Rain pounded on the tarp as if it would batter it to pieces. Tears coursed my cheeks and ran into my mouth, onto my neck. Titus raised his head and looked at me again, bewildered—a wounded lion. He started to mouth something, then closed his eyes when he could not. A small spider danced across his shirt, and for some reason I could not take my eyes from it.

Josiah lay propped up against a tree a little ways beyond. They had cut off his feet too. He lay motionless, ashen, lips lavender-white. I would have gone to him, but I couldn't leave Titus. Memory crashed through: the night the three of us were together on the mountaintop, Josiah playing music while Titus and I danced. Now great black vultures glided through the treetops.

Some small movement from Sladie caught my eye, and a flicker of suspicion crept across her face. Did she think me one of *them*? "They found out they'd been going to the meetings, didn't they? It wasn't me, Sladie. I knew, but never told anyone. I would sooner die than put Titus in danger."

She paused, looking far into my eyes, searching, it felt, for truth in them. Then the muscles around her mouth relaxed, and she put a hand on my arm. "Sweet girl, I knows you tells the truth. I knows it."

I took a deep breath. "Did the Master order this?"

"Yes, Miss Saskia," Manassa coughed. "This mornin the Massa, he try makin them tell who the others be, who go to the meetins. Titus, he wouldn't tell. Josiah doan tell neither. Gave them lashins done near killed em, but they wouldn't tell. That's when the Massa, he order the cuttin. Tried to make Isaiah do it, tried to make that slave cut his own brothers, but he refuse. He bleedin bad hisself from a whippin." She jutted a defiant chin toward the Quarters. "Massa Pesser, he refuse too. It be Anthonij. Josiah first, til he pass out. Then Anthonij done it to Titus, slow like, so's he'd tell the names. Titus never tole no names."

I looked away, past them, deep into the forest. If Titus had spoken the names, maybe they would not have cut him. My heart quickened—he had not betrayed me either. "Will he die, then?" The words caught in my throat.

Sladie breathed in sharply. "Lost so much blood. Doan know how he live through it. Doan know he *want* to live through it."

I put my arms around Titus, cradling his delirious head on my breasts, feeling my chest turn hot, then damp with cold. I put my hand to his brow and sat with him like that for a long time under the rain-battered canopy. I gazed at Sladie. She seemed to age before my eyes. Bearer of every grief man could inflict. I put a bloodstained cloth to Titus's forehead, mopping up the moisture. "Who named them, Sladie? Who turned in Titus and Josiah? Was it Hannah?"

"Doan know. May be."

Oom Samuel sat just outside the tarp, his frail form slumped against the oak. He must have been there all along. He wore not his frayed waistcoat, but a cape of antelope skins, as if to say, "This is who I am." I rose and crouched down beside him, letting my head fall on his shoulder.

"She beg him not to do it. She beg the Massa, said it be too cruel. Said, 'You go beat em, you go whip em, you go sell them boys, yust don't cut off their feets.' But he doan listen to her, isn't it?"

"Who begged for them, Samuel?"

"The Mistress, Miss Saskia. Done get on her knees and cried, she did. Lucy, she be in the room. Saw all of it, didn't she?"

Samuel and I sat silently in the rain, then I crawled back to Titus, holding him. I could cry no more. An eternity seemed to pass. Those at the house would be raging about my absence. Did it matter? Did anything now matter? I wanted to stay all night, but determined-looking slaves approached the tarp, forming a circle around us. "You gots to leave here now, Miss Saskia," one insisted. "We can't abide no Whites here now."

This burying ground was theirs, the only ground they could call their own. I peered into Titus's face, pressed lips to his forehead, ran a hand down his cheek, then—I don't know why—untied the bloodstained scarf from his neck and stuffed it into my fist. I would come back later, somehow.

The rain had abated, and a wispy sun tried to push through clouds in the distant hills, a wound of yellow boiling in the cold sky. I stumbled out of the forest and through the crusted stalks of grapevines, then along the moon-filled river. Every step felt heavy. Even dry ground seemed to suck me further and further into the earth. Every good and right thing about the world had collapsed; a weak floor that could not hold.

Over by the millhouse, under its ragged sails, I saw two figures. A slaveman was dragging a slavewoman through the door by her hair. Was this what I thought it was? I splashed over river rocks and fell against the mill's cold wall. If it weren't for Titus, I would leave this manor in a shot. The man's voice sounded angry. Was that Isaiah? And Jezza?

"Only reason you sleep wit me was so's I do it," Isaiah shouted. "Why you make me put it 'mong Titus's things? Now they go whip and cut em! Whup me too! You the she-devil, Jezza!"

The sound of scuffling, then, "Doan you blame me none,

kaffir! How I know this happen? No, Isaiah, no!"

I gritted my teeth, lest I cry out. So it *was* Jezza. *She* stole the watch. Damn that girl! Damn her eyes! God forgive me, but then and there I prayed that Isaiah would keep hitting her, that he would, in fact, beat that wretched girl within an inch of her life.

Chapter 37

May 1750 (Winter)

Someone was calling my name. Pier stumbled over stones at the edge of the river by the millhouse. When he saw me, he clambered high onto the banks, where he could look down at me. "My God, are you in trouble. We've been searching everywhere for you." His hard eyes scanned me up and down. "Jesus, you look like a drowned cat! Soaked with blood. You've been to see Titus and Josiah, haven't you? *Kaffir*-lover! Those stinking tarboys had it coming."

I clenched my fists, felt my arms tighten. How I wanted to strike him! What did he know about anything? About longing. About freedom, and passion. About love, love one could die for. Had he forgotten who had carried his limp body from the river? Who will now carry Titus? My mouth opened, but anger clogged my throat.

"I'm telling Father where you've been. You're gonna get strapped for this one for sure!" And he spun on his heels for the house.

My face was on fire—I could strangle this boy! I could strangle the lot of them. I traipsed toward the house, hands shaking, cutting my own path, not following Pier. The earth pulled on me, as if my legs were iron. Feet slipped and shuddered under dark crystals of mud. I could still hear moans issuing from the slave cemetery. Buried feet. The debris of violence.

Mistress Cingria must have seen me, for as I entered the kitchen, she sprang from behind the door and struck me across the face. "You were supposed to be caring for the children! You're covered in blood and filth. I know where you've been. No one gave you permission to go there, missy. It's none of your business, do you hear? I'll see that you get sacked for this! Now clean yourself up, you disobedient hussy!" She shot Cook a threatening look. "No food for her until I say. Is that clear?"

I glared at her, not caring. Harridan! My heart was immune to her now, immune to everyone in this house. Suddenly the Master was in the hallway, staring at me. I glared back, my eyes full of murder. He puffed up his chest and scowled, like one who knows he's been unjust but won't relent, and skulked away, Mistress Cingria running after him. What punishment would they devise for me now?

The girls' faces were frozen with grief, and an anger they dared not express. Titus and Josiah were dear to them too. Johanna touched my back gently, but I could only lean against the stone basin and scrub at my apron. Tears fell so thickly now it was hard to see. When the blood marbled into a red pool, I sobbed. I was washing away his blood!

Cook looked around, then pressed a plate of food into my hands. Beetroots and meat, like mutilated flesh. With a cry I dropped it onto the tile floor.

In my room I sat at the open window, staring out over the forest where Titus lay. There was a soft knock, then my friend stood in the doorway. "They're dying, Johanna. Titus and Josiah are dying."

"Hush. We don't know that." She sat down and wrapped her wide arms around me. Together we wept, and when I could cry no more, I told her what I'd overheard at the mill.

"That wicked, wicked girl! I'm tellin Cook! Damn it, I'm tellin the Master!"

"What difference will that make? It wasn't about the watch. It was about the meetings." I sobbed. "Titus and I were going to escape, Johanna—and I talked him out of it. We might have been on a ship to China by now. Together. Alive." She stared at me in shock. "It's my fault he was hurt. If I'd left him alone, none of this would have happened."

"Quiet now." She wiped her eyes, stood up, looked at me intently. "Titus and Josiah were digging their own graves by going to them meetings." Her voice cracked. "They're my friends too, ye know."

Some time after she left, I heard a clink in the keyhole, and rushed to the door—locked! Damnable Housekeeper! Tulip seemed distressed too, chirping loudly from his shelf. I picked him up and stroked him, feeling his wings shudder in my hands. I remembered the day Titus and I had startled a bush full of redwing starlings—they scattered like buckshot from the branches. "Look," he'd said. "Even those birds be freer than I."

The walls seemed to press in on me at oblique angles. I was falling apart, disintegrating from the inside out. I don't know how long I lay in bed.

When the rain stopped, I untied Tulip's leg. "Find your freedom, little one. Take it while you can." And flung him far out the window, into the failing light. In the yard below, by the barn door, a machete and pile of bloody rags lay on a tree stump. I slammed closed the shutters. Finally I was aware of moonlight slanting through the shutters. Without thinking, I sat up, gripped Titus's scarf, and pierced the room, pierced the house, with a fierce and guttural wail.

~

I awoke the next morning, having no idea what time it was. My eyelids were swollen nearly shut. I rose and combed my tangled hair and changed clothes. A tune was circling about in my head and would not stop. Was I going mad? I sat rocking back and forth before my lace pillow, winding thread again and again around four pins.

One two three four. I couldn't stop. A kind of manic energy was coursing my veins. Over and over the thread looped into nooses, not making lace, only cinching itself around the necks of pins. *One two three four, who will soon be dead for sure? Four three two one, is it time for us to run?* Until the pins grew fat with meaningless mounds of thread. Finally I pushed the pillow aside, paced the room, tapping crossed arms with fingers. They had to let me out of this room sometime. I'd find a way to get to Titus.

Finally a key rattled in the lock. The door opened slightly. Mistress Cingria's voice was subdued. "Go to the *kinder*room and sit with the children, Miss Klaassens." I rose slowly. I would go, not out of obedience, but because I had questions, important questions, to put to Pier. I picked up my lace pillow, intending to undo the pins clotted with thread. Perhaps ordering them would calm me.

At the *kinder*room door, I paused. Catryn sat slumped, tied by her waist sash to a table leg, whimpering, while Pier marched about the room in a wide black military hat, brandishing his *kris.* "Cry harder!" he commanded, waving the weapon in his sister's face. Then he leaned down and made pretend sawing motions with his sword across her ankles.

"What in God's name do you think you're doing, Pier?" I slammed my lace pillow so hard on the table, pins and needles spilled out. I untied Catryn. She let out a sob.

"We were just pretending!" Pier protested hotly.

I jumped up and grabbed him by the arm, shaking him almost convulsively. "What's wrong with you?" Blood was surging through my temples, ready to burst through the skin. "Don't you know this is what your family just did to Titus and Josiah?"

"Let go of me this instant!" He twisted wildly, then raised his sword in warning. I pushed him away in disgust, turned, feeling dizzy. The room seemed to grow hazy and unreal as I gathered up the needles.

"Of course I know what they did to those *kaffirs*, you stupid witch," Pier fumed. "Who do you think told Father?" I froze. When I turned to face him, he was flashing a triumphant smile. For the briefest second, something like pride and guilt flickered in his eyes, just as it had in the Master's.

"You? It was *you*?"

"Of course it was me! *I* found out about the meetings. *I* found out which *kaffirs* were attending them. It was my duty to tell Father. And I'm glad I did."

I drew my words out evenly, measured, a study in control. "Who . . . told you . . . it was Titus and Josiah?"

"Digger told me." He cocked his head imperiously, picking up his *kris*.

"Digger? Why would Digger tell *you*?"

"I made him tell. He said he knew a secret about Titus and the others."

"What do you mean, you made him?" I was barely aware of the needle I clenched in my fist.

"I tied him up and whipped him with my riding crop. That's what you do to slaves when they get difficult. You flog them." The shaking in my hands returned. "Stupid slaves. Stupid niggers," he shouted. "And stupid you, you *kaffir*-lover. They're devils, all them, and Titus is a monkey's ass."

The veins in my temples were exploding.

"Those slaves deserve what they got. They were going to run. That's why we had to cut off their feet." He slashed the air with his *kris*. I felt lightheaded now, floating out and away from my body. "Damn stinking heathen *kaffirs*! Bloody *schepselen*!"

A kind of fog obscured the room. And then apparently I rushed him. Apparently, because I barely remember it. Startled, he dropped his sword. I felt the steel of the needle hard and sharp in my hand. I gripped Pier by the shoulder, and, before I knew what I was doing, plunged the needle toward his face. In a flash he raised a hand. I felt the resistance of flesh, but could not stop—drove the needle deep into tissue, impaling his outstretched palm like a nail into fruit. Blood spurted, a long stream of it, spattering my bodice and chemise, coursing down his arm and flooding his shirt with red. He shrieked. Catryn screamed. Everything was dim and chaotic, as if happening in a dream.

Oh, God! What have I done?

Pier fell, clenching his wrist. "Take it out!" he screamed. "Take it out!" For a moment, numb, I just stared, then fell to my knees, held his wrist with one hand and, fingers trembling, tried to grasp the needle. But my fingers only slipped over wet, bloody metal. "*Take it out!*"

Behind me, a shrill, high-pitched shriek. Mistress Cingria lurched through the door, jerked me by the shoulders, and struck me hard across the face. I stumbled to my feet, made fretting movements as she tried to pull out the needle. Pliers!

Pliers will pull out the needle! Titus will have some. I took the steps in leaps and bounds. Pier was screaming, Catryn wailing. I tore past a bewildered Manassa, out the kitchen door and down the yard. Pliers!

I felt faint, dashed into the stables, looked around desperately. "Titus! Titus!" I called. Then remembered—Titus was somewhere else, bleeding. I heard a cry from outside, and through the door saw Pier on the *stoep* pouring black powder into the barrel of a flintlock rifle. Dear God! He's going to shoot! *I have to get out of here.*

I found Luther in a stall with a mare, about to uncinch the saddle. "Give me that horse!" The slave backed away. "Help me with the stirrups, Luther. Hurry!" By now the boy would be ramming the barrel for the second time, pouring in the shot. At the stable door, I saw Pier some twenty yards away, leveling the rifle at me. Suddenly he fired. *Bam!* I dug heels into the horse's flanks and we tore down the yard. Thank the Lord those guns notoriously miss their mark. I galloped through the arches, knowing Pier was reloading. I sped across the fields, past shuddering vines, following the farm road, my horse kicking up dust and stones.

I have to see Titus one more time.

When we got to the lane that flanked the forest, I slowed to a trot, looking for the opening in the trees that led to where Titus and Josiah lay. There was the same low lamenting coming from the clearing. I rode forward, making my way to where the women guarded the wounded.

But I did not know these slaves. Two hefty Black women stood sentinel before the gate, barring my way. Then I heard it—the distant clanging of the great bell. Someone at the manor had sounded the alarm! They were looking for me. "Please," I implored. "I must see Titus. Call Sladie or Manassa, call Samuel.

They'll vouch for me."

"We knows bout you. Last time you here, Titus he go into the faint," one said. "You wantin to kill him straight out?" I stared at her, shocked into confusion. I jerked on the reins. My horse pulled her head in and retreated two steps, giving a little buck. Again the alarm rang out, this time with urgency. I glanced toward the manor house—people had seen me ride this way. Go, go! I must go!

Why ever did I have to hurt a child?

I turned my horse. There was only one way out. We tore down rows of spindly vines back toward the manor house until we hit the gravel drive, galloping toward the Cape Town road. Fear tightened in bands around my chest when I heard a deadly pounding of hooves behind me. Under the shadows of the oaks, under the strident cries of guinea fowl, I veered my steed sharply, hitting the dirt road, making for the long stretch of open flats and sandy plains beyond. But I was also riding away from Titus. Would I ever see him again?

A thunder of horses beat down the drive after me, growing louder. Blood thumped like drums in my ears. My head twisted back—three horsemen led by Mr. Pesser were galloping like the wind, faster than this old steed could gallop. Their brows were hard with determination. Soon they were barely fifty yards away, and gaining. My heart collapsed into my stomach. There was no escape. What terrible cowardice made me flee? I reined in my horse, turned her around, and sat back in the saddle, facing them. That's when they overtook me.

Chapter 38

May 1750 (Winter)

People talking, rattling around downstairs in the kitchen woke me. My face throbbed. In the mirror a cheekbone looked swollen and blue. When I checked my door it wouldn't budge—locked in once again.

Last night, when the men threw me at the feet the Master, he was so angry he lunged forward and thwacked me across the face, hard. "I should send you to the Castle! They know what to do with crazy maids like you!" And so I was locked in my room until he decided my punishment. Never mind that his own son had shot at me, wounding himself instead.

In some ironic twist of fate, Pier's gun had hang-fired, smoke blasting out and blinding him in one eye. Those who knew of these things said it was probably temporary. He had rammed in the shot and fired with the needle still embedded in his palm. His fingers must have slipped in the blood. I thought of what I'd done to him and groaned.

I stared out the window. Could I tie sheets together, haul myself down the side of the building and run to Titus? And then what? Nay, too many people moved about the yard. Were they going to throw me to the mercy of the courts? Slam me into a cell at the Castle? Torture and burn me? The only person I knew of influence was Adriaan, and I could expect no help from him.

At midmorning, Mistress Cingria and Mr. Pesser entered my room. From their hard looks I could tell something had been decided. I shouted out as she jerked off my bodice and unlaced my stays, throwing them aside while Mr. Pesser looked on. I stood in my chemise and skirts, feeling raw, broken open. She handed me a cloth to hold across my breasts. "Shameful girl!" she finally uttered. Grasping me roughly, they forced me down through the kitchen, where the girls looked on, dread in their eyes, then out into the yard. When I saw a tree stump placed on the ground, my body went hot, then cold.

Mistress Cingria pushed me toward it. "Kneel!" she commanded. "Closer to the stump!"

Mother of God!

Soon the yard filled with people. From the walls of the winery, Oom Samuel and other slaves looked on, their eyes brimming with pain. Jaco stood with the girls on the kitchen *stoep*, his arms crossed. All the staff were staring at me, and they seemed to shiver too, particularly Anna. I could see her mouth silently chanting, "Going to hell, she's gonna burn in hell."

"You aren't going to chop off her head, are ye?" Johanna shouted. *"Are ye?"*

A movement from the house made me glance up. The Master stood at his open window, Pier beside him, a patch across one eye and his arm in some sort of sling. Father and son stood in uncommon solidarity. Was that satisfaction on their faces? *Schadenfreude!*

Anthonij emerged from the tack room, his thick arm slapping a *sjambok* against his palm. I actually breathed with relief.

Mistress Cingria stepped forward and tore at my chemise, forcing it below my waist, exposing my breasts. I clasped the cloth to them, but Anthonij pulled my hands forward and tied them around the trunk. Mistress Cingria bent my head low against the stump, crushed my cheek into the wood—and held down my head with a foot. The humiliation! Before I could take a breath, leather strips slashed across my back. *Jesus!*

The short whip coursed down again and again, cutting into skin, then into open flesh. I didn't want to, but I cried out. Five lashes, six, seven. I thought of Titus, and how he had borne that *sjambok* too.

Twelve lashes. That's what Johanna later told me. I didn't remember, because I passed out.

Bending me gently over a table in the cellar, Cook and Johanna washed my wounds. Sladie helped, slathering a poultice of stinging herbs and turpentine over my back and bandaging me.

"Shameful, exposing and lashing a girl that way," Cook said.

"I'm glad," I said. "I deserved it." They told me Pier's sight was coming back, and I was genuinely relieved.

"Heard what ye did yesterday," Johanna drawled.

"Who hasn't?"

"I mean, being out stealin horses like that."

Johanna always made me smile, even if this was a little one. "I'm finished here at the manor, aren't I?"

"They ain't givin ye no award," Cook quipped.

"I want to see Titus. Help me get to him."

Instead they helped me upstairs and, under orders, locked me in my room. I lay in bed on my stomach, longing to go to Titus.

Late that night, when the house was quiet with sleep, I awakened to hear keys rattling at my door. Johanna tiptoed in, asking if I could walk. "Mistress Cingria wanted to make you wash the floors this afternoon," she whispered. "Can you believe that woman? Cook told her to leave you be."

We slipped out of the house, she returning to her cottage while I, tin lantern in hand, stumbled down the path toward the Slave Quarters. At every step, shards of pain cut into my back and blood seeped through the bandages. Yet it was no more than what the slaves commonly endured.

Beyond the garden, by light of the moon, slavemen were walking, slouching toward the forest. Some bore shovels on their shoulders. Others, a few yards behind, bore a pallet—a body shrouded in an antelope skin. I froze. "Is that—?"

"Titus still be in Quarters, Miss Saskia," one said. "He not lost his shadow yet."

Not lost his shadow yet. I knew what they meant. A flood of emotions surged through me: fear, relief, then a wave of shame and sadness. "Good, dear Josiah," I whispered. "God rest his soul." Then anger's dark curtain descended like night. If Titus died too, I would help the slaves bury him. I would claw the soil for his grave with bare hands, for I wanted the earth to remember what had happened here.

At the entrance to the Quarters, Sladie held out her hand. "Titus, he been askin to see Aunt Effie, Miss Saskia. I hates to ask ye, but could you go fetch her?"

"Don't know if they'll let me out tomorrow. May I see him, Sladie?"

"Mr. Pesser not let you."

"Has Titus asked for me?"

"Nay, Miss Saskia. Only for Effie. I do be sorry."

A pain seared my heart like a branding iron. "I'll see what I can do. Heal him, Sladie. Promise me."

I got up early the next morning, before the slave bell rang, wrapped thick bandages around my torso, dressed, and slipped out of the house. Fortunately, no one had checked my door, which was still unlocked. I caught Jaco just as he was spanning the oxen for Cape Town. He got down from the driver's seat and, picking me up by the armpits, pretty much lifted me into the wagon. His face was drawn and weary. Overnight, his mouth had hardened into a grim line.

"You know you could get into real trouble for this, Jaco."

"I'm so mad about what they did to Titus and Josiah. And for the lashes ye took, Saskia. As for that prick of a boy . . . He will heal soon enough. He deserved worse."

I didn't dare tell him what I'd intended. It almost *was* worse.

All the way to Cape Town I held my sides. The rough road was hard on my back, and I could only lean sideways against the seat without pain. Looking out over stark fields of vines, I felt around for something, anything, of the old me. But only a searing numbness breathed me now.

"She came begging Titus for forgiveness. Did ye know?"

"Who?"

"Jezza. Who d'ye think? Oom Samuel said she laid her head in Titus's lap and cried. He put a hand on her forehead, real gentle like. I suppose that were his forgiveness. *I* sure wouldn't a forgiven her." Oh, Jaco! Was hearing that supposed to make me feel better? "I'm scared, Saskia. Just who are these people we work for? What more are they capable of?"

I bit the side of my lip until it bled.

Hours later, Jaco helped me down at the outspanning yard, saying he couldn't pick me up until afternoon. I stumbled up and down the hilly streets to the Bo-Kaap, anxious to see Effie, until finally the bright fruit-colored buildings came into view. The authorities considered this place a hotbed of intrigues and insurrection. Right now all that my eyes fell upon, from seedy stores to hookah tea houses, seemed proof of its dark underbelly. But the manor had its own underbelly.

The late morning sun made a low, cold arc in the sky as I stood knocking on Effie's door. When I saw her face, tears sprang to my eyes. I tried to speak, but words guttered in my throat. I looked around, glad to see she was alone, and dropped onto the settee. From my pocket I pulled out the bloodied kerchief. It sat in my lap like a small, wounded animal.

Effie lowered herself slowly into a chair. "Doesn't that belong to Titus?" Her hands shook, flew to her face. "Oh, God in heaven."

I told her what they'd done to the slavemen. Never before had Effie shown me tears, but now they tumbled down quietly. She pointed me to a cabinet where I fetched a crock of *naartjies*. The tangerine liqueur stung my throat and exploded through my chest with sudden heat. The story spilled out in broken, misshapen pieces: the missing watch, the interviews, Titus and Josiah on the forest floor, hurting Pier, his attempt to shoot me. As to my lashing, I would not burden her with that too.

Effie fell back in her chair, overwhelmed, and dropped her head in her hands. "My boy!" Suddenly she winced, and her hands fluttered to her missing leg. "Pour me another cup, Saskia."

Our silence was long and desolate, yet the *naartjies* and being with Effie strengthened me, gave me some comfort. Outside, street vendors hawked fried *samoosas*. Horses and dogcarts clattered by while conversations in Malay drifted up the hill.

"Of course I'll come back with you."

I tried to help her pack a few items, but mostly I sat on the edge of her bed staring straight ahead until my gaze fell on that statue of many-armed Shiva, giver and taker of life.

"I watched Titus grow up, you know." Effie sighed. "What a strong green sapling he was! Always, the Europeans tried to make him small, belittling him as Black and a slave, but he showed them. He grew the legs of a giant."

Legs? I breathed in sharply.

"We became lovers, Effie." She turned to me, eyes large, then reached out and touched my swollen lids. "Feelings between us were growing for a long time."

"Well, I must say, child—I did wonder if something had happened between you two." Her hand ran gently from my neck to shoulder.

Suddenly I felt anxious. "We must go soon, Effie!"

"Child! You said we had to wait for Jaco."

"Oh, Effie. How can I make this pain go away?"

She sat beside me on the bed. "We cannot. We can only suffer it. You and I must suffer it. Without bitterness." She breathed deeply. "Come here."

I leaned against her on the coverlet, letting her fold me in her arms, despite my wounds. The lappets of her cap, her crisp hair, crushed against my cheek. Her skin smelled of *kardemom*. How long it had been since someone held me as Mama had! I wanted to crawl into her lap like a babe. Fountains of grief, new and ancient, poured out. She let me weep.

"Why are people so violent?"

She breathed deeply, gazing down at gnarled hands. "Because we forget. Forget that life is sacred."

"They call themselves Christians! They're not Christians. They're devils!"

"Most of us think ourselves good, Saskia. But we hide shadowy selves, darkness buried in altars behind our hearts, to which we pay secret homage." She turned her face to me. "Don't you see how, when you struck at Pier, you acted just like those who hurt Titus and Josiah?"

I pulled from her, scowling. "I thought you were on my side." My girlhood flashed before me: my stepmother lashing me, no one stopping her. No one! I sprang from the bed. "I wanted to injure Pier, all right? Oh, Effie, I wanted to bury that needle as deep as I could into his sick little skull!"

Effie looked down. I sat back onto the bed again, weeping. She held me for the longest time. "How does this violence stop, Effie?"

"It stops with you. It stops with me. We must always stand up to injustice, Saskia. But not with more violence."

"How, then?"

"With understanding. With example. With wideness of being. Only that will change things."

The next thing I knew, I was in the hallway, throwing on my cape. Why was she lecturing *me*? "I'm going out."

The early afternoon was chill with low-slung clouds that caught like gauze in the treetops. The sky was cold and milky white, a Dutch sky. I made my way up Longmarket Street among the brightly painted cottages.

A light rain fell. Insects buzzed in the mist that rose from water furrows. As I made my way uphill, sadness wrapped me in its bandage. I felt captive, as if in a cramped cell with a door that opened inward. I wanted to run from everything. Then a terrible thought crossed my mind: what if, on the day Titus and I set out to flee, I hadn't had the courage?

The incline was steep. In a few minutes I reached the crest, and a flat piece of land on which to pause and look out over the ocean. How could a boy under my care become so full of bile? I was his nursemaid, yet I'd failed to reach him. I'd thrown him out of my heart. I'd also disgraced myself, and soon all of Cape Town would know. In time word would get back to Delft. Papa would hear of it, and Cousin Gertruyd. They would suffer shame because of me. For that I was deeply sad.

I turned and climbed along a goat path, the wind churning

up leaves and whipping the hems of my skirts. I stopped to empty my clogs of small stones, then closed my eyes, remembering the look of agony, of dismay, on Titus's face. The last time I'd seen him, his eyes were sinking below his brow. If he died . . . I could fling myself from the highest cliff, walk into those cold, choppy waves. I might go to the tanner's for some tannin to drink. Tumble into death, into oblivion . . . Did I have the courage?

Madame Remy once told me that taking one's life was the greatest selfishness, for we were demanding life only on our terms. But couldn't the world's barbarity drive one to despair? To my right a pure, thin cloud hovered over Table Mountain, stretching like an ostrich plume beyond its high bed.

I worked my way up the curving path past thorny shrubs and patches of firs to the top of the ridge, then slipped on some needles, slamming my knee on stones, startling the wounds on my back. I sat on the path, tears rising to my eyes, and laughed.

At last, panting and perspiring, I attained the summit. The whole of Cape Town stretched out below, with the silver-blue waters of Table Bay. I looked down at all the streets Titus and I had walked. If he pulled through this . . . I would find a way to marry him.

Two Hottentot boys, herding goats along the slope, caught sight of me and scampered down the mountain. Azure sea shimmered to my left, stately Table Mountain to my right, and beyond that the hills and plains that led to Rustigvallei—a place no longer home. In the distance loomed the rougey Simonsberg and Stellenbosch Mountains, the Bottelary Hills—and at their feet the wild forest in which they'd savaged my friends. Further east the rivers swelled and gushed from the rains, streaming red with iron earth. How much human blood had already soaked the orchards and fertilized the fields of this continent? How much more would spill before all were free?

I sat on a rock and buried my face in my skirts. What if I had blinded Pier? I was beginning to understand Effie's words. When you strike against evil without compassion, that evil enters *you*. And so violence goes on. Did I too contain that evil?

When was it exactly that I'd turned my back on my employers, my church, my kinsmen? To side with the slaves. I had no master now, owed allegiance to nothing, only to my own humanity. If I could find it again. I dug into myself, praying for the first time to Madame Remy's God. *Oh, Mother, give me a woman's strength, a woman's heart!*

Finally I stood up. I must go back down to face whatever it was I must face. Jaco would be arriving soon to take us back to Rustigvallei—and to Titus.

As I descended, a wide slice of sunlight shattered the ocean, splitting it into a hundred patches of gold.

~

I stopped in my tracks to see a familiar carriage on Effie's street. Who from the estate had come, and why? Inside, the Mistress was sitting on the settee. Had she come to deliver me more punishment?

"So you got out of your locked room and escaped here, did you?" The Mistress looked pale and tired. I hadn't seen her for days. "We ran into Jaco, and he told us where you were."

I curtsied so low, it was almost genuflection. "Forgive me, Mistress de Witt. I'm sorry, so sorry . . . Pier. I-I don't know what came over me." But I did know what came over me. Enough rage to hurt a child.

"A needle thrust through his hand. That's horrid, Saskia! He said you were going for the eye. But I can't always believe that boy." She shook her head and shuddered. I cast my eyes down, then glanced at Effie, begging for support. She did not give me any. Oh, Saskia, just bear it, bear it.

"Mistress . . ." I stumbled over the words. "I know that you tried to-to spare the men from . . . being cut."

The Mistress closed her eyes. Moisture filmed her lashes. She arched her back. "Pier's wounds will heal," she said with a trace of indignation, "as will yours. But Titus and Josiah's . . ." She opened her fan, fluttering it madly across her face. So she hadn't heard about Josiah. I decided not to tell her. "Catryn said Pier was shouting obscenities about them." She stared at me with eyes of pain.

"How is Catryn taking this?" I dared ask.

"She's upset. Confused." What did I expect?

"If only you'd brought my son to me, Saskia, I would have given him a good caning, and a piece of my mind to boot." I gazed at her. Would she really have? Perhaps.

"I've done a lot of soul searching the last few days," the Mistress continued. "Titus and Josiah are dear to all of us. And I know," her voice trailed off, "you and Titus were close." She paused. "I can't tell you how upset I am at my husband's choice of action!" She glanced at Effie. "Upset at so much of what we Europeans have been up to at the Cape. But what's done is done. You need to apologize to Pier *and* to his father, Saskia. Despite your punishment, you must make amends." Make amends! I blinked. No matter what I'd done, I would never grovel before either.

Effie leaned forward. "Saskia, what's that on your back?" I touched my dress. Under the shoulder of my chemise, blood was seeping through.

"How are your lash wounds, Saskia? Are you healing?"

"Yes," I murmured, looking away. "Thank you." Effie stared

at the Mistress, then at me, and clasped a hand over her heart.

Mistress de Witt turned to her. "Yes, my husband had her punished. All this brutality! I can't stand it! Mistress Huyskens, would you consider traveling back to the estate with us? I imagine you would like to see Titus. Personally, I would appreciate your company just now. My carriage is out front. Jaco and his team will follow later."

And all at once it was as clear as day. The Mistress hadn't come for me at all. She had come for Effie.

Chapter 39

All places are distant from heaven alike.
—Robert Burton

May 1750 (Winter)

Our carriage shuddered in the wind that pumped from the southeast. The bottom half of my window was cracked. Frail sunlight caught on the glass and glinted through smashed shards, fracturing and unjointing everything my eyes fell upon: the streets Titus and I had walked, the curbs where we sat sharing chunks of watermelon and cups of *rooibos* tea. Now the great plane trees were brown and leafless. What patches of grass remained were parched white-green. I thought we would live forever, together, whole. How brittle is life! It can slip away from you just like that, an icy shoe dumping you into a cold canal. It can fall from your hand like a crystal glass, shattering into a thousand pieces.

I pulled back from the carriage window—wounds of memory were too fresh. Life had become a shifting kaleidoscope viewed through broken prisms, nothing sure, no one safe. I thought of Titus lying on his cot, eyes all but lost beneath his skull.

"How could God let this happen!" I shouted.

The Mistress looked at me, startled, her own blue eyes unsettled too, while Effie rested a hand on my arm. We were approaching the edge of Table Mountain. Cape Town slipped back and away, further and further from view, as if disappearing into the mists of time. We rode along in silence.

Our eyes were caught by a flurry of small movements under the Mistress's sleeve. We stared. A dove-gray moth had worked its way under the lace and was beating its wings madly, trying to get free. The Mistress jabbed at it.

"That moth—that is how I think of things," the Mistress said. "As if we're lost, caught in a prison of threads. Life just a wretched, tangled mess." She slipped her finger under the lacework, and lifted. In a flap of gray dust, the moth flew up around our heads.

By late afternoon light, my teacher's face was copper-gold. "Perhaps now it can see the grand design." She opened a window, and the moth flew away.

For several hours we traveled the road back to the estate, lost in thought. As the sun sank low in the sky, we gazed at wide stretches of mountains and veldt, purple and blue-violet in the failing light.

The Mistress gazed at Effie, then me. "I'm separating from my husband, did you know?"

I started.

"There's a ship sailing for Amsterdam in three weeks. The children and I will be on it." She glanced at me meaningfully. Of course she wouldn't ask me to go along. "I hate it here, hate slavery. And God knows I hate the arrogance and violence that created it. We Dutch have much to answer for. With all due respect, Mistress Huyskens, I don't see a good design to any of it. I don't see why any of this had to happen."

We looked out on boney trees that cut like blades at the twilight. "I know, Mistress," Effie said, "I know. I'm still that little moth. I pray that one day I'll be large enough to understand too." Her hands fell on her crutches, knocking one to the floor. I picked it up, cradling it in my lap.

As we entered the last stretch of road, as the carriage wheels spat up pebbles and the hills swallowed the last orange rim of sun, the Mistress turned to her. "You know, my dear lady, so much of my life has been wasted. I want to get to know my children. I want to become involved in their lives. And I'd like to learn to make lace." She sighed. "I want to create just one fine thing before I leave this earth, one thing of enduring beauty."

Effie and I smiled at her almost affectionately.

By the time we arrived, I was anxious to see Titus, but my stomach turned somersaults at the thought. Was he better? The manor house drive was lit with torches. I took Effie by the hand. The Mistress had given us her blessing, so we hurried through the cold to the Slave Quarters. Like the parting of the Red Sea, the slaves made way for Effie, ushering her toward Titus's slouching body, but they closed ranks around me, barring my way. Effie waved me to leave.

I leaned against the fence surrounding the Slave Quarters, beating on it slowly with a clenched fist. Why couldn't I see him? We belonged to each other. "Unfair!" I shouted. Then remembered—no more rage, Saskia! I took several deep breaths, calmed myself as I waited. Then Sladie appeared at the door, motioning me in.

Effie was sitting at his side, holding his hand. He was conscious—what miracle had her presence wrought? Conscious but weak. The smell from his wounds hit me between the eyes.

He seemed to recede into the pillows, then turned toward me. I knelt by his side. Yes, he was aware, and at last we regarded one another. I couldn't help the tears that coursed down my cheeks. When his mouth quivered, I reached for a cup and brushed fingers of water over dry lips. He tugged at my sleeve and drew me close.

"Saskia." His voice was ragged and thin. "The waterfall. By the waterfall!"

The world seemed to spin out of time, and my stomach dropped away. "Yes, Titus," I whispered back. "By the waterfall."

~

Passing through the garden, I heard someone run up behind me, panting. It was Jezza. A shiver of revulsion surged through me. That girl now seemed not so much to appear as to slither around corners, like a dog that has deeply displeased its master. A pariah everyone snapped at. It was *her* fault that Titus now lay withering in his bed. I hastened my step.

"Wait, Miss Saskia." I was exhausted from the journey, the cuts on my back ached, and seeing Titus had pulled on me so, I didn't want to deal with her. "I nevva meant things to happen as they did . . ."

Was this her apology? Sudden anger erupted in me like spuming lava. I raised my hand. By torchlight, her eye looked swollen, face and arms stamped with wounds. Isaiah. And maybe others. Her insolence, her prickly sensuality, all gone now. In the bend of the body, only frailty. Effie's words beat at my ears: *Violence begets violenc*e. If I struck out in rage once again, we'd both be lost. I would become one of *them. Again.* I dropped my hand.

~

If all goes well, I could get to Cape Town in two days. My feet felt leaden, as if the earth rose up too fast to meet them. Jaco and Johanna offered to take me by wagon, but I'd refused. I don't know why, but I had to walk. Perhaps it was one last tendril of rebellion . . . one last stand of honor, if any honor were left me. Of course, it was dangerous. Jackals, leopards, lions, and who knows what else roamed this countryside. I didn't even know where I'd land once I got to town. I only knew that I had to leave, and leave alone. Tonight I would stop at the estate where Jaco's wife worked and beg for a place to rest my head.

The morning was gray and silent. Low clouds smudged the horizon and the wind-torn treetops. I wondered what time tomorrow I'd pass the lane to the waterfall. Snatches of his poem still burned in my brain.

The rain came to court the
Spider maiden.
He came in the morning by the
Waterfall
Catching on her web,
Courting her, turning
Lush the grass.

Did the grass there still bend where our bodies lay?

Two days ago, Master de Witt sacked me. Mistress Cingria bore the signal honor, the dark delight, of relaying the message. Cook told me it was the Mistress who saved me from the worst, from what the Master had first demanded—imprisonment at the Castle.

Where was I to go? Effie's place was tiny; I couldn't ask her to take me in. Neither could I return to the Netherlands and Papa, for I had no money for passage, and besides, such a quick return would only spell shame. News travels slowly, but it does travel. More than that, I would be too far from Titus, from every thing and every place that spoke of him. I was given three days to pack and leave, but I left in one. For last night Titus died.

Early this morning, as I gathered my belongings, Sladie came to my room and placed a bundle in my hands. Folding back the cloth, my heart shifted in its chambers. Later I took the satchel with all its contents, and when I found Jezza, pushed it gently to her chest. "Take it." She threw me a suspicious look but tugged at the knots, then drew a breath to find Titus's quill pen, inkwell, and his book on penmanship. And the horse etching he had pinned to the wall of his hut. She ran gentle fingers along each object, unfolding the etching and staring at it, until her eyes filled with tears. I almost touched her on the shoulder before I walked away. We had both suffered so much.

Sullen clouds shrouded the sun. I made my way past fields of withering grapevines, carrying only my lace basket and a few mementos. Mama's locket. The rosary from Madame Remy. Titus's bloodstained kerchief, his bobbins. Jaco offered to deliver the rest of my belongings to any place I bade him. But what did I care now for belongings? I wanted to die myself, to slip away forever beneath the skin of the earth.

Drops of rain *ping ping*ed in the dust and tapped at the hood of my cape. Then something happened that I cannot explain. There was a shift in the air—a warmth, a chill, a strange quiet. Something touched my neck, something insistent. It pressed too hard and lingered too long to be rain. I spun around—but no one was there. A shadow flickered in the corner of my vision, then disappeared. I stopped and held my breath, suddenly aware of an enormous presence hovering about me. I became very still, listened. It was he! He was gone, but with me now. A soft wind churned up leaves on the path while a great warmth, and light, like a blessing, suffused everything around me. Then all at once I felt him expand into the particles of air and scatter to the winds. *Oh, where are you going? Stay with me! Carry me with you!* But he was gone.

I clutched the handles of my lacemaking basket and, standing in wait, savored the last flutter of that phantom. An afterglow, as when one walks into a space a perfumed woman has just left. If there were some part of him that lived on, then wouldn't I too? Might we be together someday in another world?

I heard a flapping and looked down. The wind had thrown open the lid of my basket. I grabbed my portrait of Titus, his poem on the back, just before it blew away. The wind had seized a bit of unfinished lace and now danced it on the breeze until it caught on the trembling grass, rising back toward the estate. We are threads, I thought, each of us, sometimes frail, sometimes bright and strong, but spooled, luminous, from the same core, connected in one grand tapestry.

Perhaps, in the end, what I do to you and you to me affects the Bushman slumbering in the hills, the newborn babe crying in the night, the spider spinning her nest in the vines, the leopard running in for the kill, the oceans, clouds. Sun, moon, stars.

The sun broke an opening in the clouds and burned away the mist, for an instant diminishing the shadows and the ghosts that, for me, will always haunt this land. Mysteries here we may never unravel. Meanwhile we unreel, spin, and cast forth the threads of our lives as best we can. And that is enough.

A note from the author

Did you enjoy my book?

If so, I would be very grateful if you could write a review and publish it at your point of purchase. Your review, even a brief one, will help other readers to decide whether or not they'll enjoy my work. Large numbers of reviews are vital for helping indie books find readers, so I appreciate every little one and thank you for your time.

Would you like a free e-book and notifications of new releases from my publisher, AIA Publishing?

If so, please visit www.aiapublishing.com and click the button to subscribe to notifications of new publications. You'll receive a free e-book of *Worlds Within Worlds* by Tahlia Newland. Of course, your information will never be shared, and the publisher won't inundate you with emails, just let you know of new releases.

Glossary

aya or ajah — lady servant or "auntie" to children (Malay)
baas — boss or master (Malay)
banjah — primitive predecessor to the banjo (unknown origin)
bastars or bastaards — a person of mixed parentage (not necessarily illegitimate) (Malay)
biltong — dried jerky of wild or domesticated meat
bobbejaan — baboon (Afrikaans)
bobotie — a spicy meat casserole or stew (Malay)
caffer(s) — related to *kaffir*, caffers were slave convicts assigned public duties, particularly violent work for the police
de Kaap (de Goede Hoop) — the Cape (of Good Hope) (Dutch)
dhoti — loincloth worn by Indian men (Hindu)
dis kamma so — Imagine it is so (early Cape Dutch)
drostdy — local governing body (Dutch)
engageantes — under-ruffles for sleeves, often of lace or thin linen (French)
fichu — a scarf or shawl covering the neck and shoulders (French)
fynbos — fine shrubs or bush (Dutch)
grote halfronde zonnehoed — round sun hat with cutaway in back (Dutch)
houd vol — Stand firm, take a position. (Dutch)
kaffir, caffer, or caffir — originally meaning infidel, it once meant all natives of southern Africa, and eventually became an extremely derogatory term for Black and colored people (Arabic, *kafir*)
kerrie — curry (Malay)
kinder — child (Dutch)
kloof — saddle between mountains (Dutch)

kolf — golf (Dutch)
kraal — enclosure, corral, as for animals but also huts (Cape Dutch)
kreupelboom — a kind of bush used for firewood (Dutch)
kris — metal sword with undulating edges (Indonesian)
kudu — African antelope, male has long spiral horns
mejuffrouw — young woman (Dutch)
mevrouw — mistress, madame (Dutch)
mielies — corn (Dutch)
mos — syrupy juice from the first grape pressing (Dutch)
muti — totem (African)
mynheer or *mijnheer* — mister, master, sir (Dutch)
naartjies — tangerine liquor (Dutch)
nyai — concubine to a European (Malay)
oom — uncle (Dutch)
pannenkoek — pancake(s) (Dutch)
predikant — preacher (Dutch)
rusk — sweet dry biscuit resembling biscotti (Dutch)
samoosas — deep-fried pastry with spiced vegetables or meat (Urdu)
sangoma — medicine man/woman (African)
schadenfreude — joy at someone's misery (German)
schepselen — creature(s), as opposed to humans or Christians (Dutch)
schoener — schooner (Dutch)
seuntjie — sweetie (Dutch)
Sinterklaas — Santa Claus (Dutch)
sjambok — short, tough whip of hippo hide (African Dutch/Indonesian)
speculaas — spicy butter cookies (Dutch)
spoeks — spooks (African Dutch)
swarte jongen — Black boy (African Dutch)
taal — language (Dutch), referring to the pidgin Dutch spoken by slaves and immigrants
tover — magic (Dutch)
toverman — witch doctor (Cape Dutch)

veldschoen or *veldskoen* or *veldsjoen* — soft leather boots like moccasins, modeled after Hottentot shoes (African Dutch)
veldt (pronounced felt) — uncultivated countryside or grassland (Dutch)
VOC — Dutch East India Company (Dutch)
voortrekker — a pioneer, independent people who spurned the VOC and traveled into the South African interior to live off the land (African Dutch)
vrouw, frau — woman (Dutch)
windroos — a wind rose, showing wind frequency, as seen on maps (Dutch)

Research

Readers may wonder if events described in this novel really took place. They did. The kind of riots Saskia relates surrounding her escape from her father's house actually happened countrywide in Holland over several months in 1748 when angry mobs attacked corrupt tax officials. The slave uprisings discussed by the gentlemen at the Java dinner party are historical facts, including the punishment of Santrij.

I first decided to write this story around 2004. The next year I moved for three months to the incredibly beautiful wine country at the Cape of Good Hope, needing to get a feel for the land and the people. The people turned out to be wonderful and, when Black, sometimes desperately poor. It felt like scenes of paradise painted over a broiling, tense landscape.

The Dutch settled the Cape in 1652, almost a century before my story takes place. At some point, they began growing grapes, and within a few decades their wines were the toast of Europe. Every weekend, my new friend drove us to a different old wine estate to tour the historic buildings and grounds. I took copious notes of every detail of eighteenth-century life in the restored manor houses of Groot Constantia, Blaauwklippen,

Vergelegen, Boschendal, and more, many still working estates, grapevines radiating out as far as the eye can see. In the 1700s they also grew tobacco, vegetables, cultivated livestock, and fruit orchards, to supply ships sailing the Europe–Asia route. All worked by indentured servants like Saskia, and slaves like Titus.

Fortunately for me, my landlords, the Vales, loaned me hard-to-find books of early Cape living from their extensive library. I visited The Castle in Cape Town which once held prisoners. Yes, heads were once actually impaled on stakes at the gate. The guide described gruesome punishments meted out in the 1700s, even for women criminals, the very ones Titus describes one day to Saskia. And yes, women were still burned at the stake. We visited the Huguenot Museum in Franschhoek with its marvelous exhibits of lace; Burger House in Stellenbosch; and Kleinplasie in Worcester, an open-air living history museum of pioneering days; all to imbibe a sense of early life at the Cape. We visited botanic gardens, and the Slave Quarters in Cape Town, which, at least to me, still reeked of an ancient sadness. And upon return I moved to the Santa Ynez Valley where I observed lacemakers at work at the Elverhoj Museum in Solvang, CA. I even took a lace lesson under the wonderful Clara Ehrsam.

Today we can hardly wrap our heads around the atrocities Europeans (and Americans) wrought upon slaves just to ensure dominance. Dutch at the Cape may have generally been kinder than the Dutch in the West Indies, but not much. All the horrors described in this novel were, at one time or another, meted out by Dutch masters upon their Cape slaves. Unfortunately, it all happened.

Acknowledgements

A book of this nature depends on the help of many. Of all those wonderful souls who befriended and helped me in this undertaking, I would particularly like to thank the following:

Zoe Keithley, my superb editor and writing coach; Dr. Gina Briefs-Elgin, my other incredible editor; Genny Cummings who read, critiqued, and helped this book in so many ways; Mary Jonaitis, whose perceptive seeing gave me entry into the story; Yvonne Nelson Perry and Geoff Aggeler, teachers at the Santa Barbara Writer's Conference; Peter Weismiller, Gerald DiPego, David Holden, Lou Erb, Trudy Bartlett, Dorothy Jardin, and Theresa Laursen for invaluable ms. suggestions; Louise von Mecklenburg Tucker; Diane Griffin; lacemakers Clara Ehrsam and the Hale family, particularly Kristal; Clarke Buehling with information on African musical instruments; Marilyn Hill Harper, MD, for medical expertise; Thelma Boyana, Cincia Sardine and Sydwell Mbune at Groot Constantia Wine Estate, South Africa; Dr. Colin and Mrs. Dorothy Vale for scholarly expertise, hospitality in Stellenbosch, and so much help in so many ways; Pieter and Annetke Schaafsma for their scholarly expertise and kindnesses, and Gerrit Schaafsma for computer savviness; David Mwansa; Willem D. Malherbe; Max von Hofwegen on folk dances; Pieter Bestbier, owner, and Carel Hugo, winemaker at Goede Hoop Wine Estate at the Cape; Barbara Robinson for generous financial help and for gifting me with several books on lacemaking and being a reader, along with Marsha Carmichael; Carole Gochin who not only hosted me so generously in Cape Town but provided me company and transportation on many research trips to wine estates and museums at the Cape; Julie and Gary Greinke for a place to write for a time; Bill Horton, Scott Keyzers, and Vicki Mitchell for great computer help; Tahlia Newland, my publisher at AIA Publishing, Rose Newland, book designer, and Katherine Kirk of Gecko Edit who all put up with me most graciously; and last but not least, members of the Solvang Writer's Group in California.

My line "Better to be the jackal in the forest than the greyhound on the golden leash" is adapted from a quote from an early sultan of Kilwa (East African) in Margaret Shinnie's *Ancient African Kingdoms.*

Madame Remy's line "I was not aware we had been quarreling" (on being asked at her death if she would like to make her peace with God) is a downright theft from Thoreau.

The story of street fighters being stopped by a kiss to the fists is an old spiritual story I once heard, but do not know the origin.

Titus's poem to Saskia was written by me but inspired by a Bushman (/Xam subgroup) poem in the book *The Stars Say 'Tsau'* by Antjie Krog.

Also, fashion plates, the kind Saskia and Johanna pored over in the Mistress's room, probably were unknown before 1781, but women did study etchings and Pandora dolls, or "babies," dolls dressed in current fashions at the milliners.

Books that were particularly helpful were: *Amsterdam* by Geert Mak; *Slave Narratives* by Wm. L. Andrews and Henry Louis Gates; *Islands* by Dan Sleigh; *Frontiers* by Noel Mostert; *Letters of Lady Anne Barnard to Henry Dundas, 1793–1803* and *Cape Journals of Lady Anne Barnard, 1797–1798*; *Journal of a Visit to South Africa in 1815 and 1816* by the Rev. C. I. Latrobe; *James Ewart's Journal—Covering his stay at the Cape of Good Hope (1811–1814); Lace* by Virginia Churchill Bath; and *The Golden Bough* by Sir James George Frazer; Dorling Kindersley's *South Africa*; Max von Boehn's *Modes & Manners: Ornaments*.